T0374367

Adobe Kroger

Adobe Kroger

Knight Errant

Dan Sacharow

ADOBE KROGER
Knight Errant

iUniverse books may be ordered through booksellers or by contacting:

iUniverse
1663 Liberty Drive
Bloomington, IN 47403
www.iuniverse.com
1-800-Authors (1-800-288-4677)

ISBN: 978-1-4759-9008-9 (sc)
ISBN: 978-1-4759-9010-2 (hc)
ISBN: 978-1-4759-9009-6 (e)

Print information available on the last page.

iUniverse rev. date: 08/09/2017

Dedication

This book is for all of those who labor to create but have not yet achieved. Whether it's science, philosophy, art, music, writing, entrepreneurship or invention, don't give up. This world would be lost without you. Break the rules and win.

Disclaimer

The text of this book consists of an almost entirely verbatim transcription from live dictation, with all pursuant verbal nuances, faults, and tics preserved. That is to say, whatever Ms. Adobe Kroger said, I wrote. To alter the prose too greatly from its natural state, I felt, would lend an unnecessary air of artificiality to the narrative, and be nothing less than an affront to the honesty and to the subject of said narrative. I say all this only in the hopes of staving off any supposition that I was merely attempting to recreate a spontaneous, earthy, and free flowing voice for the protagonist out of whole cloth, and not succeeding.

—The Author

Chapter One

"This movie...is terrible."

That was Raine Gilham. She said it like her brain was melting, which it probably was, and I didn't blame her one bit. The fact was she was right. The movie was terrible. What the hell was I thinking, taking Jill's recommendation? Again.

It wasn't like Raine needed to say it either. If you wanted to know how terrible this picture was, all you needed to do was turn your head one way or the other and see the light flickering off row after row of maroon colored, super comfortable, and super empty plush stadium seats. And this was Sunday night on the movie's opening weekend in a downtown multiplex, too, which meant real bad buzz already murdered the flick before it even got out of the gate. But let me tell you, this movie deserved to be murdered. Oh, did it ever.

A really corny line from the main character made me face palm. I made a point of overdoing it, too, so Raine could see I was in as much pain as she was. There was no way in hell I was going to let her think I was enjoying this. I was already embarrassed enough, thanks.

Jill would pay for this. By *god*, she would pay.

You know what, I'm not being fair. Jill did in fact mention that this masterpiece was a total chick flick, but she also claimed that it was a good chick flick. That should have been enough for anyone with any taste to run for the hills, but not me! That thought really didn't make me feel any better.

At least the popcorn was good—salty with just enough butter. Unfortunately, the bright colorful popcorn bucket had a picture on it that was advertising a much better movie I saw last week, which only reminded me again how awful this one here was. When I laid eyes on the bucket after grabbing a fistful, I almost groaned again.

I'm telling you, I could have spent the last hour staring at the shadows dancing across the pastel pictures of Chaplin and Monroe on the theater's walls and been more entertained.

I tilted the popcorn bucket at Raine, and I felt more like I was throwing a drowning woman a life preserver than anything else. She was slumped down low in her seat, her feet propped up on the railing in front of us. In the dim light I could see that her beat up combat boots were mostly coming untied, and that she was twirling a finger in her chin length purple bangs. She had her hair cut short almost everywhere except for that one part, and I have to hand it to her---she managed to pull off the look. She had the crinkled-up straw from her soda hanging from the side of her mouth like a cigarette, and it bounced up and down as she chewed on it. After a second or two she noticed the popcorn bucket, and she looked down it without turning her head.

"No thanks," she said, kind of through her teeth. The straw bounced harder. "Eating would only prolong my agony."

I giggled. "Smart."

"Nah," she said. "Just basic self-preservation in reverse. I think." She shifted her feet on the railing a bit. I glanced at the movement, which made me think of another thing that should have tipped us off about this flick before we even sat down. What might that be, you ask? Well, the row in front of the railing is always the first to fill up *because* you can prop up your feet like Raine was doing. Usually, getting a center seat in front of the rails in this place was like winning the lottery (and no, I am not exaggerating). The row was completely empty when we came in tonight, though. I swear, the next time I see this row empty I am going to run away screaming.

I plunked down the popcorn bucket on the floor and it bumped into an empty soda cup that was lying on its side. The cup rolled away under the railing and over the edge. I pictured myself doing the same off of a much higher edge if I had to stay here much longer. I turned and looked at Raine.

"Speaking of self preservation," I said, "can we go?"

"No," she replied. "You said this would be good. Suffer."

I blinked.

"Umm," I said. "I take it back. You're *not* smart. You know you're letting yourself suffer right along with me, right?"

"Well worth it to see you properly punished," Raine said, with a shit-eating grin.

"Please," I moaned, grabbing the sides of my head. "My brain is imploding!"

"I never had one to begin with," she said. "But OK, fine. But you don't get to decide what we do next. Or ever again."

"OK, fine---you got it. *Anything.*"

I've had worse.

I'm not sure exactly when, since I don't go out much, but I'm sure I must have at some point. Well now that I think on it, I'm probably not the best judge of what makes a good night out since nights out aren't really my thing. I'm terrible at them. I only went out tonight mostly to stop my friends from clucking.

Scratch that, it was entirely to stop my friends from clucking. Jill most of all---I'm telling you she just would not quit. I keep telling her and everyone else that my whole purpose in life is to find new and exciting ways to be left alone, but they all keep swooping in and doing everything they can to force me to have a good time, if it kills me. It almost did, tonight. I mean, it started out OK I guess—just a girls night out before the work week got us all tangled up yet again, and I have to admit that it took less arm twisting than normal for me this time. Mainly that was because I had a huge presentation the next morning and I figured this might help me quit worrying about it for a couple hours. That was the theory, anyway. Dinner went well since I didn't really have to talk much, even though I had to at least make a passing effort at it since I just met Raine a week ago for the first time and we still hadn't really broken the ice. That's just kind of how I roll.

But after dinner Jill, Sammy, Carolina and Laurie all said they had to cut out early, before the evening even really had a chance to get going. As it turned out, Raine and (somehow) I ended up being the only ones who didn't want to pack it in. You should have heard their vague and lame excuses, too—they'd have killed you. I guess Jill figured she made up for it by recommending that horrific disgrace of a movie, and I fell for it hook, line and sinker. Raine had her doubts from the look of the poster, but like a big dumb dope I told her we could trust Jill's taste. So much for that. But who the hell knows? Maybe now that we were escaping the movie the night just might pick up. That has been known to happen from time to time, even to me.

Well, as Raine and me made our way out of the theater, I couldn't help but feel a slight pang of sympathy for those poor bastards who made that movie. I just bet they woke up every morning and thought they were making something wonderful only to end up with this atrocity. At what point, I wondered, did they realize the movie was compost? After the money was all spent, and they sat in the editing room watching the final cut, slowly overcome with crippling existential despair? What went through their skulls as they watched all those months of creative energy and hopeful anticipation get flushed and go swirling? It was like that gourmet dinner you dropped fifty bucks a plate on only to spend the night on the bowl.

You know what? Screw 'em. Their job is to entertain me. If I mess up at work I catch it, so why shouldn't they? Try harder next time. They're fired.

Seeing as that we left partway through the movie, we suddenly found ourselves with some time to waste—I mean *spend*. I guess technically we could have just called it a night, but both of us still didn't really feel like it.

It was a usual Sunday night at CityPlace, that little pretend city just outside of downtown West Palm Beach. It wasn't too crowded, not too quiet, and it was nice and brisk as mid December in South Florida usually is. Personally, I love it when it drops into the fifties; it makes the summer months of swamp ass at least somewhat bearable knowing there's a nice winter on its way eventually (if at all). You just try telling that to some of my native born friends, though. Yeesh, you'd swear we were in Siberia. I guess maybe I have a better perspective, since I lived all over the place, being an army brat. Raine didn't seem to care much, either; the girl had *shorts* on for crying out loud and she didn't seem to notice the cold one bit. Before we did anything else, we hung out for a second right outside the theater and put each other's numbers into our phones.

"That," Raine said, putting her phone away, "was brutal. We *really* need to cancel that out."

I turned and gave her a face like I was trying to say *you can say that again*, but she wasn't looking at me. She looked like she was checking out the open-air jazz diner joint across the way where some four-piece band was doing their best to cover that one big band tune everyone can hum. I started bouncing along to it before I realized I was doing it.

Raine glanced at me.

"You have good taste," she said.

"Can't help it," I replied. "I wish I knew what that damn song was called."

"That's 'In the Mood'," she said almost immediately. "Glenn Miller Orchestra, 1939. Based on a lick from 'Tar Paper Stomp,' By Wingy Manone, 1930, although the lick also appeared in 'Hot and Anxious' by Don Redman, 1931, and in 'Hot String Beans' by Joe Marsala, 1939."

I just stared at her. She smiled back, and I saw that her grin was slightly crooked, more to one side than the other, and that her front teeth were slightly larger than usual.

"Sorry," she said after a second. "I get that way when someone asks about music; it's kind of a passion of mine. You've been warned."

"Noted," I said. "Umm, so, what were we talking about?"

"Movie, terrible, need to cancel out," she answered, and I noticed a slight southern twang in her voice this time I must have missed before. "What do you wanna do?"

"Well Ms. Raine," I said, slipping my phone into my hoodie pocket and zipping up, "I'm seriously up for anything." I meant it. I am so low maintenance it's actually stupid.

"How about a drink?" she asked; a breeze blew her hair over her face, and she brushed it back behind her ear. "Straightforward enough."

I made it look like I was thinking; you know, I did the whole looking up and to the side thing and even went *hmmm*. Of course while I was doing that I wasn't looking where I was going, so I bumped straight into someone. Slick, that's me.

"*Hey,* man," said some chick's voice, and I got a flash of bright red out of the corner of my eye. I whipped my head around to say sorry to whoever that was, but for the life of me I couldn't see anyone or anything remotely red anywhere near enough to be bumped into.

"You OK?" That was Raine.

"Yeah," I answered, but I took one more real quick look around anyway. Seriously, that was weird. I just shrugged and went on.

"So, a drink?" Raine said, lowering her head a bit and looking up at me.

"Oh, oh, yeah," I said, but I think I still sounded a little distracted. "That's perfect. Wet Willies?" I pointed at the place. You could see the rows of colorful spiked slushies in the clear plastic bins from where we were.

"Nah," Raine said, and brushed her hair back again. "I think I need something more authentic after that ordeal. O'Sheas?"

"Oh *now* you're talking," I replied.

And was she ever. O'Sheas was one of my favorite spots. Not to mention it was about four blocks away, which meant a walk in this cool night air, which was just what I needed right then.

✳ ✳ ✳ ✳ ✳

A stiff breeze made me hide under my hoodie as we made our way to O'Sheas. Along the way we passed a karaoke bar where some guy was mangling a song I vaguely recognized, and before I could so much as comment Raine spat out the title, artist and year of the track, and even added some crazy obscure trivia about the goddamn producer or songwriter's wife, too. She did that same thing two or three more times in front of other bars or restaurants before we made it out of Cityplace, and my brain boggled every time she did it.

Even though I found all that pretty damn cool, I was glad to finally get to the quieter part of town on the way to Clematis Street. I don't know, I guess I just found the sudden drop in volume kind of relieving.

There were perfectly clean, empty condominiums on one side of the street that gave me the impression that I was intruding on an immaculate closed movie set, and on the other side there were empty lots of mangled grass and jagged concrete debris that made me feel like I was walking through a slum. All in all, it was an intriguing, if comically paradoxical juxtaposition. Sort of like myself.

Oooh, that was deep. No, I'm not wangsty, I promise. Well, not overly anyway. I have my moments, like everyone else, and the best I can hope to say is that they're few and far between. No, the truth is I am actually pretty seriously messed up on a fairly basic fundamental level.

Right now you're probably saying *How messed up are you?* Well . . .

The truth is I play the banjo.

I'm *joking*. Well, not about that. I do actually play banjo, if you can call it playing. Not to put too fine a point on it, I suck out loud. Banjo is bad enough but a poorly played banjo is too much to ask of anyone, so solitude helps loads there. No, banjo is just an annoying hobby that I try to keep secret most of the time. What I'm talking about is worse, and it's the reason I usually keep to myself. It's not that I hate people or anything, and it's not like I don't want to find the right person and live happily ever after someday. The problem is that even if I do, there will always be this thing about me that will most likely end up coming between us.

But I'm getting ahead of myself. Moving on.

There I was looking over the empty windows of the meticulously painted condominiums, hoping that maybe, just maybe, tonight they would betray some sign of life and prove that the whole building wasn't some plywood façade that would topple in a stiff breeze. Not surprisingly, the windows remained dark and blank.

"That movie," Raine grumbled, but I could tell she wasn't being too serious, "What the hell were you thinking?"

"Oh quit," I said, smirking. "I didn't write it, film it, shove a gun up your ass and force you to watch it."

As you can see, I have a prodigious, elegant vocabulary. Two years of college well spent; just ask my mom. It looked like Raine liked it, though. She cracked another of her crooked smiles.

"I trusted you," she said, pointing at me and doing her best to look serious. "And you betrayed me. You've made a powerful enemy tonight."

I clasped my hands together, and did my best puppy-dog look; you know, I opened my eyes a bit wider, lowered my head and looked up at her. "Wilt thou please grant me another chance?"

"Sure," she replied, and then she stopped, turned and pointed. "Here it is. Riddle me this. What do you see there?"

"See where?" I said, looking. If I wasn't wrong she was pointing straight at one of the empty lots across the street. "What, that?"

"Yeah," she said.

"What, behind that empty lot?" I asked.

"No, *on* it."

"Huh? There's nothing there."

"Wrong," she said, and took a seat on a low wall just off the sidewalk. She crossed one leg over the other, tilted her head to one side, and made like she was concentrating. "I see a live open mike music bar. Yeah. Like I saw in Savannah once." She motioned with both hands. "Over there's the hand-painted marquee---it's got a some cool cartoon on it---and there's the big window where someone can play to people walking past. You know, to lure them in. Right there's the front door. It's always open so you can hear the music, and the stage is all the way in back but you can see it from the street."

"Wha—?" I said, blankly. I was lost for a second, but then I got what she was doing. It was kinda goofy, but I had to hand it to her; she definitely could think left handed. Maybe I saw it as a challenge or something because I played along. "Oh yeah," I said, as casual as I could make it sound, and sat down next to her. "One of those would be fun around here. You play?"

"Tone deaf," she said, and she gave her head a tiny little toss to get her bangs out of her eyes.

"Tone deaf," I said, and my eyebrows scrunched up together. "You're like, some kind of music expert and you're telling me you're tone deaf?"

"A thousand percent," she answered, and shrugged. "I tried to learn to play lots of different things but I couldn't ever get it right. Figured if I couldn't play it I might as well know all about it." She tilted her head. "You play?"

"Technically yes, I guess."

"Really?" She leaned in and smiled, her eyes a tiny bit wider. "What do you play?"

I shook my head. "You don't wanna know."

"Then why'd I ask, genius?"

I looked sideways at her, and braced myself for the question I knew would follow. "Ok fine. Banjo."

Her eyes went almost all the way wide. "Really? That's freaking— I've *always* wanted to learn to play that thing. Can you do "Dueling Banjos"?"

There it was, the question that always followed. I nodded, and tried not to let my lips go tight. I just knew she would ask me that, mainly because everyone always did. It's like a reflex. I'm no genius on the five string or anything, but I already got the impression that asking for "Dueling Banjos" was about as welcome as asking a rock band for "Free Bird". But could you beat it, a second later Raine said about the coolest thing she could have said.

"Don't worry," she said, and patted me on the shoulder. "I wouldn't ask you to play that. I'd be like that asshole who shouts "Free Bird" and thinks she's the first one who did that on the whole planet. Nah, I like frailing better than finger picking anyway."

I looked at her like I couldn't believe my ears, which was pretty much the truth.

"You're shitting me," I blurted, and then wished I hadn't put it quite like that. Raine didn't seem to care, though, so I went on. "You mean, you even know there's more than *one* way to play banjo?"

"Oh yeah," she said, and shrugged. She put her palms down on the concrete and stretched her legs out a bit. "Well, I didn't until I saw Steve Martin on YouTube. It looked like he was just strumming it but he was playing melody and rhythm at the same time. It blew me away."

I didn't say anything for a second. This was eerie. I knew which video Raine was talking about, because that was the video that made me want to learn to play. I must have watched it something like a thousand times.

"Wow," I said, brilliantly.

"Wow what?" she asked, one eyebrow up. I almost winced; I've always wanted to be able to raise one eyebrow but I could never figure it out. I can't stand seeing other people make it look so easy. But, in the end I forgave her because she ended up looking kind of adorable.

"Forget it," I said, and decided to move on before I started babbling; I was still having trouble dealing with her knowing about frailing. I couldn't think of anything bright to say, so I just turned and pointed at the empty lot. "Well you wanna know what I see there? A tattoo shop."

"Really? You're an *artist* too?"

"When I was four," I said. "But then I quit improving."

"Like a lot of inkers I've seen," she said, all serious, without pausing. I started to laugh at that but only ended up snorting. She went on. "You have any?"

I nodded and turned my back on her. I lifted up the hair from the back of my neck, and let her have a look at the round Celtic knot design I had done there on my eighteenth birthday. I actually only ended up getting that tattoo because Jill really wanted to get one but was too chicken to go through with it. Finally I said I would get one first, but only if she sucked it up and got hers after.

9

"Nice," Raine said, and gently touched the skin on my neck. I could tell from how she did it that she was tracing the lines of my tattoo with her finger. "Very Celtic. Where'd you get that done?"

"Aces High," I replied. I let my hair drop down and turned around just in time to see Raine jerk her hand back. She made like she wasn't sure what to do with her hand for a second, and finally just let it drop back on her lap.

"Oh yeah," she said. "I know that place---down by the turnpike?"

"Yep," I said, grinning. "Now, I showed you mine, you show me yours." I leaned in. "You *do* have ink, don't you?"

She raised one eyebrow again, and chuckled. She knew I could damn well see the huge colorful sleeves all over her forearms, the bright patterns on the side of her neck, her fingers, and on one calf for that matter. They were kind of hard to miss, being super vibrant against her pale skin. From the way she was sitting with her legs crossed, I could also see one working its way up her thigh.

"I got a couple," she said, smirking.

"Start with that one," I said, pointing to her right arm maybe a little too quickly.

She glanced down, giggled, and rolled her eyes. "Oh yeah. Figures. That's always the one everyone wants to see. Especially guys."

"Can you blame them?" I said.

"Not really, I guess," she replied, smiling. She rolled her short sleeve up to her shoulder to give me a good view, and I leaned in to make the most of it.

The tattoo showed a naturally well-endowed nude woman standing about thigh deep in ocean water, facing a sunset with her back to the viewer. She had her head thrown back, and her hair ran almost all the way down to her waist. The lighting emphasized every last curve she had, and there were drops of water glistening all over her. It was damn near photographic quality.

"Nice . . ." I said softly, and all of a sudden I found myself running my thumb over the ink. Apparently without realizing it I had taken hold of Raine's arm when I leaned in to get a closer look. She didn't seem to mind, though. "Whoever did this is a genius."

"Yeah," Raine said. "Unfortunately he went to LA."

"Damn, too bad," I said, and I meant it. "What made you decide to get this?"

"It was a dream I had," Raine replied.

"This is you?" I asked, looking up at her.

"Oh no," she replied, shaking her head. I let go of her arm, and unfortunately that meant I didn't have that great a view of the artwork anymore. "It's not me, it's something I saw. I can't remember much specific about it really except I was walking along and I saw her. She seemed so at peace with, like, everything. Somehow I knew that and I could feel what she felt, too. I remember feeling it after I woke up, and for a while everything just seemed ...I dunno, right. Like I didn't have to worry about anything because everything was going to be fine. Not easy really, but fine." She looked down at the tattoo and tilted her head in a little shrug. "I dunno, I guess I wanted to remember that feeling. Does that make any sense at all?"

"Wow," I said, after a second. "I hate you. All mine means is that I like thick, black, symmetrical lines."

She looked up at the sky, giggled, and shifted a bit. "Oh now you're just making fun of me."

"Am not," I said. Just then another hard breeze made me scrunch up, and I did something again without realizing it.

"Yoink," I said, and leaned against her. "*My* heat."

"Umm, be my guest," she said, and I could tell by her voice that she was probably as surprised as I was. She was very warm, though. By the way she relaxed almost immediately, I could tell she must have been thinking the same about me.

"Mmm," she said, kind of lazily. "Ya know—" Before she could go on, we got hit with another breeze, this one a bit stronger than the last. She dipped her head and leaned her cheek against my collarbone. "*What* Florida?" She said. I snorted, again.

After a second or two she lifted her head a bit, and leaned her cheek on my shoulder.

"So, Ms. Tattoo shop," she said, craning a bit to look at me. "... Aren't you going to ask about these?"

Before I could ask her what she meant, she put her hand on my wrist, so I could see the skin art on her fingers. I looked down at them.

"I—I guess I should, right?" I said. I almost swallowed the first part of that sentence, but I managed to finish it.

"If you wanted to," she said. "There's plenty others if you'd rather."

"That's...cool," I said. She giggled again, and she didn't snort, either. Am I the only one on the planet that does? She straightened up then, and looked at me.

"You know, what?" She said. "All this got me thinking, and it kind of gives me an idea."

"...It does?" I asked.

"Of course," she said, and leaned in a bit like she didn't want her voice to carry. When she spoke again, she was almost whispering. "It's the dumbest idea...ever."

I didn't say anything. I just looked at her, and she looked right back at me. She blinked once.

And then she leaned in again, slowly. She closed her eyes and tilted her head. I felt her breath on my lips, so gentle it almost wasn't there at all ...I gasped, and my eyes closed on their own . . .

And then, she kissed me. It was so...soft and gentle and delicate and...perfect. For a second I completely forgot where I was and maybe even *who* I was; my mind was blown clear to pieces. I mean, this was exactly what I was hoping for ever since I laid eyes on Raine, but now that it was happening, I was almost too dumbfounded to respond.

Finally, I got something close to a thought back into my head, but it sure as hell wasn't easy. I think it went something like:

Wow. I'm really kissing her.

She had my upper lip between both of hers now, and she gently ran the very tip of her tongue across it. I gasped again. *She's kissing me,* I thought. *She's really kissing me.* I couldn't form any other thought, not if I tried. I didn't want to try.

I have no idea how long we stayed like that, but we came apart, a little. I still had my eyes closed, and the only sound I could hear was my own breath. It was coming a bit harder and faster than it was just a second ago, and my heart was racing.

"That," I whispered. "Was...the dumbest idea ever?"

Raine didn't say anything. Not that I cared. I needed more of her, and I needed it now. I leaned back in and pressed my lips against hers. Somehow I managed to keep myself from gasping, but it wasn't easy; she felt and smelled so *beautiful.*

I was so lost in it that it took me a while before I realized that Raine didn't seem to be kissing me back this time. At first I glossed over it (and who could blame me), but eventually it began to feel a little ...off.

"You OK?" I whispered.

No answer.

"Raine, is everything OK?"

No answer.

I leaned back and asked her again. She didn't respond. She wasn't even looking at me; her eyes were lowered like she was looking at my breasts.

"Raine?" I said.

She didn't say anything.

I blinked once, twice, and then one more time. I lowered my head a bit and made eye contact with her. Her eyes looked distant and glazed, like she was thinking hard about something.

"Raine, are you ok?"

She still didn't say anything. In fact, she didn't even move a muscle on her face or anywhere else.

"Are you messing with me?"

Dead silence. I snapped my fingers in front of her nose. Nothing. I leaned in a little closer.

"POW!" I yelled. Finally, she blinked.

"She *does* respond to stimuli," I grinned. And did she *ever* respond.

Raine spun faster than she had any business being able to, seeing as though at one point I was pretty sure she told me she was some kind of store manager who hated going outside and exercising. Whatever that may have been, before I knew what was happening the woman hooked me full across the face and I spun like a top. I probably spat out some lame sound like *wugh* or *gnah* or *Ggllglth* or something. It's not my fault; we all look pretty silly when we get sucker-punched.

I went down like a wet towel, but she caught me by my hood and my waist, swung me back and heaved me full on into an empty storefront like a bouncer chucking out some asshole drunk. I saw all kinds of red, white, and blue sparks dance all over the place like the Fourth of July, and I hit the dirt, hard. My mouth filled with the taste of blood, and the entire side of my face felt like someone set fire to it and put it out by slamming it with a shovel. All told, all this was about the last thing I expected Raine to do.

I was a bit hazy at that point, but I remember I heard a bunch of raised voices. I couldn't tell what anyone was saying, but I could tell by how the voices sounded that they were real mad, kind of like how a dog knows you're mad at him just by the tone of your voice instead of by what you say. Like this one time I said *Twinkie Sucker* from the back of the throat and my mom's pug started looking all sad and scared.

I heard scuffling, screaming, breaking windows, and a whole bunch of other stuff. Whatever was going on couldn't have been pretty, but I didn't have much time to think about it. Someone kicked me full on in my stomach and I rolled, and then someone yanked me up into the air and slammed me against a wall, knocking me silly all over again.

I shook myself and managed to blink back into focus, mostly; I squinted against a severe glare that I realized came from a nearby street lamp. In the small circle of light I saw someone's body sprawled on the concrete like a broken doll, and I hissed in sympathy for the poor bastard. But then I realized I still had some problems of my own. I looked down to see Raine's face half a foot below; she was holding me up like she could bench a Buick and I was far enough off the ground for my feet to dangle. She kind of looked like she was trying to explode my brain by looking at it.

"You're right," I wheezed, "This is the dumbest idea ever."

Although Raine was suddenly a lot livelier, she wasn't any more talkative. She tilted her head and her eyes began to soften, like she was looking at something over my shoulder. As far as I could tell, the only thing over my shoulder was the wall, but I didn't bother to point that out. If she couldn't see what was right in front of her, there wasn't much I could do for the girl.

"I'm sorry I picked—" I said, and spat out some blood on the *p* without realizing it. The glob landed smack between her eyes like I just hocked a massive kool-aid colored loogie. I meant to say I'm sorry I picked a crappy movie but came up short when I realized what happened.

"Oops," I said, and spat out another glob on the p, which landed on the first glob like some huge gross fat person belly flopping on you in the pool. There was no winning, so I just shut up. In that, at least, I appeared to have good company; Raine didn't move or react in any way. As weird as that was, what she did next made me wish she'd just go on staring and staying still.

A little dot appeared on Raine's nose. No, it wasn't a dot; it was a little dimple in her flesh that pressed down deeper and deeper until it became a hole. As I watched, the hole got taller and thinner until it became a line, then a gash in her face that ran vertically up and down her nose. The line stretched until it ran from the top of her forehead where it disappeared from sight in her scalp clear down to her chin.

"You OK?" I asked, slowly. Needless to say Raine kept mum. "Was I that bad?"

Several more lines sprouted outward from the center of the first line, forming a sort of asterisk over her entire face. I heard a faint squishing sound, like when you squeeze a latex glove full of Jell-o.

"What," I said, "I have bad breath or something?"

She tilted her head again and then her whole face split apart and opened like a gigantic flower. Her eyes, the halves of her nose and mouth, they were all are still there. Hell, I even saw her eyes blink, but it was like someone just hollowed out her skull and peeled it open. All along the inside of each undulating fleshy petal were rows and rows of spines as long as the first two knuckles of my (smaller) pinky.

Yes, my pinkies are not the same length, but that's really not important right now.

A gross glob of goopy goo shot out of the center of where her face used to be and hit me in my own like an open handed slap. It smelled like wet muddy sweaty socks soaked in sour milk and covered with rotten hamburger meat, and burned like a jellyfish sting. I'm not gonna lie, I gave Raine my dinner back then and there. Keep the change.

If that weren't enough, I began to go numb and limp. After a moment I couldn't feel my feet, legs, hands, hell, nothing. I tried to say something, but my tongue was as numb as the rest of me. I'm sure I sounded brilliant.

Well, this wasn't any kind of fun, and more than anything I wanted to get out of this so I could tell all my great friends, and *especially* Jill what a waste of time dating is! I was in a sort of a fix though; the Raine-thing here (whatever kind of thing she was) got the drop on me fair and square. I had to hand it to her for technique and style, and I sort of had it coming for letting my guard down. But whatever, Ms. Raine-thing had it backwards: *she* was the one who made a powerful enemy tonight, not me. Like I said, I've had worse.

I calmed myself, cleared my head, and did my best to steady my breathing. I stopped fighting the numbness and let it lay over me. The trick was to detach and disassociate. Forget and ignore. Ms. Raine-thing isn't here. That lamp isn't here. I am not here. Nothing is here, not even nothing.

There we go. I was taught well. I can do this in my sleep, and I often do. It works wonders when I need to ditch a case of insomnia.

Now it felt like I was alone, floating in the dark. The dark was so thick I could feel it compressing every inch of me; to get out I'd need . . .

The Light.

The Light they tried to steal from me, the light I kept anyway.

The Light I kept, because I refused to let it go.

There, there's a tiny flicker, so tiny it can rest on the tip of my finger. That was super tricky, but I got it. Don't think about how you'll pay for this later, that only makes the light go away. Oh, crap, I told you not to think like that, get it back. Good. That was close. Make it bigger. Bit by bit, little by little. There, now I can cup it in my palms. Bigger still. No need for finesse or elegance, just make it as big as you can, as big as it can go. It's nice and big now, bigger than my big fat thick head. Getting there, but not quite. It's got to be bigger still. Keep going, keep going. It's bigger than my old math teacher's ass. Almost there, it's bigger than I am. Don't quit, don't quit . . .

There, it's so big it's pressing against everything. This is where I needed to get, like a balloon about to pop. Almost there. Like I said, no need to be clever, just make it as big as you can and . . .

Chapter Two

I went off like a flash bomb.

There was a burst of pure white light, brighter than the sun at high noon, and a blast like ten cannons going off. Both of those shot out from me and all around me. The wall behind me crumbled, leaving behind a neatly shaped round crater, and Ms. Raine flew almost twenty yards away, getting at least three feet on the first bounce. She ended up somewhere in the middle of the vacant lot where my tattoo shop was going to be and I fell flat on my ass against the wall.

If you're confused, give me a second. When I told you earlier I was messed up I meant it. I didn't mean quirky, like I had to touch my left elbow if my right elbow bumped into something, I mean I am seriously messed up.

I won't keep you in suspense anymore. I'm a Knight. More specifically a Paladin.

I mean a real Paladin, literally blessed with the holy and cleansing light of God, and the power and authority to smite the wicked and profane. I even have an official affiliation: Acolyte Sentinel third class, Six points Cathedral, House Whytehearte, Fifth Abbey. I'm an honest to God sacred magic flinging Holy Knight.

Yes, I am. Don't look at me like that, I am.

Okay, you got me. Technically I'm only an *ex*-Paladin. Ex as in psycho ex, and ex as in excommunicated. Truth be told, I'm not supposed to be able to do all this righteous indignation magic light stuff anymore, but it can be frustratingly hard to get through to me sometimes. For example, this whole ex-Paladin thing never really took all the way, but not because my old Paladin bosses didn't try. They sure as hell went through a whole rigmarole to make sure I was just plain me, to lock my power away, but I had other ideas.

Short version: I can still do some seriously pious holy magic crap, channeling the Divine Light of love, life and creation. Don't get the wrong idea, it's not like I'm a wizard or anything, although I did have a chance to work with one or two of those in my brief tenure as an anointed warrior. When I say brief I mean I never even made it past acolyte third class, which is put near the lowest possible rank allowed on active duty before I was fired. Still, even though what I managed to learn wasn't much next to what those real spellslingers like wizards could throw around, I could still do some pretty cool stuff. Not to toot my own horn or anything, but I can honestly say I got pretty good at it, unlike most things I've attempted in my life.

Still, that thing I just did with the huge light bomb, while it sure as hell did the trick, it was not really a great thing to have to do. It's basically a last ditch survival move which wouldn't have been something a fully-fledged Knight would enjoy doing, let alone an exiled newbie like me. Let me see if I can explain why.

✶ ✶ ✶ ✶ ✶

Imagine you want a nice refreshing drink of water, and there's this man standing there with a tanker full of it. You walk up to him and hold out your cup and say to the nice man "please sir, could I have a drink?" and then the guy pops open the valve and lets the whole tanker empty out all over you.

Yeah, your cup would probably get filled to the top like you wanted, but you're also drenched and something like 99.999 (repeating) percent of the water in the tanker just rolls off into the sewer where you wouldn't want to drink it anyway. You end up with one little cup you can drink and all of the other potential drinks are gone. Basically, super inefficient.

That make sense? I hope so because that's the best I got.

✶ ✶ ✶ ✶ ✶

I got free of the Raine-thing, but I felt like a six month old dish sponge.

Well, at least I could move again, and this meant I could bless. Blessing would be one whole hell of a lot easier on me then that what I just did, which was the spiritual equivalent of a quickie standing up in the kitchen. It was inefficient, sloppy, messy, and you're spent before you know what just went on. Now that I could bless, I could take my time and enjoy the scenery, you might say.

I held out the first two fingers of my right hand, placed them on the bridge of my nose, and muttered the litany that would substantiate my Blessing.

Let me explain what I just said. Now don't jump down my throat if my explanation sucks, I never claimed to be an expert lecturer or anything. Hell, at work when I step up to the white board and bust out the squeaky dry erase I think I end up making my point even harder to understand. But here goes anyway.

First of all, as I just pointed out, magic is real. I mean, really real. There are wizards and witches and ghouls and ghosts and vampires and demons and heaven and hell and just about anything else you can think of. You need to just go with this because whether or not you buy it doesn't change the fact that it's true.

That said, I'm sure you're familiar with the concept of spells. I think we pretty much all are. A wizard or a witch wants something to happen and they make it happen usually by sheer force of will and give it juice by using anger or any other emotion that's handy. That along with their sensitivity to whatever or wherever their magic comes from makes the spell happen, and they usually seal the deal by declaring their intent, like with a magic word or incantation.

Now, wizards have different spells for different occasions. A wizard wouldn't, for example, try to make a tree grow by shooting a fireball at it. Usually. A Paladin's magic is just the same...only different. If you're a Paladin, willpower or emotion doesn't count for anything. It's all about belief and faith. And you don't need to have belief or faith in anything in particular; you only have to believe that you can do what you're trying to do and that what you're about to make happen is real.

I know what you're thinking right now; you're probably thinking *wow, that's easy! I could do that!* Sure, on paper it sounds like a snap, but if it were that easy there'd be a lot more of us out there.

Like wizards, we have different flavors of magic. People have lots of opinions on this but basically it boils down to three major kinds: Blessings, Prayers, and Exactions. From fifty thousand feet, here's the difference:

Blessings are for healing.

Prayers are for empowering.

Exactions are for killing.

In a nutshell, if you were trying to close up a cut, clear poison, or ditch a headache you'd *bless* yourself or the person. If you wanted to beef up your fists or weapons or jump higher or run faster, you'd *pray*. On the other hand, if you wanted to generally just try to end something's life by shooting the Light at it, you'd *exact*. One Knight I trained with would say something like 'B' for benign, 'P' for power, and 'E' for exterminate. I guess that sort of works.

Moving on. Just like wizards, we also have to speak our intent out loud in order to make anything happen. Why? Don't ask me, I only work here. Basically, when you speak out loud, you're opening the door and telling your prayer or blessing or exaction to get out of the house, and they can only do what they need to do once they get out of the house. That's called substantiating.

It doesn't really matter what you say to substantiate. The same Knight I just mentioned would use words like *Yeehaw* or *Thatherton* for some reason. He was pretty damn good at what he did though, so I never said anything about it. Another guy used a weird mix of Hebrew and Arabic (how's that for bizarre!). As for me, I always went with German, mainly because, let's be honest, it's hard to find a language that packs more punch. I never had any trouble believing that German would make my stuff work, because it just sounds so aggressive.

The litany I chose for this blessing was just a passage I ripped out of Psalms 9:16:

But the needy will not always be forgotten, and the hope of the afflicted will never perish.

I used Google translate to get the German, so don't blame me if it's terrible:

Aber die Bedürftigen nicht immer vergessen werden, und die Hoffnung der Elenden wird nicht untergehen.

A few seconds passed, and then the Blessing took effect. All the nasty hurts the Raine-thing threw at me just washed off and away like grime in a hot shower. I was as good as new.

Let me tell you something. If you've never experienced this (and you most likely haven't), then I can't really expect you to appreciate how incredible it feels. I might say it was like a shot of heroin on steroids but first of all that doesn't even make sense, and second, I have no idea what shooting heroin feels like.

I stood up, letting the Light fill me, course through me, and complete me. That's the stuff. Nice and easy. Oh yeah. By the time I completed my blessing, I felt ten feet tall and bulletproof. Hell, for all I knew, I was. Whatever, I was ready for twenty Raine-things now, so, where was she—

Crap, Raine was already in midair, halfway toward me. Christ, did she really just jump from all the way the hell over there? Looked like it. She landed about ten feet short, and then lunged at me like I just kicked her mom in the face.

I lifted the first two fingers of my right hand sideways to my lips and grabbed my right wrist with my other hand. At that moment, it almost felt like that one time when I was ten and my sister dared me to go in the batting cage and try to hit the fastest pitch the machine could toss. Just like then, I had maybe half a second to decide how to swing. I didn't have a chance then. Hopefully this would be different.

"*Unterbrechen*," I muttered, bracing myself. I shot out my hand, and then I let loose the very first exaction I ever learned. The Rebuke.

It was a shot in the dark, really, but I really didn't have much time for anything better. The Rebuke is a quick and dirty low-level exaction that's real useful against mindless evil stuff that's just about as low level. Basically, if the bad thing you're trying to Rebuke is the rough equivalent of a drooling, helmet-butting mouth breather then it'll be stopped in its tracks, run away, or maybe even get knocked on its ass. As it turned out, the Raine-thing got knocked on her ass, which surprised the holy hell out me. She just bounced back and hit the dirt like she was thrown from a moving train.

"Huh?" I said. I'm sure my jaw was hanging open or something. That really shouldn't have worked like that. Not even close.

Let me explain. Based on everything I saw, I was positive that Raine was possessed. Not positive-positive, more like the fake positive. But really, one second Raine was there, and the next she's some crazy flesh beast. I didn't really know what else to call it. I've dealt with demonic possessions before and they were pretty damn close to this. Typically you'd want to exorcise them, but a Rebuke can buy you a little time, if only a little. Only my Rebuke did a lot more than a little.

Rebukes shouldn't work that well against possessed people. It's true there isn't all that much left of the person once they're possessed but there's almost always enough to ignore most of what a Rebuke could dish out, because Rebukes are useless against human beings. At most I was hoping to throw Raine off balance maybe, so I could sidestep or something, but—

"That shouldn't have worked," I said, and then, as if I expected the Raine-thing to know the answer, I went on. "Why did that work?"

The Raine-thing moved a little, and rolled over. She sputtered, spat, and then got on all fours. She looked like a whipped puppy.

"Aww," I said. I guess for some reason I started feeling rotten. Ok, I know she did try to eat my face but she was a pretty nice girl all in all, when she was normal, anyway. On top of that I was only just now coming down off my rush of combat adrenaline and I was having a really hard time squaring in my head that the girl I was crushing on only a second ago was now some kind of raging flesh beast. Such is the life of a Holy Knight, I guess.

"Um," I said. "...Sorry?" I think I actually leaned sideways to get a look at her face and wringed my hands. The Raine-thing looked around like she forgot where she was for a second, and then she saw me. It was so weird. Her face had almost closed back together but not quite, and it looked like it was opening and closing just a tiny little bit in time with her breathing. Her eyes blinked again, which let me tell you, just looked plain wrong.

It looked like she was waiting for me to do something, so I did. "Um," I began, again. I'm the world's best orator, as you can see. "You ...still want that drink, Ms. Raine?" My eyes were wide open, and my mouth stretched down on one side. I looked sideways at her, hoping she would take this as her cue.

She didn't. She just fidgeted a little and went right on looking me over.

"I'll buy," I said. "Oh, not that I'm, you know, not that I'm implying you can't, I mean, I know you can pay so don't think I'm, look, if you wanna pay go on ahead, I won't say a thing. I was just thinking since...I would just...just I need Raine. That okay? Forget the paying and the drink thing. Just, is Ms. Raine down in there somewhere?"

I swear to God, that's really what I sound like when I have no idea what I'm saying. Sometimes a sentence is halfway out of my mouth and then I jump the track and dig a new dirt road in the ditch. For fun one time I left my phone's sound recorder app running for five minutes during a meeting at work where I was pitching a new project. It was horrific. I have no idea why I still have a job.

Now I'm no genius when it comes to reading faces when they're all together in one piece, let alone when they're split up in six pieces, but unless I was on something it looked like the Raine-thing was kinda scared, or maybe she was just trying to figure out what the hell just happened, and, more importantly, whether or not it would happen again. You know, kind of like when a kid walks right into a sliding glass door and you see him look around all confused for a second. The bottom line was I don't think Raine got anything I was saying.

VVVT VVVT.

My pocket shook; of course I'd get a text right now. I knew it had to be Jill, too, which means if I didn't reply immediately she'd go on texting me like a goon until I did. And you know, I was thinking just a second ago that I probably shouldn't make any moves because the Raine-thing looked like one of those bobcats or something that would see a hiker in the woods, stare for a second, and then book it once the hiker so much as breathes. In fact, the Raine-thing already edged back a bit a few times while I was talking so I was probably right.

But the thing is, when I feel my phone go off it's practically a conditioned reflex to reach into my pocket, unlock it, swipe a quick *LOL* or *ROFL* to acknowledge receipt of said text to stave off any follow ups, and put the phone back. I've broken it down to such a smooth motion you'd go nuts if you saw it; I was like a goddamn gunslinger.

I guess the Raine-thing must have thought I *was* a goddamn gunslinger, because as soon as she saw me go for my phone, she hunched back, her whole face split wide open, and she screamed like she was on fire. I jumped and dropped the phone, which only made it worse.

That was when the cops saw us.

Chapter Three

"HOLD IT RIGHT THERE!"

That was one of the cops, I guess, talking into a loudspeaker. I couldn't see who exactly was talking because they were shining their spotlights directly on us and their roof lights were sliding around all over the place too. I swear it was like they just appeared out of nowhere; three freaking cars pulled up a stone's throw away and I totally missed it.

Well, from there it got a bit crappy. The Raine-thing apparently already got it into her head that I was some kind of super big-bad that could kill her by texting at her, and now here comes all this noise and bright light out of nowhere. It shouldn't have taken a genius to figure out what would happen next, so of course I was caught totally by surprise.

The Raine-thing jerked, screamed, growled, and took off at the cops like a rabid drooling dog. I just stared for a second before I even did anything, and I swear you'll think I'm some kind of jerkoff, but I scooped up my phone before I went after her. I'm not even making that up. I really just need to chuck that stupid phone out on the highway; I swear I fidget with it for no reason at all except to fidget with it, and it's starting to annoy even me. Really, at least fifty times a day I whip it out and glance at it like I just got a text from the president of the world, like I'm fooling anyone.

Meanwhile, the Raine-thing was hauling ass. She was halfway to the cop cars before I heard the officers start yelling *FREEZE* or *GET DOWN NOW* and some other stuff I couldn't understand because it was all jumbled up together. Yeah, the Raine-thing was fast, but I wasn't exactly the tortoise to her hare. I muttered a prayer, and my body suddenly went into overdrive. I charged after her.

Now, I'm not going to sit here and tell you that I'm in shape. I mean, I might be slim if I do say so myself, but it's not from working out. I'm not into health food or yoga and I don't even so much as walk anywhere if I have a choice. All the same, my prayers carried certain perks, being who I was. Let me put it like this: I think everyone at some point in their lives whispered or thought something like *God grant me strength*. Well, the big difference between a Paladin and a normal person is that when we say that, it actually happens.

Because of that I was all of a sudden running faster than an Olympic sprinter if they were going full tilt down one of those moving airport walkways. I closed the distance to Raine before she could sink her hooks into the first cop. The cop had already fired a shot, but either he missed or the bullet didn't faze the Raine-thing. I began to wind up a second Rebuke, and I was sure that it would lay the Raine-thing out before she could do any harm—only I never got a chance to find out.

There was a flash of light, and I got hit in the face so hard I was on the ground before I knew what happened.

I rolled and tumbled a few times. The back of my head hit the dirt and bounced once before I ended up on my back, staring up at the blank, dark violet sky. I just lay there for a second, slowly realizing that my face seriously hurt and wondering how I ended up where I was. It wasn't easy; you know when you get hit hard enough you get all the wind knocked out of you? Well, I just got all the think knocked out of me. I crashed and needed rebooting.

It took a second, but I slowly began to remember where I was and what I was doing. The cops! They were in serious trouble!

I made my way up onto my knees, and stared down into the blinding glare of the searchlights. I saw some kind of movement, and I squinted to get a better fix on it. It was still too blurry to be sure, but it looked like two people scuffling, except that one was seriously beating the other's ass into another county. It was obvious that the Raine-thing was about to kill one of the cops, and I didn't have more than a second or two to do anything about it. I was still kind of dazed, and my jaw was beginning to nag at me, but I didn't waste any time on myself. I staggered, stumbled, and loped toward them, hoping I would be in time—

The person on top—who I thought must have been Raine—hit the other person on the chest once, twice, three times. I got to where they were just in time for Raine to step off with a kind of dramatic flourish—and by then I was close enough to see that it was *not* in fact Raine at all. For one thing, Raine hadn't worn an overcoat tonight.

Before I had too long to think about that, the person in the overcoat charged at me, grabbed me in one hand, and drew back a fist—

"WOAH!" I screamed, and braced myself as best I could for the punch. It didn't come.

No, that person who almost knocked my block off was not Raine. Instead, standing there like King Shit of Dicksburg, was the very last man I ever wanted to see, then or whenever. Simon goddamn Frederick fucking Bradley.

★ ★ ★ ★ ★

Simon was a Paladin, like me—only unlike me he hadn't been fired. I hadn't laid eyes on him since I was excommunicated, and I was glad of it. Too bad our time apart didn't last. His bald shiny head was glimmering in the glow of the lights, and his annoyingly perfect dark skin, nose, eyes, chin, and everything else was just how I remembered them. In his black overcoat and trousers He looked like he just stepped off of a cover of GQ, complete with all the photoshopping and airbrushing.

He dropped his fist, let go of me, and all of a sudden a huge grin split his face.

"What do you know," he said. "It's Adobe Kroger."

★ ★ ★ ★ ★

Yes, that's my name. Adobe. A brick. Don't bother asking what my parents were thinking—I made that mistake once, and believe me, the story behind the name is so stupid anything you could think up wouldn't be as bad. I'd have changed it, but I'm too lazy.

"Who, sir?" Asked one of the cops. He just came right up and called Simon *sir*, like Simon was his boss's boss. That cop and another one started looking me over suspiciously, like they were trying to remember me from that week's *Just Busted* circular.

Apparently I could have passed for any fifty of those faces, or so my friends keep telling me. Assholes.

"Oh, no worries, officer," Simon said. "She's with me. Get EMS here and clear the area. I want everyone out of here now. And make sure they take special care of that girl, too. I expect she's undergone severe trauma."

"Yes, sir."

Simon went over and started talking to another one of the police officers, gesturing like he was Patton or something, and the officer was nodding like he was actually supposed to be taking orders from this jerk. I blinked and looked around. Now that I was past the worst of the glare, I saw that there were more cars and cops around than I thought at first, maybe six cars and a dozen cops or more. Also, there was a fairly large mess of people surrounding the scene trying to get a look. Apparently I'm a huge draw.

I saw Raine lying there, or sort of; she was kind of covered up by a pair of cops stooping over her. I couldn't see much but I could see that her face was all in one piece again, and she looked as normal as I could ever remember her looking. She was still alive and well, too, or mostly; I could see her chest rising and falling as she breathed. Apparently Simon managed a pretty quick and tidy exorcism (which wasn't surprising. Simon was in a whole different league than I was on his worst day).

The cops went about their business, and Simon turned back to me, his hands clasped together behind him. I can't lie; the sight of him standing there just like that did weird things to me. No, not like that. Don't get me wrong—he was stupidly perfect looking but as you probably figured out, I don't swing that way. No, the thing was, the way Simon was standing right then was just how he was standing when he was watching my old bosses try to rip the Light out of me. He had that same self-satisfied, gloating smirk; all he was missing was a big fat *I-am-so-awesome* cigar.

My heart rate shot up like a thermometer in boiling oil, and I felt the blood rush to my ears and face. My dad and my grandpa both had high blood pressure, and I just bet I inherited it. Lord knows I'm cool enough for it. Go me.

I don't doubt I was wearing my mad all over my face, but fortunately there wasn't a whole hell of a lot of light to go around making it obvious (or so I hoped). I didn't seem to have much control over what suddenly seeing this guy was doing to me, but there wasn't any need for him to know if I could avoid it. The guy had enough over on me as it was, thanks.

I was almost shaking, but I had an advantage. In my unhappily brief vacation from Simon's presence, I had plenty of time to think up some atomic bomb insults. I was all set to properly nuke this jerk to glass, and I didn't waste any time. I wound it up and let him have it.

"H-hh-hh-"

Oh no. Not now; please, please not now. I tried to just barrel over it before it got too bad.

"—Hhh—*nnn*—"

Frog *rammit*, there I went again. My tongue was stuck to the roof of my mouth and I couldn't make it let go. I already told you I'm a wreck at speaking in general, but it gets worse. When I get super stressed or super angry or both, and especially if I have a whole lot I'm trying to say, it all tries to get out at once and I run out of bandwidth. Long story short—I'm a gigantic stutterer.

As I stood there trying to force out the next syllable, my right eye twitching, he gave me this look that made me want to stomp on his face and then he twirled his index finger like he was saying *any time, any time.* That only made me angrier, and there wasn't any chance of me getting any further. I gave up on all my carefully planned zingers and just went back to whatever came to my head.

"Oh, p-p-p—"

Oh god, the P. I *hate* the P. As if it wasn't bad enough, I didn't even sound like I was saying *puh puh puh.* Nope—I sounded like one of those sputtering cartoon jalopies. I stood there with my eyes blinking in time with my lips and my head nodding feeling like I was pushing a truck uphill.

"P-p-*piss off*," I finally managed, and I was so out of breath by then it sounded pathetic. I sure told him.

"Sure," he said, and made like he was brushing me off. "Anyway, sorry about bumping into you like that, I thought you were another hostile."

That was when the rest of my memory slammed back into place. I had made a sort of weak connection when I heard his overcoat rustling after he jumped off of Raine, but it wasn't until now that it all made sense. That's what getting clobbered in the head will do to you, I guess. See, I remembered hearing that coat of his rustling just before I got hit, and then, very clearly, I remembered seeing the bottom of his boot.

"Bumped?" I screeched, and thrust a finger at him. "Y-Y-You K-k-k—"

Arrgh, hard consonants like those are the absolute worst. When I get going I end up sounding like I'm choking on a chicken bone. One time I swear I almost gagged to death in debate class. I think I'll still catch grief for that when I'm sixty.

"You K-k—*Kicked me!*" I said, so frustrated that I almost spat out the end of it.

"Oh that's right. I did, didn't I."

I desperately wanted to call him a nasty name, but unfortunately I picked one that started with an M and my lips fused together. I just stood there, facing down, shaking my fist, looking and sounding like someone that had her mouth glued shut.

God, why do I even try?

Simon shook his head at me and clicked his tongue. "I'm all done here," he said. "You want to stay here, out of the influence of my suggestion, feel free; good luck explaining yourself to all these diligent and very curious officers, and not to mention all these bystanders who can't wait to cooperate with them. Later." He headed back up the street without so much as a glance my way.

Suggestion. Ah, I figured that's what it was; now the cop's reactions to him made a bit more sense. What Simon called a suggestion was a high level prayer that imbued the paladin with undeniable authority to every rational yet suggestible creature that wasn't sensitive to the Light. Basically, everyone within one hundred feet thought Simon was whatever boss they would have to obey. A cop might think he was a lieutenant or a captain for example, or a soldier might see him as a full-blown general. From what I heard, it was kind of flexible and changed depending on how badly someone wanted or needed someone to tell them what to do. It was very powerful and useful, and sadly I never got the knack of it. Simon just seemed to succeed at everything, though.

I watched him go for a bit, wondering if I had any chance of tearing up one of these parking meters and cracking his spine in half without being seen. It wasn't likely, but I guess at least I had fun picturing it. Realizing that I didn't have much choice, I took one last glance over my shoulder, looking for Raine. I couldn't see her anywhere; all I saw was an ambulance with a crowd around it. Finally I just gritted my teeth, growled, and fell into step behind Simon, my heart pounding so hard I could hear my blood pulsing in my ears.

I couldn't stand to look at him just then, even from behind, so it seemed a good a time as any to whip out my phone and pretend to look at it. When I did, I realized that I actually did have a text waiting; the one that set off the Raine-thing. Pleased to have an actual excuse to play with my phone, I brought the message up; sure enough, it was from Jill, and this is exactly what it said:

How is she ROLF

I swear, that's exactly what she wrote. Really, who's so stupid they typo ROFL?

I ignored my growing desire to strangle the phone hard enough for her to feel it, and I swiped the following and sent it back:

I've had worse.

✶ ✶ ✶ ✶ ✶

"So you're welcome," Simon said.

I took a breath or two, trying to calm myself a bit before I said anything; I'd be damned twice if I stuttered again. When I replied, I focused hard on each word, and that seemed to work ok.

"I don't remember thanking you," I said.

"That's my point," he said.

"Why would I thank you?" I said. "For stalking me?"

He gave me a look that said *I knew you were stupid, but you just outdid yourself.* "I wasn't stalking you, dumb shit."

"Course not," I said. "You just happened to be right there right then."

He looked up and closed his eyes, muttering something that sounded like *Holy heaven deliver us from fools*, and then he gave me a look that said *it's a chore to look at you.* He paused enough for the look to sink in, and when he talked, he made it sound like he was talking to a five year old.

"I was shadowing the nasty monster," he said.

"Raine?" I said. "You were shadowing Raine?"

"Raine? What, you named her?"

"No, you dolt," I said. "I knew her. Well, sort of." It looked like I managed to get the stuttering under control, for now. At least that was something.

"Oh really?" He said. "How so?"

I shrugged, and then muttered something.

"Come again?" he said.

"We were on a date," I repeated, slightly louder.

He blinked, and then a second later he threw back his head and laughed like a donkey. I mean, he really let it fly. He didn't hold back a single snort.

"That---explains---*everything*," he said, barely able to get himself back under control.

That did it. I stopped where I was, smacked him on one side of his chest and pointed directly into his face.

"All right," I growled, through my teeth, "Now you're starting to p-p-piss me off!"

Damn it!

He just stood there and spread his arms out. "Here I am," he said, and turned his head to the side a bit, smiling a huge toothy smile. "Lots of witnesses."

I glanced around and saw that we were standing right in the middle of a little courtyard; more than a few folks were looking our way. He wiggled his eyebrows and went on with that shit-eating grin.

"Fine," I said, and backed off. Truth be told, there was no way I could have taken Simon, witnesses or no, so it was probably for the best that cooler heads prevailed.

"Seriously," he said, and started off walking again. "You went on a date with this thing and couldn't tell what she was?"

"Lay off, she was as normal as anything all night," I said. "When she ...when she *changed* it was like spontaneous combustion. Nobody could have sensed it before she changed. Not even you."

"Sure," he said, but for some reason he didn't go on from there with an insult to my intelligence or aptitude, which was a little bit weird. I pressed on before he noticed the omission.

"I still don't see why you think I should thank you," I said. "I had Raine handled."

"No you didn't," he said.

"Yeah I did. I woulda gotten to her, and I'd have exorcised her no problem, too."

"No you wouldn't have," he said.

"Actually," I said, but he cut me off.

"Actually nothing. You wouldn't have exorcised her because you *couldn't* have."

Oh, the look I gave him. You'd have loved it.

"Couldn't?" I said. "I think I can handle exorcisms. I seem to recall a certain lady. Red and black hair?"

I think that was the first point I scored all night, but it was a good one. His eyes went a bit wider, but he got himself under control almost that same second.

"That's not what I meant, idiot," he said. Ooh, testy much? "I meant you couldn't have exorcised her because she wasn't possessed. An exorcism would have done nothing."

"She ...wait, she wasn't possessed?" I said.

"No," he said, and rolled his eyes again. "She wasn't not unpossessed."

"But that, wait, oh. But wait, if she wasn't possessed, then what was she? Is that why I could rebuke her?"

"She was . . ." he began, but then shot me a look and clammed up. "Wait, you *rebuked* her?"

"Yeah I did. I rebuked her and it knocked her flat out."

"You're such a liar," he said. "That wouldn't work."

"I am not! I did rebuke her and she went flying. I Hava—hava—ha—hava—hava—"

Oh for the love of god. I braced myself and gestured with my index finger, as though that would help. Finally, I got the rest of the thought out, but it was brutal.

"—have *no idea* why it worked." Arrgh, I thought I had it under control, but Simon has a way of getting my dander back up quickly.

"I just told you she *wasn't* possessed," he said.

"I know!" I said. "But everything I know about possessions told me she was. Wuh-wuh—one second she was Raine, the next her skull opened up but her eyes were still blinking."

"Wow," he said, and looked at me like he was amazed. "Really?"

"Yes," I said. I wasn't paying much attention at that moment, so I didn't realize he was making fun of me until later. "So if she wasn't possessed, what the hell was she then? And how do you stop it?"

"Forget it, Kroger," he said. "This is way beyond you."

"What are you talking about?"

"Did I stutter?"

I almost went after him again, but I kept it together. "C-c-congratulations," I said. "Welcome to seventh grade."

"Look," he said. "Even if I thought this was within the scope of your abilities or intelligence, which, by the way, I don't, why would I tell you?"

"Ba-ba-because there are more of those things out there, aren't there? What if I see one again? I saw kind of firsthand what these things do; they take people and use them to kill."

"Almost," he said, kind of under his breath, almost like he was thinking out loud.

"What's that?"

"Nothing. I said forget it, Kroger."

I let that slide, and pressed on. "But then you're telling me they aren't actually possessed, so I can't exorcise them? What you're saying is the only way I can stop them is to kill the person?"

"No," he said, "I'm telling you to forget it. And lower your stupid voice."

"You didn't kill Raine," I said. "I saw her—she was alive. You did something to bring her back. What was it?"

"You're an apostate," He said, and looked a little disgusted. "If I helped or sanctioned you in any way I would risk excommunication, and given how much—" He broke off a second, then went on. "I'm afraid you just aren't quite worth it, Kroger."

"How much? How much what?" I said.

"Forget it," he said.

"Ok, fine, whatever," I said. "But anyway, you've already helped me tonight, you forget that?"

"No, I didn't," he said. "You got in my way. You followed me out afterward of your own free will."

"Simon, wait," I said, and I surprised Simon and myself with my tone of voice. He stopped, and looked back at me, only half as impatiently as I was expecting. I gave him a look that I hoped said *I'm appealing to your basic decency*, and spoke very calmly and levelly.

"How did you stop Raine? Please."

I thought I saw a tiny flicker dart across his face, but it was gone in an eye blink.

"I'm only going to say this one more time," he said. "Forget it. Now, if you'll excuse me, I have a report to make. I'm going to go back to Bethesda, because, unlike some people, I can." He turned his back on me and walked off, leaving me where I was. "Go home and play," he said. "The grownups have it handled."

I just stood there watching him go for a few steps, and then he turned partway around and looked straight at me.

"Oh, and Kroger," he said. "Get in my way again and I'll smash the *rest* of your teeth in." He smiled, showing all of his own perfect teeth, and I'm sure they glinted.

Chapter Four

Well, that could have gone better. Next time, I don't care what Jill says, I'm googling the damn movie and to hell with her opinion. I swear she raves about everything.

Simon and I parted ways somewhere on just near the parking garage, which put me right near my car, conveniently enough. I didn't really feel like heading out just then, since I was only a tiny bit concerned about Raine and the others who got in her way before she tried to finish me off. Call me a busybody, but I had a nagging, insistent urge to make sure they weren't all dead.

I gave that a thought, and then decided against it. Truth was I was pretty sure the only reason I got out of there so easily was because I was under the umbrella of Simon's suggestion. I was also pretty sure going back or inquiring after Raine or anyone else would lead to bad places. It was obvious that all the commotion with the small army of cops started because someone saw Raine and me and set off the alarm, so to speak, so it wasn't too much of a leap to assume I'd be recognized. Even if that wasn't too likely, I decided it would be better to lay low for a while. Plus, I really wasn't in the best mood, and I knew myself well enough to know that what I needed most right then was quiet. Hell, that's all I ever want actually, but especially right now.

So, I turned in to the garage to find my car. I gave both the elevator and the stairs a pass and took the long way up the traffic ramps, mostly because I needed some time to calm down, enjoy the silence, and just think.

That actually didn't end up helping much, if you want the truth. All I could think about was seeing Raine lying there all alive and normal after she had just turned into some kind of flesh hungry monster, and how I had no idea how Simon brought her back. All I knew was it wasn't an exorcism, if Simon was telling the truth, which I'm pretty sure he was. Simon is obviously an asshole but he takes his calling very seriously; he'd probably take like five thousand points of damage if he even thought about lying. So that left me with some kind of bizarre new entity that caused a person to *become* that entity, but the entity didn't *possess* the person. But if I wasn't dealing with a spirit, or maybe a demon or something trying to get a foothold on our plane, then what was it?

I just realized something before I let my brain go any farther; all this time I was assuming Raine was back to normal and alive like nothing happened, but I didn't know that for sure. I didn't even ask Simon if Raine was really ok; I was too busy being pissed off and trying to get information out of Simon and treating Raine like she was some kind of goddamn math problem. For all I know Raine was catatonic or comatose or maybe even dying and I didn't even think to make the effort to ask when I had the chance. Everything was all *how did you stop Raine* and not *is Raine OK*.

That really didn't help much either.

I found my car easily enough since she was right where I left her in the corner on the third floor. She was my pride and joy; a well-worn racing-blue Ford Focus Hatchback I bought used last year at a steal. I named her Blueberry. She wasn't much next to other younger cars but she was the newest car I ever owned by a damn sight. Before I lucked out and found her I was driving a severely beat up Hyundai Excel, which was maybe the most ironic name I've ever heard for how that car ran. Don't ask, I don't even want to think about it, thanks.

I hopped in and jiggled the gearshift a few times as I was settling into the seat like I usually do, which is just one of my habits I guess. Blueberry was a stick, like every car I've ever owned. I swear I'm so used to stick that once while I was borrowing my mom's car I used both feet to brake, only she's got an automatic so I slammed the gas and the brake. Fun times, my mom'll tell you all about it if you ask.

It didn't take me long to make it back to my own little private street, since it was a gigantic four minute drive. Why did I think of it as my own private street? That's easy—because as far as I could tell I was the only one who lived on that part of the street. I lived in an old apartment house at the very end of the road, almost smack against a two story beige concrete wall that had the highway directly on the other side. Also, warehouses and other things like that surrounded the place instead of other houses. Hell, this whole slice of the town was nothing but warehouses and stuff except for a tiny trailer park next door and I don't really count that. What all that meant was it was always as quiet as death out here. It almost felt like a small corner of the world everyone drove past but never noticed.

That suited me just fine.

I pulled up to my apartment house's familiar half brick, half wooden facade and felt a sort of weird relief. You know, be it ever so humble and all that, a real home has that effect. I parked, hopped out, and even though it was Sunday night, I checked the mailbox with my apartment number on it (6). Just a habit I guess. Obviously I didn't find anything, so I just walked to the side door and let myself in.

The stairwell was pitch black dark, and I used my phone to light the way. The stairs were as loud and creaky as ever; they were those old warped kind with the strip of metal along each edge. Believe me, I tried all kinds of ways to walk up without making noise but there really wasn't any use. You're welcome to try, though. You won't do it.

I made it to the landing, and walked past the bathroom. Yes, you heard that right; there was a full bathroom on the landing. It belonged to apartment number five down the short hall to the left, where a young couple used to live until they moved out two months ago. I can't say I blame them, if I had to walk out on this landing to take my showers and everything else I'd want to get the hell out as fast as I could, too.

The other apartment on this floor—number four—was also empty. I think it belonged to a guy who shipped off to Afghanistan and it's been empty ever since. I only met the guy once, when he was on his way out for the last time, and we struck up a real quick half-assed conversation about it. I have either the world's worst listening skills or a crummy memory or maybe both, since I honestly don't even remember his name. My Dad would have been ashamed of me for that and then some; I mean that is if he were still alive to hear it. That's just me, though. A lot of the time I miss things or forget things even if I'm trying not to.

Past number four was my stop, number six. The door to number six was narrower than the others and it stuck like a son of a bitch. You really had to *want* to get it open to get it open. I mean, you had to give it a serious tug and even then it dragged along the floor so much there was a big curved mark on the linoleum where it dragged.

Again, that suited me just fine. It was a pain in the ass for visitors to get in, and that made my little living space feel all the more private. When I say little, I mean it too; I lived in the loft, at the top of one of the narrowest stairways on the continent. I swear, the stairway was so narrow you always feel like you have to sort of scrunch up or maybe walk sideways to fit. Let me tell you, moving anything up and down those stairs is its own little adventure that I don't even want to think about right now.

Well, my little loft was directly under the roof, and so the ceiling slanted down low at the walls, low enough for me to have to practically bend over to wash my dishes and stuff in the antique kitchen sink. Hell, everything about this place screamed the nineteen-thirties or maybe even earlier, come to think about it. The windows were beat up wooden frames that swung out like doors and locked shut with a hook and loop, and the tiny free standing bathtub that almost took up the whole bathroom had those little feet on it. The sink and tub were smaller than usual, too, so between that and the low ceilings I always thought I was living in more of a large dollhouse than an apartment. But the place was all mine and it was cozy most of the time, except in the dead of summer, which always showed how useless one little wall banger is. I had to go to the home improvement store and pick up a pair of those huge industrial strength fans to make it through last year, and I'm not looking forward to this year one bit.

I tossed my hoodie on the futon, which was in bed mode at the moment, and made straight for the bathroom. I needed to wash tonight off of me before I could do anything else, even if all I planned to do was nothing. I leaned forward over the sink and had a quick look in the small oval mirror I nailed over it.

"Woah," I said, as I saw my reflection. "Holy crap, did I look this bad *all night*?" If I did, I think I must have been a miracle that Raine—

I felt a slight pain in my chest at the thought, but I forced it down. No sense worrying now. I'd have to find out if she was okay somehow though. I had no idea what effect tonight's little activities would have, or even if there'd be any, but I couldn't do anything about it right at the moment. She'd be at the hospital if she was anywhere at all, and I didn't think she'd be in the best shape for talking.

I took my chin in my hand and turned my face side to side, taking it all in. I was filthy, sweaty, grimy, and gross, and there was a hell of a bruise blossoming on the side of my jaw. I kind of forgot about it while I was having it out with Simon, but now that I saw the bruise, I suddenly could feel it also. It stung something awful.

I really owed that guy, and I owed him big. One of these days, I guess, like after I kick the moon through the sun. He outclasses me by so much it's just unreal.

Just then I felt a slight twinge in my right arm. Oh, great. Wonderful. Never fails. Here it comes. This is just what I needed. Well at least it distracted me a bit from my jaw. And Raine. A little.

I glanced down at the spot on my right arm just below the inside of my elbow. There, like always, no matter how much I wished it would just piss off, was that goddamn brand in the shape of, and I'm not joking, an X.

No, I'm not a straightedge. First I'm not nearly angry enough at the whole world for that, second, I like the occasional and not so occasional junk food. No, this fantastic little X thing was burned onto my skin more or less against my will when I got my walking papers from the Church, and it's backed by one hell of a powerful exaction, one I probably would never be able to pull off. Not that I would ever want to, either.

This sweet little X wasn't just for looks, though. No, it was also one holy bitch of a seal intended to block my access to the Light, forever. That was what my old Scoutmasters decided I deserved. And the thing is, from how it looked from where they stood, they were right. They did it because they caught me using the Light for something really bad, and, honestly, looking back it *did* look pretty bad. It probably would have even if they did know the whole story behind why I did it (which by the way, they didn't, and they won't ever if I can help it).

Thing was, the X didn't really do its job. Oh, they tried to make it do its job, believe me, and as far as they know, it did. They had every right to think it worked since it came damn close, but here's the thing. I thought I needed the Light a little bit longer and I decided I didn't want to let it go.

And it worked. I have no idea how. I'm nowhere near as strong as the power they all threw at me, so I couldn't tell you. But basically they all think they took my power away, and I think I'll go on letting them think so. Well, they all do, except Simon, that is. Simon had it all figured out from the moment they finished the ceremony, and he let me know he did, too. He didn't rat me out though; I couldn't tell you why. Maybe there was a shred of decency in him after all, or maybe he's just waiting for me to screw up again so the Church could really throw the book at me. That last one sounded more like it.

But anyway, don't go thinking I'm a cool person just because I got around excommunication and kept my pally powers. The fact was, I *didn't* get all the way around excommunication, not even close. The X knows I'm screwing with it every time I substantiate something and it's not exactly happy about that. First there's the twinge, then the itch, and then the burn. Before too long the X will feel like it did right when the branding iron got me. That usually goes on for a few seconds and then it eases off until the next time. Trouble is, it's been getting worse over the last few months, and if I make too many prayers or blessings or exactions before it's had its chance to let off its steam, the burning is much more burny when it happens.

If there was anything I could point at that literally slammed a giant door shut on me, the X was it. Thanks to it, I lost everything before I even had a chance to get anything. Honestly, it was like I got kicked out of the candy store just as I spotted a shelf full of my favorite chocolate.

✸ ✸ ✸ ✸ ✸

I had it all. I finally had my life in some kind of order despite all my previous efforts to prevent that, and there were a lot of those previous efforts. Hell, I'm probably the luckiest person on earth that my family even talks to me anymore, especially my sister.

But anyway, I had it all. I had power, purpose, and, for the first time I can remember, actual friends. I was even in charge of a team, or, I should say patrol. It was one of the smaller ones, mainly I guess because I was so green. The patrol had this guy Reese Connelly, a chick named Casey Crumb and, of course, me. I don't mind telling you that the shit we saw would give most folks nightmares, either.

Casey was a damn cool chick and a hell of a wizard, even if she obviously hated my guts from the beginning for some reason I never really got. I think it was just that I was me, honestly, and I guess she couldn't really be blamed for it. But whatever. She did things that made my jaw drop, and that's coming from someone who could throw her own kind of magic around. I think that's because there was one basic thing that separated her magic from mine: I was able to make me or my weapons get a little tougher, and she could bend the whole goddamn world out of shape. Even though we never got terribly chummy, I always felt a lot safer, and, honestly, more badass whenever Casey was around. It's hard not to when you have what basically amounts to a tactical airstrike at your beck and call.

Now, Reese was, well, what the hell was Reese? He wasn't a wizard or a paladin, but a myrmidon, which is what the paladins call a non-magical combat expert. Reese and other myrmidons didn't really need magic, though. Most of them had some weird talent or other that totally made up for it, and Reese was no exception. He could turn anything you put into his hands into a lethal weapon, and that was just for openers.

Between the three of us, we kicked so much ass it's just plain stupid. Since it was our job to slam face first into bad stuff ordinary folks usually didn't even believe existed, we beat the crap out of vampires, ghouls, zombies, vrocks (which are kind of like vulture demons), three different kinds of golems, weird tentacle beasts that took giant shits on physics and causality, and even a super powerful succubus posing as the mayor of West Palm Beach. That alone was damn cool by itself, but that was nothing next to the rush I got working with Reese and Casey. If I forget everything else when I'm ninety-five and sipping everything through a straw, I sure as hell won't ever forget that. For the first time, I felt unstoppable.

So most of the time I'm the exact polar opposite of sentimental, but even after how everything went down, I still kept a couple beat up old printouts of snapshots I took of both of them with my phone. They didn't come out too good, because first of all I took them on my old phone which had a camera that was only just good enough to get by, and also because I printed the shots on a shitty printer. Still, I think I caught them pretty ok anyway. I had this super annoying habit of ambushing people with my camera phone, and if you looked at these two shots it was obvious that that's what I did. Casey was only just turning to look at me after I said *Hey Casey* and so her jaw length bob haircut is sort of up in the air like a skirt when someone twirls. Also there's a glare on one of the lenses of her hipster glasses and she looks both surprised and real pissed at me, too.

Now in his snapshot Reese didn't look surprised at all, mainly because it was damn near impossible to surprise him, or sneak up on him. That was thanks to one of his freakish talents that made him so dangerous. One of those talents was that he could read his opponents like open books, so needless to say he figured out I was a lesbian in nothing flat. He didn't really seem to give a shit, though, and he never even brought it up or made anything of it—he just ended up treating me like a guy. Honestly, given the possible alternatives, that suited me fine.

Anyway, in the shot, he's looking down at me, because he's basically a really tall stick figure, and he's making a face like he's thinking *doesn't this ever get old, Kroger?* His short blonde hair is a mess because he liked to skip showers and also because he just got done sparring with a newbie Sentinel who, by the way, he basically bent in half with his bare hands.

Like I said, Reese didn't need magic. Not one bit. His bare hands were usually enough, and God help you if he had a weapon.

Since I'm so sophisticated I went out and sprung for two plastic pushpins to stick these wrinkled up pieces of paper to the wall next to my computer desk. I'm telling you, I go all out. But to be honest, I'm pretty sure that's more than either of them did.

It's still kind of hard to believe the whole thing with these two was over in less than like six or seven months, which was my own stupid fault. Also, unfortunately Reese, Casey and miss Kroger didn't really part on great terms, which was also absolutely my own stupid fault. Those were only two of my fantastic achievements of the last year, and I could go on but I don't want to keep you here all night. Not much I can do about any of that, anyway. What's done is done. I fucked up and got excommunicated, but I kept my light for a reason. I'm not going to give it up, not at least until I do what needs doing.

Next to those two elegant mementoes was the one thing I kept from my time at home, and I think I really should stress *time* as in *time served*. It was a small photo in a cheap-ass metal frame I picked up at the dollar store, which was frankly an insult to the photo inside. It was my dad's military headshot, taken just before his deployment in the first gulf war. He missed seeing me born because he was over there, and he was almost always on some deployment or another after that. After I turned ten, shit went to shit in Afghanistan, and off he went. That time he didn't come back; an IED on the side of the road made sure.

In this picture he was a young man right out of community college, buttons bursting off his chest and looking like superman in his uniform in front of an American flag. He wasn't smiling at the camera but that was totally fake. I know that because he loved to goof around with me and tickle me until I was almost ready to throw up all over his shirt. He'd do all kinds of silly things; like, he'd put his index finger across my top lip and ask why I had a mustache or pull my allowance out of my ear like a magician or hold me up on my back so I could walk on the ceiling.

After he died, my mom went on a mad purge rampage, and threw out all of his stuff. If I hadn't grabbed this photo I knew it would probably have ended up in the garbage with everything else. She never explained why she threw out all of my dad's things, and I never forgave her for it.

✳ ✳ ✳ ✳ ✳

I rinsed off, scrunched up a towel in my face, and rubbed it all over like I was trying to scrape caked-on grease from a dirty skillet that was left out for a week. Without really thinking about it I turned and went for my computer desk, navigating by SONAR probably; now that I think about it I think I probably spend more time at that desk than in bed (and no, I am not joking).

Before I could take two steps, my whole body suddenly felt like pins and needles, as if every inch of me just fell asleep all at once. I went limp and fell backwards.

"*Awww—*" was all I managed to get out before I tumbled back and slammed the edge of the sink with the back of my head. "Awwwgh!" I said, after I hit the floor, hard.

"Son of *awwgh!*" I said, and gripped the back of my head. Man oh man was I pissed.

"You know," said a sweet, childish singsong voice that sounded like it was talking to a misbehaving dog, "You really should be less stupid and clumsy."

Chapter Five

"Crow!" I growled. "*Crow!*"

I looked up and saw her in all her blueish-white see-through glory, drifting a foot off the ground, looking almost like she was underwater. Her jaw length hair was sort of floating like seaweed and that nightgown she wore was billowing in slow motion like a giant flag in the wind.

Yeah, Crow is a ghost. A ghost I am for the time being stuck with.

"You walked right through me without my permission," Crow said. "And that is stupid. You fell down and hit your stupid head, and that is clumsy." She twisted and darted through the air, and sat down on the edge of the bathtub. She looked at me and just shook her head, the expression on her little round face looking like she was thinking *oh, you poor, poor stupid thing.*

"Thanks," I said. I staggered up, collapsed onto the toilet, and let my face fall into my hands.

"Of course," Crow said. "You know, that was pretty good advice. I'm kind of clever."

I nodded, without looking up.

"You look different," she said.

"I what?" I replied. I kept my face in my hands.

"You look different," she said again.

"Oh," I said. "Thanks."

"That wasn't advice that time," she said.

"Oh," I said. "Thanks."

"You're really stupid, aren't you?" she said.

"Sure," I said, and got to my feet. "Give me a sec, will ya, I kind of had a disappointing night."

"When don't you? Disappoint, I mean."

"Look," I said, and sort of half limped out of the bathroom, taking care not to let any part of my body brush Crow. Touching a ghost that doesn't want to be touched can have unpleasant results, as I'm sure you've just seen. "I really can't think that well right now."

"Right now?" She said.

Crow's been with me like this for about a year now, and let me tell you, it's been an absolute scream. It all started one night when I started having strange dreams that all had one small common element in them. Her.

No matter what the dream was about, hell, even if it wasn't about anything at all, she started appearing in every last one. From what I could remember at first she never even really did anything, she was just there, looking at me. Even if I couldn't remember a thing about the dream at all, I could remember seeing her standing there like maybe she was trying to figure me out; it was a tiny bit weird at first, then just this side of creepy.

After about maybe the seventh or eighth time I saw her I think I tried to make some kind of contact with her, but the second I tried to consciously do anything in the dream I snapped out of it and woke up. I was beginning to get a little bit freaked out; see I thought that maybe I was being possessed or something like that. Sometimes a spirit can do that in such a quiet subtle way you don't even know they're making you do things for them; well, I wasn't about to let that happen, thanks.

One night after I tried and failed to talk to her yet again, I decided I had enough. It was something like two-thirty in the morning, but I didn't give a flying fiddler's fuck. This had to end now. I got right to work consecrating my apartment and preparing for an exorcism.

I hate to say it, but I can't lie; Simon would have done it a whole lot faster and a whole lot better. Whatever. I got it done. I turned my tiny little apartment into a gigantic spiritual bear trap that could snap a demonic elephant in half.

After two hours, I finally got everything ready. Every last inch of my loft was covered in pure, unrefined holy power; and, now that I think about it, I kind of overdid it. I blame my lack of any serious deep restful sleep for the last week and my deep seeded certainty that my soul was being stolen. So yeah, I was kind of taking it seriously.

I said one final benediction before I went back to sleep; this one was the deal sealer. I lay there, trying to focus on how very tired I was; it took a while but I finally did drift back off to dreamland, sawing logs like a crowd of lumberjacks.

This time, I dreamt about orange polka-dot giraffe-men chasing me with bright red scimitars. I ran away from them and tried to hide in a drying machine, only the drying machine was made of glass and they could see me. Well, you can bet those angry giraffe people dragged me right out of there and threw me right on the ground. Just then one of them led this big white horse over to me, and this horse just looked down and started singing a soprano opera version of Madonna's "Vogue". Then the horse puts one of its hooves right on my chest and starts pushing down, down, down, real slow but real hard. It kinda hurt.

But then I finally hit pay dirt. Out of the corner of my eye I spotted that little girl spirit, and I quit caring about the lame ass horse and the cheesy giraffes. I turned my head to face her faster than you could believe, and then I reached out toward her.

Now, in the dream, she was probably maybe something like ten feet away, but that didn't matter. All I needed to do was declare my intent.

"*Come here!*" I said, and all of a sudden I had a fistful of her little nightgown, and the last thing I saw were her big wide eyes before we were both yanked back through swirling color like we were rubber bands.

Back in the waking world, I rolled out of bed and swung my arm like I was throwing a shot put; out came the little spirit girl thing, and she froze in midair like someone paused the DVR. I just lay there panting and sweating for a bit, looking her over. I really couldn't do much else just then because I honestly felt like I just ran a mile in six minutes against my will and ability.

"Geh…Geh…" I panted. "Gotcha. You ain't slick."

She wasn't moving, but it looked like she was floating underwater. Her gown was billowing and her hair was doing that drifting thing. Also, I could see her eyes moving all over the place, wide and scared.

"Yeah," I said. "Yeah you better be. You better be."

She let out sort of a little pathetic squeak. She couldn't really do much else; the little bitch was completely immobilized. She wasn't fooling anyone with that cute little girl shtick, demons or other evil spirits know exactly how to get past our defenses and they're totally shameless about it. I slogged to my feet and dragged myself over so I could look her face to face. I felt like I was a thousand years old.

"Oookayyyy..." I said. "Let's see what we have here, shall we? Well well."

We were practically nose to blueish-white nose. Her eyes were as big as I think they could get, and she squeaked again. I snorted.

"That was cute," I said. "Do it again." She did.

I snorted again, sputtered, and started to laugh. I was so incredibly exhausted that I thought that little squeak was about the funniest damn thing I ever heard. If she did it again I probably would have ended up on the floor choking for air or something. Luckily she didn't, and I got myself back together.

"Okay," I said. I kind of had my straight face back but I could tell it was fragile. I bit the inside of one cheek and that seemed to help a little bit at least. "Let's just see who you really are, mister!"

I've always wanted to say that, ever since I was six. I made a huge sign of the cross over her, and said:

"*Verraten!*"

She flattened out in midair, her arms and legs spread out like she was being drawn and quartered. There was a wooshing sound like we were in a wind tunnel, and she started writhing and making a real gross choking sound.

"*Oooh,*" I said. "Didn't expect that one did you?" She didn't say anything; she just went on writhing.

"Didn't think I had a holy fire enema, huh? *Oooh,* You like that? Huh? *Huh?*"

She choked and shook and struggled for a few more seconds, and then everything just...stopped. She floated in place for as long as it takes to breathe in and out, and then she drooped and sagged and just hung there, like she was stuck on a hook.

Well, yeah. That was it.

"...Huhr?" I said. I'm pretty sure I had my eyebrows up (I can never raise only one eyebrow, no matter how much I try) and my jaw was open and off to the side a little. I stood there staring like a big dumb douche, waiting for something cool to happen.

But, like I said, nothing did.

"Um," I said. "Um, Um..."

Ok look, I already told you I was exhausted, plus I was a little bit confused, so, yeah, I couldn't think of anything smart to say. Hell, *anything* to say, smart *or* stupid. I blinked a couple times, trying to kickstart my brain, and then finally something hit me. *No*, I don't mean something *literally* hit me; I mean I thought of something.

"Oh," I said. Yeah, that what I sound like when something big hits me. See, what I used was an Exaction to reveal the true identity of this spirit. It's a very abrupt, direct, and, well, painful thing to have happen to you from what I was told. Thing is, what I didn't realize at the time, and what I realized now, was that I really didn't need to use it. I was already looking right *at* her real identity. This wasn't some big mean bad monster pretending to be a little girl, it really was a little girl.

I am the world's biggest asshole.

I walked right up under her and tried to look up into her face, but her hair was slumped down and covered her completely. She twitched a little but she didn't make a sound.

Well, let me tell you, I really didn't know what to do. I tried talking to her but that obviously didn't do anything; no matter how many times I tried she didn't budge. I thought maybe she might need some soothing or something so I thought music might help. I don't know.

I popped on one of my playlists and then sat there and watched her for any movement or reaction. Lord knows some of the sadder or more thoughtful stuff sure made me get all misty, but if she reacted I couldn't tell.

I sat up watching her until the sun rose.

I wasn't sure what the hell was happening then. All I knew was I had to go to work, and there was a floating catatonic ghost right in the middle of my apartment. I was too wiped out to think, so I pulled on some clothes, splashed some water on my face and stumbled off down the stairs.

I barely made it through that day, and I came back home in a daze. I got to the top of the stairs, threw down my keys, and turned and saw the ghost floating there.

"HO!" I yelled, and tripped backwards and fell down the stairwell. I don't think the stairs missed one single part of me, either.

Yeah, over the course of the day I completely forgot about the damn ghost.

So after that I knew I had to get this under control somehow. I tried everything. I blessed her, I sanctified her, I played music for her, I talked to her, I prayed for her, I read stories to her, you name it. Hell, I even tried playing my own five-string for her, but if anything I think that just made it worse.

I knew that I could have just exorcised her and be done with it, but I already think I'd made a big enough mess of things where she was concerned already. I put her tiny little girl spirit through a meat grinder's worth of terror and I didn't doubt that there was already a barrel full of trauma or something else that was keeping her here in the first place. Maybe invading my dreams was just her way of screaming for help, I didn't know. All I know was I had to bring her back somehow if only to tell her I was sorry, for whatever good that would do.

It took damn near a week before anything happened, and it wasn't much. I was playing—no, scratch that, I was making a huge mess of 'Skip to my Lou' on my beat up five-string. I mean it, that's like maybe the world's most basic song and here I was barely able to get through it. I was just thinking then that maybe in five years I'll play it where others could hear me, and then it happened.

"*Kssshhht—*"

I almost fell off the futon. You would have too. Trust me. See, what happened was one second the ghost's face was down like always, then it changed like someone changing channels. I mean like her whole face just blinked and for a quarter of a second she was looking right at me, and I mean really looking right at me. You know, with one of those looks that just seems to go right through you?

Well, her face was back down where it was, but I sat there with my heart racing wondering what the hell just happened, and I realized then that I had scooted back a foot or two in my panic.

"Whoa," I said. I'm a poet.

Over the next few days it got better. It started happening more and more, and lasting longer, too. Before long it sounded like she was trying to string some words together in some crazy language I was sure I never heard of, but for some reason I couldn't put my finger on, it sounded kind of familiar. Obviously I couldn't make anything out of it, but I recorded some of the jabber on my phone and tried to google the words. I don't have to tell you, I don't think, but I struck out.

It took me a whole day after that to realize why her weird language sounded familiar. It was because it wasn't a weird language at all, it was English, just...backwards. Yeah, you know how something sounds when it's backwards; it has emphasis in weird places. Well, turns out I'm not completely useless after all. I popped on my headphones, loaded the sound file onto my PC, and played it backwards.

I wished I hadn't. I just sat there, stunned, listening to the file loop. I hated myself more than ever at that moment. I mean I really just wanted to die. No, I'm not telling you what it said, it's really none of your business, thanks.

Well, I walked up to her, leaned over and whispered in her ear. No, I'm not telling you what I said, either. Again, none of your business. All you need to know is that when she heard what I said, she came back completely, and when she saw me, she reacted about how I thought. She was terrified and she tried to get as far from me as she could. It took me over an hour to get her to the point where she would listen to me and God knows how long to calm her down.

I did eventually calm her down though, and I can't exactly remember how, either. All I know is, finally she got a little bit responsive, and from there I kind of eased into a basic conversation.

It went something like this.

"So," I said. "I'm Adobe. What's your name?"

"Croatia," she said. She looked like she had to think a little first, like she wasn't sure.

"Croatia?" I said. "What, like the country?"

"Like the what?"

"Never mind," I said. "Honestly, that's kinda pretty and all, but I don't think it really fits. Look, how about I just call you Crow?"

"Crow?" she asked. "What, like the bird?"

"Um, yeah, exactly."

She smiled so big you wouldn't have believed it. "OK!"

If I could, I would tell you how relieved I felt when I finally saw her smile. After everything I found out about her, about why she got into my dreams in the first place, and about why she was more or less stuck to me, I think it was much, much more than I deserved.

Like I said, that was a year ago, and she's gotten a bit more lively and confident since. She started showing up in my dreams again a few days later, but you can bet I took it in stride from then on. I kind of walked on eggshells for a long time, since I didn't think I deserved much more after what I did. When I talked to her at all I didn't do much more than make light conversation, since I really just wanted to do my best to keep her at ease, no matter what happened; hence why I didn't get all hot and pissy over my minor head injury.

I limped over to my computer desk and dry swallowed two aspirin from the bottle I kept next to my monitor. Yeah, I could have used a blessing to get rid of the ache, but, honestly, using the Light to rectify such a small inconvenience just seems kind of tacky. I fell into my chair, swung the chair back and forth a bit, and then absently reached for my five-string.

"Ooh . . ." Crow said, her eyes going a little wider. "Play an Eddie Peabody song!"

I rolled my eyes, but not too much. See, one thing I found out about Crow over the last year was that she has no real sense of time, so she forgot how long it was since she last asked me that. The last time she asked was last night, when I told her I was still working on an Eddie Peabody song, but as far as she was concerned, the last time she asked me was five years ago.

Anyway, the first time she asked me that I had to Google Eddy Peabody before I knew who she was talking about. Turns out he was some almost hideously talented showman from the nineteen-twenties who played just about anything with strings, but in particular he played a four string banjo in ways that would make a speed metal guitarist's hands cramp. I watched one video of the man playing and all of a sudden I felt about two inches tall.

Oh *yeah*, I'm sure I could play like that, if I live to be seven thousand.

"I'm still working on it," I said.

"Oh, ok," she said. "Could you learn "St. Louis Blues", I love that song."

"You know it," I said. She always said that, too.

After seeing Peabody play and after I got over the crushing sense of inadequacy, I did realize that all that did at least help me pinpoint Crow's rough point of origin, so to speak. If she liked Peabody, I figured she was probably even way older than my grandmother. Poor thing.

I began to strum the banjo, and gave "Cripple Creek" a try; like usual I failed to hold rhythm for very long. I guess it wasn't god-awfully bad but no one would have dropped a penny in my hat on the street. Crow looked like she liked it, though. Sounds of home maybe? I don't know.

Just then I thought of something. It was a really good idea, or at least I thought so.

"Say, Crow," I said.

"Hmm?"

"You know how you can visit my dreams?"

"Yeah. So?"

"Do you think you could visit someone's *else's* dreams?"

Chapter Six

I woke up the next morning feeling all satisfied with myself. Crow was so excited about my idea that she went right off and got right on it. I had no idea if it would actually work or how long it take, but I was so pleased that I thought of it that everything just seemed dandy as hell.

I don't use that word nearly enough. Dandy.

I went off to work that morning with a skip in my step, and arrived a full half hour early, which let me tell you, is a huge accomplishment. Not that anyone cared or that it made any difference. See, I'm salaried and I work a sort of results oriented job, so they don't really see my hours so much as my output. I'm a web developer, specifically a PHP web developer, for a financial research and publishing firm, which is every bit as exciting as it doesn't sound for someone who isn't in the field. I have a kind of odd problem of being unable to rave or complain about my day to most of my friends, since they'd almost need a glossary. Eventually, I just simplified it to "I take data from one place, do stuff to it, and then put it someplace else." Once they got that, I could just say stuff like, "Today sucked because I couldn't get data from someplace", or something. Still, it didn't exactly make for a fun conversation, so eventually I just quit trying.

Today, though, today would be different. Today was a big day since my team was about to present our progress report to the whole business. We've been working on a home grown content management system to replace the out dated, hacked together atrocity we'd been using for the last fifteen years, so it was kind of a huge deal. Needless to say, I was pretty sure that if we blew them out of the water I could just take the rest of the year off, seeing as that we were a whopping two weeks from Christmas break. I really ought to be nervous about it, but for some reason I was just in too good a mood for that.

I just strode in through the lobby liked I owned it and said a nice chipper "good morning" to the receptionist. She was used to how I usually went dragging through there so my bright attitude kind of caught her off guard a little, I think. Anyway, I swiped my badge and let myself in; the receptionist smiled then, since she was used to having to buzz me in because I forget my badge a hell of a lot.

Up the stairs I went, and then, like always when I walked past HR, I looked up. They have this little dry erase board hanging there right outside their door, and they scribble something that's supposed to be inspirational on it every morning. Today's offering was:

"Ability is what gives you the opportunity; belief is what gets you there."

I've seen this one twice so far. If I miss the daily message I can't properly start my day, and I'm not even joking. I think it's some kind of crazy ADHD or OCD or whatever the hell, I can't keep those straight. Whichever it is, I haven't missed the message in months, except for that one time.

See, that one time, I came to work and the dry-erase was blank, and I almost had a fit. Of course, I didn't realize I came in on a holiday until like twenty minutes later after I walked around and saw no one else was in the whole building.

As I approached my cube, I saw my team members John, Armando, Cade, and Mitch all gathered around sipping coffee, or in John's case I'm pretty sure it was tea, from the break room. John always drank tea, and it seemed to fit since I think he came from Redding, England, and had the accent to match. He even called thermoses 'flasks', which threw me for a loop the first time I heard him say it, let me tell you.

"Glad you could join us," John said, lifting his paper cup like he was toasting me or something. "You can settle a dispute we're having."

"No shit?" I replied. "What's that?"

"Which of us you would take out if your fancies lay in that direction." He swept his hand around at the other guys.

"All of you at once," I answered without pausing. "I thought I already told you all that."

"Yeah," Mitch cut in. He was an interesting dichotomy that I realized was becoming more and more common to see these days: A brilliant programmer who looked and sounded for all the world like a full-on football jock. "Except we don't share too good."

I shrugged. "Buyer's market. Deal with it. So they fixed the coffee machine finally?" I pointed at Cade's cup.

"Not sure yet A, " Cade replied. Cade was an older guy from Vietnam, and most of the time he just called me *A*, my initial. It was kind of his thing.

"I saw someone doing something to it," Armando said, and I have no idea where his accent came from but he claimed it was Romania. "But I didn't get close enough to see what it was."

"I'll take the risk," I said. "Need to be in ship shape for the 9:30."

"What's going on at 9:30?" John asked, sounding as deadpan and sincere as hell.

I snorted, rolled my eyes, and went off to the break room.

At 9:30, all five of us were set up in the big main cafeteria room, a projector shining a large, pretty company logo against one wall. There had to have been someone from almost every business unit crammed into the place, and even though the room was huge with plenty of seats and tables, some people had to stand. I'm thinking all together there had to have been at least eighty people or more. On top of that, this little shindig of ours was being streamed over the Internet to our other offices in LA, New York, Boston, and Georgia.

Yeah. This was sort of a huge deal.

Armando was the team lead, so he introduced us and gave a quick overview of the project before turning it over to John. That was super smart because while Armando is a freaking genius, he's about as warm as a snowcone. John always did a better job with the speaking thing, mainly I think because it's hard to screw up when you sound like someone straight out of Monty Python.

Anyway, John went through his demo and took some questions, and I could tell that everyone was seriously eating it up. Even though some features weren't ready yet, John explained them perfectly and I could see people in the audience looking at each other and nodding.

Finally John started wrapping up, which meant it was my turn to show off my part of the project. John was a tough act to follow but, in my own humble opinion, my part was the really cool stuff. I was honestly nervous as hell, but then I remembered all the late hours and weekends I put in making sure this all was just perfect, and that helped. A little. I think.

"No more questions?" John asked, looking around the room to make sure. "Right then, let's move on to the templating tools, which I'm sure is something you've all been waiting to see. To that end, I yield the floor to Ms. Adobe Kroger. Thank you."

Everyone clapped, and John smiled and stepped aside, making room for me in front of the screen. The he remembered he was still holding the remote to advance the slides and switch over to the laptop display, so he stepped back and handed it to me. I took it, turned around to face the audience, and—

I was face to face with Crow.

"HO!" I yelled. I stumbled back toward the wall, and I ended up falling over the desk that had our laptop on it and knocked them both over. The cable connecting the laptop to the projector got yanked out and the screen on the wall went blue and said "connection lost". Something else must have gone wrong too because there was a huge squealing noise like microphone feedback, and then an even louder buzzing sound, and then some kind of stuttering beep. It sounded like a really bad Atari 2600 space shooting game, on full surround sound.

And for all I knew, all this was going out cross-country.

Oh, who was I kidding. Of course it was going out cross-country. Live and uncut.

"What's wrong, idiot?" Crow asked. She was still floating right there as calm and natural as you please. John and Cade ran right past her like she wasn't even there, though, and started helping me up. I wasn't sure what to make of their and everyone else's non-reaction to a god damn ghost right in front of them; maybe they saw plenty of ghosts already and seeing another wasn't any big deal, or maybe it was that they couldn't see Crow at all. I had a sneaking suspicion it was the second one. I thought it was safe to assume they couldn't hear her either, but since I never saw Crow outside of the loft before I had no idea.

But wait, it got better. All of a sudden John and Crow started talking at the same time.

"Are you all right—" John said.

"—and I found—" Crow said.

"—looks as if you took a—" John said.

"—and you're naked—" Crow said.

"—perhaps you—" John said.

"—upside down and backwards—" Crow said.

"Wait, which?" I said brilliantly, probably to both of them.

"Which which?" Crow said.

"Sorry?" John said.

"Um," I interrupted. "I'm sorry, hang on, one a time?"

"What are you—" Crow said.

"—one at a time?" John said.

This was obviously doomed to failure. I thought listening to two songs I didn't know by heart at once while talking on the phone would have been easier. I held up my index finger, trying to gesture at Crow without making it look like I was doing that.

"Hey John," I said. "Um, hold that thought a sec."

"Sorry?" John said.

I won't bother going into the rest of the presentation in detail, but suffice to say it was a mess. It didn't help that while I was trying to get everything together Crow kept right on talking, and she kept getting more and more irritated and got louder and louder when I didn't answer. Finally, though, I got through it, although I don't really remember how. I know I stuttered a lot.

Finally, though, the meeting was over, and everyone started filing over to the tables set up along the side to get donuts and coffee. I jumped on this chance to get the hell out of there without anyone really seeing. I told my team I'd be right back, and, when I was sure their backs were turned, I mouthed *come on* at Crow and beat it.

★ ★ ★ ★ ★

I was finally beginning to calm down a bit as I walked across the cube farm. It was obvious that no one could see or hear Crow but me, since she kept on jabbering as we walked past person after person who didn't so much as flinch at her. Well, now that I think about it that may not prove anything. After all, these are the same people I would walk past, look in the eye and say "Hello!" and they would make eye contact back at me but say nothing at all. Hell, maybe they saw Crow and didn't care; who the hell knows? Important thing was Crow followed me through the building without any incident.

Of course, no one could see or hear Crow, but everyone sure as hell could see and hear me—so the first thing I needed to do was find someplace where I could talk to thin air without anyone seeing. I knew just the place.

VVVT VVVT. VVVT VVVT.

There went my phone. I did my gunslinger thing; a quick glance at the screen on its way up to my ear told me it was my grandmother.

Ugh. Oh well. She'll leave like seven hundred messages and fill up my mailbox if I don't just get it over with now. I took the call.

"Hey grammy," I said.

"Is this Adobe?" my Grandmother asked. She always started the call like that, which I never quite got. She's calling *my* phone and she has to make sure it's me who answers? Wow.

"Yes it is," I said.

"Oh well, that's just wonderful," she said. "I'm just so happy, thank you for taking my call."

Yes, she always said that too, like I'm a talk show host or something. One of these days I swear I'm going to pick up her call and say *hello, Martha in Seattle, you're on the air.*

"Of course," I said. "So, you landed ok?"

Here's the deal. She was flying in for Christmas like she always does, and we always got the whole family together and did the hallmark thing. I was her youngest grandchild, so to her I never really grew up, even though I'm twenty-two.

"Oh yes, it was delightful," she said. "Absolutely delightful. Your mother and father will be taking me to Disney World with your sister, which I'm happily anticipating. So, tell me all about your job."

I swear I inherited my conversational skills from her side of the family. Every time we talk it's like an interview. Well, we shot the breeze for a while as I led Crow down the stairs, back through the lobby, and across the courtyard. Then my Grandma got around to the question I was hoping she would forget to ask.

"So," she said, and her voice got all hopeful and sweet. "Will you be joining me for Church while I'm down?"

I cringed. See, she's maybe the most devout person in the solar system. I'm not knocking her or anything---I mean she walks the walk. She's got a heart of gold and can seriously make friends with a convicted murderer and make him want to take up needlepoint if you give her five minutes. But at times it can get to be a bit much, and while most of the time I just let it all roll right off my back, this one particular request was only a little bit sticky.

Here's why. I *cannot* set foot in a church. Period. *Any* church. It doesn't matter what denomination. It's not like I don't like them or they creep me out, I mean I literally am *unable* to go inside one. It was a little side effect of being an excommunicated Paladin. I tried once, and, well, forget it. It really, *really* hurt. I actually almost ended up in the ER.

"I'm sorry, I don't think I can," I said, making my voice sound as reluctant as I could. I think I did an okay job.

"Oh now why?" She said. "I've come all this way."

"I'll be really busy at work. End of the year and all that." That was a big fat lie. Half the floor would be on vacation next week and now that the big presentation was over everyone was in severe coast mode. Not to say I didn't have a lot to get done, but nothing major was going to hit production until after New Year's so the worst was over.

"Well how about for Christmas service?"

"Umm," I said. If there's one thing I say way too much, it's *umm*. I need to hire a speech coach or something.

"Oh come now, dear, it's not like you'll burst into flames."

Wow, a zinger from Grammy. I didn't know what to say to that, and on top of that it practically hit the bull's-eye dead center.

"Well," I said, trying to sound casual. "Fact is I just might. I never stuck around long enough to see."

That got her going for sure. She let out one of her big full on belly laughs that kind of sound a little slower than other people's belly laughs. I didn't think what I said was all that funny, but apparently it was.

"*Ooh* my goodness," she said, and laughed kind of from her throat a few times before going on. "You are *sooo* precious my dear."

Fortunately she didn't press the issue from there. She'd go with my mom, and whatever boyfriend my mom had this month, and of course my perfect sister like always, and I'd be the selfish brat who couldn't be bothered. She didn't say as much but the implication was always there. Whatever. Not like I had a choice.

She thanked me again for taking her call and wished me an "up" day like always, and then I hung up. By this time I was just about where I needed to be, which was by a clump of trees on the far end of the courtyard.

"Are you going to stop walking sometime?" Crow said.

"Yeah, actually," I replied, and walked on into the little grove. "Right in here."

"Why did you go here?" Crow said. "Looks stupid."

"I like it," I said. "It's my thinking place."

"You think?"

"I do my best."

"Try harder."

I didn't have the energy to retort. Instead I just took a seat on a stump. "Ok," I sighed, looking right into her blueish white face. "So. What the hell are you doing here?"

"What?" Crow asked.

"What the hell are you doing here?" I repeated. "You trying to get me fired?"

"What's that mean?" she asked.

"Never mind," I said. "How did you get here? How did you find me? I never told you anything about where I work."

"Oh, that's easy," she said, and then she swooped a bit and sat on a smaller stump across from me. "Once I've seen your dreams, I can go right to you whenever I want." Her eyes rolled up and to the left, like she was thinking. "Like there's a door I didn't see before."

"That so?" I said. "There a reason you just decided to show up here? What if other people could have seen you?"

"No one else can see me or hear me, stupid," she said. "Only you."

I was about to ask how she knew that, but then my mind darted back to a year ago and that goddamn sound file I played backwards. I really, really didn't want to go back down that road, thanks. I let it drop.

"Ok forget it," I said. "Obviously everything's fine, but I still need to use my mouth to talk, and how'd you think I'd look sitting talking to nothing? Damn stupid, that's how."

"You mean for a change?" she said.

"Damn it, I'm being serious."

"But you look stupid."

"Would you just...ok, forget it."

"I came here because you asked me to anyway," she said. "Don't you remember?"

"I—wait, what? I asked you to come here? When?"

"You said 'let me know when you know for sure.' Well, I know for sure, so I came to let you know."

I paused for half a breath, and then I lit up like you wouldn't believe. Remember when I asked if she could visit other people's dreams?

"Oh! That's *right!*" I beamed. "Is Raine OK?"

Crow nodded. "She's been sleeping a long time but she woke up and she's fine now. She wasn't even all that scared. I could tell 'cause she only had lots of nice dreams. I already told you all that but I guess you weren't listening."

"No I—I mean—oh that's *great!*" You have no idea how good this was to hear—that Raine was ok and apparently none the worse for wear, and I knew for sure because Crow got a first hand, up close intimate look at her subconscious. I'm telling you, even with the disaster that just happened I felt fantastic.

But just then something clicked. Something I managed to make out in the garbled mess of words while John and Crow were both talking at once.

"Hold on," I said. "Just upstairs, a second ago, when I was on the floor, did you say something about naked?"

She nodded. "Oh yes. You were naked in every dream. She had seven of them."

My cheeks got hot, but I kept my face straight. "That so? Seven?"

"Yup. Just a whole bunch of naked you. In one of them you were in a shower and all gleaming and—"

"That's cool," I said, and cut her off with a swipe of my hand. I really wouldn't have minded hearing more about it under normal circumstances, but from Crow it just seemed odd and wrong. "More than I needed thanks. And I think I remember something about upside down and backwards? Yeah, that's OK also. You needn't elaborate."

"Oh yeah, that," she said, giggling. "That was hilarious!"

"I'm sure it was. Look, that's fine." I slumped and massaged my temples with my thumb and forefinger. "I'm just glad she's OK and all. Thanks, Crow."

She shrugged. "Wasn't hard. Kinda fun."

"Fun? You like your dream walking, don't you?"

She nodded. "Yeah."

"Well that's great," I said. "Because I'm about to ask you to do it again, to someone else."

"Yay! Who?"

"A little someone named Simon Frederick Bradley."

Bing.

That was my IM going off.

I was buried in code with like fifteen windows open and I couldn't have found the icon on the taskbar if it wasn't flashing bright orange. Turns out it was Jill. She's one of those types that love to use a super big colorful italicized font so her stuff takes up like the whole damn window and crushes my poor default font like a grape. Oh, and she types in all caps and the only punctuation she uses is a thousand question marks. Yes, in this day and age, she still does that. Anyway . . .

JThames: WELL HOW WAS IT???????

AKroger: How was what?

JThames: YOU NO LOL

AKroger: What, the meeting? Weren't you there?

JThames: NO U NO I MEAN THE MEETING WAS HILARIOUS LOL BUT I MEANT LAST NIGHT WITH RAINE LOL

AKroger: Thanks a lot. Well, as for last night I guess I'm alive so pretty ok.

JThames: COME ON DETAILS GIRL I NEED DETAILS HOT DETAILS

AKroger: There isn't a whole lot really. The movie sucked so we cut out early.

JThames: SHE TRY TO KISS U OR ANYTHING????????? OR MAYBE MORE????????

AKroger: This stuff is logged you know.

JThames: OH OOPS LOLWELL ANYWAY R U GONNA SEE HER AGAIN U GOT HER NUMBER RIGHT??????

AKroger: I did, but it's not looking like it at the moment. I don't think we clicked.

JThames: OH AW =(WELL U WANNA COME MEET US TONITE AT SHEAS??????? KARAOKE

AKroger: You mean Shea's in Boynton or O'sheas by me?

JThames: OH SORRY I MEAN BY U U CAN MEET JASON

AKroger: Well, I don't know. Rain check? I have a lot to get done here.

JThames: BOOOOOO ITS RIGHT NEAR U I CAN EVEN DRIVE U SO YOU CAN DRINK A LOT =) WELL LET ME KNOW IF U CHANGE UR MIND MAYBE U CAN BRING RAINE U SHOULD CALL HER SHE WAS SO CUTE

AKroger: Hold on, I think you said the magic words.

JThames: WHICH 1's??????

AKroger: Drink a lot. I think maybe I could use a blitzing after this morning.

JThames: YAAAY C U TONITE

Chapter Seven

Even after the crap morning I had, and all the lame wisecracks I put up with all afternoon, not to mention the doodles on my cube's whiteboard showing me slipping on banana peels or whatever, I was still in a damn good mood for the rest of the day. Hell, I even got sent links to a video of me falling over that already had over a thousand views. "Presentation fail" it was called. Wonderful---with my luck it'd go viral. Still, all in all I didn't really care. I knew Raine was all right (and a little more I'll need to find out more about later). Not only that, but I kind of felt like I was on a roll. I sent Crow off to do her dream-walking thing, and she took off like she heard the ice cream truck. Well, Simon, if you don't feel like telling me what's going on, maybe I'll just find out anyway.

Jill was super stoked about me coming along to the pub tonight, too, since she really wanted to run her latest potential guy by me for approval or something. She always does that, as if I have any idea.

The rest of the day flew by (which is a miracle in a job where you just sit and stare at a screen), and I was out the door at five on the dot. I made it down to the parking lot faster than anyone in the world could have even if I gave them a ten hour head start. I hopped into Blueberry and before I even completed my three-point turn out of the lot, I fired up my music. I turned it almost all the way up, rolled down the window, and then the godlike funk groove of "The Streetbeater" sailed out all over the road. You less cultured types might recognize the song easier if I called it the theme to *Sanford and Son.*

I did my absolute best white girl head bob as I made my way out to the expressway, and even did full on air harps. If you don't air harp to this song, you need to join the human race.

★ ★ ★ ★ ★

I went home, changed out of my work duds, and pulled on my favorite jeans and black tank top. Crow was nowhere to be found, which absolutely almost never happens, so I took that to mean she was off doing what I asked. Judging from how fast she managed to get back to me last time, I figured I'd probably get all the information I wanted by the next morning. Yeah, I was feeling just fine. Wasn't I just the smartest thing, too.

Anyway, I had a little bit of time to kill before meeting up with everyone, so I took the chance to run through my exercises. No, nothing like cardio or anything. Every now and then I just need to brush up on my Paladining.

Yeah, I never made it near Simon's level but I never really had the time to really find my feet before I was politely asked to leave. Still, even if I do say so myself I wasn't exactly hopeless at it. I picked up enough to get by, you could say.

Well, a Paladin is at the core a righteously wicked badass on a whole mess of different levels, but the package is never complete without their sanctified weapons and armor. Obviously when the church bounced me I wasn't allowed to keep any of my gear or weapons but a ren faire freak like me always knew where to find stuff.

Over on a set of hooks I screwed into the slanted ceiling hung my two swords. On top was my main one—a reproduction of a Model 1860 light cavalry saber. I called him Sherman, and I loved loved *loved* him. He was light, quick, easy on the wrist, and just plain fun. Plus, since I was an Army brat, I got all stuck on US military history, especially the civil war, so any sword that was photographed on Jeb Stuart's lap was good enough for me. My other sword was a copy of an Indian sword called a Talwar, and his name was Slinky. He was kind of cool looking but not as easy or comfortable as Sherman, so I mainly kept him around to keep me from getting too lazy.

Now don't go thinking I'm some kind of one trick pony. My Paladin training covered all kinds of different weapons besides swords, but it's hard to find or for that matter afford most of the kinds of things I got to use before I was let go. Plus, it's just kind of easier to pass swords off as decoration, so I stuck with them.

So, I took Sherman off his hooks, lay him on the floor, and knelt in front of him. This was something we all did regularly, kind of a throwback to the vigil from the old old old days, except we did it to make sure we were always properly focused on the importance of the relationship between our weapons and us. See, when a Paladin bonds with a weapon, it's kind of a huge deal. When I shared myself with Sherman, he became a whole hell of a lot more than just an old sword; he became a living extension of my strength, power, will, and command of the Light. If I really put everything I had into him, he could slice through a telephone pole. Not that I ever actually did that. Intentionally. More than once.

I just knelt there for a bit, clearing my mind and letting my energy go down.

"*Ich im Namen des Lichts segne,*" I whispered. "*Ich gebe meinen Geist und Seele.*"

I held out the first two fingers of my right hand and made a slow pass over Sherman.

"*Stärke, Nützlichkeit, Schönheit.*"

I felt a sharp tingle as the air between my fingers and Sherman's blade shimmered like a mirage, and then Sherman gleamed with a faint blue light for half the time it takes to blink.

He was locked, cocked, and ready to rock.

I went through as many of my sword drills as I could comfortably fit in my tiny loft, which wasn't all that terribly much but It was better than skipping practice entirely I guess. I thought that one of these days I would have to see if I could just transfer my lease to one of the bigger apartments on the second floor (but no, not the one with the bathroom on the landing).

Right about then I saw Jill's car pulling up down below, so I finished up, hung Sherman back in his spot, and grabbed my hoodie. Time to go be social or something.

There was already a crowd when I got to O'Shea's, and it was all mostly our group. Let me tell you, when Jill gets everyone together for karaoke, she doesn't mess around. Of course, the show was run by a friend of hers so it's not hard to understand why she made the effort. There were at least thirteen of us including me, and we ended up sliding together almost every table to make room except for one or two small round ones.

Everyone called my name when I came in, and I went around shaking hands or hugging or high fiving and all that and took a seat.

It probably took a whole whopping second before someone showed me the video of me falling over on one of their phones, and I did my best to just laugh along with it. Luckily, Jill was right there at the end of the table and she pulled me aside and dragged me along to the bar before I had to deal with it too much.

"Okay," Jill said, after she ordered up a drink for both of us. "I need you on top of your game tonight, A-K."

Yeah, you heard that right. A-K. Jill started calling me that ever since she realized my initials sounded close to AK-47. You know, like I was wild and crazy like an assault rifle or something. Don't ask me, man. I didn't have the heart to tell her it was stupid, like calling someone named Dan *Dan the Man with the Plan*. Jill just had that kind of brain. I dealt with it though, since at least she doesn't know my middle name is Francine. Who the hell needs to be called AFK?

"Top of my---? What---I don't *have* a *game*," I said. "Weren't you there this morning?"

"Oh please," she said. "As far as I'm concerned you're the only game in town."

"I still don't know why."

Like I said before, it was always my job to look over Jill's potentials and give a full report of my first impression, which she would either take to heart or not depending on the flip of a coin. I got saddled with this duty apparently because I called that the last four guys she tried to hook up with were total duds and I turned out to be right. Of course, if you were to ask me about guys I'd always come off indifferent, so it probably wasn't all the guy's fault. I could have been totally wrong and shot down a winner more than once for all I knew. Whatever the case was, she thought I was some kind of genius at spotting a *yay* or a *nay* and so here I was being asked to do it again.

"Ok, look," she said. "I really like this one, A-K."

"Really?"

"Yeah."

I sighed and my eyes went up. I came just shy of throwing my head back, but I think I sort of halfway did it.

"What's that all about?" She said.

"Dude, you *always* say that. About all of them."

"I do not," she said. "I really think this one is it. Like honestly."

"More *it* than Chris? Or Jake?"

"Oh, shut up," she said, but she was kind of laughing at herself as she said it, I think.

I shrugged. Right about then our drinks came. Jill's was her usual, a Long Island Iced tea. Mine was my usual, a Guinness. The head was still settling on mine but I could tell it was damn near perfect. On top of that the bartender made a flawless shamrock in the foam; I love it when people go that extra mile. Well, I didn't waste a second. I upended the glass and let it start flowing downhill.

"So where's Raine?" she asked. "She coming tonight?"

I shook my head, but that was all since I was still busy chugging my drink and I had no intention of stopping until the glass was dry. That was always how I drunk. I always said it's a crime to let any drop of Guinness sit any longer than it has to, so I had to down them in one go.

"I heard she really liked you, though!" Jill said. "Or, that's what I heard, I think."

I was about halfway done, so all I did was shrug.

"Are you serious? She was so cute," she said. "You're telling me you didn't even like her a little?"

I held up a finger, which basically meant *shut up until I finish please.* Jill got the hint. She clammed up until I got my last few huge gulps out of the way and started tasting dregs. I exhaled, dropped the glass back on the counter and rapped the surface twice with my knuckles. The bartender, some chick named Brianna, scooped up the glass. I smiled at her and she smiled back before she hustled back to the taps.

I guess now that I didn't have a drink to hide behind it meant I had to think of some way to answer Jill's question (not that I really wanted to). The fact was, I think I liked Raine a hell of a lot more than just a little. I don't think I ever believed in bullshit like love at first sight but if that wasn't what happened it came pretty damn close. Raine wasn't just cute like Jill said—the girl was fucking stunning. I mean she damn near knocked the breath out of me the first time I saw her, and on top of that she was quirky, creative, funny and she cut me slack (sort of) for making her sit through a rotten movie. And that kiss. Wow. That was the thing dreams are made of, make no mistake. The only real problem I saw was she turned into a monster and tried to kill me---which wasn't exactly something I could point out. Instead I just copped out and dodged.

"Look, I told you," I said, doing my best to sound bored with the whole thing, "We didn't click. I don't really think I'm clickable. Could we talk about something else, please? This really isn't my thing."

"Not your thing? Are you kidding?" she said. "Raine almost makes me want to go for my oral exam."

"Her?" I said, deadpan, without missing a beat. I looked at Jill like I was offended. "What about me?"

"*Heey,*" Jill said, in a goofy sexy way, and leaned in and gave me a full-on motorboat. It tickled like hell, and I started to laugh but all I did was sputter and choke. Everyone at our table started hooting, hollering, and clapping. I know one or two of them were snapping shots with their phones, too.

"You damn tease," I said, and pushed Jill away. "If you can't bite, don't growl." She just laughed her fool head off at me.

★ ★ ★ ★ ★

I had enough time to demolish a second Guinness before Jason, the guy Jill wanted me to check out, showed up. Turns out he came all the way from Indiantown up north and had trouble finding the place. Indiantown. Wow, that's really remote. It's one of those places you can drive through without noticing since it's barely bigger than a turnpike rest stop. Hell, you go too much further and you'll drive straight into Lake Okeechobee.

So Jill immediately introduced me to the guy, obviously. When I told him my name he asked me to repeat it since obviously he couldn't believe anyone could have such a name but he pretended it was because he couldn't hear me. Whatever, I'm used to that whole act. Every now and then I wish my parents had just called me Tracy or something.

As the night went on, it turned out Jason was actually pretty ok. I mean he was ok looking I guess but nothing that would stop you in your tracks at fifty paces or make you crash your car. Of course, I'm not the best judge of that but you get my point. Thing was, he was all friendly and talkative and actually real funny, and he seemed comfortable enough being surrounded by over a dozen strangers. That, by the way, is something I could never pull off if my whole family were held hostage and I'd get a twinkie besides. And even better, he wasn't overconfident or cocky or full of himself, either. He didn't seem like he was putting on some kind of cheesy phony act to make himself look awesome; I could tell Jason was just being Jason, and Jason was as comfortable with that as anyone I'd ever seen.

Jason seemed to talk to me a whole hell of a lot, too. Well, not like we could help it much, everything we said to each other just led to something else as easy as anything. He had almost all of the same interests I did, and when he heard I played banjo (I left out the part about me sucking at it) he didn't even mention "Dueling Banjos". No, instead he said he was teaching himself fiddle and always wanted to jam with a five-string. He said something about the—and I swear this is exactly what he said—he said that the...what was it, the interplay or counterpoint or something like that between those instruments is almost sexual. Yeah, he really said that. Sexual. Can you beat it? I thought that was hilarious and I almost choked while chugging my Fourth Guinness.

"So, say your fiddle gets my banjo pregnant," I said, giggling, "You think they'd have a fretless?"

Jason and I thought that was about the funniest damn thing anyone ever said, and we cracked up, pounding the table. I saw Jill tapping him on the shoulder but he just held up one finger at her and kept on laughing with me.

A little while later (I forget how long, but I'm pretty sure Jason and I had a few more crack-up sessions in the meantime, one about him treating me to a lap dance on my birthday and another about something to do with how lame tech job interviews can be), Jason dared me to go sing something. He even plunked down the huge catalog in front of me and almost knocked over my fifth Guinness. I said I would go sing but if only if he did a duet with me no matter what I picked. On top of that, I said, I wouldn't tell him which song it was until we went up and he would have to sing whether he knew the song or not. He told me I was on, and we did a pinky swear thing on it, so he couldn't back out.

I really wanted to get him good so I tried to pick a super obscure tune, something some white boy from Indiantown couldn't ever possibly know. I thought I had him when I picked "Kal Kya Hoga" from that 70's Bollywood movie my dad loved called *Kasme Vaade*. Yes, this karaoke dude had a Bollywood song from the 70's. He was just that damn cool.

But get this. When Jason saw the song come up on the monitor, you know, where it says the title and the key you're in (in this case, A minor), he jumped right in like the song was "Row Row Row Your Boat." He didn't even miss a beat. He even did the tongue-rolling thing perfectly and he made the gargling chicken noises, too. He even did some dead-on accurate Bollywood dance moves while I was singing my parts. I was laughing so hard I almost couldn't sing. I swear this guy was hysterical.

We had the whole bar clapping and whooping and singing like you wouldn't believe. As cool as the karaoke dude was for having the song, I think it goes without saying also that Jason went up like a thousand cool points for both knowing the song and singing it; I made a mental note to tell Jill to consider hanging on to this one. Trouble was, I didn't see Jill much after Jason and I got up to sing, but I was so smashed I didn't know what the hell was going on, honestly. The hours shot by, and I finally said goodbye to everyone, although for the life of me I still couldn't find Jill. Jason gave me an extra big hug and even hoisted me up off the ground and made this goofy growling grunting sound. For my part I squealed and kicked my legs in the air like a goddamn idiot, and some of the guys yelled at us to get a room. Everyone's a comedian.

I had maybe like the equivalent of ten beers sloshing around in me, but I still insisted that I was top of the line perfectly fine to drive home. They all bought it, but I sure as hell didn't. Then I remembered that I didn't actually drive here tonight, so that didn't matter. No, Jill drove me, and I couldn't find her anywhere.

Once I managed to pass on that information, Jason offered to drop me off. I gave him a big hug and told him he was a super great guy but he didn't have to put himself out like that. (Actually, that was what I wanted to say, but I think I actually said *you don't have to come out like that* instead.) I told him I could walk home and that the fresh air might just do me good. He insisted though, and said it would be safer if I got a ride rather than walking home alone. I came this close to telling him I've beaten up demons with my bare hands, but somehow I kept my mouth shut. Instead I just ended up giggling and saying something stupid like "You're a swell kid." I'm not sure, exactly.

I really don't remember much until I was already getting out of his truck and started stumbling like a moron up to the side door of my apartment building. I think he called after me and asked if I needed any help, but I just waved my hand and kept going. A few steps later I took out my keys and almost immediately dropped them.

"Yeehaw," I said, and dropped down on all fours, scrounging around in the gravel. It didn't take me long to realize I wasn't having much luck. I couldn't see a damn thing. If I wasn't bombed to pieces I probably would have thought to whip out my phone and use it for light, but I was, and I didn't.

"Oh you have *got* to be *kidding* me," I grumbled, making huge circles in the grass and dirt. I thought I found the keys twice but they were just twigs. Christ, of all the times—what the holy hell was I thinking, getting bombed on Monday night? What was I, fifteen? Wow, never again. I was sure I'd actually stick to that too, for maybe a month.

Just then I heard some footsteps in the gravel behind me.

"Need help?" that was Jason. I turned around and ended up looking straight into his flashlight.

"*Ah,*" I said, and covered my eyes.

"Oh, sorry," he said quickly, and lowered it. "You all right? Couldn't help but notice—"

"Oh no, this is just—" I made a face and swept my arms. "This is just—no I just—I got it."

"Got what? You drop your keys?"

"No, I got it," I said. "Really, I got it, but thanks."

"You sure? I got a light."

"Yeah, I got it—yeah. No problem, I got it—umm, yeah, no, no I totally don't."

He laughed, and I have to admit I did, too. He walked up and shone his flashlight on the ground near me.

"That help?" he asked.

"Oh god, yes," I said. "You're a god damn lifesaver, man. Glad one of us is prepared."

"Aim to please," he replied. "Oh, wait---I think I got 'em."

"No shit, where?" I asked. I whipped around and saw him holding them up, shaking them a bit back and forth.

"Heeere you go," he said, and plopped the keys in my hand. "Hang on to these now, you hear?"

"Yes sir," I said, and got up. "Thanks, I really didn't feel like calling my landlord. The guy's a creep."

"No problem. Glad to help."

I went over to the door and fumbled a bit trying to find the right key, but again it was so dark I couldn't tell which was which. Sure as hell, Jason came to the rescue again with his flashlight and I finally found it.

"Man," I said. "I must look like such a goon right now."

"Nah, I think you're as far from that as you can get, if you want my opinion."

I turned around, leaned against the door and pointed at him with a key.

"You better watch out, mister," I said. "If you keep this up I'm going to have to give you a triple A rating. And then Jill's gonna drag you out ring shopping by lunch tomorrow."

"The what?" he almost spat out. The look on his face was so damn priceless that I lost control and laughed at him.

"What's so funny?" He asked, sort of grinning along with me.

"Oh-oh, yeah," I managed finally, "You know, that was the whole reason Jill wanted me along tonight, right?"

"No, what?"

"She wanted me to check you out for her," I said. "And you know what?" I tapped him on the chest for each word I said next. "I-think-you're-freaking-awesome." A second later my eyebrows came together and I went on poking him in the chest, shoulder, and upper arm.

"Holy shit," I said, leaning in for a better look. "Is this all like totally solid muscle?"

"Uh," was all Jason said.

"It is," I marveled, and pinched him a couple of times, like I needed to be sure. "You're like, carved out of a mountain, man."

"...I try...?" Jason said, hesitatingly.

"Try, hell," I retorted. "You're, like the straight goods top to bottom, dude. I'm not even joking. You're like, everything Jill could ever deserve. Hell, more if you want my opinion. I'll make sure she knows, too, you can bet on it."

"Umm—I, damn. Ok. Thanks, I...think?" All of a sudden he looked a little uncomfortable. I tilted my head.

"What's that mean? You don't sound too excited. Yeah, Jill's a little flaky but she's not—"

"No, no," he interrupted. "No, that's not what I mean. I mean, yeah, Jill's a great girl but I don't think it'll work out."

"Oh," I said. "Oh. Well now that stinks. What did she do? She always badgers me for that information when this happens. Could you like, be specific? It'll help if I don't have to make something up again."

"Oh no, nothing specific. Guess we just didn't gel." He paused a second, and then went on, like he wasn't too sure if he should or not. "…Not like I think we did, anyway."

My eyes opened up a bit wider, and then one corner of my mouth stretched downward.

"Ooo," I said. "…gotcha."

"…gotcha?"

"I, I mean, that's…umm…"

"Is that a problem?" He asked, a little nervously.

"A little," I replied. "Dude, I'm . . ." I gestured at him with both hands a couple times. "You know, I'm…"

"…Completely?"

I nodded.

After a second, he nodded too, slowly. "Yeah. Gotcha."

"Look, I'm—"

He looked away. "No no, that's all me. I guess I should have known better, but, you know, it's hard to pick who you fall for."

When he said that, my stomach got tighter for a second, like someone just jabbed me down there. I honestly didn't know what to make of that. I think I must have twitched or something because he looked back at me.

"What?" He asked.

"Umm," I said brilliantly. "I—I mean, look, I'm . . ." I gave him a real soft, pitying look that wasn't fake in the least. "I'm sorry, I think I gave you the totally wrong idea. I was just trying to be, you know… friendly."

"Oh no, no," he said quickly. "You didn't do anything." He kind of smirked, and then: "Damn Biology. Then at least I could have had a shot."

I bit my lip, and then I said the first thing that popped into my head.

"…My dad always said you shouldn't waste your ammo on a shot you can't hit."

"Your Dad's a smart man," he said. I could tell he was trying to keep his voice under control. "And lucky to have a daughter like you."

Something about what he said just then hit me, hard.

"Really?" I asked. I looked at him like I really needed him to be sure or something.

"Yeah," he answered. "Completely really."

"Look—" I stammered. "No-you're-I'm, I didn't mean to—"

"Nah," he said, looking down at the ground. "It's on me for getting my hopes up. Sorry, hope I didn't make you mad or anything. 'Night."

He turned and walked away, and I just stood there, watching him until he disappeared into the dark.

Damn it.

Once I got upstairs, I fell onto my futon and just sat there a second on the verge of tears, feeling like the worst person in the world. Somehow or other—although I knew it didn't make any sense—I felt like *I* was the one who just got kicked to the curb instead of the other way around. I took a couple of hard breaths, and then without realizing what I was doing, I ran to the window, hoping to catch Jason before he pulled away. By the time I got there, though, I saw that his truck was gone.

"*Fuck*," I cried, and slapped my palms against the glass.

Feeling like someone just punched me in the stomach, I turned, walked slowly back to my futon and sat back down. A second later I felt so lonely it was literally painful. I dug for my phone, found Raine's number, and more or less out of desperation, I texted her:

Call me, thinking about you.

I stared at the text after it went through for several seconds, hardly believing I'd sent it. Jeeze, what the fuck did I do that for? Did I forget the fact that Raine was hospitalized? Why didn't I text *are you feeling okay, I'm worried about you* or something? Why didn't I do that earlier today for fuck's sake? Crap on me anyway. I started sinking down into a seriously dark mood, amplified by like a thousand percent by all the booze in me.

I wanted to just collapse right then and there but I knew if I did that I'd be fully dressed, including shoes, and sleeping like that always makes me feel like ass. Since I already felt like ass, I decided one ass was plenty and thought it might be a good idea to strip down a little.

Right after this nap, I thought.

Chapter Eight

The first thing I could remember thinking after that was maybe I must have left a window open. Or maybe it was all my windows. It sure as hell was cold enough for that; in fact it was goddamn freezing. Yeah, that had to be it, I forgot to hook the windows and that's why I was also soaking wet. The rain must have come in from the windows or something; I hate when I forget to latch them and man oh man was I cold, I really needed to get up and—

Holy sweet *shit*, let me tell you something about pain. It's there to let you know that something just ain't right and you need to do something about it before the pain turns to damage. Fine, ok, I get that and that's all cool. But, am I the only one who thinks pain should fuck off once it's delivered its message? I get it, I burned my hand and I yanked it off the hot greasy skillet before I would have left skin behind, now thank you and drive through. Oh no, pain is like a roommate you hate but can't kick out.

All that was the next thing I remember thinking, after I tried to sit up and my whole body, head to foot, screamed at me to please *please* stop being an idiot and lie still. My head suddenly felt like I had a pair of electric drills tearing into my temples, and my arms and legs felt like someone really huge and strong grabbed them with both hands and twisted in opposite directions. My ribs felt like they were doing their best to poke my lungs full of holes and my stomach felt like my colon was wrapped around it, if that even makes any sense.

I started to let out the best swears I knew as loud as I could, but moving my jaw felt like running raw flesh against sandpaper so I couldn't even have the satisfaction of finishing. I had to settle for growling, and I don't mind admitting that my voice cracked which made me sound like a boy who didn't finish puberty.

I told my eyes to open and at least they listened without making a scene like every other part of me. Trouble was it didn't really seem to do a lick of good. I couldn't see a thing. Well, not at first anyway.

I gave my eyes a second or two to adjust and then I could sort of see dark shapes moving back and forth, kind of swaying. A second or two more and I realized those shapes were...were those *tree branches?*

Wait. Was there a hole in my roof I missed before? Why the hell could I see tree branches? And another thing, I knew my futon isn't exactly a memory foam mattress but I remembered it being a little more comfortable than this. I mean, it felt like I was lying on soaked, filthy mud for Christ's sake.

Upon further review, I found that I *was* in fact actually lying in soaked, filthy mud. Wait, why did I bother to say that the mud was filthy mud? As opposed to what, gleaming clean mud? Oh, forget it. Moving on.

Now, I had no idea what the hell was going on, but after I took a second, I think I could be sure of a few things: First, I was probably nowhere near my futon, or my windows, or my whole goddamn loft either. Next, I was somewhere outside, and I was mostly prone. Also, it was dark, wet, and freezing. I could hear high wind blowing through tree branches and heavy rain slapping the ground or leaves and splashing in shallow puddles.

The hell?

I thought for a moment, trying to somehow retrace my steps to make some kind of sense of all this, but then my head and body seemed to realize that I was misbehaving and pounded the crap out of me. I stopped trying to move and think until everything calmed down.

Right then I heard something that wasn't me. It was someone else's voice right nearby, a chick's from the sound of it, and whoever it was didn't sound happy. In fact, whoever it was sounded like she was in as much pain as I was. I doubted it, but I gave her the benefit.

Ok, so I knew two more things at this point. There were at least two of us here, wherever *here* was, and we both needed a hell of a lot of help. Fortunately, I was me, and by that I mean I was a Paladin, whatever Simon and his friends had to say about it. I was equipped to help us both in just the way we needed.

Of course, like when the oxygen masks drop in a plane, you have to help yourself before you help your kid. I cleared my mind, and called on all that lovely training I got to relax myself completely. It took a little longer than usual to get where I needed, but hey, look at my circumstances before you give me a hard time about it.

It took a hell of a lot of work, but I managed to remember the litany I needed to fire off the blessing I wanted to use. It was the one I ripped out of Psalms 9:16, and I really ought to have this thing down cold, but, oh well. Try reciting the alphabet backwards while someone sings an annoying novelty song in your ear and you maybe might get how hard it was to get my brain going.

When it finally came back to me, I went for it, reciting the litany in some kind of messed up slow motion, and my voice sounded like I was chewing nails. I went on through it anyway, and I believed every last word I was saying. Once I got the last syllable out, things started happening. I felt the light build ever so slowly but it was definitely there, like a hot bowl of chicken soup on a cold winter night, except better in ways I'm not really smart enough to describe. Trust me, it's the stuff.

After a minute or so, I was able to move enough to sort of scoot up into a sitting position, and after another I could move my arms. The first thing I did was touch my face with both hands, and then the real relief began. Oh my sweet Christ it was so incredible I almost felt like smashing myself up all over again just to have another chance to feel it. But even I'm not that much of a moron.

The pain in my jaw went away, and then I could smile without feeling like my whole damn face would fall apart. It was about then that I realized I was mostly naked, which went a good way toward explaining why I was so damn cold. Well, I had a tank top and underwear on, but that looked like that was it. What the unholy hell was I doing way out here in my underwear in the middle of the night?

I decided I would worry about that later. The light warmed me up a little, and I was in good enough shape to move if I took it easy, so I crawled over to the poor little moaning chick a few feet away to have a look.

Just then there was a lightning flash, and I got a better look at her for a second before the thunder made me flinch. She looked like someone who just heard Nirvana and Pearl Jam and flipped but didn't do that great a job at putting together the outfit. It was like she had the basic ingredients for a grunge suit but never really got the hang of it. Her flannel shirt had like five different color schemes, she had what looked like a mini version of Doctor Who's twelve mile long scarf, and her sneakers looked like Chuck Taylors but were really some weird generic imitation. Whatever, at least she had enough sense to be out in the cold fully dressed, unlike some other idiots I could think of at the moment. Also her hair, which looked like it was cut in a kind of bob, was blazing stoplight red. I mean, Ketchup red. Primary red.

I knelt beside her, and reaffirmed the blessing by reciting the litany again, just to be sure. It never hurts. I felt the light fill me again, and once the warmth got to a good point I laid my hands gently on her back. She flinched and jerked away from my touch at first, sort of hissing through her teeth like you might when someone dumps peroxide on a cut. Yeah, it hurts, but it beats gangrene all hollow.

"Awwwww man..." she said. Her voice sounded about as beat up as mine felt, but I could tell she maybe watched a lot of surfer movies because she had that whole relaxed beach bum pothead thing going on. "Seriously, what the hell just happened, for real?"

She turned and looked up at me. There wasn't much light apart from what my hands were giving off, but there was enough to see that she looked extremely confused.

"Who're...wait...what?" she said, and then she looked at my hands. She looked back at me, then at my hands again. A second later her eyes went wide and she just freaked.

"*Gerruff!*" she said; she swung her arm and clocked me clear across the face. I got knocked over and ended up cheek down on the ground; I saw the chick doing a kind of crab shuffle away from me. She went straight through a puddle and sent gross water and splashes of mud everywhere. "Awww, no way, no way, no way!" She was seriously going ape shit. "You just, you just, awwww...you just..." She got up on her hands and knees and started rooting around in the dark. "Where, where, man, where the crap is it..."

I don't think you need me to tell you what I was doing while all this was going on. But just in case you weren't listening too close up till now, I'll tell you. I just lay there looking stupid, and after a few seconds I let loose with, all together now:

"Ummm..."

I eventually decided I should get back up. When the chick saw me move, she started freaking out again.

"You," she said. "You just keep your hands away, kay?"

"Me?" I said. "*You* hit *me!* Who the hell are you?"

She was still reaching around all over, patting the ground like a crazy person.

"Why don't y'all just leave me alone, man? What all did I do?"

"What?" I said. Yep, that was all I could think of to say. Boy, can I spin my wheels or can't I?

"Don't I do everything you all say?" the girl asked, but I had no idea *who* she was supposed to be asking. "When don't I? Like, never!"

"Can we…" I said; at least I didn't just say *what* again that time. It looked like I finally managed to find first gear after grinding the hell out of the gearbox. "Can we back up and start over?"

"Naw man," she said. "I think I done that plenty."

"Can you…hold on? Stop doing that, I can't think!" I wasn't kidding. She kept splashing and scrambling and it was making it real hard to straighten my brain out.

"Crap," she said. "I can't find it, man!"

"Find what?"

"My ticket outta here, man."

"Your what? Will you just stop?"

She did, but I don't think it was because of anything I said. I think she just realized she wasn't going to find whatever this *ticket* thing was and gave up. She slammed the ground hard with both arms and then sat sort of on her knees and put her face in her hands. She looked like she was about to cry.

"Fine, man," she said. "Do whatever. Just make it quick and leave me alone, 'kay?"

"Look," I said, and it was obvious I was getting a little cheesed off by now. "I don't know what the hell you're talking about. I don't ha-have the first damn clue. I don't have any idea who the hell you are or why I should care or why you think I'm going to do anything to you, got it? I don't even kn-know where the hell I am or what I'm doing here in my underpants, okay?"

That shut her up all right. It took her about seven seconds before she said anything. When she did, I felt a little better about my brilliant brain.

"…What?" she said.

"Oh f-f-f-f-forget it," I said. I wanted to say something else but I couldn't make it happen. That's just great, I really could have used a good solid swear, but whatever. I got up, shook a second, and did my best to look around. There wasn't a damn thing in sight that told me where I was, or for all I knew, where I was miles from. Lightning flashed again, and all I could see were trees, tall grass, and bushes.

It was so freaking cold, even though I was warmed up by my little bit of light my jaw was chattering and I folded my arms without realizing I did it. Boy oh boy did I feel like a colossal douche for all that talk about loving Florida winters, let me tell you.

"*Where the hell am I?*" I yelled, more or less at the air around me. "I swear someone better tell me or I'll—"

A thunder blast drowned out the last part, and that seriously pissed me off because I finally got out a hell of a good swear. I didn't even get to hear myself say it. Figures. I wound up to let loose again but I slipped, fell, and landed flat on my ass in the mud instead. I tried to get up but I only slipped again and landed on my back this time.

I didn't do anything for a little bit. I just went on lying there, letting the rain hit me full in the face. I thought about trying to get back up to see if I would land face down next time but in the end I just stayed right where I was.

I basically just closed my eyes and counted to twenty in my head. I really figured I needed that or else I'd probably end up thrashing all over the place trying to punch out the mud. I'm not even kidding, when I get really pissed that's about as rational as I get.

Before I could get to sixteen, I heard something. Wouldn't you know it was that chick again. What, was she still here?

"...You..." she said.

"WHAT?" I really hated being interrupted before I got to twenty. Perfect. Now I had to start all over. "W-w-hat the f-f-f—"

Arrrgh.

I gave up on what I was trying to say, and took a huge breath and tried to picture what I wanted to say in my head. People tell me that should help when I got stuck, but whatever. The chick went on like I didn't say a thing.

"You ..." she said. "...wait, you ...hold it ...you..."

Oh *man*. She was really starting to annoy me. I still owed her a slug, too. Maybe if she got close enough—

But what she said next really threw me. She said:

"...you...*healed* me?"

"...What?"

That *what* came from me. I was back in *what* mode. At least it wasn't *umm*, that was something. Well, she got my attention good. I sat up.

"You healed me, man," she said. "A second ago I was all banged up so bad I couldn't even roll over. I just realized I was moving around a lot, so...that's what you did. But...but you guys don't do that, man."

"*You* guys?" I said. "What's that mean?"

"...What?" she said.

Wow. We were talking so much alike there may as well only be one of us here.

"...You said," I managed, "You said *you guys don't do that*. What's that mean?"

It took a second for her to say anything, but when she did, I got thrown all over again.

"...Well...*Paladins*, man. You guys don't *heal*."

"...Wait, what?" I asked. I really have no business making fun of people for being slow. I really don't. "...You know what I am? You know about us?"

I wasn't used to that. I wasn't exactly officially a Paladin long enough to figure out much, but I did know that we sort of went under the radar because, well, once you got into the order, you got slapped with one hell of a severe Exaction that forced you to clam up if you so much as tried to talk about the possible existence of Paladins. Think of it as a non-negotiable and inviolable non-disclosure agreement. You could try to fight it, I guess, but it would fight back much harder than you ever could, and it would win, even if it meant killing you. Needless to say, I had no desire to test the limitations. Basically the only way around the gag was to talk to some other person who was already authorized to know about it.

I got the idea that a few higher up government types might fall into that category, but that was it. Then there was this chick, who seemed to not only know about us but also had one hell of an opinion, too.

"Duh," she said. "That's one thing I can't ever forget." She sat down and leaned back; her butt landed in some mud and made a squishing sound. "You all won't ever let me forget. I just wanna be left alone, man, I ain't hurtin' nothin', that ain't who I am, you know? But y'all think you make all the rules an' no one else can't do nothin', man. I can't help bein' me, you know? But y'all make bein' me a felony, man. Y'all ain't never done nothin' but make me wonder why I just don't step in front of a train."

Woah. OK, so obviously I was missing something here. A whole *lot* of somethings.

"I don't have any idea what you're talking about," I said. "For real. I don't have any idea what's going on, I just saw someone hurt that needed help, that's all."

I could see her dark shape move a bit, she was looking up at me, I think.

"And I'll tell you something else," I said. "You seem to know about Paladins and it's obvious you don't like them. Well guess what? As much as you don't like them I just bet they hate me ten times worse. If they saw me they'd probably kick my teeth in before saying so much as *happy t'see ya*, and worse if they found out I could still heal batshit crazy people like you. I'm not allowed."

"...That ain't true man," she said.

"Wanna bet?" I retorted. "Look."

I muttered the same blessing I did before, and my hand lit up blueish white. The chick flinched and almost backed off again until she realized I was just using it for light to show her my right forearm. She looked down and saw the big X branded there, and then her eyes went wide.

"Ohhhh," she said. "Wow. Oh yeah." She nodded, like she just solved a seriously hard problem. "Uh...what's that mean?"

"It means," I said, and let my hand go out, "that they kicked me out. As far as they're concerned I'm not a Paladin anymore. I got expelled from Pally U. So if you wanna yell, yell in *their* direction. I ain't got nothing to do with whatever you're pissed about."

She didn't say anything for a few seconds; maybe her gears were spinning, I don't know. But finally:

"Wh...Wait, you're serious? You ain't even prevaricating, man?"

Wow, that was random. She just plunked down that big word out of nowhere. It was one I knew, though, or at worst I probably could have figured it out from how she said it.

I shook my head. "No, I'm not." I muttered the blessing again, and my hand lit up. "See, I shouldn't even be able to that anymore, but I can. If they caught me at it, I'd be better off just jumping off a cliff." I paused, and then remembered that I was in Florida. "Well, first I'd have to go somewhere that *has* cliffs, then do it."

She didn't say anything to that, but looked at my hand like I was about to use it to burn off all her skin. Since the last thing I wanted to deal with was another freak out, I let the light go off.

"I don't even know why the hell I just told you all that," I said. "I don't even know what I'm doing here or where *here* is or what the hell just happened. It's all a complete blank. One minute I'm in bed, the next..." I spread my hands, motioning at everything around me.

The chick just sat there for a bit. I was beginning to get even more annoyed at her than I already was. Before I could let her know that, though, she spoke up.

"Ohh . . ." she said. "...makes sense, man."

"It does? Mind sharing?"

"I cleaned up," she said, "and you got cleaned up too by oops. A little harsh, but I can't do nothin' 'bout it now but wait for it all to come on back to you."

"What?"

"Forget it, we don't got time. Help me out, man, we gotta find my focus."

"Your what?" I said. If my conversation with this chick was any indication, no army of people could help her find her focus.

"Forget it, man," she said. "It's a big flat wood bat, like they play that weird British game with. I need it to get us the rest of the way home, man. I was so wiped out I only got us halfway there. That's why were in the middle of nowhere."

"A cricket bat?" I said. "What good would that be?"

"Can't do nothin' without it, man," she said, and began to root around again. "That's what."

"That didn't really answer anything," I said, helpfully.

"Oh wow," she said, and I got the idea that she was maybe trying to sound excited but her voice still came out in the same slacker drawl. "Got it!"

"Is that right?" I said. "Hooray?"

"Hang on," she said, and I could see her getting to her feet. "I gotta do this quick an' I'm all outta stash."

"Wait, you're out of what? And what do you gotta do quick?"

"This," she said; there was a flash of reddish light, and then I felt like I got clocked across the melon with a two by four.

Or maybe I clocked a two by four with my head. That's actually more what it felt like, if you want the truth.

Chapter Nine

I came around who the hell knows how long after. It could have been a second later or a year later, I have no way of knowing. All I did know was that for the second time in recent memory I had no idea where the hell I was. I felt like I was being pressed flat against a hardwood ceiling and I was somehow managing to drool up onto it.

"Awww, man..."

That wasn't me; that was that chick. I still had no idea who she was and what was going on and, let me tell you, *that* more than anything was seriously starting to piss me off. I kind of moved around a bit and saw that I was lying on a sticky, dirty hardwood floor that had a weird smell I couldn't place. I was next to what looked like an old bed with wooden legs, and I could see under the bed from where I was; there was a whole bunch of random stuff there, like single socks with holes in the heels, candy wrappers, three soda bottles, and this big travel trunk covered all over with what I guess were bumper stickers with what were probably names of bands on them. I couldn't recognize most of them, except one:

For Squirrels

I groaned and sat up. My head suddenly felt light and I almost fell back over, but I shot out a hand and caught the side of the bed. I got steady, and then I glanced around, looking for that redheaded chick. I found her lying on her side, next to some huge antique pipe organ that was loaded down with mismatched piles of books and papers and old, brownish photos of unhappy looking people. Not one thing looked like it belonged there, but just like someone threw it there to get it out of the way.

"Crap," the chick said, like she just woke up. "How long we been out?"

"You're asking *me?*" I said. "Ok, that's enough. *Stop.* Who are you?"

She looked over at me all confused, like she forgot what I just said. After a second she seemed to get it, though.

"Oh," she said. "Oh. Sorry. Smoot."

"What?"

"Smoot," she said again. "I'm Smoot, man."

"Smoot?"

"Yeah."

"...Smoot?"

"Yeah, that's what I said."

"Your parents hated you, huh?"

"Huh?"

"Never mind," I said. "Like I should talk. I'm Adobe."

She looked at me all confused again. One eye narrowed a little and kind of twitched.

"...I thought you were a Paladin."

"...What?" It was my turn to be confused.

Just then Smoot jumped like someone zapped her with a static shock, and then her head whipped around. She looked off at the hallway for a second, and then she thrashed her arms and legs and shoved herself up to her feet.

"What? What is it?" I said, but Smoot ignored me. She just stood in place a second, and then twisted to look left, right, and left again. Then she like charged off in some random direction and knocked over a mountain of boxes and broken picture frames and a few plates and a teakettle and what could have been an easel or maybe a half built bookshelf. She bent almost in half and rummaged for a second in this pile of junk and then came back up with a tiny black pouch in her hand.

"What the . . ." I said, but all I could do was watch. She scooped up a natty old book from somewhere on the floor---I couldn't see from where---and then she smacked the book into the little pouch. There was a little purple puff of smoke, and then she threw down the book, and then she swung the pouch in the air and I got covered by a large puff of purple smoke.

All of a sudden, I felt real weird. I mean, weirder than I just did a minute ago, anyway. It almost felt like I was melting and freezing at the same time. Yes, I know that doesn't make sense, but I'm not smart enough to describe it any other way, sorry.

"OK man," Smoot said, whispering real loud. "Don't move an' don't talk, unless you wanna jump off a cliff!"

She tossed the pouch away and turned her back on me. Now, I hate to say it, but I'm not even joking about this next part. Right after Smoot tells me if I don't want to jump off a cliff I should sit down and shut up, I came about a millimeter from asking "Why" out loud. I mean, yeah, I didn't really know shit about Smoot or why I should trust her, but most of the time if someone says to do something if you don't want to jump off a cliff, you really oughta just give them the benefit of the doubt. Not me. Not this kid. My mouth was halfway to making the "W" sound when I heard what sounded like a door being kicked in, and then a whole bunch of footsteps and pissed-off sounding voices.

A second later, four people stepped into the room, and I swear to God I almost died right then and there. There was no way I would forget any of their faces as long as I lived, and maybe even a little while after.

They were Paladins. Not just any Paladins, either, but the same four who excommunicated me.

✱ ✱ ✱ ✱ ✱

As if I wasn't already confused enough. Everything between getting home from the bar and waking up in the middle of nowhere half naked next to this Smoot person was a complete void, and now here I was sitting in a pile of junk staring down the four people who did their absolute best to ruin me. All four of these people had their own little part in that ceremony they forced me through when they tried to rip me away from the Light.

There was Brother Wolfe, built like a wall in every sense of the word, who I could probably fit inside of like he was mechanized battle armor. The man could rip me to pieces with his pinky if he felt like it, and the kicker was he was something like seventy years old but he didn't look anywhere near it. His neck was like as thick as my thigh, and my whole face could almost fit into the palm of his hand.

Wolfe was the one who held me in place during the ceremony. He could have done it with one hand and texted out for pizza with the other.

There was Brother Holloway, the stump to Wolfe's tree. He wasn't a small guy but he had a habit of staying close to Wolfe so you really had no choice but to see him as small. He always had this beard that made him look like twice as old as really was because the tips of it were going grey. He was probably Philipino or something, but his accent made me think he was South African. He liked to smile a lot from what I remember, but the smile never hit his eyes.

Holloway was the one who recited the litany of excommunication, and each syllable made me feel like I was being dunked in boiling tar.

There was Sister Marsh, who may have been a knockout but she dressed way the hell down. Not a shred of makeup, and she kept her hair tied back tight in a bun. I think she also never got smiled at as a baby because her face only came in one flavor: Scowl. I'd say she looked like some old school marm or something but now that I think about it, even dressed down she was too pretty for that.

Marsh was the one who rang the bell, closed the book of the gospel, and snuffed out the candle. But that wasn't all she did that night. But first...

There was Father McCormick, in the center of them all. McCormick was old and looked it, but he was probably in thirty times better shape than I've ever been. I swear he's gotta be some kind of robot because he never looked tired or even put out, no matter what. He also had this way of talking that never failed to creep me out, even before I got excommunicated. He talked kind of like Mr. Rogers, all the time, even when he was obviously about to boil over with seething rage. The man scared the crap out of me since I had no idea when the top would blow and I'd be literally vaporized.

McCormick was the one who actually substantiated the exaction that sealed the deal. For style he took a red-hot poker and dragged it across my arm twice in a crisscross pattern, which left the shape of a huge X, and then shot an exaction into it that hurt so much I swear it must have destroyed every nerve in my body.

The only one missing from this happy family was Simon. He didn't do anything himself at the time, but he bore witness and didn't bother to hide his glee.

All of these people would probably not be thrilled to see me just at the minute, unless of course they felt like beating someone until you couldn't even recognize them. Not that I had done anything new that they knew of (I hoped), but just because it would have been fun. The thing was, even though they were no more than seven feet from me and facing me, they didn't seem to notice I was there. I wasn't exactly upset over that, but all the same I have to admit I was as confused. Still, if they were perfectly happy to ignore me, I was perfectly happy to let them.

Smoot stood there facing them with her back to me, and they just all stood there with their hands behind their backs and almost buried her with pissed off looking glares. With Wolfe there Smoot looked almost exactly like a kid who got caught screwing up by her daddy.

"Your focus," McCormick said, without even saying hello first.

"Oh, oh, right ma—uh—sir," said Smoot. "Lemme get it."

"Thank you," said McCormick, but I could tell he didn't mean it at all. Mostly he looked bored and irritated. Smoot stated rummaging in the mess, and she looked real scared while she was doing it, too.

"This place is revolting," Marsh said. "How do you stand living like this?"

"I dunno," Smoot said.

"Of course you don't," Marsh said. Oh *man*, do I hate that woman's voice. She talked that way to me all the time. To this day I still fantasize about punching her teeth in and watching her choke on them all.

Smoot looked around for a second or two and then came up with that cricket bat of hers. She almost tripped herself up getting back to McCormick because she was going so fast. The chick was spooked out of her mind, and I saw Marsh almost crack a half a smirk watching her, but I may have been hallucinating.

"Here sir," Smoot said, and held out the cricket bat sideways on the palms of her hands. McCormick took it from her almost like he wished he had a giant pair of tweezers. Marsh curled her lip, and Holloway looked like he was trying not to cringe but it got away from him a little anyway. Wolfe looked like he couldn't care less.

"What is that stench?" Holloway said, and glared at Smoot like she just stepped on his toe.

"...huh...?" Smoot said.

"Oh, forget it," Holloway said. "Father, take care to avoid infection. It appears vile enough to endanger even you."

"Rest assured," McCormick said, "I shall. Wizard, this is absolutely nauseating."

What? Wait, did he just say *wizard*? Who's a wizard?

"Sorry m—sir," said Smoot. "I guess I got it a little messy . . ."

Wait, Smoot's a *wizard? That* is a *wizard?*

"Enough," McCormick said. "Tell me, wizard. What shall we find when we complete our audit of this...let's call it a focus?"

Smoot moved a little side to side, and then she answered.

"Umm...yeah, I can always remember my spells."

"Congratulations," Marsh said. "Would you like a round of applause?"

"Please, sister," Holloway said, with one of those half smiles of his. "I'd rather not draw this out any longer than necessary."

Marsh glared at Holloway, but didn't say anything back. McCormick ignored both of them, and just looked at Smoot like he was saying *well?*

"Umm..." Smoot said. "Five evocations—a direct force blast and a hold into an internal expansion into a total spatial reversal." She paused for a second, like she was waiting for the Paladins to say something. If that's what she was doing, they didn't say a thing, and so she went on. "And then a greater mass amnesia and then two recalls."

"Two? McCormick said. "Why two? You were alone, were you not?"

Smoot didn't answer right away, and I pictured her swallowing.

"I messed up the first time, sir," she said. "I pushed myself too hard an' only got halfway home in the first try."

"I see," said McCormick. "That would appear to mesh well with your demonstrated level of competence, but all the same—Marsh?"

Marsh stepped forward and looked down at Smoot so hard I could almost feel it from where I sat.

"Look at me, wizard," she said, like the last word tasted bad. Smoot tensed up, and I saw Marsh's arm move. A second later she spoke up.

"Nothing the wizard said is a lie," she said. "but she may be leaving something out to avoid lying directly."

"Oh please," Holloway said. "She's hardly smart enough for that."

Marsh glared at Holloway again, and Holloway glared right back. Holloway looked away first, and then Marsh looked back at Smoot.

"Who released you, wizard?" said Marsh. "Who authorized your focus?"

Smoot just stood there. I could see her shifting a bit, though, like she was kind of going from foot to foot.

"I...I..." Smoot said.

The Paladins inched in a bit, boxing her in.

"It was none of us," Marsh said. "And there is no record to be found of its authorization. Who was it? We will find out once we audit your focus anyhow. But you can tell us now and you may be dealt with less grievously. Or not."

"I...I...I don't *know!*" Smoot said. I don't think I've ever heard anyone so scared.

Marsh grabbed Smoot's face between her thumb and first finger, and then jerked Smoot's face up. I heard Smoot make a little *gack* sound, and then Marsh stared at Smoot so hard I thought the chick's head was gonna explode. A second went by, and then another, and then one more. Finally, Marsh, she just grit her teeth and growled.

"*Onthullen,*" she said.

Oh crap.

Marsh just used the same exaction I used on Crow that one time. Guess who taught it to me in the first place? If you guessed Marsh, you win. She used a Dutch word to substantiate it, but, like I said before, the word you use to substantiate doesn't matter. The effect was the same. But forget all that; the important thing was that she was using that same exaction on Smoot, and I don't have to remind you what it did to Crow when I used it, and next to Marsh I was just a green trainee. This sort of thing was what Marsh lived for.

Smoot stiffened up and started to make a super gross choking sound, like she was drowning, and then started shaking like she was having a seizure. Watching it, it felt like it went on for like six hours. Finally, though, Marsh chucked Smoot back onto the bed, and shook her hand like she was trying to shake off something disgusting.

"Well?" McCormick said.

"She genuinely can't remember," Marsh said. "She is so monumentally stupid she can't remember a damn thing from one moment to the next."

"An anterograde amnesiac," Wolfe said, and I think that was the first time I ever heard the man talk. His voice was just what you'd think it would be, too. It sounded like an earthquake, if that even makes sense.

"An idiot," Marsh spat. "Although I did manage to extract something. She is, in fact, hiding something from us, although she can't remember what, where, or how."

My heart sped up like someone suddenly floored the pedal. I'm pretty sure I gasped too, but to be honest I wasn't sure and I can't really remember. I do remember I held my breath, though. I thought I saw Marsh look over in my direction, too, but that was probably just my imagination.

"There is nothing the wizard could have willingly hidden from that Exaction," Marsh said. "As I suspected, she is useless." She looked down at Smoot, who was still sort of squirming around on the bed like she was trying to wake up after being knocked out. "If she was ever anything else."

"Very well," said McCormick. "Wolfe, if you please—" he handed the cricket bat to the silent giant, who took it without making a peep. "—and now—" he took a step toward Smoot, but Marsh held up a hand in front of him; McCormick looked over at her and raised one eyebrow. For some reason just then I was jealous that he knew how to raise one eyebrow. I have no idea how my mind works sometimes, I really don't.

"Yes?" he said.

"If I'm not overstepping myself," Marsh said, and then jerked her head a tiny bit at Smoot.

McCormick looked at Smoot, then at Marsh, and then he nodded.

"Very well," he said. "But be quick."

"Yes, father," she said.

All of them except Marsh turned and walked out. McCormick first, Holloway next, then Wolfe. Marsh waited until they were all gone before she looked back at Smoot.

Marsh just stood there for a second or two, and I could tell her breathing was getting harder and heavier by the moment. Suddenly she just about dove onto the bed, grabbed a fistful of Smoot's shirt, and yanked her up until their noses were almost touching.

"Since I know you're too stupid to remember anyway—" Marsh said, and then she hauled off and decked Smoot full in the face. Smoot yelped and her head whipped back like she was in a car crash.

"Shut up," Marsh snapped, and pulled Smoot back close again. "I want you to know that one fine day, I'm going to kill *all* you shits. You got that? *You got that?* And I'm going to start with you. I'm going to enjoy every second of it."

Marsh stood up off the bed and dragged Smoot with her by her scrawny little neck, and then Marsh held her up like she didn't weigh an ounce. Smoot obviously couldn't breathe and she was using whatever strength she had to grab at Marsh's hands. Blood was streaming out of Smoot's nose and her face was almost the color of her hair.

"We're going to find the one who helped you," Marsh said, "And we'll throw a special party for you both. Think on that, if your brain can handle it. Until then—"

Marsh pulled back her free hand, like she was going to deck Smoot again, only she wasn't making a fist. Her hand was open, like she was going to smack her instead.

"*FORNEKTE!*" she howled, and then hit Smoot in her chest like she was pushing her. There was a blast of blue-white light, and Smoot half grunted, half yelled, and fell back like she got clotheslined. She disappeared behind the other side of the bed, and I heard junk collapse from everywhere. Even though I couldn't see from where I was, I'm sure she got buried in it; I heard her moaning a little after everything settled.

"I suggest you be good, wizard," Marsh said. "Not that it will change anything. And now I really must be off."

With that, she turned and walked out, but first she took one last look over where Smoot landed and grinned in a way that made me want to punch her face inside out.

Chapter Ten

What the hell did I just witness?

I hardly knew what to think. I really didn't even know where to start. But after a second I realized that what I thought didn't matter a good goddamn because there was something a lot more important for me to do. That is, I needed to know if Smoot was okay. I didn't know her from a hole in the ground but what the hell did that matter?

For the first time since Smoot sprinkled that weird purple shit all over me I tried to move. I felt a weird prickly sensation like you do when you try to move your arm or foot after it fell asleep, but only for a second; the feeling went away as quick as it came, and I stood up.

"Smoot?" I said. "You still with me?"

I couldn't see her from where I was, but I heard her groan and then it sounded like a few random pieces of whatever shifted around a bit, like maybe she was trying to move but couldn't really put a lot of energy behind it.

"Hang on," I said. "I'm coming." I decided not to try to slog through the junk and hopped onto the bed instead. I crawled over it and saw Smoot lying there on the other side looking like a broken doll. There was blood smeared all over one side of her pale face and she was breathing real slow and weak. Her eyes were almost but not all the way shut and all I could only see the whites of her eyes.

"Holy shit," I said. "Stay there, don't move."

Don't move. That's actually what I told her. Really? What, like she was about to do back flips? Never mind.

I got down on my knees next to her and did my little German litany thing. When I finished, her nose was back in one piece and she was coming back around. I couldn't do anything about the blood on her face, though. That would need regular old boring cleaning with water and paper towel or something.

She blinked, took a deep breath and looked straight up at the ceiling for a few seconds without doing anything else. She reminded me of an old, beat up computer that took days to boot up.

She looked left, and then right, then at me, then left, then up, then right, and then kind of did a double take and looked right at me.

"What do you want, man?" she said. Her voice was scratchy and flimsy, kind of like she just finished yelling for three hours straight.

"Smoot, it's me," I said. "Adobe. Remember?"

"What's a Doh-bee?" she asked.

"No, I'm not a *Doh-bee*, whatever that is. That's my name." I patted my chest. "Adobe Kroger."

"Oh. Nice to meet you. Where are your clothes, man?" she asked.

I think that was the first time I took a good look at what I was wearing, or mostly wearing. I was apparently dressed in my blue R2D2 Underoos and tank top, and that was it. Funny, I didn't even remember putting these on.

"That's a great question, Smoot. Tell you what, I'll get back to you."

"Okay," she said. "What do you want, man?"

After she said that I thought of a computer program that just kept looping recursively back on itself. "I don't want anything," I said. "I just want to make sure you're okay."

"Oh," she said. "Well, no, I think I'm really kinda not really okay."

"I guessed. How can I help?"

"Umm…" she said. "I dunno. I think I could really use a bed, my back is screamin' at me, man."

So I helped her into bed, but only after I offered to fire off another blessing to get her condition into a better condition. The second she saw my hands shimmer, though, she panicked and told me to keep away with that "dark shit, man." I couldn't see what else to do, so I let the blessing drop and promised I wouldn't come at her with that "dark shit" again. She calmed back down, but it took a while, and I waited until she was done before I lifted her up.

She couldn't get up on her own, and she looked even paler than she did before---almost as pale as a sheet. Her forehead, temples and upper lip were all sweaty, the skin around her eyes was all red and puffy, and she was kind of trembling. She couldn't even really help move herself much, but that wasn't any big deal, really. I wasn't feeling too hot just then either but she probably weighed less than the clothes she had on. It was like carrying a huge skinny housecat, and I put her down super careful because I was scared I would break her in half.

She seemed to be a bit happier once she got the soft mattress under her; she let out a sigh and sort of melted down into it. I left her to it for a bit and ran off to find something to clean her face with.

✶ ✶ ✶ ✶ ✶

"You...wow," I said. "...Umm...so...yeah. So you're a wizard?" It wasn't the smoothest way to break the ice, but that was all I could think of at the time. I was sitting by her on the bed and just finished cleaning up the mess Marsh made of her face, and the silence was getting to me. I managed to find the makings for tea somehow in the wreck of a kitchen one room over, and she was cradling a steaming tin cup, sort of. It looked like it was gonna slip out of her hands at any second, because her hands were so shaky.

"Unfortunately, yeah, man." She looked right at me, and, even though she looked like absolute hell otherwise, her eyes were bright emerald green and as deep and soulful as you could imagine. I mean they looked as deep as the middle of the ocean.

"...Why unfortunately?" I said. I didn't realize it at first but I paused to stare back for almost a whole second or more. Her eyes were just that fascinating. They almost looked like they belonged in a painting.

She just shook her head and shrugged, like a person too exhausted to care.

"So, Umm...those Paladins, they never saw me. That thing you did, did you make me invisible?"

"...What thing?" she said.

"Right before they all came in, you did something to me, and they couldn't see me."

"...I did? Why'd I do that?"

"You don't remember? It just happened like ten seconds ago!"

"It did? What did I do?"

"That's what I'm asking you!"

"Oh. So what did I do?" She sounded like she was seriously curious, like I knew something she didn't.

"Seriously?" I said.

"Yeah," she said. "Was it cool?"

"You really don't remember?"

"...Remember what?"

"You like—" I made like I was grabbing something small in my hands, "—and then you—" I smacked my hands together, "—and then you—" I pretended to throw something.

Her eyes got a little narrower and her eyebrows tensed up. A half a second later her mouth opened a little bit. She looked like she was trying to solve one of those math problems that take up half the blackboard in her head.

"...Oooohhh..." she said. "Ohhhhh...yeah, I think...yeah. Looks like Mimic Powder, man."

"What?"

"Mimic Powder," she groaned. "Look, basically it can make you look like whatever it touched last before you used it. I had to grab the first thing I could find. I just made you look like a pile of books."

"...You made me look like books?"

"Yeah, man. You weren't invisible but they couldn't see you anyway. I remember kinda that I wanted to make sure they couldn't see you but I couldn't use my focus or else they'd find out. I think." She breathed out and lay back. "I dunno, I'm really not feelin' too hot, y'know?"

She sounded really bad, and I mean *really* bad. "No kidding," I said. "What did Marsh do to you?"

"Who's Marsh?"

"That crazy chick who just smacked you down. Don't tell me you—"

"Oh, oh yeah," Smoot said. "Oh yeah." She chuckled, and to be honest it sounded so painful my own throat hurt just listening to it. Then she just lay there for a bit, and then sighed real heavy before she answered. "She shut me off, man."

I blinked. "Shut...you off?"

She nodded. "Yeah-huh. Like a light."

"What's that mean?"

"I'm off, man," she said, like she was telling me water was wet. "I can't do things."

"What things?" I said. Here we go; I was sounding just like her again.

"*Any* things," she said, and held up a hand and wiggled her fingers. "Like that."

"She…" I started to say, but all of a sudden my precious little X started to itch, and also—this was new—it started throbbing too. It never did that right off the bat before now, and I didn't think that could mean anything good for me. But whatever, there wasn't any point in wasting any time thinking about that now. I'd just have to grit my teeth and take it when it got worse, like always.

"She blocked off your magic?" I said, rubbing my arm.

Smoot grunted. "May as well just kill me, man. Would be more entertaining and less...painful—" she shook, and then she started heaving.

"What is it? What?" I said; Smoot just shook her head and her cheeks puffed out. I put two and two together and snatched up the first thing I could find that would do the trick, which in this case was a little cardboard box by my foot. I got it under her mouth just in time for her to let it all fly. I honestly have no idea how so much stuff could come out of someone so tiny; I think she lost an organ or two along with it. When she finally finished, she slumped back and moaned real quiet out of the back of her throat.

"Man," she said. "I wish I could forget when she does this, but I can't ever."

Now give me a second for yet another example of how fast my brain works. It took me this long to finally register something Smoot said while the Paladins were grilling her, and only just then when Smoot said what she just said. As it turns out, this little thing I just finally registered may have helped me understand my situation a little more. They asked her something like *what would we find when we audit this focus* and she rattled off a whole bunch of stuff I didn't really follow, except for one.

…And then a greater mass amnesia…

If you could picture a chimp in a science project trying to make sense out of an internal combustion engine, that would be me right then. The only things missing were the little confused *Ooo-ooo-ooos* and random pokes at the big scary thing it couldn't get. It took almost five seconds for me to realize why my brain was trying to tell me that I really should think that little phrase Smoot said was important.

I did get it eventually, but it came over me so slowly it was like thick tar being poured over my head. My mouth made a big stupid looking O.

"Hey, Smoot?" I said, and even now I sounded a little doubtful. She didn't say anything, she just groaned.

"What was that you said about greater mass amnesia?"

"...the what?"

★ ★ ★ ★ ★

I felt like I was chasing my own tail for a few minutes trying to jog her memory until I remembered something else she said. She told McCormick that *I always remember my own spells.* Oh really? Well that could give me someplace to start I guess.

"Ok," I said. "Smoot, do you remember the spells you cast tonight?"

She nodded. "Oh yeah, man. A direct force blast and a hold into an internal expansion into a total spatial reversal. And then a greater mass amnesia and then two recalls."

Wow. Almost word for word what she said before, like it was cut and pasted or something.

"Ok," I said, motioning with my hands sort of like I was trying to say *okay, let's get on with it,* "SO, you cast a greater mass amnesia?"

That did it, finally. She nodded, and it all came pouring out like someone dumping a bucket over your head. She said that one thing she always had to do after she finished up the job she needed to get done was to, as she put it, "clean up" any witnesses. What she did was wipe any memory of the last ten minutes or so clear out of any person who saw anything. Sometimes she needed to only do it to one person, sometimes a few. But in some cases she needed to wipe whole crowds, or sometimes the things she was trying to make them all forget were so traumatic that she really needed to pour it on. In those cases, she needed nothing less than the A-bomb of that spell, greater mass amnesia. That was obviously the spell I got slammed with, and she said she was sorry but that was why I couldn't remember anything. She said it may come back to me eventually, if at all, but there were no guarantees.

"So you're saying," I said, "That I completely lost ten minutes?"

She nodded her head yes. "Somethin' like that, I guess."

"Ten minutes?" I said. She nodded again.

"Only ten minutes?"

Nod.

"What the shit could have happened in only ten minutes?" I said. "I was asleep in bed, and ten minutes later I'm . . ." I waved my hands at everything.

Smoot shrugged.

"Ok, never mind," I said. "Oh, I have an idea. You said that you needed to clean up after you finished your job."

She nodded.

"Do you have any idea what that job was?"

"...huh ...?"

Okay, I'll skip the tail chasing part that followed, and just go right to the end.

"Are you serious?" I said. "You can remember what you cast but not *why* or on *what*? How the hell does that brain work?"

I know, I was being really mean just then, but my patience was burned. My little hissy didn't last long, though, because Smoot just stared back at me, all pale and shaky and weak, and shook her head and shrugged. She looked like she wanted to say *I'm so sorry, please don't hit me*, but couldn't get it out.

I had to back off.

✷ ✷ ✷ ✷ ✷

Well wasn't this just fantastic. I still didn't even have a single solitary clue where I even was. Oh, and it was a work night, too, and only a Tuesday on top of that. I didn't have my phone, my wallet, nothing, and for all I knew I could have been in another part of the state. Or hell, another state.

Smoot wasn't especially helpful, either. Here's roughly how it went. I'll paraphrase, and I forget which order these came in, if it matters.

"Where am I, Smoot?"

"...you're in my house, man."

"I mean where am I. What city."

"What which?"

"Do you have a computer?"

"...Wha ...?"

"Ok, do you have a phone?"

"Which?"

"Do you have a car?"

"...why?"

"Do you know if there's a payphone anywhere?"

"What's that?"

"I'm afraid to ask, but do you have any money?"

"Huh?"

"What time is it?"

"...night?"

"Are we anywhere near civilization?"

"...maybe?"

There may have been more to it, but I think you get it now. In the end I just asked if she had any spare clothes. Turned out she did, and, as I expected, it was a t-shirt and baggy jeans. She even had a spare pair of beat up converse knock offs, although I really didn't feel like going anywhere near her socks. Once I was slightly more covered up, I decided the next step was to get the hell out of there. Paladins seemed to like showing up here out of the blue, and besides, I did all I could for Smoot. I tried one more time to help her but she wouldn't let me near her with my blessing, and then she started almost begging me to leave her alone. Fine. Happy to oblige.

Well, first I had to get my bearings, and, seeing as Smoot seemed to be somewhat incapable of helping, since she basically just fell asleep and started snoring louder than someone twice her size should have been able to, I just stepped outside.

Into sheer nothingness.

Chapter Eleven

Well not literally. But wherever I was, there wasn't so much as a speck of light. Or any background noise, unless you count a dull breeze. It looked like it was raining a while ago since the ground was littered with puddles here and there and the air was a little bit misty.

It looked like I was on some kind of dirt cul-de-sac that was mostly mud at the moment surrounded by really tall thick trees. Once my eyes adjusted I saw that the cul-de-sac led out onto a dirt road, which kind of looked promising.

I tied my hair up in a knot, since it was getting a little irritating, and then I was on my way.

I'll cut to the chase. I walked and walked and walked. I must have walked for a thousand years. I eventually found a paved road and followed that for a while until I found a traffic light. Then I picked a direction at random and followed that for a while. The few street signs I did see really weren't any help since they were just numbers. There was nothing in sight except an occasional ranch house or something. There were no streetlights and the sky was all overcast so there wasn't even any moonlight; basically it could have been anywhere between midnight and sunrise and I had no way of knowing if I wasn't just going in circles.

The sky was beginning to lighten up by the time I found a little convenience store that looked like one of those ones that people forgot about and just bump into by accident when they're lost. You know, kind of like I just did. There were a couple of cars parked out front with Florida plates, so at least I knew I was still in the same state. I walked in and asked to use their phone, and I'm sure I looked like some kind of runaway homeless prostitute or something. The old lady must have felt sorry for me though since she let me use it.

Now here comes a whole new problem. I didn't know anybody's number. No, I'm not kidding. Who would when you just plunk the numbers into your phone and press someone's name when you want to call them? I must not have laid eyes on anyone's actual number since I entered them a year ago.

I just stood with the handset to my ear and my finger hanging immobile over the keypad. The old woman looked up at me for a second, and that started making me a little nervous for some reason. I get that way when I'm on the spot sometimes.

Finally, though, a number popped into my head: Jill's work phone. Thankfully, Jill is one of those overachievers that didn't mind being on call as long as it meant she got a free company phone out of it. I remembered her work phone number because I got a call from it a few days ago and it displayed the number since I didn't assign it to a contact yet. I saw that number in my recent calls plenty of times because I was too lazy to add it to Jill's profile. Looks like that laziness paid off.

Without any further delay, I pounded the keys.

My call went to voice mail three times before Jill finally picked up. When she did, I almost had to duck away from the receiver, she yelled so loud.

"*All right! Who is this?*"

"Ow," I said. "Relax, it's me."

"Me?"

"Come on," I said. "Quit messing around. It's Adobe."

"Adobe? Wait, what? Oh my Christ, what the hell is it?"

"Love you too," I said.

"Where the hell are you calling from? You know I don't answer blocked numbers. I thought you were some telemarketer from India. By the way, did you *notice* what time it is?"

"Oh, sorry, I didn't realize," I said, and then I turned to the old woman. "Say, what time is it?"

"Half past six," the woman replied.

"Oh," I said. "Thanks. Yeah, it's half past six."

"*I know that,*" Jill said. "What do you want?"

Wow, she sounded a lot more pissed than I would have thought, even though I woke her up. I wasn't sure why, but that didn't change anything. I needed help one way or another.

"I need a ride," I said.

"You...wait, what? Wait, what's wrong with your car?"

"I don't think anything's wrong with it that I know of," I said. "It's just not where I am at the moment."

"Where are you?" She said.

"Hold on," I said, and turned to the woman. "Where am I?"

I have to hand it to the old woman, it must have looked like she was talking to an amnesiac but she didn't miss a beat.

"Indiantown," the woman said.

"Indiantown," I repeated into the phone.

"...You're...wait a second. Why are you in Indiantown?" Jill said, and she sounded all of a sudden really calm.

"Umm . . ." I said. "Long story?"

"Suppose you tell it?"

"What? Look, can I get a ride or not? I'm seriously stuck."

"What are you doing in Indiantown?" She still sounded calm, if a little bit shaky, almost like she was trying not to shout.

"Can we talk about that later?" I said. "I'm serious, I'm stranded here."

"Get a cab," she said. She sounded pissed again.

"What?"

"You heard me. Get a cab."

"Huh?"

"Did I stutter?"

Oh. Oh man. If there's one expression I am sick and tired of people throwing at me, it's that one. It's so goddamn old, for one, and for another, it's a super cheap shot and anyone who knows me knows how sore I get. Even Simon of all people uses it.

"What's your p-p-problem, man?"

"Oh, now I know it's you for sure," she said, and hung up.

I had to call her four times before she picked up again. When she did, she yelled into the phone, and asked me about Indiantown again. Wow, what was with this third degree about Indiantown? What was the big deal about Indiantown? It was like she had an answer to her question already in her head and just wanted me to guess what it was. My brain doesn't work that way when it's fully functional, let alone when it's exhausted.

Finally though, I managed to get a word in and tell her that I didn't have my wallet or my phone or anything and that I was seriously exhausted and desperate. She said to call a cab anyway and just pay him when I got home. I said that cab fare from here to my house would break me since I just paid all my bills. Then she said I should have thought of that before I drank five pints of Guinness last night.

That was when it clicked. "Wait," I said. "Oh."

Oops. It took a while, since I had to shift my brain in a totally different direction, but I did finally make an association that kind of made sense. Jason, that guy from last night was from Indiantown. Once I made that connection, everything else about Jason last night came flooding back almost all at once. I guess I sort of shoved it to the side to make room for dealing with whatever the fuck happened afterward. I had no idea how much Jill knew or not, but judging from her voice, things didn't look good at all.

"Oh what?" Jill said. "What the fuck is going on here?"

"Umm...can we please talk about this when I don't have five strangers staring at me?"

We went back and forth a bit more but in the end she agreed to pick me up. I hung up, but only after I realized that I didn't tell her where in Indiantown I was. I got that information from the old woman and passed it along to Jill, who sounded pissed that I realized I forgot.

Chapter Twelve

The ride from Indiantown to my apartment was probably the most uncomfortable ride I'd had in years. I don't think it really helped matters much that I showed up in what looked like a set of big guy's clothes, either. I did the whole "It's not what it looks like" thing but it wasn't like I could give any kind of good explanation. I didn't even have one for myself, let alone for Jill. Thing was, looking back it had to have been obvious to anyone paying attention that Jason and I spent most of the night looking like we were the ones on a date. From the conversation I had with him outside my apartment, I even found out that's what Jason wanted. And then, I even had some kind of bizarre momentary second thought about him after I turned him down. That made the least sense to me out of all of it. I still had no idea what had been going through my head at that moment; I knew it was nothing rational but it was there anyway. Regardless of any of that, I knew nothing went on between me and Jason, but now I still felt like I tripped over a corpse by accident and fell into a pool of blood and landed on the murder weapon just as the cop's searchlight got me.

Me and Jill barely talked the whole way, except for about five or six quick sentences, and that's only if you count "Hi" and "Hey" as sentences. Subtract two from the above count if you don't.

Turns out last night at the pub Jill quit having fun pretty quick and left. A little later she tried calling Jason but his phone kept going right to voicemail. She texted the hell out of him, too, but he never replied.

"That is weird," I said. I didn't really know what else to say. "Weird" seems to be one of my safety net words, like *umm* is.

"Isn't it?" she said.

I couldn't think of anything else to say, and neither did Jill apparently. I just did a lot of bottom lip nibbling and pretended to look out the window. Jill was obviously as pissed as pissed gets, and it didn't even really seem to occur to her to ask why I needed a ride from her if I did in fact do what she thought I did. I mean, if it were me and I got the call, I would have thought the guy was a jerk who just kicked her out the door without so much as cab fare. In other words, I would have thanked her for helping me dodge a bullet. Not Jill. Or at least as far as I could tell because she wasn't saying anything.

★ ★ ★ ★ ★

We pulled up Old Okeechobee road and I noticed there were a few more vehicles parked out front of my apartment building than usual. I say that with only a twinge of irony because there were maybe three cop cars with their lights flashing and a big van as well as a huge huge diesel dualie with an extended cab that almost stuck out into the street.

"What the—?" I said.

I didn't have much time to think about it. Jill practically swerved in to the nearest open spot and slammed her car into park. She didn't say anything or even look at me.

"...thanks," I said, and decided that was all I should really say at the moment. I let myself out and made a huge show out of closing the door super gentle. Jill barely gave me enough time to pull my hand away before she started backing out way faster than she needed to. A second later she was tearing off down the street like she was going for a ten second quarter mile, and she didn't apparently give a shit that there were a number of cops watching the whole thing. I guess that pretty much said it all.

"Aww, screw," I said, and rubbed my eye with the palm of my hand. I really didn't feel like doing anything except sleeping for the next seventeen years. I had a feeling though that sleep was the thing I was furthest from just at the minute.

Well you can bet Jill's hasty retreat drew attention to me. Two cops made their way over to me pretty much right then and there. As soon as I figured they were close enough I gave them an exhausted look, rolled my eyes and shrugged.

"Women," I said.

I got roughly neither of the cops to laugh at that pathetic crack, and they immediately started in on me.

"You live here?" One of them said.

"Yeah," I said. "Number six. The loft." I pointed vaguely at the third story window, as if the cops didn't know what the word *loft* meant. "What's going on?"

"You say you live in the loft?" The other cop said.

"Yeah," I said, and all of a sudden I felt a yawn coming on. I let it out and exaggerated it to give me a second to think. "I was over at a friend's last night. What's going on?"

"I think you better come with us," said the second cop. "This should be interesting."

If by interesting he meant holy sweet screaming shit, then he was right.

The cops led me up the stairs, presumably to the spot in the building that all these police people found so fascinating. My heart sank and seized all at once when they swung around to my little narrow stairway and I realized it was my own little private pocket of quiet that had brought them running. I don't know why I held out hope that it was no big deal even as I got halfway up the stairs; they wouldn't have sent out this many cops for a noise complaint.

My jaw almost fell completely off when I laid eyes on my loft, or, more to the point, what was left of my loft. The only way I can think of to describe it was it looked like someone yanked it inside out like a giant sock. Everything was torn up, smashed, broken, beaten in, and strewn all over to the point that it wasn't recognizable. There were two people that I could see kneeling and looking through the wreckage, which was two more people than there had ever been in my loft before besides me.

That was when I noticed the smell. It was almost catastrophic, like a shit-covered corpse, and I almost gagged after inhaling it once. It was like being sucker punched, and no, I am not exaggerating. I think I actually would have preferred being sucker punched to this, thanks.

Anyway, I barely had time to process this overload before the first cop called out:

"Detective, there's someone here to see you."

"What?" called a voice from over near the bathroom. "Who?"

"Unless I miss my guess," said the first cop, "It's the late Adobe Kroger."

It took me a second or two for what the cop said to sink in. When it did, though, I was more confused than ever.

"Wait," I said, and looked at the cop. "Do you just say you think I'm dead?"

"A fair assumption, given everything," said someone else. I turned to look.

There stood a man about maybe in his mid forties, bald and a little on the chubby side but not too much with a well trimmed black goatee and Buddy Holly glasses. He looked about as threatening as a math teacher until you saw his eyes, which looked as bright, keen and penetrating as a brand new freshly sharpened kitchen knife. It was obvious that this man was the opposite of an idiot, which is the opposite of what I could say for myself.

He pointed at something off to the side. When he did, another one of the people there, some chick in a blue jacket marked *forensics* across the back in yellow stooped down to pick something up. It was a clear zip lock baggie, and as she got closer I was able to see that it had my wallet in it. I made a motion toward it but stopped myself midway.

The man in the glasses saw me move, though, and his eyebrows went up. He took the baggie from the chick, opened the baggie real slow with his latex gloved hands, and then took out my wallet. He flipped the wallet open, held it up, and looked back and forth from it to me.

"It would seem," he said, "That we have a match. This changes things a little."

"In the dark here," I said. "What's going on?"

"Hold on," he said. He reached into his pocket with his free hand and took out his phone. He tapped the screen with his thumb, and a second or two later he grinned.

"I thought the picture looked familiar," he chuckled. "Presentation fail."

I scowled.

"I apologize," the guy said, kind of quickly. I have you at a disadvantage. Detective Cartwright. Pleased to see you in one piece, Miss Kroger."

"Umm, I'm pleased to see me in one piece, too," I said. *Christ,* that video. "What happened here?"

"Seeing as that you're here," Cartwright said. "And as we've already established, in one piece, I was hoping that maybe you could tell us."

He paused for a second, and smiled.

"Or, at the least, get us on the right road."

"Umm…" Guess who that was.

"I'm sorry," he said, and opened my wallet again. "You are in fact—" he squinted at the wallet—"Miss Adobe Francine Kroger, aren't you?"

Oh for the love of god. I really, really hate being reminded that my initials are AFK. I don't know why, it just irks me. I guess it could be worse, I mean, I had a friend whose initials are POS.

"Yeah, that's me," I said.

"I take it then," Cartwright said, "That you weren't present for these festivities?"

"No," I said. "What festivities?"

"If you weren't," Cartwright said, "Then where were you?"

I paused only half a second, and I think I kept my eyes from moving up or to the side, but I'm not sure.

"I was at a friend's."

"I see. Fortunately for you, it would seem. Sergeant!"

A thirtyish looking woman with short brown hair stepped out from the back of the loft.

"Yes sir?" She said.

"I would like you to meet our victim, miss Kroger."

The woman blinked.

"Miss Kroger?" She asked.

"Yes," Cartwright said. "Amazing. I'd say this changes everything, doesn't it?"

"It would seem so, sir," she said, and then she tilted her head a bit. "Say, isn't she—the Presentation fail girl?"

Cartwright waved his hand. "Sergeant, the scene's yours, now. For Miss Kroger's safety I'm going to bring her back to the station and get some things sorted. Send along her effects once we've gotten what we need from them, and please be gentle, I'd say she's been through enough so far this morning?" He put my wallet back in the bag and handed it to the woman. I felt a bit miffed at that, but because I didn't exactly have my head screwed on straight I let it slide and didn't realize it until later.

"Yes sir," she said, and turned around and walked toward the back of the loft, calling out to the others there. I watched her go, and then my jaw almost fell off when I saw that the whole back wall of the loft was blown out. There was nothing left of it; there were two or three people silhouetted against the early morning sky and I could see over the highway wall.

"Holy—" I said. But that was it. I couldn't come up with anything else to say or think.

"Yes," Cartwright said. "You can see why there was a cause for concern. Now, if you would please, come with me."

"Wait—what?" I said. I was still goggling like a brain dead idiot at my missing back wall, and so I barely said a thing as Cartwright shuffled me out. In fact, I kept looking at that huge hole until I got walked down the stairs and couldn't see it anymore; by then I just let myself get swept along for the ride.

✴ ✴ ✴ ✴ ✴

Before I knew it I was in the back seat of some black Crown Vic staring at the back of Cartwright's huge bald head. I think it was the smell of his cigarette that snapped me back out of my shock. He had one hand on the wheel with a Marlboro half gone between his first two fingers and he was yapping into his cell phone.

"No, as it turns out, she's fine," Cartwright said. "Uh huh. That's right. No worries. Right." He tapped his phone with his thumb and put it down.

"Where are we going?" I said, after a second of quiet, mainly so I could keep from showing how irritated I was getting all of a sudden. I couldn't help it; I really, really wanted my wallet back. I felt weird without it. Seriously. The more I thought about it, the more confused I was that they didn't at least give me back my wallet. I should have just reached out and grabbed it and to hell with them needing to look it over, but I couldn't think of anything quite so practical at the time. Mostly all I could think of at that time was what the fuck happened to my house and, on a slightly related note, if this isn't what happened in those ten minutes Smoot made me lose I'll eat my own face. What the hell could it be?

Come to think about it, I just remembered my phone should have been back in my wrecked loft somewhere, too. I really needed to fidget with it now, whether it still worked or not, and I'm embarrassed to say that my left hand, my designated phone hand, clenched when I thought about it.

"We're going someplace safer," he said. "Until we can sort everything out."

"What's...everything?" I said. "What the unholy crap just happened?"

Cartwright glanced up into his mirror for a second before he said anything.

"I think," he said, "What's more important at the moment is what *didn't* happen."

"What's that?"

"The small matter that you weren't, as we initially thought, killed."

"Oh. Yeah. I guess that's something." Leave it to me to miss the big picture.

"Yes, isn't it?"

"Yeah. So, now that I know what didn't happen, mind telling me what *did* happen?"

He looked up into the rearview again, took a drag, and then exhaled before he answered.

"Briefly," he said, "Early this morning your landlord arrived to pick up some tools from his storage shed in the back yard, only to find that said storage shed had been completely destroyed. Before he could think too hard on that he also realized the state of your apartment. He said he was able to see the damage from where he stood because as you saw the damage was rather extreme."

"Rather?"

"Yes," Cartwright said. "Naturally he was curious to see if the damage was as bad as it appeared at a glance, and so he made his way there and found his fears confirmed. What had happened to the young single female tenant, he thought, for her car, the blue focus, was still in its usual spot out front. Naturally he assumed the worst and shortly thereafter, we arrived."

"Now, it's fair to assume that, after a cursory examination, that the tenant of that apartment was in a bad way, wouldn't you say?"

"I'd—say so?" I said. "It looks like an eight inch shell went through it."

"Quite. But now clearly, you are not in a bad way," Cartwright said. "So either the perpetrators are seriously bad at what they do, or what we had there wasn't murder. Since that's obvious, what do we have?"

"Ummm," I said. "I have no idea." I was beginning to get a little irritated by this guy's tone. If I didn't know any better I would have thought he was hamming it up for a camera somewhere. If he was I was so not signing any release.

"Of course you don't," Cartwright said, "and neither do we, now. There are two other possible explanations that occur to me at the moment. One would be general all-purpose burglary, but, as far as we can tell anything that may have been worth anything, and that frankly isn't saying much at all, has been either been destroyed or left behind."

"What's the other explanation?" I said. I almost felt like the straight man in a vaudeville act at this point. Holy crap, who the hell actually talks like this? Plus, did he really have to get in a little dig at the fact that I'm mostly completely broke?

"Rather overzealous vandalism," Cartwright said.

"That's not vandalism," I said. "That's demolition."

"Well put. And yet the damage was fairly localized. Your car was untouched, as was all the other apartments in the building. And here's another odd part."

"What's that?" I said. Like I said, I almost felt like he was making a "Yo' mama is *so fat*" joke and it was my job to say, "How fat *is* she?"

"There are two occupied apartments on the first floor of the building," he said. "And, given the state of the loft, I hardly think whatever happened there could have gone unnoticed by them. So naturally we made it a point to inquire." He paused, almost as if he was waiting for me to prompt him. Finally, I did.

"Well, what did they say?"

"That's the odd part. None of them were home, although, as your landlord confirmed, all of their vehicles were still parked out front. In fact, one of the unit's doors was half ajar, and after a glance inside we found that the TV was left on and that there was a half eaten pizza and an open two liter bottle of soda on the coffee table. Also the tenant's cell phone, keys and wallet were still strewn alongside the pizza."

"So...what, he just ran off?"

"You know as much as we do about that," Cartwright said. "The other unit was similarly abandoned, as if the tenants left in a hurry. That more or less left us without any witnesses, since we tried the mobile park next door and no one can remember hearing or seeing a thing."

Of course, I thought, after thinking that over for about half a second. *Greater mass amnesia. If I got hit then why not them? Even if they did see anything...*

"Does that mean anything to you, Miss Kroger?"

"What?" I said. Then I realized that I must have nodded or something when I made the connection a second ago, and Cartwright spotted it. I tried to reply without making it look like I was dreaming something up, and I'm not sure how well I did.

"Yeah," I hazarded. "Those people keep to themselves mostly from what I saw."

"Yes," he said. "So it would seem."

We went back and forth more or less like that for a few minutes until we arrived at the station downtown. Cartwright led me in to the lobby, and said a few things to a blue uniformed clerk behind bulletproof glass while I stood around with my arms folded. Finally, he swiped his ID badge and opened a thick wooden door that had a tiny little square glass window high up enough for me to have to go on tiptoe to see through. He held the door open with one hand and motioned me on through with the other.

He led me through a room full of people sitting at desks with outdated computers and piles of mismatched folders on them. I'd tell you more about the place but we walked through so quickly I barely even had time to take it all in. I basically was able to glance at some cubicle wall and think *hey, it's a Lego Yoda* and then we were suddenly in a bland hallway with a plain white linoleum floor, buzzing florescent lights and light brown doors every fifteen feet or so on either side. Cartwright stopped, opened the second one on the right and stood holding it open, looking at me.

I peeked in; all the room had in it was a table with two chairs on either side and a camera in one corner of the ceiling.

"What is this?" I said, and smirked at him. "I'm being interrogated?"

He chuckled. "Oh, no," he said. "Just need to get some information for the report. Also I want to see about getting your effects back as quick as I can. I'm sure you have some phone calls you need to make and what not as well, so just have a seat for a minute. Do you drink coffee?"

"Black," I said.

"Excellent. I think I can scare up some donut holes, too. Would you like some?"

"Wow, I should get my house destroyed more often," I said, and walked in past him. He just chuckled again, said he'd be right back, and closed the door.

I took a seat and tried to make myself comfortable, but that was completely impossible. The chairs just flat out sucked, and I tried all four. They may as well have had nails sticking up out of them and they made my back bend all weird. I did finally manage to find one way to sit in one of the chairs that didn't make me want to just give up and stretch out on the floor; I had to sort of slump diagonally into it and prop one arm up over the back. I let my head fall back and let out a deep breath. Maybe it was because I still didn't quite process everything yet but all I could think of was that I was going to be late for work and I couldn't call in.

So I sat. And Sat. And Sat.

I could go on but I think you get it now. I felt like I was simulating time-lapse photography. I swapped chairs, walked laps around the table, made funny faces into the camera, and counted the notches in the ceiling panels. There wasn't a clock anywhere in the room, and of course I didn't have my phone so I had no way of knowing how long Cartwright abandoned me for. I really started craving coffee before long, too. Oh, and glazed donut holes. Then all I could think about was a huge plate of silver dollar pancakes and bacon. I was actually so hungry I was about to start gnawing on the table.

✳ ✳ ✳ ✳ ✳

All of a sudden I heard the door shut, and my head shot up. Turns out I had my head down on the table and fell asleep, for how long I have no idea. My eyes wouldn't open all the way and I couldn't see much of anything but a bunch of brown and white blurs around a black blur. The black blur moved, and then:

"I knew I should have killed you," said a woman's voice.

A whole lot of things happened all at once just then. My heart froze, my stomach wrapped tight around itself, and my lungs just quit altogether. I couldn't help it, really. You may as well have told me to dunk my hand in boiling water and not yank it right back out. See, there was only one person that voice could belong to. My little X began to throb again as if just hearing that voice set it off.

I squinted and the blurs sharpened up. Not that I needed them to in order to be sure, but hey. Just as I thought, there she was, and this time she could see me as well as I saw her.

"Hello, Marsh," I said. "What's up?"

Chapter Thirteen

I was actually proud of myself. My voice didn't shake or crack and I didn't stutter. It was all a bullshit act, and I'm pretty sure Marsh didn't buy it at all, but the small things are important and all that.

I'm not sure why I bothered though; it was extremely hard to bullshit Marsh, and I should have known that better than anyone alive. Marsh has a sort of history of finding me out and making sure I get it in the teeth.

She just stood there for a second, her face about as expressive as a wooden doll. As usual her black hair was tied tight in a little bun with a braid wrapped around it, and like always she somehow pulled off looking hot without a speck of makeup. To this day I have no clue how she does it. You got the impression that if she didn't go out of her way to look as dull as possible she'd cause pileups picking up her mail, and this is coming from me, who would like nothing better than to see her get run down by stampeding bulls. I call 'em like I see 'em, that's all.

She was wearing her mandarin collared black uniform shirt which almost made her look like a priest, and over that she had on a black overcoat which was cut up front just above her midriff and went down just past her knees in the back, almost like tails on a dress tux. It was the same uniform I got to wear for a while, and I don't mind telling you, seeing her in it wasn't exactly doing wonders to improve my composure. See, stripping me out of that very uniform was part and parcel of the excommunication ritual.

She pulled out the chair directly across from me real slow and deliberate like, and she managed to make sitting down look as graceful as a ballet routine. She put her hands together on the table in front of her just as graceful, almost like she was made of mercury or something, and then looked me straight in the eye. I had to look at the bridge of her nose because somehow I just couldn't do any more than that. She always seemed to get the better of me that way.

"So," she said. "What shall we talk about?"

"I'm guessing the w-w-weather is out?" I said. She didn't flinch.

"I suppose you thought that was clever," she said. "Waste any more of my time and I'll start taking liberties."

"Like w-w-what?" I said. Yes, I really did say that. I don't know how I got the nerve, or why I was suddenly so stupid, but I did. Maybe I had flashbacks to bullies I wished I'd stood up to, or maybe I was just beyond irritated from hunger, exhaustion and confusion. Who the hell knows? Point is, I said it. Before I could blink Marsh decked me across the face and I was flat on the ground with my chair on top of me. I didn't even have enough time to be shocked before she heaved me up and threw me back in my chair like she was tossing out the trash. Then she lifted her foot and pushed me—chair and all—back against the wall so hard I may as well have been hit by a truck. The back of my head bounced hard against the wall, and my chin hit my chest. I looked up without lifting my head, rolling my eyes as high as they could go. There was Marsh, almost nose-to-nose with me, leaning into me with a hand on each armrest. Her face was as blank as it was when she came in.

"I guess that camera's off?" I said. Wow, I really don't learn, do I? I plead stupidity and smashed brains. I mean the first words out of the woman's mouth were *I knew I should have killed you*, not to mention she just clocked me, oh, and don't forget that if she somehow managed to work out that I could still manifest the light, I'd be about ten thousand times more fucked that I already was. All that and there I was poking her with a stick? If I don't win the Darwin Awards this year I'll eat my boots.

"I'll hurt you in ways you couldn't possibly imagine," she said. "You, who would take the gift you were given and defile it with blasphemous, profane depravity."

"Say what—?" I said. I couldn't really help that, either. I really, *really* can't stand it when people speak all elegant and dramatic like that. It's like they think they wouldn't sound cool if they just speak like a human being. "You trying out for a play?"

She hurled me one handed across the room like I didn't weigh a thing. I hit the wall just below the ceiling, bounced, and smacked the ground in a face plant that would probably win me an Oscar if I were a stuntwoman. My face hit the ground and I tasted blood. Wow. I know Marsh never really liked me, but this was beginning to look like she thought I not only murdered her whole family but also ate them smothered in ketchup. She heaved me up again, and this time she slammed me against the wall with one forearm against my throat. Holy sweet crap, If I didn't know any better, I'd swear she came into the room with every combat prayer she knew blazing; what she was doing was like killing a cockroach with a bazooka.

"Are you finished, Kroger?" she said. She sounded calm as hell; she wasn't even breathing hard.

I couldn't answer because she was pressing too hard against my neck. All I could do was make gross choking noises. It was probably for the best, really. Finally I just nodded my head up and down real fast.

"Good," she said, and eased off the pressure. She yanked me away from the wall, and I gasped for air. She didn't give me any time to get my breath back, though. She just swung me around like a toy, pushed me back into the same chair she knocked me out of in the first place, and then she shoved me back in toward the table. I just sat there, stunned, and she walked back around to her own chair. Then she did that graceful sitting-down thing and the hands-in-front-of-her thing just like before.

"So," she said. "What shall we talk about?"

My hair was mussed all over every which way but mostly in my face; it kind of felt like I was looking at her through a weird shaggy black curtain. I really didn't feel up to getting slugged again so I thought for a second, and gave the best answer I could think of.

"I don't know," I said. My throat was killing me with each word, but I tried really hard and kept it from showing. "My house was destroyed."

"Oh, that is a good beginning, but that would only be the beginning," Marsh said. "We have far more ground to cover than that. Why don't you go on?"

I wasn't about to mouth off again, thanks. Frankly I have no idea why I did in the first place. Defense mechanism or not, it was a *stupid* defense mechanism. I may as well have jumped out from behind cover and yelled *Here I am, shoot me, shoot me* at some guy wearing an *I want to kill Adobe Kroger* shirt and holding a mini gun.

"I...it looked like...I...I don't know," I said. My head was really starting to hurt. I tried to think of something else to say, but every time I tried the little vein on my temple throbbed. Not to mention the X on my arm felt like it was burning a little. Oh, and also I was still just a little bit scared out of my shit. After all, this woman could probably bend me in half before breakfast on her worst day, and she hated my guts to begin with and I'd already pissed her off.

All that and then there was the small problem that I really, *really* didn't have jack shit to say. I decided I'd better say something though, if for no other reason than to keep her talking instead of caving in my face.

"It was just—destroyed," I said finally, without making a move to fix my hair. I actually liked it just how it was at the minute. "Almost like someone firebombed it. I didn't even get a good look around, the detective got me out of there before I could say anything."

"Yes, Cartwright does his duty well," she said. "He saw to it that we have plenty of time alone. Now, why don't you go on? Tell me what happened last night."

She was talking so calm and quiet and soft I was almost more afraid now then when she had me pinned against the wall. I could tell she was on the verge of exploding, and I really, really, didn't want that.

What could I do, though? Tell her *duh, I don't remember?* Yeah, she'd buy that no problem. Could I tell her I had no idea what she thought I did or why she was beating me down? Oh yeah, that'd go down even better.

"I...don't know," I said. Seriously. That was the best thing I could think of.

Marsh narrowed her eyes a bit.

"Perhaps you didn't understand, which hardly surprises me. I believe I told you to go on, not to continue wasting my time. I gave you this chance to offer some small opportunity to rise above and repent your invidious actions, which is far more than you deserve. I do not actually require you to tell me anything, as you can hide nothing from me I do not allow you to."

"I'm..." I said, but I paused for a second. What the hell was I supposed to say? Explain that I actually couldn't tell her anything about last night whether I wanted to or not? If I did, how was I supposed to explain that? Tell her that a wizard cast a greater mass amnesia and blew it all away? Yeah, assuming Marsh believed me, I'm sure it would take her roughly one second to put two and two together and then go and rip Smoot apart after she was done with me. I didn't know anything about Smoot's situation but it wouldn't have taken a genius to figure out that Smoot was on borrowed time with Marsh and that the other Paladins couldn't give a shit one way or the other.

I had no way out of this, unless you count throwing some chick who protected me under the bus just for a small chance Marsh would beat less shit out of me than she already planned to. So basically, I had no way out of this. Look. I'm not like those characters in movies or books that come up with brilliant stuff on the spot that actually took the author weeks to work out. I was tired, starving, scared, and in a hell of a lot of pain. Not that I had too many ideas to begin with, but if I had any before, I sure as hell didn't now.

So, there I was. I began to say something and paused. I took a deep breath and went on.

"I'm not trying to hide anything from you," I said. "I don't know what happened last night. That is the Lord's truth."

I thought I saw the corner of Marsh's mouth twitch. She didn't say anything for about ten seconds. Finally, though:

"Look at me, Kroger."

I froze. For a moment I thought I must have imagined hearing her say that, maybe because I really, desperately didn't want to believe she actually said it. I think I must have froze for too long though, because all of sudden she grabbed my face between her thumb and fingers with one hand and yanked me forward so hard I almost felt like she was going to rip my whole head off. I had maybe a second to realize what was going on before I heard her voice snap at me like a whip.

"You dare speak so freely of him, source of the blessed light that has forsaken you as you forsook it? I will not have it."

"W—whu—?" I said; that was the best I could do with my mouth all scrunched up.

She pulled me up out of my chair, threw me face down on the table, and then grabbed my arm with her free hand. I don't think I have to tell you which arm she grabbed, either. In case I do, though, I'll go ahead and tell you anyway. Long story short, she grabbed me right on the X.

Remember a little while ago when I talked for a bit about pain? Well, forget it. Just then Marsh showed me that I really had no idea what I was talking about. All I could remember was hearing her say something that sounded sort of Norwegian, and then there was nothing else but...

How can I put this?

Imagine that a volcano could feel pain. Now imagine it erupts and it's also wide-awake for the whole thing. Maybe it might feel a little like what I was feeling, except not nearly as bad. I may have screamed, but honestly I'm not sure. I could kind of feel my throat working but my voice sounded far, far away, almost like an echo. The pain was over in maybe less time than it would take for the sting to wear off after someone slaps you in the face, but believe me, that was above and beyond was what necessary to come within a whisker of knocking me completely out.

"Remember what you are, apostate," she said. I could barely hear her over the pounding in my ears; my heart was trying to punch a hole in my chest and I was panting like I just tried to catch up to a train. "There's no point in foolishly making this harder on yourself."

It took me a second, but I got why she flipped out. It was because I said the L word, and not the cool one you're thinking of, either. Marsh is about as blindly fanatical as it gets, and I guess I should have known better but *that's the Lord's truth* is just an expression my dad used as long as I can remember. I couldn't imagine what she might have done if I let a *goddamn* slip.

I think that must have officially ended her patience because she quit messing around right about then. I didn't even have time to catch my breath before she yanked me up and shoved—no, actually, slammed—me against the wall. I didn't even have time to slump down before she got over the table, grabbed me, and hoisted me a foot off the ground.

"Look at me, Kroger," she said.

My head just hung there. I was still blinking myself back into focus.

"I said look at me," she growled. She banged me against the wall again, and forced my head up. I had nowhere to look but right into her eyes whether I wanted to or not, and that was not a happy place to be. It was like staring down into my own grave.

"As I said, Kroger, you can hide nothing from me I do not allow you to. Yet still you have done your best to try. Very well, on your own head be it."

I knew this was coming; not that knowing gave me any chance to stop it. Marsh looked right into my eyes, or through them, if you want the truth, and clenched her teeth.

"*Onthullen.*"

Oh.

Crap.

Chapter Fourteen

Every now and then something happens that you won't ever forget, no matter how hard you try. I have a lot of those stuck up somewhere in my mess of a skull, and most of them are just silly crap that I wish would stop taking up space. Like for instance, when I was around five or six I was watching an old rerun of *Family Feud* at my grandma's house. I knew it was a rerun because the color was all washed out and the clothes looked straight out of the seventies. But anyway, like usual at the beginning the walls came open and the families standing behind them got introduced before the game started. Well, this one family had what I thought was a guy dressed in a black suit at the very end, but when the person's name was called it was a girl's name. She had short hair and looked almost head to toe like a guy, except of course she wasn't. That was the first time I ever saw what was basically a severely butch chick, and I thought to my little self:

Wow, I'm never gonna forget that.

Why, I have no idea. But I didn't, and to this day every time I tell myself I won't forget something, that image from Family Feud pops into my head all on its own. It's weird.

Then there are things I can't forget because they were either so very unbelievably awesome, like how I felt the day I got my first blessing to work, or because they basically left a scar on me the size of a skateboard, like what Crow told me in that backwards sound file. I won't forget either of those, not even if I live to be one hundred twenty.

And then, there was this. This was something else entirely. This I won't forget even if I get reincarnated a thousand times. Maybe even two thousand.

I'm talking, of course, about Marsh's Exaction. In order to have any chance of explaining just how much it hurt to be hit with it, I'm going to need a minute to collect my thoughts. Bear with me.

Ok, I think I got it. Imagine you have a super deadly deep dark secret, or maybe a whole bunch of them. Every day you lose sleep or almost throw up worrying that someone somewhere may just find out about one of them, because if they do, not only will you be executed in the slowest, most painful way possible and then go straight to hell but everyone you love would push each other to get in line just to be able to spit on you before you died.

Imagine what you may go through to keep anyone from finding out, or even getting within a mile of finding out. You'd go through anything, even dying. Imagine the worst possible torture you could take without breaking and going crazy, and then ramp it up just one tiny extra bit. You'd sing like a choirboy just to make it stop and before you know it, all your terrible secrets are out and you're totally screwed. You're stripped down naked, and I don't mean just your clothes. I mean your skin, your flesh, your bones, your mind, your soul. Everything. You're nothing but a gibbering pile of mush.

That's what this exaction I learned from Marsh does to you. The one I used on Crow, that poor, innocent little girl spirit. Just thinking about it made my stomach sick, and that was when I only heard kind of second hand how devastating it was. Now that I felt it myself . . .

I will never, ever forgive myself for using it. Not ever. In fact, I think I deserved twice as bad as I got from it for even thinking of using this Exaction in the first place.

★ ★ ★ ★ ★

I had no idea where I was or what was happening. The best way I can think of describing what was happening, or, what I thought was happening was that I was hanging in midair in the dead center of a giant tornado, one of the really huge, dark, evil looking ones that look like the end of the world. I couldn't move or talk, not that either one of those would have done any good at all. I was too busy being stabbed by hundreds of invisible daggers, or that's sure as hell what it felt like, and also every second or so it was like some big invisible hand grabbed a chunk of my flesh, then twisted, and then pulled. Every time it did, I swear it ripped a piece of me off with it, and I caught a quick flash of some small piece of my past, like I was channel surfing.

I saw myself sledding down a snow-covered hill on my big blue plastic toboggan at my grandma's old farm. There was a real steep drop off at the bottom about four feet high onto a dirt road, and I launched off it at top speed. I went airborne for almost a whole second, and then I slammed on the dirt road, hard. My sled went one direction and I went in the other. I ended up on my back and I couldn't get up because I was all bundled up in a massive snowsuit. I heard my sister laughing at me.

Now I saw my sister hanging from a high branch on a tree she was climbing. The branch was bending, bending, and it snapped! She fell ten feet. I heard my grandma gasping.

Now I'm digging out my dad's military headshot from the garbage before it's lost forever. I have no idea why my mom is throwing out everything to do with my dad, and I never asked more than once because she just got seriously angry. Who cares? I'm saving at least this one little thing and she can go fuck herself sideways.

Now there was my old 'friend' Gabby who caught me picking my nose in fourth grade. She spread that around and I was so mad...

Oh no, there I was in second grade, I pulled my friend Josie down from the wall and on top of that bush. She needed stitches. I felt like a murderer. We were never real friends again.

There I was in kindergarten, I was in the center of a circle of kids chanting "Dopey's going hyper, Dopey's going hyper!" Dopey. I really hated that nickname ...I kept squeaking at them to "Shut up" but they just drowned me out.

And there was more, and more, and more. There wasn't any order or rhyme or reason, just one after another. Marsh was tearing these memories out of me like she was ripping off a piece of duct tape from my skin all in one quick pull. She was going to know every last thing about me when it was over. Everything. Including...

Including that sticky little thing about my excommunication not taking all the way.

I tried to scream but all I could do was gag and choke. Smoot was totally right. This was dark, dark shit.

Wait...*Smoot!*

In between all of that mind-blowing agony, I realized that if Marsh was going to find out about everything I had, she'd also find out all about Smoot, that Smoot helped me.

Yeah, at this point I still had no idea what Marsh thought I did, but obviously it was nothing that would earn me a lollipop. If Marsh found out that Smoot helped me, I think that would be all she wrote for her, as they say.

Smoot could have just turned me in or done nothing but let me sit there when the Paladins came for her, and that would have been that. But for some reason she didn't. She hid me, and put herself into maybe five hundred times more trouble when she did too, and all because she just did what she thought was right.

I couldn't let that happen, not if I could do anything at all. Trouble was, what the hell *could* I do?

Well, I guess maybe there *was* something I could do. Of course there was. But, if I actually did that thing I could do, it'd be over. Marsh would find me out and I'd be done for. Wait, hold on, what the hell was I talking about? Marsh was about to find me out anyway. I'd still be done for, but the only thing that would change then was that she'd find Smoot out also.

Well now that sure made my decision for me. That was all I needed. Time to go. Just needed a second or two...I hoped it wasn't not too late.

$$\ast\ \ast\ \ast\ \ast\ \ast$$

This is very very hard to do. It's very very hard to concentrate.

I wasn't really expecting it to work, and I didn't think I'd be able to do anything afterwards, but that really didn't matter. I was fucked inside out either way. The whole point was just to cut Marsh's Exaction short. Once I did, I figured she probably wouldn't bother to try it again, because she'd be roughly too pissed to care. If I could pull this off in time . . .

This was my only chance. It was something I could practically do in my sleep, which was a good thing, because at the minute even something so simple was like trying to recite *King Lear* while rolling down a rocky hill in a garbage can. I couldn't imagine trying anything even remotely harder. Like hell.

I just needed that first...
It Hurts—little ...so—much—spark ...Holy shit, I did it.
Catch, bitch.

★ ★ ★ ★ ★

"*Unterbrechen!*" Yeah, I rebuked her.

I swung my arm out more or less at Marsh, and let loose my belief that she was an evil, evil thing that needed a foot up the ass. That part was actually as easy as it sounds, if I do say so myself. I felt the light build and release like a shot out of a gun.

No, it didn't actually hurt her. Honestly I don't think I even hit her, or came anywhere close, not that I would have done much of anything if I did. Rebukes aren't meant to actually hurt living things, only to scare or knock out supernatural, evil things. But I didn't need to hurt Marsh; only surprise her, and that much I did just fine. She dropped me, fell back onto the table, and, wouldn't you know it, her damn exaction stopped dead in its tracks.

So sorry. Sincerely.

Like I said, she dropped me, but my legs didn't feel like getting out of bed yet. When I landed and could have really used their support, they gave out like they were made of paper and I almost fell over. Luckily I got my arm out in time and only ended up on my knees; I really didn't think it would be good to smack the floor with my nose.

I had enough time to take two or three breaths before I heard Marsh speak up. I wasn't looking at her but I'm practically positive her face started out white and stiff with her eyes wide open and then melted real slow into a butt ugly snarl.

"You . . ." she said. "You ...you . . ."

Those really aren't the kind of *yous* you want to hear; especially not from Marsh.

"...*Defiler!*" She shrieked, or I think that's what she said. The only reason I'm not sure is because at about the same time she said it, she cracked me in the face with one of her steel-toed boots. She went on yelling a whole bunch of things and slammed me against the wall over and over again so hard I was knocked almost clear out of my skull.

After who knows how long I stopped feeling the bang of the wall against my head, but Marsh kept on shaking me just as hard. I didn't know what to make of that. Maybe she finally split my head open and I lost all feeling. Who the hell knows? At that point I really didn't care, I really just wanted it to end one way or another.

But it didn't. In fact she went on shaking me and shaking me, and yapping something or other I couldn't really make out, or at least I couldn't at first. Somehow after a few more seconds I came back enough to understand her.

"Come on, stupid," she said, like she was more impatient than wanting to rip off my head. "Wake up! She's really strong!"

Chapter Fifteen

What the hell did she say?

"Wake up, idiot!" Marsh said. "I can't hold her forever!"

"...whu ...?" I said. "...mmhuh?"

"Come on, hurry up! She's really strong, and really *really* mad!" I managed to get my eyes open, and I saw Marsh there, just like I expected. Only something wasn't right. Thing was, well, it was Marsh's face, but it also wasn't her face. Does that make sense? I ...no, ok, I guess it doesn't. What I meant was I was looking right at Marsh's face, but Marsh had an expression on that didn't belong at all. She looked scared, and almost, well, like, girlish?

"Are you even listening, stupid?" she said. "Wake up!"

At that point I must have put on one of my best classically confused faces, because Marsh clicked her tongue, groaned and rolled her eyes.

"It's me, idiot!" she said. "*Me!*"

I blinked twice and went on staring, like I didn't have a single brain cell to bend sideways. Finally though, somehow I made some kind of vague connection. Don't ask me how. I tilted my head and one of my eyes went narrower than the other.

"...Crow?" I said.

"Yes, idiot, I'm in here and she's really really strong, what do I have to do?"

"You—you're—you—I—"

"What do I have to do?" she said. "Tell me!"

"You—you—wait, you p-p-possessed her?"

"She has to do what I make her do," she said, and then she rattled out this next part super fast: "But she's trying real hard to kick me back out so shut up and tell me what I have to do!"

"Badass," I said; and Marsh—or, I guess, Crow, looked at me like she was seriously irritated. I held up a hand and nodded.

"Ok ok ok," I said. "I—here. I know. Hold on a second, first let me—" I twirled my finger in front of my face. Crow rolled her—or, I guess, Marsh's eyes and sat back.

I tried to clear my head, or what was left of it anyway, and whispered my trusty litany. I have to tell you, getting the light to listen to me just then was probably one of the hardest things I could remember doing, unless you count that week at work I was put on bug duty.

Soon enough, I felt that sweet warmth build and flow all over and through me, and the pain just melted and trickled off, kind of like snow on a slope during spring thaw. I let out a huge breath and slumped back against the wall; I think I must have used up most whatever energy I had left to pull off that blessing, or it sure as hell felt like it anyway.

"Well?" Marsh—or I mean Crow, said. I looked up at her, and I could see that her face was kind of twitching a little bit, as if she had some kind of nervous tick. "What now?"

If Crow was expecting some kind of masterstroke of genius from me, she would be seriously disappointed. My mind was a complete blank, but in the end, I guess that kind of worked out. I had no ideas, and since I was basically backed straight into a corner, it wasn't too hard to figure out my only possible choice.

"We need to get out of here," I said. "The cops are obviously with Marsh, so you need to make it look like you're escorting me out of the building. Can you do that?"

She nodded. "Think so. But what after that?"

I shrugged. "Dunno. First things first."

I had only two choices once we got back out into the hallway. Basically I could go back out the front door or I could try to find some other less obvious way out. It didn't take long to decide that the best thing to do was just to walk right back out the front door, for a lot of reasons. First, that was the way I came in and I actually knew how to get there. I had no idea how long Crow would be able to go on holding Marsh, but since Crow looked so impatient I figured it wasn't all day, and so I figured I wouldn't waste any time wandering around. Second, it would have looked a bit strange having Marsh look like she was lost, and not to mention I just wanted to zip on by before anyone could have a chance to strike up a conversation.

So, the front door it was. I had Crow walk sort of behind me so I could lead her and look like I was being lead at the same time. I told her to just make Marsh frown a little without overdoing it and keep her eyes to the front.

It started out easily enough, except that I almost walked right out into the big cube farm at the end of the hall with blood still all over my face. That would have been fantastic. Luckily there was a water fountain nearby, so I wet my hands and rubbed myself down like crazy.

"Hey Crow," I said in a loud sort of whisper, while I was doing that. "Can you, I dunno, can you tell what Marsh is thinking in there?"

She nodded, and twitched. "Yeah, kinda sorta. She really really wants to kill you, you know. She hates you. She's basically shouting it."

"I figured," I said, and wiped my hands on the inside of my pockets. "What the hell does she think I did? Can you see that?"

I saw Marsh strain, grimace, and grit her teeth. Finally, she growled. "Can't…she's going to…need to…" She bit her lip, closed her eyes tight, and then finally relaxed.

"Ok, ok, never mind," I said, "I get it, let's get out of here while we can."

Man that sucked. I didn't bother to ask, but I'm pretty sure what was going on was that Crow had Marsh in a gigantic full nelson, and when Crow tried to dig down into the woman's head, Marsh came close to wiggling out. So, I didn't dare ask any more questions, which was what I really needed to do at the minute. Like for instance, how much Marsh saw while she had her exaction on me or maybe even how she was able to thrash me against the walls a thousand times without anyone even hearing. Well, I wasn't sure if no one heard or no one cared or whatever, but it seemed weird that she was able to do all that in the middle of a Police Station. I made a note to ask Marsh about it sometime later when she was a little more agreeable, like maybe at her funeral.

"Okay, come on," I said. "If anyone tries to talk to you, just blow them off or something."

It didn't take long for me to realize that it wouldn't be as easy as I thought, because once we got into the cubes, I saw that it was much bigger than I remembered. Cartwright marched me through the first time like I was on rails, and we were through it before I knew what happened. Now that I had to find my own way back through, I had no idea where to go. Everywhere looked the same, and to top it all off, there was more than one door in the place. In fact, from where I stood, there looked like there were four or five. Oh, and they all looked the same, too, with those tiny little square windows near the top. I looked for exit signs, and couldn't see a single one.

Hell, I couldn't even find the Lego Yoda, which was the only landmark I could remember.

I didn't stop or even slow down though, because at least four people, two patrolmen and two in regular suits saw us as we came in. They were all talking to each other and didn't really do much more than glance at us, but all the same I really didn't think it would be smart to stop and get my bearings. Like I said, I didn't want anyone to have any chance to talk to Marsh, so I just picked an aisle in the cube farm and hoped for the best.

We got about six steps down the aisle, and then I heard it.

"Excuse me, Agent Marsh?"

Oh crap. I stopped dead in my tracks, and, of course, so did Crow. I looked back, and, a split second later, Crow did the same thing. One of the guys in the plain suits was standing there with a mug of steaming coffee.

"Blow him off," I whispered with my mouth shut. I have no idea if Crow heard me, but I didn't think it wouldn't have been too smart to say it any louder.

"Sorry, real busy," Crow said, and turned back around and gave me a little shove. We started walking again, hopefully at a nice casual pace. "No time."

"I know," the guy in the suit said, and he went on talking. He raised his voice, as we got further away. "Detective Cartwright wanted you to see him before you...oh wait, there he is. Detective?"

You're kidding me. This wasn't getting any better, not at all. We managed to get all the way through the aisle and there were at least three doors along the wall. I had no idea which one to go to, or if any of them were even the exit. Like I said, I didn't see any signs. I didn't have much time to think it over, though, because sure as hell, here came Cartwright, sort of hustling a little up the aisle we just walked through. He was carrying a Styrofoam cup wrapped in a napkin in one hand and a plain manila folder in the other.

"Ah, good," Cartwright said. "Sorry if you missed me, I was out of my office. It took a little longer than I intended."

Crow just stared at him for a second, and then swung back around and gave me another little shove.

"Sorry, real busy," she said. "No time."

"Oh, I know, I know, I apologize," he said, and reached out a hand to Marsh's shoulder. He didn't use very good judgment, though, because he used the hand holding the cup to do it. He spilled a good-sized splash of coffee all over Marsh's coat.

"Oooops," he said. "Oh, I'm sorry, here let me—" he put down the cup on the nearest desk, bunched up the napkin, and started patting at the mess with it.

Crow made Marsh look down at the mess on her shoulder, and then at Cartwright. Then she swung back around and gave me another little shove. "Sorry, real busy. No time."

"Oh but wait, didn't you want this?" He said, and held out the manila folder. Crow swung back around, and I saw her face twitch. I swear I saw Cartwright go pale.

"I'm ...nnn—busy," Crow said, in between some more twitches. Cartwright didn't say a thing, but held out the folder a bit more. Crow looked down at it for a second, and seemed to think it over, wondering what the hell to do.

"I'm so sorry," he said. "Here, and go ahead and send me the bill for your coat."

Crow looked down at the folder, than at Cartwright, and then her top lip jerked up a little, so she kind of looked like she was snarling. Finally she reached out her hand, slowly, a little bit at a time, like she was almost fighting against it. She grabbed at the folder once, like she was trying to snatch something out of a fire, and missed. She tried again, and that time she grabbed hold and took it.

"Thank you," Crow said. Her eyes were wide and she gave Cartwright a smile that was all teeth. "Good...*bye!*"

"Oh, uh, yes, goodbye—umm—" he looked at me, almost like he was noticing me for the first time. He did a real small double take with his eyes, but looked back at Marsh quickly. "Let me know if you need anything else?"

"Sure will," Crow said, and then swung back around and gave me yet another little shove. "Real busy." I went off toward one of the doors, hoping Cartwright would just turn around and walk away.

"Excuse me, agent Marsh—?" he called.

"Real Busy!" Crow said, and this time she didn't stop or turn around.

"I'm sorry—" said Cartwright. "—but the exit's the other way."

★ ★ ★ ★ ★

Well, thanks to Cartwright's help, we found the door to the lobby. Crow wasn't looking all that happy, though. She opened the door for me, and shoved the folder into my hand.

"Is that the way out?" She whispered. I nodded.

"Good. Wait for me out there. I have to throw out the body."

"You what—?" I said, but before I could say anything else she went back inside and was gone. The big heavy door clicked shut behind me with a sound that echoed through the empty lobby like a cannon shot.

Ok, great. So now what?

I didn't have very far to go from here, technically, but for some reason it felt like a thousand miles. I glanced at the desk with the bulletproof glass, and there was the old man in blue, looking down and writing something. It was so quiet I could hear every last stroke of his pen. He glanced up at me, and I nodded at him and smiled as nicely as I could. He didn't nod back or anything; he just went back to what he was doing.

Ok, I thought. *Quit messing around.*

I took the first step, and for some reason I felt like I was walking into one of those old Mayan temples with booby-trapped floors. Every step I took I expected to set off some kind of blaring alarm that would drop a huge steel cage right on top of me. I wasn't paying much attention to myself but I just bet I was hugging the folder to my chest with both hands and walking like I was on a tightrope. Subtle I ain't.

I made it to the big glass doors somehow without setting off any traps; amazing, I know. I swung the doors open, and then all of a sudden everything got real noisy and bright. It was all busses, cars, and sunlight, almost like someone flipped a switch and the world suddenly turned on. I walked out onto the sidewalk, and I couldn't shake the feeling that someone, somewhere, had me in the crosshairs of a sniper rifle, just waiting for the word to blast my brains all over the concrete.

I didn't know where I should stand, but right in front of the doors didn't really seem like a hot idea, so I sidestepped a little and tried to act cool and normal, as if every person passing by on foot or in cars was about to point at me and yell *There! There she is! Get her!* That's how far gone I was. The adrenaline from a minute ago was long gone, and I was about to collapse right where I was. My legs were shaking, and I was seeing spots.

All of a sudden I heard a scream. A really loud, high-pitched scream, like you'd expect from the chick being chopped up in a horror movie. It started out loud but got even louder and louder, like it was coming closer or something. I looked up and down and all around but I couldn't see who was doing it. Then . . .

KRAK!

I jumped at the noise, which sounded like a combination of someone hitting a side of beef with a baseball bat and a thick tree branch snapping in half. I spun around and saw a pile of black fabric, twisted limbs and blood mashed all over the sidewalk about thirty feet from me. I blinked and squinted and realized that wasn't just any old pile of black fabric and blood. No, that was Marsh.

A bunch of people started bellowing and yelling stuff like *OH MY GOD* or *HOLY SHIT* or just a bunch of random noise I couldn't make out. A second later Marsh was swarmed and I couldn't see her anymore.

Just then Crow herself swooped in front of me; she was free floating and bluish white as always. I have no idea which direction she came from, it was almost like she just appeared right where she was.

"What now?" she said.

Chapter Sixteen

"I—" I said brilliantly. "Umm—"

This wasn't happy. It would probably take no time at all for this place to be crawling with police, and here I was, the last person Marsh was with, and my fingerprints were all over this folder thing, whatever the hell was in it. I know for a fact that even if I was smart enough to make up any kind of story on the spot that would explain any of this away, which I wasn't, by the way, I was truly and royally screwed from either the cops or definitely my old friends the Paladins.

I needed to get the hell out of here, and I had maybe less than half a minute to do it.

"Crow," I said, and I whipped my head around every which way. I may as well have been an owl. "Him! Grab him!"

Crow followed my finger, and saw a middle aged guy driving a hot looking red Audi. At the moment he was stopped in traffic and looking at the commotion, so I hoped he missed me pointing at him. Crow just shrugged, and then swirled and dove through the air at the guy like a heat seeking missile. She disappeared into the car, and a second later the guy rolled down his window and called out to me.

"Now what?" the guy said.

★ ★ ★ ★ ★

I just about ran over to the Audi. I didn't care at that point if I looked suspicious, I needed to get as far from here as I could as fast as I could.

"Open up and move over," I said.

The guy opened the door, undid his seatbelt, and started squeezing over into the passenger seat. It was taking a while.

"Hurry up," I said.

"This suit's tight," Crow made the guy say.

137

"Then rip it, I'll pay him back!" I said; I hoped no one overheard me. Finally he got over and I hopped into the driver's seat and slammed the door. Traffic had already begun to move again so people behind me were laying on their horns good and loud, but that also meant I had a clear path right ahead of me.

"Hold this," I said, and chucked the folder onto the guy's lap. Then I adjusted the seat (this man had to have been a foot taller than me), got the car in gear, and took off.

"Where are we going?" Crow said through the guy.

"South," I said.

✶ ✶ ✶ ✶ ✶

I drove extra careful. I was too afraid to do anything else, which was a damn shame because I just now realized I was driving an Audi S5, which had to have at bare minimum three hundred and fifty horsepower. This was the kind of power I've wanted at my fingertips since I was ten, and I didn't dare do shit about it now. I couldn't even appreciate the beauty of the interior. Figures.

I made my way to the highway by the most direct route I could think of, and slowly merged onto the southbound ramp.

"Crow, your timing could not have been better. I love you, you know that?"

"Whatever," she said, or the guy said. Ok look, from now on, I'm saying *she* when Crow made the guy talk, even though the body was a guy. Just go with it. "I only came back to tell you what you wanted to know. AND I need you to stay alive for now, stupid."

"...Right, I know," I said. "Believe me, I know."

"Do you want to know what you wanted to know or not?"

"The what?" I said.

"Wow, you're stupid. You told me to jump in someone's dreams, remember?"

"Crow, I—wait, what—OH, oh, oh, right!" I did ask her to jump into Simon's dreams yesterday, and with everything that happened between then and now I clean forgot. Apparently finding out about how Simon stopped the Raine-thing wasn't as high a priority as other stuff.

"Well," she said, "do you want it or not, because I can just go home, you know."

"No, wait, don't!" I said. I think I actually had a mini heart attack.

"Ok, fine," she said. "It was hard, just so you know. That lady back there was strong but that guy—"

"Simon," I said.

"What?"

"His name's Simon."

"Why are you telling me that?"

"I just wanted to be sure we were talking about him," I said.

"Of course we are, idiot. Who else would we be talking about?"

"Right," I said. "You're right. Sorry, go on."

"Okay, are you sure, or are you gonna keep talking?"

I pursed my lips and shook my head.

"Well he—" she said, but then stopped and glanced at me with her eyebrows up. I just looked back and kept quiet. After a second she nodded and looked impressed.

"Well," she went on, "Like I said he was really strong. I almost got caught right from the get go and besides that he almost never sleeps. I think that's why I could get into his dreams finally, because he was super tired. But I got in there and had a look around. It was really really hard to find anything about what you wanted because he keeps everything hidden up real good. But I finally found something about something he called a *koo*."

"A coup?" I said. "C-O-U-P?"

She looked at me all exasperated like. "Ok, are you really gonna keep doing that or…"

"Sorry!" I said. "Shutting up now."

"C-O-U-P spells *coop*, idiot," she said. "I said *koo*, not *coop*."

I nodded but kept my mouth shut.

"Ok, so Simon's all after this koo thing. Said the wizards were trying to do it. Said the wizards were tired and angry and there was one wizard who wanted all the other wizards to do a koo. Said the wizards figured they were allowed to do a koo because they're slaves."

She looked at me, and, after making sure I kept my trap shut, she went on.

"Simon thinks that there was this one wizard that wanted all the other wizards to do a koo, right? So Simon thinks that one wizard is making weird monsters. You know—"

She broke off, opened her hands in front of her face like a venus flytrap, and made a gurgling sound in her throat. My eyebrows went up. She obviously meant the kind of monster that Raine turned into.

"—those ones," she said. "Simon thinks that one wizard I just talked about is trying to make the Paladins attack other bad monsters because the Paladins think those bad monsters are making these (she did the thing with her hands in front of her face again) weird monsters. That's what that one wizard wants the Paladins to think. Said the Paladins are about to start a war with the wrong guys and then the wizards will do a koo behind the Paladins backs while they're fighting the wrong guys."

I looked over at her, and she looked right back at me. We just stared at each other for a few seconds and didn't say anything.

"Now you," she said, and nodded at me.

"Now me what?" I said.

"Now I mean you can talk now because I'm done."

I didn't have much to say except that I was so hungry I'd probably start digesting my own organs. I didn't think I'd ever be able to gather my thoughts until I took care of that, and I really, really needed to gather my thoughts. Crow just basically info dumped a ton of dirt over me and I had no hope of processing all that and everything else that happened in the last who knows how many hours without eating. On top of that, I had to bless a lot and that burned a lot of calories.

So, I did something I'm not particularly proud of, again. I pulled off the highway about five exits down and drove through a McDonalds. Yeah, I'm not proud about eating McDonald's food, but that was only part of it. Thing was, I also used the man's card to pay for it.

Ok, it was like six dollars. I'll slip it under his door when I get the chance sometime. I mean it.

I sat parked way off in the corner of the lot, and devoured the egg and bacon sandwich so fast I don't even remember what it tasted like. I sat there, letting it settle, and munched on the hash brown and sipped the cold, pulpy orange juice through a straw. Every swallow made my eyes roll up into my head, and I felt like a noble woman on her third helping of leg of lamb.

Crow just kept the guy sitting there. Obviously this ordinary guy was a hell of a lot easier for her to keep than a full-blown Paladin.

"Where are you going, besides South?" She said.

"Las Olas," I replied. "Around there."

"What's Las Olas?"

"A place where I might find help, I hope."

"Who'd help you?"

"Hopefully, an old friend who's still an old friend," I said. "Though I haven't seen him much since you showed up."

Crow glared at me. "That's not my fault," she said.

"Oh I know, I know," I said quickly, and shook my hand at her. "I'm just saying it's been that long. We didn't really part on the best terms, but I don't have any other ideas."

Crow just *hmmphed* and looked away from me, out the window.

"I want to go home," she said.

I stopped chewing and looked at her. I was about to say something, and then I thought better of it and just kept quiet.

★ ★ ★ ★ ★

Now that my stomach was mostly full, I could finally ignore it and get my brain in order. I sat back as we made our way down the highway toward Fort Lauderdale and just let my mind drift around everything.

First of all, my apartment was destroyed last night, and I'm positive I was there for the whole thing, whatever it was. Problem: I couldn't remember a damn thing about it because—

This wizard Smoot blew my memory away. How I got wrapped up with her I have no idea. I'd never met her before and as far as I know she sure as hell had no idea who I was. Of course, she probably couldn't remember what she had for lunch five minutes after eating it, but that's something else entirely.

Oh, and this wizard Smoot was apparently some kind of prisoner in her own house. And the same night my house was wrecked, four Paladins show up in hers. Not just any Paladins, but the main four.

When I say main four, I mean the *main* four, or at least as far as I know. Ok, before I go on, let me take a minute to explain what I mean.

Like I said before, I didn't get too far up the ranks while I was still allowed to be a Paladin, so I only got an overview of how everything worked from the top down. Here's more or less what I figured out.

Paladins are secret and not all at the same time. *Not* because there *are* some who know about us, and *secret* because, like I said before, whoever knows about us *literally cannot* speak, write, text, draw or *hint* about us without a powerful Exaction basically ending their life if they push too far.

We work in and around all levels of government in lots of different ways, passing off for ordinary people. Some of us are US Marshalls, some FBI or CIA or NSA agents, some serve in Congress, some are on the President's cabinet, and one of us serves as the Doctor on Air Force One. There are at least five of us in the House of Lords that I know of, and a fair amount in MI6. I think we have a few in the Knesset, too. Basically we have a lifeline through every major power structure all over the world, and I'm not exaggerating. If I left any out it's just because I didn't think of them. Chances are, even if I didn't mention them, they're lousy with us anyway. Paladins, and the people who work for them, are both the backbone of the world's political power, and also are the first and last line of defense against that messed up supernatural shit the mere mortals aren't really equipped to deal with. We're pretty much everywhere, but as far as just about everyone is concerned we don't exist (with the possible exception of a few higher up folks).

Now, Paladins have our own little separation of powers, to lift a phrase from civics 101. There are four branches all together. There's the Exemplar, the Templar, the Judges, and the Sentinels. Don't ask me, I didn't pick the names.

As far as what the four branches do, I only really know exactly about the Sentinels, since that's what I was. The Sentinels are basically your beat cops or foot soldiers that go out and kill and break things, so if you're picturing a knight with a sword and shield mixing it up with the hounds of hell, it's a Sentinel you're thinking of. I couldn't really tell you about the other three without saying *I think* or *maybe* about a thousand times each, but here's what I do know. Basically the Exemplar are so freaking powerful they're almost half angel, half human, and there's only ever thirteen of them at a time. The Templar are kind of like assistant Exemplar who are in charge of the smaller regions, each one of which has a Judge with Sentinels under them.

But whatever, the point is there are those four branches, and each one has their number one guy or gal. As you've probably already figured out, the four heads of these branches were McCormick, Marsh, Holloway, and Wolfe, the same four I saw at Smoot's.

Now that's a big deal because the four heads of the Paladin order wouldn't get together and personally deal with something unless there was a serious mess to take care of. The last time I saw them together was when I was excommunicated. That was a huge deal because, as I found out just before that bit of awesome went down, I was the first Paladin to receive that honor since something like the 1800s! Aren't I just the absolute shit? I told you.

So, why would all four of them show up at Smoot's place? Yeah, there was something about Smoot or what she did that they all figured was a tiny bit important. If it was something she did, which I sincerely believe it was, it was something I was probably there for, since I was hit with Smoot's amnesia spell. It also had to be something that was seriously messed up since Marsh was ready to tear me limb from limb with her bare hands over it.

Oh, yeah. Marsh.

If I wasn't in twenty feet over my head in a pool of piss before Crow made Marsh jump out a building, I sure as hell was now. I was practically positive Marsh would live, even after what happened, because:

A) She is one holy hell of a damn bitch, and
B) She's a mother-fucking Paladin.

I've already told you how I bounced back from next to nothing using a blessing I learned when I was still soaked behind the ears, and that was me. Marsh was the head of one of the four major branches of our order, and on top of that she was brilliant and a freaking psychopathic fanatic. She could get hacked in half and she would still drag her torso after something she thought needed to die, and she wouldn't even blink doing it, either. A tiny little thing like a three or four story drop wouldn't do anything more than slow her down.

She'd bless herself back to perfection ten times better and faster than I could ever dream of doing, and then . . .

She knew a couple things about me she didn't before. Like:

A) I still have my powers and

B) I got help from a free roaming spirit who took over her body and threw her out a window.

Paladins are supposed to destroy or purify free roaming spirits, not use them to subvert the free will of the living and force them to try to kill themselves. To say the least, the order looks down on that activity. You can bet Marsh would be ready for Crow next time, and she probably would bring a few friends along. Or, who knows, she'd probably just sick the cops and the National Guard on me, too. Lovely.

Don't forget I had no money and no way to contact anyone. Oh, not that my list of people I could contact was too long anyway. Who was I going to call? My mom? My sister? My grandma? Are you out of your mind? Assuming for a picosecond that I was actually able to tell them anything about what was going on without the gag order ripping me apart from the inside, what was I supposed to tell them? *Hey, sorry I don't call or text unless I'm guilted into it, but I happen to be a fugitive holy knight who is about to have the most powerful secret society in history dog me across the whole planet because of something I can't remember doing. Oh, and while you're at it, could you do this laundry I brought over and make me a pie?* Forget whether or not they'd look at me like I just grew a third head, I also had no idea what kind of trouble they were already in let alone what more trouble I could brew up for them by even thinking about going to them for help. So scratch them.

Ditto all of my friends, not that Jill would lift a finger to help me just now anyway. Hell, Jill would probably hold me while Marsh turned my face inside out and then ask to switch places. Scratch them, too.

All that plus as far as I could tell from what Crow said we were on the verge of some kind of wizard revolution, because, the wizards were slaves? I didn't remember anything about wizards being slaves, but I guess I remembered them being the least happy out of all us, usually. At the time I thought they were just jerks or something, but like I said, I was basically the equivalent of some new employee still on her probationary period and, on top of that, I miss stuff easily.

Oh well, not much I can do about that either way at the moment. First, I needed help, and I needed it in a severe way. There were only two people I could take a chance at asking now, and those were my old teammates, Reese Connelly and Casey Crumb. I only had one real flimsy idea of how to find either of them, and I had no idea how thrilled they'd be to see me anyway. Best idea I had, though.

★ ★ ★ ★ ★

I was so wrapped up in my own head that I missed the exit I wanted which meant I had to get off at the next one down and swing around back north. That wasn't fun at all, since there was a big pile-up there that I didn't know about until I was all up in the jam. Whatever, it wasn't like I had anywhere else to be, unless you count work. I needed to get to a phone of some kind and call out, because I really didn't need the extra-added stress of losing my job. No, I wasn't going to use the man's mobile phone, either. The last thing I needed was to leave any trace that I'd been anywhere near this car, thanks. Of course, I did use his card, but I didn't have any choice. I only hoped that he either didn't miss the six bucks I spent at McDonalds or he'd write it off as a guilty indulgence on the way to work that he forgot about or something.

We finally got past the delay and swung back north. The traffic was much better in that direction so I got to my exit in no time flat. Once I got off it was all about landmarks. It'd been a while since I'd been down this way, and I really need to keep my eyes peeled since I didn't know the streets too well. I knew I didn't want to go east toward the beaches, and that was basically it, so I turned left at the light and tried to find something I recognized. It didn't take long. A few blocks up the road I saw the Revolutions nightclub on the left, which is exactly what I needed. I could find my way from there.

"OK," I said, and took the folder from the guy's lap. I almost forgot about it, and I had no idea what was in it, but I figured leaving it behind wouldn't be brilliant. "Crow, I'm gonna pull over in that gas station, kay?"

"OK," she said.

"I'm gonna leave you with the car and the guy you're in, okay? If you can, find out where he needs to go and get him there some way or other. When you're done, can you find your way back to me?"

"Are you gonna be dead before I get there?" she asked.

"Not a chance," I said. "I told you, the only thing that'll kill me is getting you home, and that's only if."

She looked at me a second, and her eyes narrowed. "You sure?"

I nodded back. "Yeah. Now one more thing." I parked alongside a pump. "See if you can find out where he lives. I owe the man six bucks."

✶ ✶ ✶ ✶ ✶

I watched the Audi disappear down the road, and then it was all me. I think, now that I was alone, I finally began to understand just how alone I was. Honestly, what the hell was I thinking? I wasn't anywhere near smart enough or tough enough to pull any of this off, not that I had the first damn clue what I was trying to pull off.

Some parts of me felt small, stupid, and useless right about then. Other parts kept telling me to give up and turn myself in somewhere and wait for all this to get over with one way or the other. Others said just to run and hide and hope everyone thought I dropped dead under a bridge. All of those parts of me sounded like they really knew what they were talking about, too.

But then one small part of me basically cold cocked me, knocked me down and started stomping on my stupid face, yelling a word every time its boot connected:

"*Suck-it-up!*"

For some reason that part of me sounded a little like my Dad, and, I'm not surprised, it also sounded the most persuasive. Having a military dad does that to you. I decided in the end to listen because, you have to admit, he had a pretty good point.

I walked across the street, and I did that really super annoying thing where I didn't so much as slow down and let cars miss me by inches. I really hate when idiots do that to me, but hell, I guess I'm exempt from my own standards.

Chapter Seventeen

I walked down the side street toward the Revolutions nightclub. I never actually went here to hang out, but from what I hear it's not all bad if you're in the area. Not that it made any difference. Right now the place was just a landmark to my only possible idea for getting out of this mess I was in, so it could have been a polka-bingo joint for all I cared. I highly doubted that it could have passed for one, though, what with all the beer and radio station banners plastered on the second story railway.

The place was all over yellow with white trim, and there were even little bits of the front wall painted pastel blue. All that stuff honestly made me think more of canaries on bright summer days than anything else. My sister told me it used to be dingy grey and black. I tried to picture the building with those colors and, I had to admit, it did improve it a bit in my head. Of course, the only color I can coordinate at all is black, so, of course I'd think that.

I walked on alongside the place and there was some guy in a backwards ball cap sitting on the concrete in front of the box office. He looked up at me and I think he was about to ask if I had any cash but then thought better of it when he realized I was probably as broke as he was. Smart guy. He looked away from me almost as soon as he saw me.

I started to keep my eyes peeled, because I knew the spot I needed was somewhere around here. I knew about what it looked like, but not exactly where . . .

I passed by Revolutions, some little open-air patio place right behind it, then what looked like a bar . . .

There it was. In between the bar and the next building over was a narrow alleyway that was closed off by two tall grey doors. One of the doors was graffiti tagged with what looked like a Pac Man ghost with a plus sign on his forehead and the words *Qjita Gang Bang* scrawled over his head. I didn't remember the tag, but I sure remembered the doors. I looked closer and, thankfully, they weren't locked or even closed all the way. Call me lazy, but I'm glad I didn't have to climb over them.

For some reason, instead of just opening the stupid doors all the way I found it necessary to slip sideways through the opening. I have no idea why. Maybe I was still scared to death of leaving any trace that I'd been anywhere near and I thought I was actually accomplishing something by doing that. Who knows? I've given up trying to make any sense out of my head a long time ago. It's pointless.

✶ ✶ ✶ ✶ ✶

As soon as I entered the alleyway, it got real noisy. There had to have been maybe fifty air conditioning units lined up on the ground from one end of the alley to the other and they were all yelling at the top of their lungs. The alley was so narrow I actually had to side step those big grey boxes to get by.

I walked past a pair of big metal canisters marked *nitrogen* and an electric box tagged from top to bottom with the letters *UG* over and over again. Then, about halfway through the alley I found exactly what I was looking for. There on the left was a huge door, propped wide open with a big plastic bucket full of wires and things. There was a small piece of paper with the message **Please <u>DO NOT</u> use this door** taped on the door with blue duct tape.

This was exactly where I needed to be, or where I hoped I needed to be. If this didn't pan out, I was truly and completely out of ideas.

✶ ✶ ✶ ✶ ✶

I poked my head in the door and had a quick look around. There really wasn't all that much to see, just a hell of a lot of grey, damp concrete, big white buckets like the one holding open the door, fifty pound bags stacked four or five high on palettes, and a whole bunch of brown boxes wrapped in plastic stacked off against one wall. Through a door I could see a large empty room that had basically nothing in it but a huge concrete floor that really looked like it could use some pressure washing. I honestly felt like if I hung out here for too long I'd catch the crud.

"Umm…" I said. "Anyone here?"

148

I waited for a few seconds, but the only answer I got was the air conditioners buzzing outside. I dropped the folder on one of the boxes, took a few more steps inside and raised my voice a little.

"...Hello? Umm...Reese?"

Nothing. Not a peep.

All of a sudden it hit me how stupid an idea this was. What made me think there'd be anyone here, let alone someone I needed to be here, just because I needed him to be? Please, life doesn't work like that.

Then again the door was propped open, and, I guess it sort of looked like someone was doing some kind of work here. Of course, it could be anyone. Or, it could be no one and they just left the door wide open when they left. Or, I could just be stupid and I have no idea what I'm talking about. Yeah, I agree; it was most likely the latter.

That didn't stop me from trying again. Or maybe it was that I wasn't ready to admit I hit a dead end.

"Reese?" I said. "Anyone? Reese?"

As you may have already figured out, the only thing I heard was the echo of my own dumbass voice. I looked up and around and side to side but if there was so much as a flicker of movement or sound I missed it completely. Well now this was a dud if I ever saw one.

"Of course," I said, and spun on my heel and made my way back out the same way I came in. "So now what am I gonna—"

That was as far as I got before I got slammed in the back so hard I went flying forward out the open door and landed flat on my face on the floor of the alleyway.

★ ★ ★ ★ ★

"What the—" I said, or started to say anyway. Before I could get any farther someone grabbed me by my hair and shoulder and flipped me over on my back. A half second later I had my arms pinned at the wrists off to the side and someone was sitting on top of me. It was a kind of skinny guy with short blonde hair and a real thin face; hell, he almost looked like a human whip if you want the truth. He had a five o clock shadow twice over and he was snarling like a real pissed off attack dog.

"—Reese!" I shouted. "Get the hell off me!"

"Shut up!" he howled. "The only reason you're still alive is because I need to know something."

"Get-OFF!" I said, and started struggling with everything I had, but it didn't do any good. Reese was skinny as hell but he was all wiry muscle. The man was a beast, plain and simple. I couldn't budge him. "Are you *nuts?*"

"Where's Casey?" he said. "Tell me or I'll kill you, I swear!"

"What—?"

"Shut up! You know! Tell me!"

"Get-Off!!!"

"Where is she? What did you bastards do to her?"

"You crazy—" I growled. "DON'T-MAKE-ME-*PRAY!*"

All of a sudden the look on Reese's face went from 'psycho killer' to 'squirrel that just saw an oncoming semi five feet away'. I didn't give him any more time to think about it, though. I wound up the prayer in my mind, gave it the full power of my faith and belief, and let it fly.

"F-f-f—"

Oh, you have got to be kidding me!

Reese slammed his forehead square against my nose. I felt and heard the bone break—the pain was like an million volt electric shock and blood spattered all over my face.

"AWWWWW!" I yelled, but I managed to resist the urge to waste any energy swearing at him. If I do say so myself that was probably one of my proudest moments. Instead, I turned my head to the side and—

"F-f-*festigkeit!*"

Oh hell yeah.

The power tore through me like a shot of the best stuff you've ever thought of. If you've ever jumped out of a plane or maybe got launched on one of those extreme roller coasters that go from zero to one hundred twenty before you know what's going on, then maybe you have some idea what it felt like. I mean, I literally felt like I could knock down a building with my pinkie if I wanted to.

Of course, all I had to do was chuck Reese off of me, which wasn't nearly so hard as that. I forced up my hands, and he didn't push back any harder than a two-month-old baby would have. His eyes went wide and his whole face looked like he just caught his parents doing it. I grabbed a handful of his shirt and threw him off to the side like a Frisbee; he bounced off an air conditioning unit and slammed into the ground on his side.

I got up and walked over to him. On the way I mumbled my favorite litany, and passed my hand over my smashed nose. In a second it was, as far as I could tell, as fit and fine as ever. Whether or not it was all messed up and crooked looking I had no idea. I think this was maybe the tenth time it'd been broken in the last twenty-four hours.

Reese was on his butt now, sort of scuffling backwards. He wasn't looking scared anymore, no, just incredibly mad.

"You think you can just walk in here and—" he said, but I cut him off. I really didn't have so much as a speck of patience just then. I mean, I knew I needed his help and all that, but the man did just attack me and break my nose, so I was a little pissed off.

"Shut up!" I yelled. "Calm down goddamn it!"

"You keep away from me!" He said. He scuffled back a bit more, and then stood up.

"I don't have any clue what you're—" I said, but then Reese whipped up one hand and chucked a rock right at my face. He must have scooped it up when he was on the ground or something. I flinched without thinking; I couldn't help it. Next thing I knew Reese just disappeared right in front of my eyes in a blur, and something slammed into my lower back, hard.

"G-g-gk—!" That was me. Oh my sweet *Christ* that hurt, so much I think my whole body went into shock and I couldn't even scream. I jerked forward a little but stopped short. I couldn't move a muscle. I was completely paralyzed standing up.

"Sorry," said Reese. He was behind me, and he put his chin on my shoulder. Damn, the guy got the drop on me, but good—for some reason I completely forgot about that freaky talent of his. Somehow or other he's able to move so fast you can't even see him, but only for a half of a second at a time. That doesn't seem like too much until one second he's in front of you and the next he gets behind you and sticks something in your back, like he just did. I'm damn lucky all he had was his fists. Small comfort.

He moved his mouth a little closer to my ear before he went on.

"Normally I don't hit girls," he said, "but you don't really count, do you?"

I ground my jaw a bit, and some drool dropped out of the side of my lip. It took a lot of work, but I got my mouth to move.

"I know I—fail at chick, but you oughtta gimme *some* credit."

"You wish," he said. "One more chance. Where's Casey?"

"Hate to break your bu-huh-ubble," I groaned. "But I ha-have no idea what you mean."

"Did I stutter?" he said.

Really? Even though I was in so much pain I could hardly stand it, I rolled my eyes. I don't think Reese saw.

"That's a new wuh—one," I said. Well, fuck me sideways. Here I was, the only person who had a chance of helping me just attacked me, broke my nose, and was about ready to gut me groin to gullet. Oh, and I had no idea why, like usual. I mean, like I said Reese and I didn't really part as bosom buddies or anything but this was way over the top. Do I just have the world's most shitty memory or was I really missing something here?

Oh, and that little *did I stutter* dig of his cut a hell of a lot deeper than it should have. Reason being that I maybe had a way out of this little problem, but not if my mouth got stuck. There wasn't any way in hell Reese was going to let me substantiate a prayer if he had a chance to stop it. He'd already shown that. No, he'd probably just finish me instead if he thought I was trying. I had to calm down, clear my head, and to do that I needed time. Maybe I could buy some if I got him thinking he was on top. Well, he really was on top anyway, but I couldn't let him think that had any chance of changing.

Thing was, he didn't give me the time I needed. He just walked around in front of me, so I could see him, and bent down and picked up a rock. It was a big one, like the size of his whole hand.

"Well?" he said. "Where is she? I'm going to count to five, and then I'm splitting your head. I don't give a shit what happens after."

No, obviously he didn't. He looked me straight in the eye, and it felt almost like he may as well have been pointing a gun right at my nose.

"One," he said.

"Reese—"

"Two."

"I'm t ...t ...t ...."

"Three."

"You really n-n-need to ...."

"Four." He lifted the rock and made like he was about to pitch a fastball. He was really going to do it. Holy shit. I had to stop him somehow, but he wasn't listening to me. All he wanted was an answer I couldn't give. My only chance was a prayer, but I just knew I wasn't going to have enough time to substantiate it thanks to my unpredictably defective mouth.

Wait. That was it!

I don't know how I thought of what I did next; I'm honestly not this smart. But that doesn't matter. Fact is, I *did* think of it, and literally just in time, too.

"FI—"

"She's in p-p-p . . ."

He stopped short, and his eyes opened up a bit. That was all I needed.

"She's in—p-p-p—*Panzer!*"

Oh my Christ, finally. I almost gagged on the word, but I completed the prayer. What I was trying to do was encase myself in a solid barrier of holy power, which is stupid tricky to maintain. You really have to believe that you're protected or it just won't work, period, and that is about five hundred times harder than it sounds. It's really difficult to *unbelieve* that a baseball bat will crack your skull, for instance. It took me weeks to get it right when I learned it, and that was some seriously brutal training.

Anyway, I honestly hoped I had enough faith in myself at the moment, because I was about to need it one whole hell of a lot. Reese growled at me like he was trying to imitate a bear or something, and threw the rock right at my face. He put his whole body into it, from his shoulder to his feet.

The rock hit me right between the eyes. My head snapped back and I almost stumbled over, but the impact didn't hurt at all. It was like someone just tried to push me off balance with his fingers. I straightened out as much as I could, leveled my head back, and gave him a real ghoulish grin. I bet I looked like a ghoul with blood still all over my face, too.

"You!" he snarled, and then he tackled me like I was a quarterback behind my own goal line.

I didn't have a chance of getting out of his way or resisting at all, so I went down good and hard. Hitting the ground didn't hurt, but since I didn't exactly recover from his shot to my kidney I still felt like my whole body was being ripped apart in over thirty different places. I wanted to scream, but I couldn't get enough breath.

"You're dead Kroger," he growled. "You're dead!" At the same time he said that he hauled off and clocked me a good one across my face. My head whipped to the side and my cheek hit the ground, but other than that I didn't feel anything. He did it again, and again, and again, and my head went back and forth and back and forth, but that was it. Finally, he stopped, and glared down at me with his teeth clenched. He was breathing really hard, and looking down at me like he was trying to figure something out.

After a second he looked side to side, leaned over, and picked up another rock. I say *rock* but honestly it looked more like a broken piece of a concrete block, those ones that looked like a squared off number eight. He hoisted it over his head with both hands.

"Oh my *God!*" I screamed, my eyes as wide as they could go, and then he slammed the block down right on my face. I managed to turn to the side a bit so the block landed with a real gross squishy thud on my cheek. The block was heavy as hell, and I got pressed down flat into the ground, but it felt no worse than if someone just gave me a real rough peck on the cheek.

He raised the block over his head again.

"Oh, come on—" I said.

Thud.

"Gimme a—"

Thud.

This was getting extremely annoying.

Thud.

I started mumbling my little restorative litany, keeping my mouth moving as little as I could.

Thud.

There we go...I felt like I could move again, sort of, but to be honest all of this abuse and blessing and abuse and blessing without any kind of rest in between was seriously beginning to wear me down. I've been running on an egg sandwich and an orange juice since O'Shea's last night and I was getting real close to burning all the way through it already, or it sure felt like it. Not to mention the *X* on my arm was really beginning to hurt, more than usual. I couldn't afford any more screw-ups, not now.

I waited until he lifted up the block one more time, and then I whipped up my left hand, caught the block in my palm, and pushed it right back at him. I really would have rather punched *through* the block and landed my knuckles clean on his nose, but I did the next best thing and beaned him full on in the face with the block instead. He went over and down like a puppet someone got tired of playing with, or, at least I *thought* he did at first. Turns out I forgot how well this guy was able to roll with punches; he did go down, but then he just did a somersault and ended up sitting up straight. Before I could get to my feet he was already hauling ass down the alleyway like he was trying to break some kind of record.

"Reese!" I said, and then sprung up and took off after him. He was in ridiculous shape, and on top of that he had a hell of a head start on me. I couldn't let him get out of the alley with such a huge lead or I had a feeling he'd lose me before I could blink. I remembered that he could only do that speed blur thing of his every so often because it took serious effort, but for all I knew he could have been about to do it again any second.

This called for yet another prayer, which gave me a whole other problem. I was already maintaining two prayers and I didn't dare let either of them drop while I still needed to deal with Reese. I wouldn't stand a chance without them. The man always made me look positively stupid when it came down to hand to hand scrapping and that didn't look like it changed a bit since we last met. He was damn near a genius with blades or any other kind of beat stick you could think of, like his fists for example, and then there were those freaky skills of his. You already know about his little blur of motion trick, but that's just one thing he can do. He also has a fully circular field of vision, and no, I have no idea how that works. Suffice to say that somehow he has eyes on the back of his head and on both sides of it, too. You literally cannot sneak up on the man, or even flip him off when he turns his back (I've tried both). Ah well, hell with it. But in order to catch him, I needed yet another prayer.

"*Geschwindigkeit,*" I hissed through my teeth, and substantiated one of the two combat mobility prayers I managed to learn.

Ok, before I go any further, here's what I mean by combat mobility prayers.

As you've probably figured out by now, I can do a whole lot of really cool things that let me kick all the ass you can think of. Trouble is, everything I can do is limited to my arm's reach; that's just the drawback of being a Paladin. Wizards can blast things to mulch from a hundred yards without even thinking about it, but we sort of can't. You have to get all up in something's business to really cut loose, and it would really suck if what you needed to wail on were able to keep six feet or more away from you, like for example, Reese was doing right now. That's where combat mobility prayers come in. Remember back when I was trying to run down the Raine-thing before it could reach the cops? That was what I was doing right now. I can, when the need arises, run over twice as fast as people who worked all day at running their whole life, and that also includes Reese.

★ ★ ★ ★ ★

I started closing the gap real fast, and Reese obviously knew it. He didn't have to turn around to see it, which is such a hugely unfair advantage I almost want to call bullshit, but there it is. He made it to the end of the alley, where there was another set of tall grey doors blocking off the entrance, and these were padlocked. Reese didn't give a shit, though; he leapt against the side of the alley, pushed off and up like a goddamn ninja and rolled through the air over the top of the doors.

Show off.

Well, I sure as hell couldn't do anything nearly as cool as that, so don't bother asking. What I could do though was whip out the other combat mobility prayer I knew. Which one would that be? I'm glad you asked. Suppose the distance you need to cover to reach the bad guy you're chasing is vertical instead of horizontal?

"*Springen*," I muttered, and then I pushed off the ground with both feet. I went up and kept going a lot longer than I should have. Hell, I could have dunked on a twenty-foot rim if I felt like it. Luckily all I had to do was get over those doors, which I did with something like ten feet to spare. It wasn't all that graceful, though; my arms were spinning like windmills and my legs were moving like I was running on air. I only hope no one was filming.

Thanks to the speed I built up charging down the alley, my jump had a hell of a nice long arc to it. I ended up landing—or skidding, if you want the truth—clear on the other side of the small side road, and, this is probably the coolest thing I'd done in a while—I whipped my head around and ended up looking Reese right in the eye. Turns out he was running in the exact same direction I jumped and I went straight over him; I ended up totally cutting him off, by accident.

I heard some woman's voice from somewhere scream in surprise; well I guess it isn't every day you get to see someone move like that. As for Reese, he stopped short and his face suddenly went all panicky.

"Woah!" he yelped, but that was it. He slipped a bit, but then he spun on a dime and ran up the road, back toward Revolutions.

"Wait!" I said, and jumped off like a javelin after him, hoping to tackle him, but he did that blur thing of his and sidestepped me. I hit the ground hard and rolled, and he kept right on going like he didn't miss a single stride. He did that unnecessarily showy ninja tumble flip thing of his and hopped up onto Revolution's second floor railing like he was in the circus or something. He didn't even pause before he landed on the walkway and started toward the fire escape that led up to the roof.

That was trouble; I couldn't let him leave my sight or I'd never find him again. Then all he'd have to do is wait me out until I couldn't keep my prayers up and then finish me off, or just disappear altogether. Reese was damn good at disappearing and I was damn bad at finding things.

I jumped up after him, and had no trouble at all making it to the second floor walkway, but there was only one small problem. I did another one of those long arcing jumps and I couldn't exactly stop in midair or anything so I had to use the wall to stop. I hit it head on and bounced off it like a rubber ball and almost fell back down over the rail; by the time I got myself together Reese was almost halfway up the fire escape to the roof. I didn't have time to chase him that way so I leapt up onto the railing, grabbed a drainpipe with both hands and feet and heaved myself upwards. I shot up, grabbed the edge of the roof and pulled myself onto the surface; I got there just in time to see Reese jump onto the roof himself about thirty feet away. Once he got there he started running like he was on a bridge with a train right behind him.

Well, he could run as fast as he wanted, since at the moment I was still faster. The trouble was, how could I catch him? I couldn't stay out of his line of sight, and he could just step out of my way faster than I could follow if I tried to grab him or tackle him. He'd also probably run rings around me if I managed to get in close anyway. Eventually he'd wear me down, even with my prayers going, unless I could wear him down first...

I sort of got an idea just then. It wasn't all that much of an idea, but I guess it was something, and something is always greater than nothing. In this case it was *barely* greater than nothing, but . . .

Off I went, giving it everything I had. I took about four big bounding steps and then jumped toward Reese, and this time I came down at him feet first.

I was about half a foot from him when he blurred away. That was about what I figured; he'd want to make sure I was real close so my field of vision would be narrower and I couldn't tell where he ended up. What he didn't count on was that I had a pretty good idea where he was going anyway, whether I could see him or not. Here's why.

Reese was an absolute monster in close combat, and that didn't just mean he was good at using his fists, either. He had a natural knack for reading his opponents, and we were on the same team once upon a time. If he forgot from our time together that I was a lefty, I'm pretty sure he figured it out by now. He would have sidestepped off to my weak side, just like he did when I tried to tackle him ten seconds ago. I hoped.

I landed, planted my feet, and twisted a bit to my right. Then I pushed. Hard.

✻ ✻ ✻ ✻ ✻

I slammed into Reese like a charging bull. I heard him go *ooof* and we were tangled all up in each other, and then for a second or two it was real messed up and confused. I was grabbing every which way I could for some part of him but he kept slipping out, until finally I somehow got a hold of one of his wrists. When I realized I managed that, I squeezed, tight.

"Aaooow!" he yelled. "Get off you crazy—"

Something hit me in the side of my head, then right on my nose. I wasn't sure but it could have been his elbow or knee or who knows, both. I didn't let go of his wrist, though.

"That felt like a kiss, man," I said. "I'm not—"

That was all I could say before he yanked his arm all around and broke free. I couldn't believe it, but his wrist just slipped right through my thumb and fingers and I couldn't keep hold at all. The smart thing for him to do at that point would have been to run, but he didn't. What he did do was grab my wrist and try and twist and push me down, which would have worked great if I didn't have all my prayers going. It was like some three year old was trying to move me, honestly.

I twisted back and wrapped my arm around his and grabbed hold. I have to hand it to him, he didn't so much as flinch—instead he swung his free hand and got me right between the eyes. Four times. Like *thunk-crack-whap-bam*. Whatever, I yanked him in closer with my other hand and got him around the chest so we were locked up side by side in a sort of police come-along hold. He kicked me across the kneecap, punched me in the stomach and grabbed my head and slammed my face into his knee. I would probably have mashed into unrecognizable mush by now if not for my prayer; I swear it was like being on the safe side of a glass cage with a pissed off tiger swiping at you.

"Are you done?" I said, and wrapped one of my legs around one of his. He wasn't anywhere close to done. I took one in the temple, on the chin, on the nose, and he tried to knee me in the face again but I had him locked down way too tight. He growled.

"I apologize in advance," I said. "But I'm bored now."

I pushed forward with my leg and back with my arm, and we both fell backwards and hit the roof like a pair of clattering saucepans. I think I knocked him out.

Yeah, I knocked him out.

Chapter Eighteen

"You're a goddamn freak, Kroger," Reese said.

For the moment he was sitting pretty, mainly because I had taken off his shirt and used it to tie both his hands behind his back to a pipe.

"You think?" I said; I was sitting about ten feet away on an AC unit. "You ready to talk yet, or should I keep watching traffic?"

"Like I give a shit," he said. "Where's Casey?"

"Is that a yes?" I said.

"Where-is-Casey?"

"Reese, I haven't laid eyes on her since Coral Castle, so I couldn't tell you. She wouldn't complain, either. She hated my guts."

Reese snorted. "Of course. Can you blame her?"

"I have no idea," I said. "I thought she was really cool, and I told her that, too. But for some reason she hated me from hello. I don't have the first damn clue what I did to deserve that, either."

This time he chuckled and his shoulders shook, then he leaned his head back, looked up at the sky, and sighed.

"What's that about?" I asked.

"Really?" he said. "You're serious?"

"Reese," I said. "I've had a motherfucker of a morning and you're tied to a pipe. How about you just cut the shit and be straight with me?"

"Fuck you," he said.

"Fine, I'll go first," I said; I got up and started pacing around. It took me a second or two to decide what to say, since, honestly, I was running on practically zero sleep. Finally, though, after running my hands through my hair a time or two, I thought of something. I took a deep breath.

"Casey and I never got on," I said. "And I don't know why. I haven't seen or heard from her since Coral Castle, and she never really had anything nice to say to me before that, if you want the Lord's truth."

Reese didn't say anything, so I went on. "If something happened to her, which, apparently something has, I didn't have anything to do with it. All I know was that she was a hell of a damn wizard and I'd be dead without her. Oh, and the same goes for you, Reessss—"

I stopped, hissed, and grabbed at the brand on my arm. It had been irritating me for a while, but now it was impossible to ignore. I bit my upper lip and waited for the pain to go away, which it didn't.

"Hope that hurts," he said.

"You win," I replied, my jaw tight.

"Didn't realize I got you so good. Guess you're not invincible after all."

"You really didn't," I said, straining against the pain. "Gnnrgh!"

"You could have fooled me. That's where I grabbed you."

"Just ...shut ...up a—gnnrgh—hnnngh—*yyyyeah!*" With one last huge explosion of nasty, the burning finally stopped and began to ease off. Wow, it was *never* that bad. I let out a huge breath and sat back down. I started panting like a puppy.

"That's right," he said. "Next time I won't be so gentle."

"Quit flattering yourself," I said. "That was something you had nothing to do with, at all."

"Sure," he said. "I gotcha."

I got up, walked over and knelt next to him. He flinched.

"Oh, calm down," I said. "If I wanted to beat up on you, you'd already be a stain. Here."

I held out my arm right under his face. Even after what I just said, he shut his eyes and turned away, like he thought I was trying to punch him.

"Stop, you know I'm a lefty, idiot," I said. "Look!"

He looked down, and did a tiny double take when he saw the brand. After a second his eyebrows came together and his mouth stretched down on one side. I couldn't really blame him, the brand and the whole area around it was red and irritated, like massive sunburn.

"The Hell's that?" He said.

"My s-s-severance package," I said, and let my arm drop. He looked me right in the eye, and, although I had no idea what was going through his head, I decided to take a chance. I sat down next to him, leaned back, and relaxed.

I waited for a few seconds before I said anything, mostly to make sure he was okay with me being right there. As far as I could tell he was at least putting up with it. I let out a breath and looked at him.

"Yeah," I said. "I'm in seriously deep shit, Reese."

Neither of us said anything for about fifteen seconds. Finally, though, Reese spoke up.

"Umm," he said. "When did that—?"

"Almost five months ago," I said. "Like right after Coral Castle."

"Woah."

"Yeah."

"Wait, so, you got nailed, too?" He asked.

"Too?"

His face got dark all of a sudden. "What, you thought me and Casey got off with a wrist slap?"

"I don't know, I wasn't—"

"Bullshit," he said. "You kicked us down the stairs, asshole. Do you have any idea—"

"I kicked you—what? Wait—hold on—"

"Do you know what they did to Casey?"

"Reese—"

"No, shut up!" He glared at me. "She was already a wizard, Kroger, and then she got blamed for what you did! What the hell did you think would happen?"

✷ ✷ ✷ ✷ ✷

I was about to try and finish my thought that he kept interrupting, but then what he said kick started something in my brain. And not just what he said, but also how he said it.

She was already a wizard.

The way he said it, it was like saying Casey was already screwed to begin with before anything else happened. Like it was a simple fact of life, like saying *just so you know, that huge truck was already rolling downhill without brakes, of course it was going to crash and blow up, duh.*

My head was all over the place what with everything I went through in just the past few hours, but, just then I was able to start putting things in some kind of order. Sort of. All of a sudden I pictured Smoot, and what she said when I first met her:

I can't help bein' me, you know? But y'all make bein' me a felony, man. Y'all ain't never done nothin' but make me wonder why I just don't step in front of a train.

I remembered how Marsh beat the tar out of Smoot, and how Marsh said she'd *kill all of you shits.* It was obvious McCormick and the others weren't exactly tripping over each other to stop her, either. Was it because . . .

She was already a wizard?

I remembered what Crow babbled on about while I was busy trying to get as far from Marsh's point of impact outside the courthouse as possible. My head wasn't on straight at all then, and it didn't help that I wasn't expecting anything like what Crow actually said, either. Thing was, I sent Crow after Simon to find out what he knew about the Raine-thing and how he brought the real Raine back, and what I got was a whole mess of stuff about how wizards were slaves, which I almost didn't process fully at the time because it was so out of left field. Then I remembered Crow said something about Simon thinking there was going to be a coup because the wizards just couldn't take it anymore.

Where the hell did all this come from? I was there, for crying out loud. I was a Paladin, and I fought alongside wizards and talked to them like I would have talked to anyone else. There was always some kind of massive disconnect, though, especially with Casey. I thought it was just because I wasn't likable or something, but . . .

Was it because of this? Could I really have missed so much that was right in front of my stupid face? Was that why Reese just laughed at me when I mentioned Casey hated my guts?

There was obviously some big gap in my understanding, and I had a feeling that if I wanted any chance of moving forward here I'd need to at least know how big it was.

"Reese," I said. "What?"

"What did you mean, she was already a wizard?"

"You kidding, right?" He said.

"No, Reese, I'm n-n-not," I said. "I honestly—"

"Are you blind, stupid, or both?"

"Yes, I'm dumb as a rock. Can we move on? What did you mean by *she was already a wizard?*"

He didn't say anything to that, but he turned to me and started looking me over, like maybe he was trying to figure out if I was bullshitting. I looked right back at him and didn't so much as blink.

"You're not yanking me around, are you?" He said. "You really don't know?"

"All I know is I have two eyes and an asshole," I said.

"...how could you not know?" he said.

"I wasn't in very long. I never even got my health plan."

If I was expecting him to laugh, I had a feeling I'd be waiting a while. Instead, I just asked him again.

"I really don't know. Could you tell me?"

He went on looking at me for a bit and then just and shook his head, leaned back and sighed.

"How long do you have?" he said.

✶ ✶ ✶ ✶ ✶

So, Reese told me all about it, but first he made me get a pack of smokes and a lighter out of his right front pocket. Just about then those nasty cancer sticks looked like ice cream cones to me, and I begged him to toss me one. He said to go ahead, since he couldn't really stop me anyway. I lit us both and then I held his up to his lips for him when he wanted a puff.

The more Reese talked, the less I realized I knew. It wasn't all that easy to hear since he was talking about something I was a part of after all. But it wasn't like I could say he was lying, since I saw firsthand just what he was talking about, and then there was what Crow told me.

I'll keep it as short as I can. Reese said that wizards were only allowed to actually *be* wizards if the Paladins said so, and anyone who found a way around that little rule never ended up happy. The Paladins made sure in lots of ways, and none of them were all that terribly good for the wizard. They did stuff like binding the wizard's power to a focus so every spell they did could be tracked, and locking the wizard's power out completely when the wizard wasn't on the job.

That was what Marsh did to Smoot right before she left. Reese said they did that same thing to Casey all the goddamn time, and that it was brutally painful when they did that, like being hit by a car. On top of that, Reese said, Casey almost always caught a fever and got sick for days after. I mean the messy kind of sick. When I remembered how Smoot looked after Marsh left, I couldn't say he was exaggerating.

Reese said that after Casey got shut down she wouldn't even be able to work up enough magic to light a match until the Paladins decided they needed her again, and she never knew when that would be. It could be again that same night or the next month. One time, Reese said, Casey went almost three months completely locked down.

Casey told him that it's been like this as long as she could remember. She said the Paladins came calling almost right after she realized she could use magic, and from then on, it was as if she had no life of her own whatsoever. No privacy, no rights, nothing. She was sealed up, locked away, and became, as Reese put it, a non-person.

When I asked him about her family or why she didn't try to go to the police or something, he just looked at me like I had a brain the size of a pea, which I probably did to ask that question, honestly.

He went on to say that he had no idea when all this started or why. He said maybe there was a war or something, or maybe some gigantic disaster, but in the end it doesn't matter. Basically, as he put it, wizards are nothing more than tools to be used and thrown out when they stop working. As if that wasn't enough, he said some of the most powerful and brilliant wizards in the world had to suck it up, smile and get bossed around by little punk ass Paladins, like, for example, Adobe Francine Kroger.

"Wait," I said. "I never b-b-bossed Casey around."

Reese gave me a look that kind of said he thought I was a moron but he also felt a little sorry for me.

"Kroger, think, you idiot. They made you the leader of our little team before you had the faintest idea what the hell you were doing. By then Casey had been doing things you couldn't even believe or understand for those sanctimonious shits for almost ten years."

I blinked.

"It was nothing but a cheap-ass insult," he said. "She wasn't even allowed to say a damn thing unless she was answering you. Hell, remember when she snapped and told you what she was really thinking that one time?"

I nodded. Casey really ripped me a new one that time, and, honestly, I deserved every bit of it, and some more besides. "Yeah. I told her she was right, and I even apologized."

"Well, that's great. They tossed her into shadow anyway."

"They—wait, they tossed her where?"

"You don't even know about that?"

"No. I have no idea what that is."

He looked at me like he was super irritated. "Well, a year in the hole would be a goddamn party next to it. And it was all thanks to you. Do you see why you may not be her most favorite person ever, Kroger?"

"But I didn't—"

"You're one of them, Kroger. Look at it like this. Some big pizza joint makes a really shitty pizza and the driver drops it off. The driver didn't make it, but who the hell else are you gonna yell at? To you, that driver *is* the store. See? To her, you were the guys who ruined her whole life."

"...I didn't—I didn't know," I said. I couldn't think of anything else.

"And then," he said. "There was Coral Castle. Do you know what they told us afterward?"

"What?"

"They said you told us Casey went crazy. That she caused it."

"What? That isn't what happened!"

"Well, that's what I said, but, hey, they never took much stock in my opinion."

"But I didn't—wait, they told me *you* ratted *me* out!"

"Well," he said. "I kinda did. It *was* your fault, you know."

I took a puff and leaned back. I couldn't really argue with that.

"Ayup," was all I said.

"Did you even get done what you were trying to do?"

I shook my head. "Nope." I exhaled, letting the smoke out real slow before I went on. "I fucked up. Crow's still here."

"Nice," he said. "Good job, Francine."

"Save it, I deal with it every day, thanks."

"Good to hear," he said.

"Your *face* is good to hear."

"—What?"

I waved my hand. "Oh, forget it. If you or Casey wanted to get back at me, I'm afraid they beat you to it." I held out my right arm under his face again.

"So then they gave it to you," he said.

"Yep. Excommunicated."

"So, what does that mean, they fired you?"

I nodded.

"So, if you were fired, why would Casey head out to your place last night?"

Chapter Nineteen

"Why would what?" I asked.

"The last I saw her was last night," he said. "She said she was going to the store."

"Going to the who-hah?"

"That was code," he said. "She's from Pittsburgh."

"Wha? I don't—Oh, wait. *Kroger*. The supermarket. I get it. That's kinda stupid, Reese."

"She said it, not me, Francine."

"She'd call me...the *store*? Really?"

"Yeah. I know it's lame. Point is, she'd only say that when she was headed out with you. And she'd only do that if she were forced to. And you know what? As you probably guessed, she never came back last night. From you."

"But—now wait, I didn't—" I stopped dead right there, because, finally, despite all odds, I made some sort of weak connection. Truth is, Casey could very well have been at my place last night, and I just didn't remember. It all seemed to keep coming back to those ten goddamn minutes Smoot wiped out, almost like they were important or something.

"Oh," I said.

"Oh what?"

"Oh I mean—um, ok, what I mean is—well look, here's the thing. I *could* have seen Casey last night."

"You what?"

"I *could* have seen Casey last night," I said again.

"Well what's that mean, Kroger? You either did or you didn't."

"Actually, it could be neither, or both." Almost as soon as I said that, I realized how stupid it was. I looked to the side a little and made a face at myself.

He blinked. "—what?"

"Never mind," I said. "Look, this is what I mean."

Before I could make any other brilliant statements, I decided just to let him have it. I told him everything I could remember from last night on, including the part about me forgetting all about ten minutes or so thanks to some wizard named Smoot. I told him about my wrecked apartment and how Marsh came within an angry mule's kick of beating my brains out over whatever happened that I couldn't remember. He listened without interrupting once, which I have to say, made it a hell of a lot easier to keep my thoughts straight. I'm serious; if someone jumps in with a question while I'm talking, most of the time you may as well have just thrown my whole train of thought off a cliff.

"So," he said when I finished, "what you're saying is…"

"What I'm saying," I said, and then looked sideways at him and made loops with both index fingers on either side of my head, "is apparently there's some seriously fucked up shit going on and I have no idea what it is."

"How long does a greater mass amnesia last?" he said.

"No clue. I don't think it actually ever wears off. You'd have to ask a wizard."

"Like Casey?"

"Reese, I told you I don't know—"

"I heard everything you said, Kroger, I didn't have any choice. I know you don't know, or at least that's what you told me."

"I told you the truth," I said. "I'm completely against the wall here, and—"

"—and you need my help," he said.

"—Yes. Given what you just put me through, the fact that I'm still asking for your help should show you how goddamn desperate I am."

"Fine," he said. "You got it. I'll help you."

"I—whu-what?"

"What," he said. "You don't want my help now?"

"—No...no! I don't mean that—I mean, just like that?"

"Yeah."

My eyes narrowed a bit. "What's the catch?"

"Simple. You help me find Casey first." And then he brought his arms out from behind his back and stood up. His shirt was bunched up in one hand. "Let's get going."

I stared at him, eyes wide, and more than likely my jaw was hanging open, too.

"You just—wait—how long have you been free?"

He gave me a look like he couldn't really believe what I just said.

"Come on, seriously?" he said. "Like ten seconds after I woke up, if that. If you want later I'll teach you all about knots." He held up his right hand, three fingers up. "Made it all the way up to eagle."

One of my eyes twitched. "...you were a boy scout?"

"No Kroger, I was a brownie."

"Oh whatever. But if you were free—why didn't you—?"

"Obviously you wanted to talk really, really bad," Reese replied. "Thought after all that effort the least I could do was see how full of shit you were."

★ ★ ★ ★ ★

Well, I figured I really didn't have much to worry about with Reese at the moment. He could have ended me easily if he was free the whole time since I had no prayers up and I had my guard down on top of that. He had to have known all that, too, but he just sat there and heard me out instead. Good. My chances just got better by something like a half a percent.

Trouble was, I solved one problem and inherited another. Miss Casey Crumb was missing, and I had a feeling she wasn't enjoying herself much. In fact, given what I witnessed with Smoot, Marsh's unpleasant mood, and what Reese told me about Casey's shaky relationship with the Knights, I'd be amazed if she had enough intact bones to count on more than one hand.

I had no idea how I was supposed to help Reese. Still, what choice did I have, really? It wasn't like I could turn him down. It was this or nothing. Oh and hey, who knows? Maybe if I get Casey out of whatever she's in, she may actually decide to help me too.

Yeah, that's exactly what'll happen. Moving on.

So we went back down to the street, and got more than a few glances on the way, but I just ignored them and kept walking along like I owned the place. I had no idea if there were any witnesses to our little meeting besides that woman who saw my record-breaking long jump, but since everything stayed relatively quiet so far I thought we were in the clear. Still, I figured it was better not to hang around in the open, and it looked like Reese agreed.

"This way," he said, and we skirted across Revolution's front walkway. "It seems to me that the best way to get what we both want would be to jog your trashed memory."

"Looks like it," I said. "I don't see where else to start."

"Well you happen to be in luck," he said. "Turns out I think I may have a solution."

"What's it gonna cost me?" I said.

"I already told you," he said. "Casey."

"I know that. What else?"

He glanced at me, but didn't say anything.

"What else?" I said.

"Really? Are you seriously going to make me ruin the surprise?"

"I am in exactly the wrong mood for surprises," I said.

"Fine, if you insist," he said. "I also want this shit with the Knights to end as of now. You're going to help me and Casey disappear, for good."

I looked at him like he just asked me to strip to my bare ass and dance. "What do you think I am, wit-sec?"

"You're resourceful. You'll figure it out."

"Did you miss where I said the Knights are after me, too? What makes you think I could make that happen?"

"You'll figure it out," he said, again. "Or, if you think you can handle your situation yourself, l-l-ots of l-l-luck, Francine. Oh, and lest you forget, I have no problem ratting you out."

I didn't say anything for a second or two; I just gave him my absolute best death glare. All he did was smile back at me.

"...I love you?" I said.

He shrugged, reached into his pocket, took out his lighter and smokes and lit up again. I guess he took pity on me because he let me steal another one, which I lit off of his.

"You wouldn't happen to have a phone, would you?" I said, after a nice hearty exhale.

"Not at the moment," he said. "I'm not pleased with my current family mobile to mobile data plan. I'm exploring my options."

I gave him a dirty look. "Well is there a normal phone in there somewhere?" I pointed down the alleyway as we passed by.

Reese made a huge sweeping motion with one arm. "Did it look like it? We're kind of in the middle of remodeling. Check back in a month."

"Errrgh," I groaned. I leaned forward and rubbed one eye with the base of my hand, letting my cigarette dangle. "Well, I need one, soon."

"Tell you what," he said. "I'll get right on that." He took another drag. "But first, we got someplace to go, and I'm afraid I'll have to insist that we put a rush on it."

"Where's that?"

"You won't like it," he replied. "Not one bit."

I gave him a real tired look.

"There is so much I don't like right now," I said. "What the hell's one more?"

We walked across the street to the parking lot, and Reese led me over to a severely abused looking pickup truck with a hood that was a different color than the rest of the body. Seeing a vehicle in such sorry shape gave me flashbacks to the pieces of junk I had to live through, and made me appreciate blueberry all the more. Man, what I would have given to have that car just now. And my wallet. And my phone. Christ, I felt like a castaway.

Reese's truck sounded like a wounded animal. Everything it did made a groan or a grind that made me wince, and then there was the stench. I don't mind the occasional smoke but Reese was a freaking chimney, and I almost couldn't stand how overpowering and stifling the air was in the cab. I couldn't roll down my window either, because the handle was missing, and besides that it looked like the glass was sealed shut anyhow. There were butts everywhere and also about fifteen empty beer bottles, which confused me to all hell since I had no idea how Reese could abuse himself like this and stay in such perfect shape. I'm telling you, I want this man's secret in the worst way. What I wouldn't give for a washboard stomach like his.

I wasn't sure where he was taking me, but from what I could tell he was heading north. That was all I could figure out since I really didn't know the area.

"Hey," I said. "Could we stop at one of those gas stations? I really need a phone."

"Relax," he said. "There'll be a phone where we're going. I really don't want to double back in this traffic."

I let out a breath and leaned on my hand, but I didn't push it any further than that. Truth be told I didn't have a particularly good feeling about any of this, and that was before Reese came right out and said that I wouldn't like it. Thing was, Reese went from wanting to kill me to wanting to help me a little too easily, even if he made it obvious he was only helping me for his own sake. Or no, wait. He said it was actually mostly for Casey's sake; which, once I had a minute to think about it, made a lot more sense. It was actually kind of stupidly easy to see once I saw it.

"Say," I said. "Were you and Casey like—" I let it hang at that.

"None of your damn business," he snapped. If that wasn't a yes I'd swallow my own face.

"Hey man, that's cool," I said. "I didn't realize. Sorry. How long you been?"

"I said none of your business. You want to get out right now?" He hit the brakes, but before he could come to a full stop I waved him away.

"No, no," I said. "Ok, sorry, I'll drop it."

"You better."

"It's dropped."

"Good, shut up."

"It's shut."

"Fine."

✷ ✷ ✷ ✷ ✷

"Here we are," he said. He pulled up, pushed down the parking brake with his foot, which sounded like that creaking sound you make out of the back of your throat, and then killed the engine. The truck shook and rattled for a few seconds before it finally quit; Reese barely waited for the rattling to stop before he opened his door and got out.

"Where's here?" I asked, and got out of the truck. I didn't have the first damn clue; I looked around, as if that would have done any good, which by the way it didn't. I may as well have looked at a circuit diagram and nodded sagely. I remembered Reese turning off of Federal and taking a lot of back roads but I lost track real quick. It looked like we were in one of those large concrete lots behind a row of shops in a plaza, except it looked like it hadn't been used since I was in diapers.

All I knew was, this place just felt wrong. It wasn't necessarily the overturned shopping cart that was missing a wheel, or the illegible half assed graffiti on almost every visible surface. It wasn't the chunks of torn up concrete with grass growing up through it or the barbed wire fence with huge pieces taken out of it, either. Or the three story boarded up concrete block buildings that looked like they belonged in a war zone and were covered in condemnation notices. Or the metal barrel peppered with holes just sitting off by itself like it was waiting for a bus. No, it was much more than all that. I had a feeling that this place could have looked like a storybook country town and it would still weird me out.

Reese was right. I didn't like it.

"This way," he said, and took off walking. He didn't even bother to make sure I was following, either. Couldn't really blame him, it wasn't like I wasn't going to. That didn't stop me from wishing he had picked someplace else, though.

✶ ✶ ✶ ✶ ✶

The place actually got worse, which I have to admit didn't so much surprise me as impress me. I'm serious, that was one hell of an accomplishment. We walked maybe two hundred feet and went down between two of those big boarded-off buildings, and then the place went from *okay this is weird* to *get me out of here, now.*

The ground, the rocks, hell, even the air seemed to be whispering to me—or, *at* me might be better—without making a sound. Then I got a very uneasy feeling, like I just walked into some room where I really didn't belong and then the whole room went real quiet and everyone was staring at me.

I had a sudden very small ache and a touch of vertigo. It wasn't enough to make me fall over or anything but it was enough to make me pay attention. I think I must have flinched real obvious like though, because Reese noticed.

"Knew you wouldn't like it," he said. "Suck it up, though, it's all we got."

"What is this place?" I said. "It's weird but it almost feels like this place doesn't like me."

"Probably, but don't take it personal. It's less *who* you are than *what*."

"Oh. That helps. Thanks. But not really."

"Keep up, Kroger."

I did my best to do just that, but every time I took a step it got harder, like the ground was getting thicker and kept trying to grab at my feet. It didn't feel like I was stepping in mud or anything, actually it was more like my feet were very slowly becoming magnets. My heart almost stopped right there, because the last time I felt anything like this very, very bad things came of it.

"Reese, this is really bad," I said.

"I know," he replied. "But I don't know what else to do. You asked for my help, this is all I got. Let's go through here."

He led me up to one of the buildings, and let me tell you, calling this place a building was being kind. It was at best half built at the moment. I followed him through what was left of a door, and stepped into what looked like a cross between a rundown crack house and a bombed out war zone. The gross feeling I felt outside almost came close to doubling once I got in.

"Reese," I said. "You feel that—?"

"Feel what?"

"That—right there. You're telling me you can't feel that?"

"No, I can't," he answered. "What made you think I could feel anything? You're the Paladin."

"Coral Castle," I said. "That's what it feels like. Where the fuck did you bring me, Reese?"

"What about Coral Castle?"

I whipped my head around in every direction. I felt like I was about to be shot from like twenty-nine different angles.

"Come here!" I said, and grabbed hold of him by his shoulder. Before he could say or do anything I rolled around so we were back to back.

"What the hell are you—"

"Shut up and stay close!" I touched the bridge of my nose with the first two fingers of my left hand and held my breath. For some reason or other that always helped me focus; I guess it's a mental thing, like putting everything on pause. It took about half a second to get my brain in the right place, and then I let out a much larger than necessary exhale.

"Kroger, what—"

"SHHH!"

For some reason he listened and kept quiet from that point on, which I have to admit, was a pleasant surprise. That was good because I needed to remember a whole different litany that I spent *weeks* learning.

This litany, like my favorite, most frequently used one, was also ripped straight out of the Bible. In this case, I lifted Ephesians 6:11, and once again used my elite Google translate skills to dump it into German:

"*Tragen sie die volle rüstung rottes an, und die können den schutz gegen die listigen anschläge des teufels haben.*"

Or, *Put on the whole armor of God, that ye may be able to stand against the wiles of the devil.*

This blessing I just finished was sort of a nice little life preserver if you happen to be drowning in evil. I would eat my shoes if that weren't exactly what was happening, since I knew the feeling oh too well. Paladins have a sort of trained affinity for these things; it's almost as automatic as smelling rotten food after you get it right. But this, what I was feeling now, was like diving into a dumpster. The evil was almost literally punching me in the face with brass knuckles.

As soon as I finished the litany, warmth built in my body, like I just stepped in from a blizzard into a cozy cabin with a crackling fire. It was a massive relief. The warmth and light spread out from me and made a kind of invisible circle just big enough for both Reese and me with a foot or so to spare. The difference between now and a second ago was ridiculous. Before, I felt like I was sort of being poked, pinched, and prodded over every square inch of me. Now, I felt almost like I was in a soothing hot shower.

Who the hell needs heroin?

Here's another cool little thing about this blessing, aside from how stupidly awesome it feels: It also does something else pretty damn nifty. I already told you about the first exaction I could ever do, the Rebuke, right? Well, this was sort of a weaker, constant area-effect version. The effect is strongest in the circle itself and then diffuses out for another ten feet or so, getting fainter as it goes. Unfortunately, I didn't have all that much time to enjoy the blessing. That nasty evil feeling outside the circle ramped up by almost ten times, almost like I had just caught it jerking off and it was super irritated at being interrupted. I felt the evil close in on me like I was caught in a tightly packed mosh pit with a crowd of huge guys five times as big as me. Finally, though, I was able slowly push it back out as far from me as I could manage.

And then, you'll never guess what happened. Reese just walked away from me, and said:

"That good enough?"

"What?" I said, and I'm sure I did one of those goofy double takes, too, which almost broke my concentration. "What the hell are you doing?"

"You here or not?" Reese called out. "That good enough?"

"Indeed it is," said another voice, after a couple of seconds. It was deep, smooth, and silky, like an extra thick chocolate milkshake spiked with arsenic. "Welcome, Paladin."

Chapter Twenty

"Reese!" I hissed. I would tell you I was confused but I hadn't quite gotten there yet. "What—?"

"Adobe Francine Kroger," Reese said, apparently to the air. "Acolyte Sentinel third class, Six points Cathedral, House Whytehearte, fifth abbey."

What? Why did Reese just recite my whole entire affiliation, into thin air?

"Whytehearte, is it?" Came the voice again. And then the air about fifteen feet in front of me moved weirdly, like a mirage. "I daresay you may have gone above and beyond, Reese Connelly."

"Save it," Reese said. "We're all waste deep in shit and sinking. In case you forgot that, have a look around you and compare it to where you just came from."

"Temperance, my friend," said the voice, which was reminding me only a tiny little bit of Barry White. I mean, it was deep enough and all, but the accent was wrong. It was more of a rich southern drawl.

"Who the hell are you and what do you want?" I said, and held out my left hand with two fingers and my thumb out. "Don't make me reveal you!"

The voice just laughed, real slow and deep. It sent a chill through me.

"I wouldn't dream of having you exert yourself, child," the voice said. "I apologize for my impertinence."

"The what—?" I asked, but I didn't have time to go much further. Weird stuff started happening before I could. The air directly in front of me began to crackle and blur, and then, well, it looked like it started to melt. I know that doesn't make any sense, but I'm telling you that's what I saw. The air molded itself into a human shape like it was ice that melted and then poured itself into a human sized ice tray. It was a pretty crazy thing to see; I have to admit that even in my line of work I hadn't ever really seen anything like it. I tilted my head and blinked.

"Oh come on," Reese said, almost groaning. "Skip the goddamn theatrics; you're cool, you're awesome, you're bad-ass. We get it. Hurry up!"

The human ice shape turned its head to look at Reese, and then after a second I saw its mouth move. The deep voice came out of it.

"You're an artless thug, you know that, Reese?"

"Whatever," Reese snapped, and then he tapped at his wrist like he was wearing a watch.

The iceman lowered his head and sighed. A second later, he looked up and all around. "Oh, all right," he said, and this time the voice sounded a lot less deep, and the drawl was gone also. Now, it sounded more like he was from the Bronx than anything else. "The asshole blew the effect anyway, folks. Come on out. There's only one of her."

"You sure she's alone?" Another voice, this one a girl's, said from somewhere I couldn't see.

"She is," the iceman said. "It's legit. Come on out."

"Reese," I growled. "What's this?"

Reese didn't say anything, but I got my answer real quick, not that I really needed it. The ground, the rocks, and bits and pieces of wall all around the ice figure started to shift and move. Or, that's what it looked like at first anyhow. After a moment I could see that is wasn't the rocks that were moving; actually I was just seeing a whole bunch of seriously camouflaged...*things* stepping forward. They had been standing right out in the open the whole time, just from my angle they blended perfectly and I couldn't see them. The more they moved, the more I could make out their basic shapes—like when you finally see the picture hidden in those annoying 3D prints—and let me tell you, some of those shapes didn't look exactly human. Not even remotely. One of them looked like a freaking dung beetle with a long, long, snake-like neck and a triangle shaped head, and another one looked like a human hand walking on its fingers, except that it had like twelve fingers and no thumb.

One by one the camouflage texture (if that's what you want to call it) started to crack and flake off, and I could see all of the creatures clearly. The thing that looked like a dung beetle with a long neck turned out to be...a dung beetle with a long neck. No, seriously, that's the only way I could describe it. Like it was a snake that got stuck in a bug's mouth and decided it liked the arrangement. The human hand with too many fingers ended up looking kind of like a flat football with elephant trunks for legs. There turned out to be a lot of those things, of different sizes, kind of skittering and slithering around everywhere—including behind me. It looked like they had me completely boxed in.

Then I saw a couple of slightly more human looking figures, and when their camouflage dropped off, I saw a girl with shoulder length black hair and maroon colored lipstick. She looked about my age, but kind of skinnier. Next to her there was a smaller, skinnier boy with scraggly dark brown hair and skin, and he was looking at me like I was every boogey man you've ever heard your parents warn you about. I mean, the kid just looked terrified.

A second or two later the ice guy's skin cracked and flaked off also, and I could finally see who I was dealing with. I don't mind saying it was a bit surprising. He was a short, balding, middle-aged guy with aviator shades, a bright orange Hawaiian shirt, khaki slacks and penny loafers. He had a bushy mustache that completely covered his mouth and a little soul patch on his chin. Needless to say, the man looked downright ridiculous, but that really didn't matter. It didn't take me long to realize that the vile, evil energy that was pounding me from all sides was mostly his fault. Whatever the hell this guy was, ridiculous wasn't it.

"Things sure are happening fast, huh?" The bald guy said, and he sounded like someone born and raised in New York, not someone hamming it up and throwing in a bunch of *fuggedabouddits* to sound like a New Yorker. He started pacing back and forth and motioning all over with his hands. "I mean, last night my club gets raided and torched, same with my dog track and Jai-lai court, and I barely get out with my life, saved 'cause I was out havin' one hell of a lucky smoke. So I haul ass to this dump, the only place I'd have a prayer—" he nodded at me—"pun intended, to hold out until I could think of some way to get the hell out the country before my head ends up on a plate." He motioned at me with one hand, and I could see he was wearing a seriously flashy gold wristwatch. "And now a myrmidon drops my passport straight into my lap. You did good, Reese."

"I'm not doing you a favor Bob," Reese said. "You're going to help me spring Casey Crumb."

"Crumb?" The bald guy---Bob I guess---raised one eyebrow. Turns out he was yet one more person who could do that besides me. "No shit, they got her too?" The dung beetle with the long neck stirred a bit, and the girl with the maroon lipstick glanced at it. The brown haired boy looked up at the girl and then at me, looking as scared as ever.

"What else could have happened?" Reese answered. "She disappeared. You want this Knight—"—he pointed at me—"you get me Casey."

"This Knight," I interrupted, talking through my teeth, "Is standing right here. Reese, what-is-going-on?"

Bob looked at Reese, and Reese nodded. A second later Bob turned toward me. I couldn't tell if he was looking at me or not since I couldn't really see his eyes.

"What's going on?" Bob asked. "What's going on is there's someone new in town. Someone the Knights can't touch. I'm guessing maybe they don't like that. They think I'm in on the whole thing, or so they say. Figures they'd realize I'm one of the few who could probably pull something like this off, but they seem to forget that I'm also one of the few who ain't goddamn stupid enough to try."

I felt the dark energy in the place try to squeeze me again, almost as if it was responding to Bob's mood. I focused on my blessing and forced it back again.

"What did that mean?" I asked.

"There are only 13 Knights that call themselves 'Exemplar' on this planet," Bob said. "And wouldn't you know it, the one presiding over all of North America happened to pay my casino a visit, personally."

"McCormick?" Reese said, and you could sure as hell tell that got his attention. "He came *personally?*"

"Sure as shit," Bob said. "Now, I can say without any false modesty that I'm one of the baddest mother fucking warlocks in the southeastern United States, and I have to say I came damn close to crapping my pants."

My stomach dropped. Oh, great; now it made sense. Bob, by his own admission, was a warlock. This was absolutely fantastic, and here's why: A warlock is basically the same as a wizard, only as far as I know they were a lot more rare and they sure as hell never worked with Paladins. This was because even though they did a lot of the same things as a wizard, a warlock's magic was a hell of a lot darker.

In fact, their magic was as evil as it gets, which certainly went a long way toward explaining why this place rubbed me the wrong way. I never had the pleasure of meeting a warlock until now, because they were usually considered above my pay grade, but I managed to pick up the basics. Although warlocks were lumped in with demons most of the time (which was fair I thought since warlocks sure liked to work with them), the Knights left warlocks alone most of the time since they were so powerful, influential, and in their own little twisted way, useful. All that meant that as long as they didn't force the Knight's hand, they got left alone. Bob must have been one of those---that is until now, anyway.

"Well, what did McCormick say?" Reese asked.

"Just like I told you," Bob said. "There's some new beasts in town that apparently the Knights can't do shit about. I mean nothing the Knights do does anything to 'em. Hell, from what I heard they basically cancel a Knight out, like rubber and electricity. Now, like I said, I wasn't there when McCormick came knockin', but one of my people got out somehow and told me that McCormick accused me of makin' these beasts. Can you beat it? What, like I'd be that much of an idiot? But get this, they found a bunch of these crazy things all caged up in one of my kennels. I don't know how they got there. Next thing I know, my livelihood's smashed and I had to run for my life."

"What?" Reese asked. "New *beasts?* What's that about? What are these things?"

"Fuck if I know," Bob said. "But we caught one. I was hopin' to maybe squeeze it to find out, but the damn thing doesn't speak any language I've ever heard of, and I speak fifteen. The whole thing reeks of a frame job, but fuck if I know how I can prove it." He motioned at the girl with the maroon lipstick and the brown haired boy. "Ok—I've blown enough time talkin'. Stacy, Eustace, get everything together. Thanks to Mr. Reese, we're getting out of here."

The girl and boy (who I guess was Eustace) nodded, and ran off into another room.

"All right Reese," Bob said, and then he turned to look at me. "You wanna do it or should I?"

"What are you talking about?" I snapped, even though I knew damn well what was coming.

"You're from House Whytehearte," Bob said. "And so is McCormick. I imagine that means he's got some kind of extra soft spot for you. He's going to let me and mine out of the country, or he'll get you back in six easy installments. Simple enough?"

I gritted my teeth. The energy of the place was getting even stronger, and I was beginning to have to try extra hard to breathe.

"So, like it or not," Bob said, "You're coming with us. Reese, you wanna do her?"

"I don't got my gear," Reese answered, casually. "And this place doesn't help me anyway. It'd take too long."

"Fair," Bob said. "I got it then. I could use a little workout."

Bob looked at me, and I glared right back at him. To be honest I felt just like I did when I was seven and was about to go down my first super steep roller coaster drop at Cedar point.

"Subdue," Bob said.

The air all around me began blurring and shaking like I was looking at it through a handheld camera with a scummy lens, and my ears also clogged up like they do when you're on a plane and the air pressure changes. That was uncomfortable enough, but then, one by one, little brown shapes started leaping out of the air. Or actually, it was more like they were tearing *through* the air like it was rice paper. That may be a little hard to picture, but I'm telling you, that's exactly what I saw.

Those little brown shapes looked like floating chocolate pudding at first, but then they all fell, or splatted on the ground and started changing. Out came little tentacle looking things that turned into arms, hands, legs, and feet, so that they looked like little brown blobs with limbs. Then the center of the blob opened up and formed what I could only describe as a smaller circle with rows and rows of tons of tiny needle like teeth.

Oh, perfect. *Imps!* I couldn't help it, I groaned out loud.

Christ, I *hated* these things. Imps are basically tiny little monsters that are just minor manifestations of magic power made solid, and they're completely blind and five times as vicious as a cornered rat. By themselves they weren't too much of a much, but they almost always came by the truckload, and it didn't look like this warlock was sparing any expense.

Before five seconds went by I was completely surrounded by so many of these little things I couldn't even count them. Each one was about as big as a good-sized teddy bear and I could already see super gross slimy crap dripping out of their maws. I groaned again; that slimy crap was bad news and then some. We're talking venom that could do everything from paralyzing you or blinding you or it just might cut to the chase and kill you. You never really knew until it hit you, and that wasn't exactly easy to avoid. Especially now that all I had between them and me was a shabby t-shirt and jeans. I would have given my right arm for my old light combat gear right now.

It would have been nice to have a few seconds or so to think of what I should do, but come on, haven't you been listening? These things never happen that way. They all leapt at me immediately, and at once.

★ ★ ★ ★ ★

Ah well, at least I had some training and a little bit of raw instinct on my side. Not to mention I managed to keep my blessing up. Go me.

"*Unterbrechen!*" I yelled, and twisted to one side and thrust out my hand. I caught three of the little monsters in one Rebuke, and they blew apart like they were hit with a high velocity bullet. Bits and slimy blobs went flying everywhere, and then all three let loose with the famous and annoying parting shot imps are best known for. They each expelled a green cloud of gas that lingered in the air a lot longer than you'd think gas should. You didn't want to be anywhere near that gas, because if you inhaled it, it could easily do the same thing their venom does, which is something I learned the hard way.

That little bit of loveliness is why I spun to the side. I shifted my legs and went right on turning, away from the gas. I grabbed at another imp and got a hold of him right on the top of his pulsating, bulging—well, *head* I guess.

"F-f-*festigkeit!*" I said, and went the rest of the way through my turn and chucked the imp like a discus. He went straight through four of his buddies and sent them flying every which way. The discus imp kept right on going and turned into a black and brown stain on the side of the nearby building. His gas cloud poofed into play right after.

I blew up four more with another Rebuke, and then the rest were all over me. I ripped one off my back, another off my hair, a third off my ribcage, and another off my right arm. I managed to kick one so far he went splat against a boarded up second floor window and used another one like a bat to swat two of his friends away.

"Reese!" I yelled, as I stepped on an imp, grabbed it by an arm, and ripped it in half. I couldn't see Reese anywhere, but I figured he was still in earshot. I didn't have any time to look for him, either; I punted the imp away and twisted before his gas could get me. "Reese! *I will feed you your own balls!*"

I was sort of doing ok for a while, but the problem with imps is that you can win and still lose. The imps don't have to survive to mess you up, and besides, they're only there to soften you up for the creep that manifested them anyway. I was covered in nicks, scratches, and bites, and the gas was getting seriously hard to miss. Since I only had my fists to use my reach was pitiful, so I ended up killing way too many of them way too close up. Even my Rebukes had at most a five-foot range. I've seen Simon stretch them out way further, but I'm not him, am I?

My body was starting to go numb, and I was seeing spots. Between the gas and the little bits and pieces of venom wearing me down I was about to capsize, but somehow I managed to kill the last imp by grabbing it and spiking it like a football. It smashed into the pavement and what I guess was its ass went straight through his face like a fly on a windshield. I had to step back to avoid his gas cloud, but when I did, I lost my balance, slipped and ended up sitting hard on the concrete. I looked up, and sure as hell, there was Bob right where he was when this whole little fracas started. He was just standing there like a statue with his hands behind his back, staring right at me.

"Wow, not bad," Bob said. "You got some stuff there, kid. I'll give you a breather. Only fair."

"*Would you knock her out already?*" Reese growled. "I coulda done it by now."

"Hey," Bob said. "I may be a monster but I ain't inhuman. She's got heart; may as well see if she can do anything with it. Plus, I have to admit, it's kinda fun; not often I get to smack a Knight around."

I was panting hard, and I got lightheaded for a second, but I did my best to keep glaring at the bastard like I was still some kind of big bad tough thing. He stared back at me with a whole different kind of look, and I felt like I wanted to throw up, again. It wasn't just the look he gave me, either; I was, after all, loaded up with imp poison.

"Okay," Bob said. "In the interest of time, breather over. Game on."

Bob held out his hand toward me, and then ...well, let me tell you something, if you've never been in serious pain and nauseous to boot and then had someone try to devour a piece of your soul, you have no idea what you're missing.

I knew I had to bless or I was toast, either from the venom or Bob's spell. As I got ready to chant my litany, though, my body seemed to be begging me not to. For some reason I seemed to remember that there was something vaguely important I was missing, but I didn't give it too much thought. All I knew was I needed to patch myself up yet again and block the warlock's power or nothing else really mattered.

Out came the litany, and all of my wounds disappeared, along with, I hoped, the venom. Next I reaffirmed my other blessing, and the Warlock's spell backed off.

I got up on my feet, hoping that I looked as fresh and fine as ever. I'm not sure how well I pulled it off, since I wobbled a tiny bit, but if the Bob saw or cared that I was faking, he didn't let on. In fact, he didn't do a damn thing but go on staring at me.

Well, that is, at first.

"Haven't had this much fun in a while," he said. "Now, let's see how strong you really are."

★ ★ ★ ★ ★

Before I knew what was happening, I felt like I weighed about a thousand tons. I'm telling you I just went *thunk* like I was a beached whale and my bones were being crushed by my own weight. I tried my best to yell or scream but I couldn't even get any air into my lungs. My cheek was mashed hard against the pavement, and there was a small chunk of rock or something digging into my skin like a super annoying blunt knife.

I could move my eyes around, for what good that did, but that was about it. This pressure went on for about five or six seconds before it finally let up.

"Quit wasting time," I heard Reese say. "Okay, you had your fun, now knock her out already."

"...An artless thug *and* a killjoy," Bob sighed. "I just bet you're the life of the party."

"You—wait, who's *that* guy?" Reese asked. I saw Bob turn to one side, and I managed to turn myself enough to see what Reese was talking about. The girl with the maroon lipstick—Stacy, Bob called her—was lugging what looked like another guy along with her in a severely wicked looking hold. The guy was almost doubled over, so I couldn't see his face, just the top of his head.

"Oh, that," Bob said. "Careful with it, Stacy, it's stronger than it looks."

"I got him," Stacy answered; her voice sounded raspy, abused, and exhausted, like she was a smoker who spent a lot of time yelling. "He's worn out. Probably starving. No clue what it eats or even *if* it eats."

"Ok. Well," Bob went on. "That, Reese, is one of those things I was telling you about, the one from my kennel. Whoever planted those things there is gonna regret being born."

"Just looks like a guy," Reese said. "What is it, some kind of ghoul or something?"

"I wish," Bob replied. "Ghouls are easy. I ain't never seen nothing like this thing. Fast as a cat and strong as a freakin' ox. And he may look normal now, but here, take a look at this."

Bob took a step over, grabbed a fistful of the guy's black hair, and lifted the guy's head. For one quick second the guy looked just like a totally normal, ordinary average guy in maybe his late twenties, and then—

And then, his face moved in six-separate directions. One second his face was all in one piece, the next, it split apart-into six fleshy petals, like a gross, messed up flower.

Just like Raine's did.

"The hell?" Reese said. "Oh man, fuck, it stinks. Does it have to come with us?"

"Yes, it does," Bob said, "I gotta find out where or who they're comin' from. Maybe I can figure out how to tear that info outta what passes for its brain."

"Okay, fine, whatever," Reese said, and then a second later he grabbed me by the neck and shoulder and heaved me up to my feet. He got me into a sort of sloppy full nelson, and I half slumped, half stood, mostly with his help. I couldn't help but lay eyes on the flesh-flower-monster-thing, and when I did, I saw the petals widen slowly, almost too slow to notice.

"Will one of you *please* just punch her out?" Reese said, sounding a little impatient. "She's done. If I do it I'm afraid I'll kill her."

"With pleasure," Stacy replied. She was glaring at me with eyes that may as well have been death rays. "Bob, hold this a second, wouldja?"

Stacy released her hold on the flesh-flower-faced-monster-thing, and then it happened, almost too quick for me to follow. The monster-thing spread its flesh face wide, squealed, lunged at me, and slammed into both Reese and me and knocked us over like dominoes. I remember screaming (or trying to, anyway) and then Reese heaved me off of him. I was airborne for maybe half a second and then hit the ground, fortunately face up.

And then, something else happened.

One time when I was around five or six I was at my grandmother's farmhouse in Pennsylvania. She had this huge farm that went on forever, and her driveway circled around this little ravine that had this giant tree growing out of it. My bedroom window faced that little ravine, and the tree was maybe thirty feet away from the glass. Well, one night that huge tree got hit by a bolt of lightning that tore straight through half of its trunk. Between the crack, boom, tearing bark and wood the noise was so strong and deafening that I felt like I almost got turned inside out. Well, if that didn't actually happen I sure as hell got knocked out of bed. That kind of noise, and that power, was about what I felt when the blast of of red light suddenly blew off right between me, Reese, Bob, Stacy, Eustace, the flesh-beast, and everything else and knocked us all flying.

I had no idea where I was for a second. My ears were ringing, and I couldn't even tell which way was up. For that matter I needed a little longer to remember where I was and what just happened. When I did, though, my insides felt like they just jumped straight up and were trying their best to tear themselves out of my body. I got the hint; I managed to push myself up a little, and then I saw, standing about fifteen feet away, in the rubble—

"...Smoot ...?" I said, kind of. I got the feeling it would have hurt too much to raise my voice. Hell, I could barely scare up enough strength to move.

It was her all right. She had her back to me so obviously I couldn't see her face, but that didn't matter a damn. There wasn't any way for me to mistake her for anyone else, since it's not often you see a tiny, scrawny little pale chick with short bright primary-red hair, a giant multi-colored rainbow flannel shirt, big baggy jeans, brown satchel, imitation Chuck Taylors, scarf and a cricket bat. She's kind of distinct. Her clothes made her look like she went into the dryer with them and she was the one who ended up shrinking. I mean she was *swimming* in those clothes. She had her cricket bat in one hand slung diagonally across her back like it was a giant sword or something that was still in its sheath.

The air all around her was crackling, snapping, and humming like she was an entire electrical substation all by herself, and every couple seconds or so something that looked like a little arc of red lightning danced on her cricket bat and made a soft little *pop*. Wow. I'm telling you the power seemed to be just pouring out of her like she was some kind of radioactive object. If I had any trouble believing Smoot was a wizard before, I sure didn't anymore.

★ ★ ★ ★ ★

"Where man? Where is it?" Smoot said, in that slow motion stoner's drawl of hers, and she looked left, right, and left again real quick. Then she shifted her feet a bit so she was facing a new direction and did the whole looking around thing all over again. "Where'd it go, man?"

"...ughh...what the hell...?" That was Bob. I couldn't see where he was, but I don't think it would have been a stretch to assume he was about in the same situation I was.

Smoot suddenly stopped, and it looked like she was focusing on someone I couldn't see. "Oh, sorry man," she said. "I musta come in hot again by oops."

".... Holy living *fuck*," Bob said, his voice all tense. "That's—Oh, fuck me, not *you*! She's with them! Get her!"

"Huh—?" Smoot said, and then, calm as ever: "Woah."

It looked like that big dung beetle with the long neck and every single last one of those little flat football things with elephant trunks for legs just jumped at her all at once. What happened next was ...well, I don't know what else to call it but, screwy.

I've seen wizards do some crazy stuff, but Smoot just . . .

Well, here's what happened. It looked like all of the creatures just stopped in midair and stuck right where they were, frozen in place, as if they had all just slammed into huge invisible sticky glass walls. Next, it looked like these invisible sticky glass walls swung up and over Smoot's head like they were covers of a giant book. When they were about vertical, the invisible walls came together and smashed all of the monsters into gross green pesto paste, which rained down all over the room.

"NO! You bitch!" Bob growled. I could see him now, his shirt was torn and he didn't have his shades anymore, and he looked seriously pissed.

"Sorry man," Smoot said, in that same drawl. I swear I don't think this girl knew how to raise her voice. "So did you see where it went?"

"What?"

"The thing, you know, with the thing?" Smoot said, and put her hand in front of her face and spread her fingers. "Umm, wait a sec..."

Bob didn't wait a sec. He growled, made some slick looking sharp and fast hand gestures---like he was saying something in sign language---and then a pulsating, crackling black sphere about the size of a medicine ball shot out of one of his hands and straight at Smoot. She had enough time to flinch and hold out one of her own hands like she was telling a car to stop, and then the sphere hit her. There was an explosion of dark green and blue energy, and Smoot stumbled back a step.

"Woah, wait," she said. Again, she still sounded slack and slow as hell. "I just wanna know where that thing is, man."

"The hell!" Bob shouted, and then he made another gesture, and sent four spheres at Smoot this time; they all swung around at came at her from four different directions. Smoot held out her hand again like she was trying to catch them. The spheres hit Smoot one after the other. The first one made her stumble again, the next one made her stumble more, the next almost knocked her over and she grunted, and the fourth one made it look like she just got punched across the face. She wobbled in place and her cricket bat slid down off her back and she almost fell over completely. She braced her bat on the ground and managed to keep from falling over, though.

Bob didn't give her any time to recover. He wound up yet again, and this time he held out both hands. A thick beam as black as crude oil shot out at Smoot. She somehow got her cricket bat up in front of her like a shield or something, and the bat started crackling with red lightning. The black beam hit the cricket bat and there was a red, green and blue explosion that sent a shock through the ground and air. Dust and stone and debris shot around everywhere like shrapnel.

It was a hell of a sight, tiny little Smoot standing up to that onslaught of unholy power, but it didn't look like it was going to last long. It was like watching someone trying to stand up to a fire hose, honestly. She kept sliding and stumbling back, until finally, she got knocked all the way across the room and into the wall, with her flannel and scarf flying. When she hit there was a massive blast of red energy that tore down parts of the walls and ceiling all over the place.

Would you believe, though, that she was still conscious?

"Harsh, man," she said. She was slumped against the wall, and somehow she still had a hold of her cricket bat. "You didn't need to do all that."

"It's all you deserve, you fucking traitor," Bob snarled making his way over the debris. "You're dead!"

"And you're borrowin'," Smoot said. "Borrowin' from this place. You're cheatin', man. That ain't fair."

"No such thing," Bob said, and he started making some new gestures. "Not no more. When they send you all bets are off!"

A second or two later, Bob's skin turned as dark blue as it could get without being completely black, and his eyes went solid white. His neck got thicker, his jaw larger, his shoulders and chest wider, and he just burst out of all his clothes. Basically he slowly turned into a freaking nine-foot tall mass of solid sinewy muscle, with four giant arms as thick as my whole body. He hunched over, slammed the ground with all four of those massive arms, and let out a roar like you wouldn't believe. His jaw spread wide open like a goddamn snake, and most of his teeth were as long and sharp as daggers.

Oh my Christ, this Bob was for real. I heard about this, but luckily I was never asked to stare it down myself. Bob just did one of those things warlocks were known for: He merged his soul and body with a demon's. In this case he merged with a full blown Pit Lord, a demon brimming over with such power that someone told me that in order to beat one it once took a judge, five sentinels, three myrmidons and a wizard.

And here Bob was going to go against little 80-pound Smoot? Umm, overkill?

★ ★ ★ ★ ★

Smoot didn't even really flinch as Bob let out that massive roar. She also didn't flinch when he held up all four fists and they started glowing dark blueish greenish black. No, she just relaxed, and made a little gesture like she was flipping a coin. A little blur of motion about the size of a half-dollar spun through the air in front of her face. She opened her mouth a bit and then snapped it shut almost immediately; when she did she had what looked like a hand-rolled cigarette in her mouth.

Bob's solid white eyes went wide, and he let out another of those gigantic roars. He drew back all four fists and the blueish-black energy around them got larger and brighter and started to crackle with green lightning.

Smoot just blinked and slid the tip of her index finger against the tip of the cigarette, and then the tip glowed with a tiny speck of orange light.

Bob thrust out all four fists at once, and four black and blue beams as big around as logs shot out at Smoot, and she had no time to move out of the way. No, she just raised her arm again.

★ ★ ★ ★ ★

Remember what happened when Bob and Smoot went head on a second ago? Well forget all about that little love tap. This was like a 20-pound hammer on an anvil. There was a massive blast of red, blue, green, and I don't know what all else and everything just got thrown all over everywhere, including me. I don't think I could have done a better somersault if I took gymnastics for five years straight. I landed hard and rolled, and ended up flat on my back, again. I couldn't hear a thing except for a faint ringing, and I was beginning to think that I'd finally been knocked stone cold deaf. It was actually kind of a relief. For a second it almost felt like I was far away from all this fucked up shit that kept on happening, and that kind of felt comforting.

I couldn't make myself move, and, to be honest, I didn't really feel like moving. I could still see flashes of red out of the corner of my eye, but I didn't really seem to have the energy to care about what was going on. Not anymore.

That is, until I saw the flower-faced-flesh-monster jump on top of me.

I think it was nothing but total panic, but somehow I had enough strength left to catch it by its neck with both hands just as it lunged. Every muscle in my arms, shoulders and wrists screamed at me, but I didn't let go. I still really just didn't want to die. Not yet. Before I could do anything else, though, I felt a very *very* sharp chill tear through my whole body, like I was suddenly thrown into a freezer. I hissed and my muscles tensed, but luckily the chill didn't last more than it takes to blink. That was nice at least, but the monster-thing was still trying to close its maw around my freaking face. I screamed in sheer frustration and rage, but it only came out like a miserable, pitiful hoarse screech.

And then, I reacted almost instinctively. I remembered Raine. I remembered what I did to swat her away when she attacked me. If I could just maybe knock this thing off, maybe I could still get out of here. I wound up whatever Light there was left in me that I could grab, like I was clawing at an almost sheer cliff wall, trying desperately to stop sliding before I went over the edge.

"Unterbrechhhh—"

As soon as I began to substantiate the Rebuke, I was struck with such terrible pain my voice broke off before I could finish. My belly, my chest, my legs---they all felt like something with massive sharp teeth was tearing into them.

It was too much. Suddenly I felt like I was falling, and then everything went blurry, then black.

Chapter Twenty One

I know this sounds stupid coming from a Pala—ok, I mean *ex* Paladin, but I honestly have no idea what happens when you die. Not the foggiest. Note that I didn't say *after* you die. I said *when*. You'd think I'd have all that sorted out in my head, but I don't. I sort of had the impression that maybe death meant peace. Or maybe relief. If what happened next was any indication, though, apparently peace and relief were the things I was furthest from.

The next thing I remembered, I heard a mess of garbled, mushy mumbling sounds, like I was at the bottom of a swimming pool trying to listen to some person talking up top. Wait. Make that *two* people talking up top. One voice was low pitched and the other one was a bit higher.

Wait, I thought. *Isn't that—?*

A second later I finally began to understand the gibberish. I only caught the end of a sentence, but it was enough.

"...could have killed her!" A guy's voice said, and I swear I almost recognized the voice but I couldn't nail it down completely.

"Sorry, man," said a slack stoner's voice. "I found the thing, though."

"—Smoot?" I said. I got my eyes open but all I could do was squint against a severe glare.

"Perfect," said the guy's voice. "She's back with us. Step aside. Keep Reese and the others where they are."

It was right then that I finally figured out who the guy was. I got my mouth moving again.

"—Simon?" I said. I probably would have sounded a bit more surprised but I honestly couldn't dredge up the energy. I felt like I was sedated to hell and gone. The best I could manage was confusion.

"Stop talking and stop trying to move," Simon said. "You're blunted."

"Hwuh?" I said. "Can't see."

"Quiet," Simon said. "I said you're blunted. Hold still."

Blunted. Even as half wasted as I was, I figured out what Simon was saying, and it made perfect sense. It was what I almost remembered when I blessed myself that last time, and it was why I felt that horrible pain when I tried that last Rebuke. When Simon said I was blunted he basically meant my body was completely beat to shit and had nothing left to burn. Remember when I said that praying and blessing burned a lot of calories? Well I meant it. Sure, it's awesome to kick ass and make yourself more durable than steel and bounce back from severe injury, but that all comes at a big price. You can't just keep healing yourself or keep punching through walls all the damn livelong day without fueling up. Eventually your body will literally start consuming itself to heal itself, if you follow me. To put it simply, there comes a time where praying or blessing is as dangerous to you as your enemy is. To make it even better, you won't even realize it until it's too late because in case I haven't made it obvious, most of the time channeling the Light is damn powerful natural high. One second you're a small god, the next you're a pile of rags.

Blunting was one of the most basic concepts covered during my training, and usually I managed to avoid doing it to myself, mostly because I was afraid of it. Trouble was, since this very awesome day began I've been more or less forced to throw prayers, exactions and blessings around like candy on maybe four hundred total calories, and now I was paying for it. Blunting isn't easy to bounce back from, either. I've heard of Paladins going into a coma over it, even if their bodies are perfectly healthy otherwise.

Ever have one of those lives where *nothing* goes right?

"Kroger, you still with me?" Simon said.

"Hwuh?" I said.

"Good enough. I'm going to revive you slightly. I realize that's slightly inadvisable in your current state, but I'm afraid it's also slightly important. Deal with it."

"*Yagonnado Whaaaaa?*"

Yeah, that was me. Before I knew it, it was like I was injected with about five thousand gallons of pure adrenaline. One second I was pleasantly mellow and stoned, the next, my heart almost blew up, my eyes shot open, and I gasped like I just got done holding my breath for seventeen days. I choked, gagged, coughed, and started thrashing all over the place like I was covered in fire ants. Before I could go on bouncing all over the ground, though, Simon pinned me down.

"*Revive slightly?*" I screeched, as soon as I had enough breath to do it. My voice cracked and scratched like I was a smoker my whole life.

"That's right," Simon said. I could see him real clearly now. His face was about a foot from mine and he was weighing me down with his whole body. "You get it all out?"

"You get WHAT all—uh...uh...uh..." I started panting, and my heart went on racing, but the rest of me seemed to be relaxing a bit. "...uh...uh...yeah."

"Ok," Simon said. "I'm going to step off you now. In spite of how you may feel, you're in very bad shape, Kroger. You're on borrowed energy. You need to stay right where you are and remain calm, or there could be permanent damage."

"...uh...uh...permanent?"

"Yes," he said. "You're blunted. Damage done to yourself by your own Light cannot be reversed. Remember the scorched earth analogy?"

"...uh...uh...oh yeah. But wait, you told me to be calm and you just shocked me awake?"

"There was no choice. Time is short and I needed you fully conscious and cognizant."

"...Uh...why...? Don't...wait...are you, are you turning me in?"

"What?"

"M-Marsh sent you, didn't she?"

"Marsh? Heh. No."

"Then who sent you?"

"Call it a whim," Simon said. "And no, I'm not turning you in; if I was, you would have been tried and sentenced already. There's no time for this. Just forget that for now and look over there."

I looked where Simon pointed, and here's what I saw.

There, standing practically dead center of the room we were in was none other than Smoot. No doubt she was a hell of a neat little sight, but I'm pretty sure she wasn't what Simon wanted me to see. I'm thinking the money was in the five figures several feet off the ground, pinned against the wall, and shimmering all over in red light.

They were (based on what I could see of their clothes) Bob, Stacy, Eustace, Reese, and the monster-thing. Only, the monster-thing wasn't the *only* one with its face split apart like a flower. No, *all* of their faces were split apart.

"Kroger," Simon said. "I recall you asked me what to do if you happened to encounter one of these creatures again. I must confess at the time I didn't think it likely that you would ever be that unlucky again, let alone twice more in as many days. You can imagine that got me to thinking."

"What...?" I said. "Wait, *twice?*"

"Yes, Kroger," he said, and pointed to Reese. "This is once, and last night would make twice by my math."

"Last night? But I—oh."

"Good, I knew you could do it."

"But, wait, no, I—"

"No time," Simon said, and then he motioned to Smoot. "I have to get her back before she's missed, especially after last night. We may already be too late. Now be quiet and listen, Kroger."

"I—"

"Smoot," Simon said. "Let Reese loose, but only just enough, understand?"

"Yeah, man," Smoot replied. "Here goes. Easing off now."

"Good," Simon said, and then he turned to me and began talking fast. "Now, Kroger, I wasn't able to intervene last night for reasons we'll worry about later. The point is I need to know why these creatures seem to be fixated on you and I would have loved to find out last night but oh well, here we are. I have an idea but I need confirmation do you understand?"

That last sentence sounded like it should have had a comma in it but Simon just barreled through it like a comma would have wasted too much time.

"Yeah, I understand," I said, which was a big fat lie. "Well, what do you need me to—"

I didn't have time to finish. I saw the Reese thing jump through the air at me with its star shaped maw spread wide open. Before I could blink it was on me, and then it closed that big maw around my entire face. If that wasn't a perfect way for my morning to end I could even begin to think of what would be. I couldn't see a thing, I couldn't breathe, and my face felt like it was on fire. Not just any fire, either; I mean one of those grease fires you try to put out with water before you remember that water won't work on it. I tried to scream but my mouth was full of some rancid goo. I choked on it because there was nowhere for the goo to go.

I could sort of hear Simon's voice, but really muffled. It sounded like he was saying something like *I said Let him loose just enough!*

And then everything faded out.

Finally. Some peace.

Chapter Twenty Two

Well, not really.

Hoo-ray.

"That's it," said some voice I didn't recognize. I guess it was a woman's voice, but who knows; I've been wrong on the super simple stuff before. "Now hurry up, she may be coming around any time."

"OK," said another voice, or I think that's what it said. It was kind of lower pitched and I could only hear the bass of the voice, but I heard two syllables and I figured that was a good guess. Then I heard both voices mumble some stuff I couldn't make out for a few seconds, and the voices got softer and softer like they were getting further away.

I got my eyes to open most of the way, but there wasn't much light to go around. I could tell I was on some kind of a cot that felt like more of a rough canvas sling that was sagging under my weight. Every time I moved or shifted the canvas made a creaking, stretching sound and the whole cot swung a little. I also thought I was covered with a real natty, thin blanket but it turned out to be a filthy beach towel.

The air felt a little thick and musty, and I could smell a real faint rotten odor, like dirty wet socks. I ached all over, like I was ninety seven, and I had a taste in my mouth that I couldn't even begin to describe, so don't bother asking. My head was throbbing, my heart was going a lot faster than it should have been, and when I took a breath my chest rattled. I mean it really honestly rattled.

I had no idea where I was, but it didn't take that much for me to guess I'd hate wherever it was. I didn't know if I should look around or run for it, but I had that decision made for me when I tried to get up and my whole body yelled at me. I yelled back at it, sort of; my voice cracked all to hell and I just sounded like I was whispering. God, I hate that. I hate when it happens to me and I hate hearing people talk like that. I swear when someone's lost their voice and they insist on talking sounding like that it takes all my strength not to tell them to shut up.

So I did manage to get about halfway up before the pain made me freeze, which meant I had nothing else to do but fall halfway back down. That didn't end well for me because the cot rocked a bit and then tipped completely over, and I went with it. I rolled off and slammed on to the floor like a huge pile of fish someone just let drop out of a net.

I had the wind knocked out of me for a second, and all I could do was lay there, cheek on the dirty wood floor, and stare at a pile of dirty laundry. That was all I could see, and clearly that was where the dirty sock smell came from. I hurt so bad I couldn't stand it, and I wanted to scream but of course I couldn't.

Christ, What a fucking day. The only thing missing was... well ...um...I didn't even know, what the hell could've added to this?

For a second I actually forgot about the pain I was going through and started thinking of things that could have added to this most perfect day, like maybe the floor I just landed on could break and I could fall into a septic tank or something. That thought was funny enough to distract me, and when I finally got my breath back, I wheezed and laughed instead of yelling.

It was one hell of a laugh. It was scratchy and miserable, like one of those hoarse laughs where it's nothing but breath. The more I pictured that septic tank the worse it got. Then I figured if I was going to land in a septic tank it might as well explode and shoot me up in the air in a giant geyser of steaming shit. That killed me all over again. I have to tell you, that laugh sounded horrible but it was also probably the best laugh I could ever remember having in my whole life.

I remember, as I lay there cackling like a crazy stoned hyena, that I wished I could call up this laugh next time I really needed it. Like when I was having another really screwed up day, or when I just needed a basic little pick me up. That would have been awesome. I'm sad to say, though, that I have yet to ever get it back.

"You ok?" That wasn't me. That was yet another voice I couldn't recognize. That was getting to be a habit. At this point I would have given up a year's pay just to be back in my cube where everything was goddamn routine.

"Sure, why not," I said. "Good an answer as any."

"I hear you," said the voice. "Here." A second later I was pulled up into the air by what must have been a pair of super beefy hands, and when I got vertical I ended up staring directly at one of the most fucked up, most ugly faces I've ever seen. I mean it was so ugly it was like getting punched.

"HO!" I said, and my eyes went as wide as I could make then go. That was the best I could do. I'm telling you I was taken completely by surprise and so I basically flipped my shit on pure reflex. The big beefy hands let me go, and I fell right the hell back down and I if you think I landed in a comfortable position you're crazy. As an added bonus I went face first into the pile of clothes, and, I swear I am not making this up, I ended up somehow with a mouth full of the stuff. How the fuck that happened I don't even know. Pure talent.

"The hell's your problem?" said that same voice. It sounded deep and tough but also kind of ...I don't know, *floofy*? Is that even a word? Oh whatever, if it wasn't I just invented it.

I gagged, coughed, hacked and spat out what I realized was a grimy sock. I didn't know what it was covered in, and I never bothered to find out. I think it's better that way, honestly. Some information you just don't need to get by.

Then, I remembered what I just saw. You know, that face I saw that was the reason I was back on the floor and swallowing socks. I guess my brain temporarily overwrote the sight. For some reason, I looked up.

There was the face again, about five inches from my nose.

"Glah!" I said. I mean I literally said *glah*. Seriously. I jerked and rolled back into the dirty clothes.

Ok, by now you're probably thinking about what a complete dipshit I am. I guess that's fair, I mean, even someone as anti-brilliant as me should have guessed that I wasn't in any kind of mortal danger. I woke up a second ago on a cot, not tied to a chair in some dank interrogation room or chained to a wall in some kind of medieval dungeon with skeletons all over the floor. Whoever was in charge of this place, whatever this place was, obviously wasn't trying to make me uncomfortable.

But that *face*—

I don't even know how to describe it. I could try but I don't think it'd make much sense to you. Here, let me try to think of some kind of comparison.

Ok, how about this. My mom, for all her faults is probably one of the bravest people I know, but she absolutely cannot stand the sight of a cockroach. I mean, she turns to putty and screams and runs the other way as fast as she can if she even sees a dead one lying on the floor. Dad or me or my sister always had to take care of them for her, every single time. Now Dad, my sister and me couldn't understand why of all things, cockroaches freaked my mom out, and neither could my mom. She couldn't tell us what it was about cockroaches that made her lose it; she said she knew it was irrational but she couldn't help it.

It was the same thing with this face. I took one look at it and the only thing that mattered was getting the hell away from it. Everything about it was wrong. The eyes, the nose, the teeth, the bulging cheeks, they were all in the wrong places. Not just the wrong places, either, the really *really* wrong *wrong* places. When I said earlier that looking at that face was like being punched, I mean that literally. My reaction to seeing that face was just as automatic as reacting to being punched.

"Are you done?" said that same voice. It sounded real impatient and maybe a little worn out too. "I realize you can't help it, but, after several centuries this gets old."

"Umm," I said, but I didn't look up. "I guess that voice belongs to the freaky face guy?"

All I heard was a huge sigh, and then footsteps walking away from me. After a second or two, I worked up the courage to look up. I was alone.

I was alone in a room that looked like a place people put stuff just to get it out of the way for a second and then forget all about. It was dark, grey, dingy, dusty, and cluttered as hell. There were boxes stacked all crooked six feet high, empty picture frames, pot and pans, broken pieces of lumber, huge knots of electrical wire the size of basketballs stuffed into buckets, a hand truck that was missing a wheel, and a couple cots like the one I was in. There was also a light bulb hanging overhead with a long string dangling from it, but when I tugged on it, nothing happened. There was some light coming in to the place from a crack in a curtain on the door, though. I guess that's why I was able to see that face, whatever it was.

Just then I heard some voices, I guessed from the other side of the curtain. They didn't sound abnormal or anything, but who am I to judge that kind of thing, right? Whatever, since there wasn't anything to do in this room or anywhere else to go that I could see, I decided to hell with my better judgment and peeked through the curtain.

There was another room on the other side of the curtain, this one looked like a sort of cross between a kitchen and a living room and den all crammed into way too small of a space. There was a small square table that sat up high, like bar height, with piles of stuff all over it. The table was about a foot from a tiny kitchen counter with an electric stove only one step above a hot plate. Right in front of that stove were two people with their backs to me. One looked like an older woman I guess, kind of short and hunched over, and the other looked like a linebacker, except, his skin was grey. I mean battleship grey, like he was in a black and white movie.

I took one small easy step into the room, and I bumped into a stack of dishes that was piled on the floor with my foot. They all fell over and slid everywhere, and my foot came down on one of the plates when I tried to do a little clumsy jerk and hop past the mess. From there it must have looked like something out of a Buster Keaton movie because I slipped like I was on ice, did a split and then grabbed at the table to stop myself from falling. That didn't go too well though because I didn't get a hold of the table, I actually got a hold of a plastic trash bag full of stuff that was sitting on the table instead. Well I went down and took the bag down with me, and the bag took god knows how much shit from the table down with it. Wouldn't you know it, the trash bag was full of what I guess had to be a bunch of metal things, maybe kitchen utensils judging from the ruckus when everything landed on me. I couldn't even tell you what else came down on me after the plastic bag, all I know was, it was heavy, and loud.

"Wow," I said, after everything finally quit falling.

Before I knew it, there were two faces looking down at me. One of them looked like a beat up, wrinkled catcher's mitt, and the other...

I hissed and flinched when I saw the other face. It was ...well ...I *think* it was the same hideous face I saw in the other room, but maybe the low lighting in there made it seem a lot worse because when I looked at the face now I didn't completely flip out. Don't get me wrong, I still could barely stand the sight of it, but . . .

"She's more fully awake, now," the ugly faced dude said. His voice was deep and...*floofy.* "Her reaction isn't as extreme."

"It must be a difficult existence," catcher's mitt face said. If I had to bet money on it I'd have no problem going all in on this being the owner of the first voice I heard, the old woman's.

"I bear with it," said ugly face, and out of the corner of my eye I saw him shrug his massive shoulders. "I'll go tend to the incubus and the dryad if you don't need me, ma'am."

"Yes, thank you," catcher's mitt said. "They need fresh water and you may wish to check their pans while you're at it."

"Yes ma'am," Ugly face said. "Up you go."

Ugly face leaned over and hoisted me up, but he didn't turn me around to look at him. He just plopped me on my feet and let me lean against the table.

"Steady?" Ugly Face said.

I really was only barely steady, but I nodded. I heard Ugly face walk off, open a door and shut it.

✻ ✻ ✻ ✻ ✻

"He's a baku, if you want to know." That was catcher's mitt; I turned to look at her. Now I'm not exactly tall but catcher's mitt was the opposite of tall. I actually had to look down to look her in the face, which I haven't done since I babysat kids in their single digits. She was dressed head to foot like a Russian immigrant from the nineteenth century, complete with a scarf over her head and one of those waist apron things.

"A who?" I said.

"A baku," she said, and she stooped down to pick up some of the stuff I knocked over. "He eats nightmares. I imagine you were seeing your own nightmares in his face. That's an unfortunate side effect, but as you can see, it lessens the further you get from sleep. He means no harm by it, but he can't do anything about it, either. Poor little lamb."

"Baku, what is he, a demon?" I said, brilliantly.

"Technically, I suppose," she said, and handed me some junk, which I put back on the table. "Although to be fair, comparing him to what you first think of when you hear the word demon would be like comparing a kindly, elderly janitor to a serial killer."

"Huh?" I said.

"Suffice to say," she said. "That neither you nor anything other than the distress caused by a terrifying dream has anything to fear from him."

"Okay," I said. "Umm, whoa. Look, sorry about the—" I made a big motion at the crap all over the floor. There was almost nowhere to put your feet.

"Oh, nonsense," she said, and lifted up the trash bag. "It really wasn't the best place for all that, but unfortunately space is at a premium here."

"Right," I said, and then I tilted my head a bit, narrowed one eye, and looked sideways at her. "So—on that note, who are you, and where am I?"

Catcher's mitt set the trash bag back down on the table and brushed her hands off on her apron.

"You may call me Dalvya Eveneshka," she said. "And you're in my home, which I have to admit is a very curious anomaly, especially given the current state of things."

"I'm sorry, what?" I said.

Eveneshka walked past me, went over to the tiny stove, and then plopped a large saucepan down on one of the coils. "Well you see," she said. "It isn't often that I see a Paladin sit on this side of their transactions."

I blinked, but then I shook myself. Why was I surprised for even one second? Of course this woman would know what I was. She did just talk about that baku demon thing as casually as if he was the mailman, and besides, it's becoming trendy for other people to know everything and for me to not know anything.

"What transactions?" I said.

Eveneshka didn't say anything, but she spread some oil on the saucepan. A second later she started cracking eggs open into it; they sizzled and bubbled for a bit and then she started scrambling them with a spatula.

"I'm sorry if I'm sound dense," I said, "but my brain's taken a hell of a pounding today and it was never top of the line to begin with. So bottom-line it for me. What's going on?"

Eveneshka just went on scrambling for a few seconds, and then she looked over at me.

"Do you just do as you're told without so much as asking what you are being told to do?"

"Huh?"

"Thoughtless power," she said, and shook her head. "I can't decide if it's more of an injustice or tragedy."

"Do you answer any questions, ever?" I said. Yes, I was getting snarky. Oh well.

"I'm not sure it would be of much use," she said. "It's clear you lack the knowledge to understand, and perhaps even the knowledge needed to grasp the knowledge to understand—"

"Does anyone talk like a real person anymore?" I said.

"—or the temperance to learn," she said, as if I hadn't just cut her off.

"That so?" I said. "Well guess what. I've made a whole career out of being underestimated. Why don't you just cut the cryptic bullshit and try me. You may be surprised."

"I already have," she said. "Have what?"

"Tried you," she answered.

"What's that mean?" I said. Eveneshka didn't say anything (big surprise) but she scooped up the scrambled eggs and put them down in a rectangular aluminum pan. After that she started up another batch of eggs.

"You have encountered the dybbukim," she said, finally, after she put some bread into a toaster that had four slots. "Have you not?"

"The what?"

"You do not even know of *them?* What sort of blindly obedient storm troopers are they spitting out these days?"

"I'm getting really tired of having to say "what" over and over again," I said. "How about you just save time and assume I don't know anything."

"No need to assume what is plain fact," she said.

"Fine, ha ha, I'm stupid," I said. "I can sit here and listen to that shit all day, I'm used to it. But just because I don't know something now doesn't mean I can't figure it out later."

"Is that so?"

"Yeah. So go ahead and get your cryptic bullshit fix, and when you get bored of that, let me know."

Eveneshka kept quiet while she plopped some more eggs into the pan. She didn't say anything until the toaster popped.

"If you want bullshit, missy," she said, "I'll be happy to show you."

She handed me the aluminum pan full of eggs and toast and walked past me.

"When I said I had already tried you, I meant that quite literally," she said. "Your mind is as difficult to miss as an oncoming train."

"My mind?" I said.

"Your ignorance screams at me like a starving baby," she said. "It's almost offensive. An intermediate with a tenth of my ability couldn't help but hear it."

She walked on toward one of the doors, and I damn near asked another of my genius questions. In this case, it would have been: *Wait, what, you can hear my mind?* But miraculously I kept my mouth shut. Of course she could hear my mind; she basically laid it all out for me in plain English when she called herself an intermediate.

Well, ok, it was plain English for someone with my kind of training. It's kind of a sketchy thing to understand, but basically an intermediate is halfway between worlds. What that means is they can see and hear things from all worlds, and a person's soul and mind are sort of in-between worlds, too. Long story short, she can see the channels us non-premium subscribers only see as a big blank screen. I have no idea how it works or why some people can do it and others can't or how or why someone becomes an intermediate. I must have been absent that day.

I figured the best thing to do at that point was to just cut the crap and go along with it. If she was an intermediate then there really wasn't much point to bullshitting. I'm not sure if she could really literally *hear* what I was thinking, but if she was worth anything she sure as hell could tell when I was full of it.

"Right through here," she said, and pushed open the door. "I imagine it's best just to show you."

★ ★ ★ ★ ★

And so, show me she did.

On the other side of that door was something I never thought I would ever see, mainly because it didn't exactly fit into any experience

I've ever had. I know what you're probably thinking right about now. You're thinking that since I was a paladin and all, that I saw all kinds of crazy stuff and it would be a lot harder to shock me, and you'd be mostly right. I wouldn't say I was shocked really. I was mostly confused. Like seeing something photoshopped in where it doesn't belong, and the guy who did the photoshopping sucked at it. You know, like it's so obviously fake it's just stupid?

Yeah, it was kind of like that, because what I saw there made just about as much sense. If I had to give it a name, it would be ...hold on ....

Ok, yeah. It was a Demon hospital.

Chapter Twenty Three

I'm sure that sounded stupid as hell, and I'd have to agree with you. But I don't know what else to call a room lined up with cots and beds with big honking huge ugly ass demons in them, complete with nasty looking IV stands plugged into various parts of their scaly, slimy, or blubbery bodies. I mean there were big red demons with hooves and tails that almost looked like they were ten sizes too big for the bed, one that looked like a giant gross wet blue eel, one that looked like a vulture with hands and legs, something that looked like a pulsating pile of tar, one that literally looked like a giant elephant turd with three mouths, one that looked like a mound of red bowling balls glued together that was leaking blue kool-aid, and even what looked like a giant wasp with a rabbit's face. Oh, and the whole place stank like five thousand barnyards that were only used to store cow crap. When that stench mixed with the aroma from the eggs and toast I was holding, I almost threw up right where I was standing.

"Oh give that here," Eveneshka said, like she was trying to show me how to tie my shoes and she just got sick of watching me get it wrong. "I won't have you fouling up that food."

I was more than happy to let her take the pan. I got my stomach back under control but it was a mission.

"Horace," Eveneshka said, and a ways down the line of beds I saw Mr. Baku straighten up so I could see him. I figured it was the Baku since his skin was grey as steel, but if it was him his face didn't even make me flinch this time. In fact, it wasn't even half bad to look at, honestly. "Horace, how are Monolu and Eustace?"

"It appears Monolu is finally becoming regular again," Horace said, in that deep floofy voice. "Eustace appears to be fine; Shock mostly. We can probably discharge him presently."

Eveneshka nodded and walked over to a beat up looking nightstand next to the blue eel's bed. She put down the aluminum pan and started spooning portions of egg onto some paper plates she had there.

"I'd like to keep him a while longer, all the same," Eveneshka said. "He's just a boy and he was transposed by a dybbuk, after all."

"That poor child. I blame Bob," Horace grumbled.

"Bob was desperate," Eveneshka said.

"He was stupid," Horace said. "I was glad to see the back of him. Things are difficult enough without fools getting themselves in over their heads."

"These days, we're all getting in over our heads," Eveneshka said. "None of us could have dreamed it would come to an edict, and that includes Bob. I daresay it's only a matter of time before they find us out. I'd be astonished if we don't get raided tonight."

Horace shook his head and walked up between the rows of beds. As he walked by the pile of tar, it bubbled and spluttered.

"Hang on, it's coming," Horace said, and waved his hand at the tar. "We've only got so much."

Horace walked by me and gave me a quick glance. I looked right back at him without blinking this time; his face was actually pretty pleasant looking. His eyes went a bit narrow and he huffed.

"Dalvya," he said, and he walked past me and through the door we just came in through. "When will she be leaving?"

"Once Bradley returns," Eveneshka said. "Between you and me, I'll be happy to see the back of her, too."

"Between you and me," I said, "I'm standing right here."

"Yes," Eveneshka said, and went on without bothering to look at me. "Yes, you are. I take it then, that if your brain doesn't work, at the very least your eyes do?"

"Umm . . ." I said. "Yeah."

"Well then use them!" she said. "You spoke of bullshit? See what you and your kind have wrought."

★ ★ ★ ★ ★

I almost just came right out and admitted right there that she lost me, but I figured I'd at least make a show of trying to figure it out. If anything, I figured it may make me look like less of a total dolt, but I'm pretty sure it had the exact opposite effect. Like when you're explaining something to someone and they nod at you and say 'yeah' even though it's obvious they have no clue what you're saying because you saw their eyes go blank.

Finally, I just gave up trying to be a cool person, which never works for me anyways.

"I don't get it," I said. "What do you mean?"

Evenshka just did one of those *Ehh* things old people do and threw up one hand like she was sick of the whole world.

"What's that for?" I said. "I've already agreed that I'm an idiot, so skip it. What do you mean by 'what my kind has wrought?'"

Before she could say anything, and, believe me, she looked like she had a whole hell of a lot to say, I heard Horace call from the other room.

"Bradley is here," he said.

"Oh good," Eveneshka said, and then she looked like she forgot all about me. "Well, see him in. I do hope he's made some progress on our little problem." She left the room the same way Horace did, without so much as a look at me; in fact, I had to sidestep a bit because otherwise I'm sure she would have just bowled through me. I stood where I was for a second, glanced around at the room full of demons, and then realized that staying there would be kind of pointless. So, I followed her.

Horace was right there by the table I knocked all the junk off of, holding another door open; he held up one hand toward the room like he was saying *come on in.* A second later, looking like he just stepped off a military parade, was none other than my good friend Simon.

"Ah, You're awake, Kroger," he said, after a quick glance my way. "Fantastic. We need to go, now. I hope you've eaten."

"Actually—" I said.

"—Can I assume by your urgency, Bradley," Eveneshka said, "that you have solved the pattern?"

"Yes, I believe I have," Simon said. "However in order to validate my theory and take the requisite action, there remains one last thing to do."

"Ai," Eveneshka said. "I pray, Bradley, that this is one last thing easily accomplished?"

"Not at all," Simon said, and gave Eveneshka one of those massive shit-eating grins of his. "Quite the opposite in fact. However, I believe I may have found the best possible solution given the time we had to work with."

"Is that so?" Eveneshka said. "What is it?"

"No, no," Simon said. "We can't chance someone like you knowing that; the Judges have intermediates of their own. I've put you at enough risk as it is."

Eveneshka nodded. "I suppose you're right at that," she said. "But, small price to do what's necessary."

Simon nodded also, and then looked at me. "All right, Kroger," he said. "Let's go."

"Could we—" I said, "Could we, I don't know, come to a complete stop for a second?"

"No," he said, and he spun around and went back out the same way he came in. "We need to move, now."

"But I haven't even eaten since—"

"You heard him," Eveneshka said. "I spoon-fed you soup for the last six hours, not that I could spare it. Now go, little miss Presentation fail!"

Chapter Twenty Four

Before I could say anything, Eveneshka was shooing me out the door like I was some obnoxious kid she wanted out of the house while she cleaned up. You know, she had her palms out toward me with the fingers facing down and she was swinging her hands like they were brooms.

"Hey, what, wait—hey—" that was about all I was able to get out before I was through the door; Eveneshka slammed it so quickly she almost bopped me in the ass with it. I spun, grabbed the doorknob and turned it, but Eveneshka must have already locked it because the damn thing didn't budge.

"Move, Kroger," said Simon, and I turned back around. I saw that I was in a narrow hallway, maybe about sixty feet long with a light bulb on the ceiling every ten feet or so. One wall of the hallway was just slats of board that I could see through and went ceiling to floor. Storage units, I guessed.

Anyway, Simon was already halfway down the hallway and walking so fast that if he went any faster he'd have to jog.

"Wait, hold up!" I said, and started off after him.

"No time," he said, and didn't even bother to slow down or look over his shoulder at me.

"Well what's the hell's going on? Where are we going?"

"To the fair," he said.

✶ ✶ ✶ ✶ ✶

"What? The fair?" I asked. We were almost to the end of the hallway; there was a large door that was just a little wider than usual doors at the end. "Wait, the Broward County fair's over!"

"No, not that one," he said. "I'll explain on the way."

He just kept going, and I really didn't have any choice but to follow him. I mean, first of all I had no idea where I was, what time it was, or hell, even what *day* it was anymore. Plus, I clearly wasn't welcome where I was anyway. Also, who knows, maybe Simon had a phone I could use?

Yes, I'm serious, that was about the extent of my thought patterns at that minute. I could only process so much at one time, really.

Simon got to the door and shoved it open; the door led to the outside and I could see from where I was that it was pitch dark. Lovely. The last I remembered it was still somewhat early in the morning—God knows how long it's been since then.

I made it to the door before it swung shut; the cold night air smacked me in the face and I heard cars driving by in the distance somewhere. I saw that we were in some alley that was just wide enough for a wicked looking black Mitsubishi Evolution parked there about twenty feet down. Simon raised his hand, and the taillights flashed.

"Get in," he said, again without looking at me. "We have to drive. I can't risk exposing Smoot again until we have no choice."

I didn't bother asking any more questions. I figured he'd just tell me to shut up again anyway, and I really didn't want to hear it, thanks. I just ran right up and kept my hole shut.

★ ★ ★ ★ ★

For some reason I automatically went straight for the back passenger side door, maybe because I really didn't want to sit next to Simon, like, ever—even now that he seemed to be trying to kind of help me out. If you want the truth, that made me more uncomfortable than anything else. I couldn't even begin to guess why he would do that, and as you saw, no one including Simon seemed able or willing to tell me much to clear things up. It was like everyone except me had everything figured out between themselves, and everyone also needed something from me but thought letting me know what that was would be a huge waste of time.

And it wasn't all that fair because I was basically lost and confused as hell. When you don't have a leg to stand on in it's kind of hard to put your foot down, you know? Whatever. Moving on.

Simon stopped me from opening the back passenger door and pointed to the front one. I just groaned real quiet so he couldn't hear me, opened up that damn front door and slipped in.

"How are you feeling?" He said, as he got in next to me. He didn't sound like he actually cared about how I was feeling, more like he was checking the oil in his car or something.

"Ummm...." I said, as he started the car. "—shitty? Do you have the first damn clue what I've been through in the last ten hours—"

"Save it, Kroger," said a voice from behind me. "I told him everything you told me."

My heart jumped. I spun around in my seat, and all of a sudden I was face to face with—

"Reese?!"

"You win," Reese said. I didn't even notice him sitting there in the backseat. I probably wouldn't have ever noticed him if he hadn't spoken up.

"*I'll kill you!*" I screamed, and got ready to deck him with everything I had. Unfortunately I wasn't in any kind of good position to do that, since I was a lefty and I'd have to swing around the goddamn seat, so I ended up just sort of grabbing at him like we were about to start a slap fight.

"STOP!"

That was Simon. Holy shit, was it ever Simon. He must have thrown some kind of exaction behind his voice because I stopped before I knew what the hell I was doing, spun back around and slammed against the door like I got smacked.

"There's no time," Simon said, and started to drive.

"He—they—all of them were ready to kill me," I said, and I tried my best to sound tough, but I failed miserably. I was either incredibly pissed or still a little bit in shock from the force of Simon's voice or both, so my voice trembled a little. I hated the sound of it.

"They wouldn't have killed you," Simon said. "That warlock and all the others were desperate but not insane. They needed you alive. If they weren't at the end of their rope they wouldn't have been hiding in a dark pocket."

"What—dark pocket?" I said.

Simon gave me a look that said *Really? I have to explain this?*

"It's a small, localized area of densely concentrated evil," he said. "It gave him power he couldn't have otherwise dreamed of. Small wonder he was squatting there. He probably could have stood up to a full patrol of Knights of twice your ability." He shrugged. "He even gave Smoot a rough turn."

Oh, so *dark pocket* is the official name for that kind of place. Of course it would have an official name.

"Well," I said, and I straightened up a bit. "Whatever the fuck, I sure as hell almost died." I turned and glared at Reese. "And he—"

"Don't start," Simon said. "Feel free to sort out all your trash later. Put it away now."

Simon glanced over at me, but I didn't say anything. He went on.

"They all just wanted to get past the edict," Simon said. "They were exercising the only available option they saw, which was that they thought they could trade you for their freedom. It was the same with Reese. They were both driven to their last resorts."

"What's the edict?" I said.

Simon looked at me like I had three noses. I don't mind telling you that my blood pressure shot way the hell up right then.

"Oh, that's it!" I growled. "I don't give a shit what you think of me, Bradley. I've been one hell of a good sport about everything, between getting beaten to death about a thousand times since I went to bed last night, one of those times, I might add, was courtesy of the lovely and talented Marsh over something I don't even remember doing! And this mother fucker—" I pointed at Reese—"thinks I had something to do with his goddamn bitch ass girlfriend—"

"Watch it, Kro—"

"Shut up, Reese!" I said. "With his goddamn bitch ass girlfriend disappearing so he knocks me under about forty seven trains. Then I'm forced to pray so much I almost rip my own god damn body apart, then I got *Griselda* back there insulting me about *god* knows what every time I take a breath, then you brush off my almost getting killed like you couldn't give less of a shit, and then you can't even answer one simple perfectly reasonable question without making one of those faces of yours? *Fuck* you and whatever you need out of me. Stop the car."

Simon then surprised me by doing just that.

As it turned out, we were pulled over on the side of I95 northbound, overlooking what I recognized after as second as downtown Miami.

"Get out," Simon said, and he didn't really sound angry but his voice definitely said *do it or else.* For a second I thought he was actually going to boot me out of the car and leave me, but instead he got out himself. He walked around the front of the car and stood in front of the guardrail, looking down at the city with his hands behind his back.

After a second or two, I finally got out, closed the door behind me, and walked over to the guardrail. It was chilly, especially with the wind starting to pick up; also, the highway was busy, so there was a big woosh as a car or truck drove by us at seventy miles an hour every few seconds.

Simon didn't say anything or even look at me. He just went on staring out into downtown. I leaned forward a little, sort of hugging myself against the cold, and looked at him sideways.

"Well?" I said.

"Tell me everything you want to say," he said, without looking at me. "Get it over with."

"What?" I said.

"Like Reese said, he told me everything you told him. I don't like you, Kroger, not in the slightest, and I don't doubt it's mutual. But that's irrelevant now. What we're about to try and do is just the smallest bit more important."

"What's that?" I said.

"We're going to stop a war."

"...say again?" I said.

"We're going to stop a war," he repeated.

"Oh." I said. "Oh. That's it?"

Chapter Twenty Five

"That's it," he said. "If we have time, maybe afterward we can hit happy hour."

"Simon," I said, a little impatiently.

"Hurry up and say what you want to say," he said. "We're on a tight schedule and I don't want to get bogged down with any more bullshit."

"What bullshit's that?" I said.

"All of these 'personal' issues of yours. Vent them all out now."

"Oh. Just like that, huh?"

"Yes," he said. "Just like that. You, me, Reese, at the moment we are tools that need to perform a very specific, very important task. What happens to us or what we think or feel beyond that task jeopardizes the lives of far too many."

I didn't say anything for a second. Simon looked over at me and raised one of his eyebrows; again, I wished I knew how to do that.

I looked right back at him and clicked my teeth a couple times. Then, finally, I just hauled off and punched him right in the face. He didn't try to move out of the way or block it or anything, even though I know he totally could have, since I'm positive I telegraphed the hell out of that punch. No, all he did was roll with it, and then almost immediately he whipped his head back and looked right at me like nothing happened. Would you believe he raised one of his eyebrows at me again?

"That was for kicking me," I said.

★ ★ ★ ★ ★

Well that sort of got the ball rolling. From there I just let him have it, telling him every last thing I could think of. He didn't interrupt once or even blink. I told him about his piss poor *I am so much smarter than you* attitude, about all the times he bullied me while I was learning the ropes, about how he stood back and smirked while I was getting excommunicated; you know, basically about how he treated me like shit in general. Then I went on about how today I was swept along without knowing what the hell was happening, and how I was for all intents and purposes on the run from the Knights, and how I have no idea whether or not he was just in the process of turning me in to them now that they obviously knew that I could bless and pray even though I was excommunicated.

"I already told you," he said, finally, "that I have no intention of turning you in to the Knights. I would have already done it long before now if I did. However, even if I did want to, I couldn't."

"What? Why?"

"Because as of this morning, I'm officially on the run from them as well."

"*What?*"

"They tend to frown on the unauthorized use of wizards," he said. "Especially given the current climate."

"What? Wait, you mean Smoot?"

He nodded, and then he took a breath before he said anything else.

"Kroger," he said. "I know everything is moving very fast, and if I'm curt it's only because there's so much we stand to lose if we fail. By so much I mean *everything*, by the way. You and I both took an oath, if you recall."

I nodded. I remembered it. I could still recite it off the top of my head, too.

"Well," he said, "Right now, the only thing between us and them—" he waved his hand over downtown—"is our prompt, decisive action. I admit, I need you, and I don't think I can succeed without you. So, I won't ask you to like me, but I'm going to have to ask you to trust me. Can I expect at least that much?"

I didn't say anything to that for a second. The fucked up thing was, I couldn't just tell him *no* just like that, even though I sort of felt like it. The truth was, despite how he treated me overall, Simon had lots of chances to seriously screw me over and he didn't do it. He never told the Knights that I still had my powers. If he had acted any different, I'd have been in an even deeper hole than the one I managed to dig myself in. Simon was at least consistent; if I wasn't putting anyone in danger, he didn't seem to care what I did. So, in the end, there was only one way I could answer his question. I nodded.

He nodded back. "Good," he said, and then he turned back to the car. "Are you finished for now, or do you have anything more to say?"

"Umm—" I said. I wasn't sure what to make of politeness from this man. "Wow, umm, well I mean I might think of something I left out later, but I guess, no. Not really, no." I meant it, too.

"All right," he said. "Then let's go. We've wasted enough time."

I watched him go for a second, and then I looked out at downtown. Simon had made a good point, there sure were a hell of a lot of people out there, and if he could find a way to suck it up and play nice-nice with me long enough to put them first, then why the hell couldn't I?

★ ★ ★ ★ ★

We were making some pretty good time now that we were north of downtown and the traffic had thinned out a bit. Simon was filling in all of my blank spots along the way. It turns out he was on the trail of those monster-things, like the one Raine turned into, for quite some time.

"So," I said, "Those flower-face-monster-things are called *dybbukim*?"

"Correct," Simon said. "Commonly referred to in Jewish mythology as wandering spirits. That isn't entirely incorrect, but it only tells a part of the truth."

"What's the rest of it? And how'd you find out when you say the Knights don't have the first damn clue?"

"The Knights on the whole tend to be a bit myopic," he said. "With exceptions."

"They tend to be dick fuckers," said Reese, kind of under his breath. "Without exceptions."

"If a means to a solution doesn't fit neatly in their paradigm," Simon said, "I've found that the Knights typically discount it. I, on the other hand, didn't allow myself that luxury."

"What's that mean?" I said.

Simon glanced at me. "I acknowledge my own limitations. I like to seek out ways to complement my limitations rather than force the world to work within them."

"Oh," I said. "What's that mean?"

"It means," Simon said, "That I sought out a consultant. It wasn't exactly easy, given how we tend to treat intermediates."

"Oh—" I said. "You mean Eveneshka."

"Exactly. It was a minor mission to gain her confidence, to put it lightly. But she put me on the right track."

"Which was?"

"That there was more to these dybbukim than I had initially thought. Quite a lot more, in fact. But to put it as plainly as I can, they're people."

I let that hang in the air for a second before I said anything.

"Wait," I said. "That's it?"

"Yes," Simon said. "That's it."

"But that doesn't tell me anything," I said. "You just said there was more to them than you thought."

"There was."

"But then you said they were just people?"

"Yes. But not just any people. They are the *first* people."

I looked at Simon and raised my eyebrows; I made believe that I was only raising one, even though I knew that was ridiculous.

"Umm," I said. "You lost me. What do you mean first? What, our ancestors? We evolved from that?"

"No," Simon said. "We didn't come from them, but they came before us."

"They came before us, but we didn't come from them?"

"No," he replied, and then he took a breath. "Listen, Kroger, I'll just have to be blunt. How much do you actually know about God?"

"God? Whoa, where'd that come from?"

"Well, what do you know? This is key."

"Oh—Umm what do I know? Umm...Wow, which version? I don't know, I mean I actually read the Bible cover to cover once, and I honestly have no idea if all that is even about the same guy. If so, he's a bit crazy."

"Fair point," he said. "But what would you say is one of the chief overriding themes of Christianity, Judaism, Islam or any other monotheistic religion?"

I actually had to ponder that for a second. "Umm, I dunno, that—I guess that we should love and obey God and he's great?" I held out both hands in a shrug and shook my head.

"Yes, that's on the right road," Simon said. "Would you say also that it's taught that God is perfect?"

"I guess that's the idea," I replied.

"Well, that's the thing," Simon said. "He isn't. Long story short, when he first created the world, he was young and inexperienced. When he was done, he was—dissatisfied. So, he abandoned his first attempt and tried again."

"Wait," I cut in. "You're talking literally here?"

Simon nodded.

"...First attempt? What are you saying?"

"Just that. He made a world, filled it with people, and he didn't like the result."

"The result? What, you're telling me that's the dybbukim?"

Simon nodded. "And then he tried again."

"And then tried again—? Us?"

Simon nodded again.

"So—but—then where'd the first world and the dybbukim go?"

"Abandoned."

"Abandoned where?"

"The best way to explain it," he said, "Is that they're on the same space, but further from God."

"Further from God? How, but, how could it be further if it's on the same space?"

"Their world essentially exists on another plane, very close to ours. But it's closer to the absence of God, or what we might call Hell."

I blinked. "Umm, so what, it's here, but it's not? Like what, an alternate reality?"

"No, a very close simultaneous one."

"Then, how, and why the hell are they showing up now, in our..." I made a couple hand gestures, like I was trying to figure out the best way to put what I needed to say next, "...space?"

"That," Simon said, "Is why we're going to the fair. I had no leads or theories since there was no rhyme or reason to their appearances, until last night. They've attacked you specifically three times in rapid succession, and we need to know why. Our only hope is that there's information in that gap in your memory that we can use."

"Well, what if there isn't?"

Simon looked at me. "There has to be. Kroger, just so you know, the dybbukim couldn't have entered our world without help. They would need the sort of help that only a certain oppressed group could have the ability and the motive to provide."

"Wizards," Reese said.

"Exactly," Simon said. "I have sufficient evidence to conclude that a certain small number of wizards plan to overthrow and destroy the Knights by instigating an all out war between the Knights and the Scions."

"Who are the Scions?" I said. I hated asking all these questions but what the hell else could I do? Every time Simon opened his mouth I felt more and more in the dark.

"They're a powerful cabal of demonic entities, essentially our opposite number. The only reason we haven't come to blows on a large scale to date is that it would result in mutual assured destruction. So, we've had something of an uneasy peace which should endure, unless one side or the other were given no choice but to act."

"...So," I said, "I guess what you're gonna say next is that's already happened."

"For all practical purposes, yes," Simon said. "Whoever is behind this has played their part to perfection. As far as I can tell neither side knows they're being played against the other, and both sides believe they're under all out assault from the other."

"How do you mean that?" I said.

"There's been an enormous recent increase in violent supernatural activity, and no fewer than a dozen wizards stand accused of collusion with the Scions. Under interrogation, and even revelation, many of those wizards have given the names of several powerful vampiric and demonic entities responsible, all in the South Florida area. Personally, I think that's absolute trash, since a vampire lord employing a knowing wizard against the Knights just to cause a little fuss would be about as bright as spray painting a swastika on the wailing wall and adding your name and address under it. Nothing would be accomplished and everything would be lost. It doesn't fit at all, but needless to say Marsh and her Judges have jumped on it with both feet."

"And fists," I said, and rubbed my chin.

Simon looked at me a second, and nodded. "She reacted about how you'd expect. She petitioned the Templar of the region for the edict, and by petitioned, I mean she browbeat him."

"Browbeat?"

"Marsh is, how shall I put it, ambitious. If there is any Knight who wants to one day be one of the thirteen Exemplar, it's her."

I shuddered. "Oh hell no."

Simon nodded. "So suffice to say, she got the edict. She forced it through so quickly since she managed to get McCormick's full endorsement. Very few Knights would gainsay him, even other Exemplar."

"And the edict ...is what?"

"Long story short, South Florida is under house arrest. Everywhere from Key West to Jupiter is completely locked down, and any 'dark' entity that steps so much as one toe out of line won't live to regret it. Meanwhile, the Knights haven't been sitting still waiting for them to make that step. At least twelve businesses and homes that I know of were 'expunged' in the last two days alone—" he nodded at me—"including our friend Bob's, and I don't think the Knights are exactly taking a break at the moment, either."

"Expunged," I said. "That's a polite way of saying demolished, isn't it?"

"Demolished would also be too polite a word," Simon said. "And if you think the Scions are just going to roll over and take it, then you're either an idiot, or you're Marsh. The only reason we haven't seen any full-blown retaliation yet is probably because they're not going to settle for doing anything halfway. Between the edict and the actions taken to enforce it, the Scions have become a giant, cornered rabid rat, and we all know how those behave."

"So the Knights and Scions are about to go ten rounds, and when they do, what then?"

"Then the wizards make their own move, and take down as many from both sides as they can while their backs are turned. This has been a long time coming, but I believe it hasn't only because an adequate means has not yet been available. The dybbukim are that. They are the perfect weapons."

"How so?" I said. "They didn't seem all that tough, I mean, the first time I saw one I just Rebuked it and it went flying. I almost felt sorry for it."

Simon looked at me, and I could have sworn he was halfway to making another one of his faces, but if he was, he kept it under control.

"I didn't believe you then, and, forgive me, I still don't," Simon said. "They're extremely resistant to just about anything a Paladin can throw at them. Believe me, I've tried. The only way to stop them is to flat out kill them with pure mundane brute force—which isn't easy, given their strength—or, as I discovered with Eveneshka's help, to transpose them."

"Transpose them?" I said.

"They enter our world by, if you will, *trading places* with their counterpart here. I developed an exaction that reverses that, permanently."

"Permanently?"

"Yes, Kroger, permanently. No further transposition for that person is possible."

"Oh," I said, and I tried to keep my amazement out of my voice. I had a hard time processing the fact that someone could just develop an exaction that powerful successfully when I had enough trouble making minor changes to ones others taught me. Well, I guess it was Simon, after all.

"I've been trying for some time to make sense of the dybbukim's appearances," Simon went on. "I've only been able to do so with the help of a wizard, because otherwise there was no way for me respond in enough time. Naturally this posed a quandary, since I would have to employ a wizard against the explicit orders of my superiors. What if the wizard were caught and interrogated? Even if he or she had no intention of betraying me, there is always revelation."

"No shit," I said. I was still feeling the aftershocks from Marsh's exaction.

"And so," Simon continued, "I was rather blessed to come across our friend Smoot, who was uniquely qualified to obviate that problem."

I blinked, and then all at once I remembered what Wolfe and Marsh said after Marsh tried her little revelation exaction on Smoot.

She genuinely can't remember. That was what Marsh said. *She is so monumentally stupid she can't remember a damn thing from one moment to the next.*

And then Wolfe said: *An anterograde amnesiac.*

"It's because she's an amnesiac!" I said.

"Correct. Her short term memory lasts for only a few minutes; it's practically impossible for her to give up information that no longer exists."

"Wow," I said.

"Anyway," he said. "Suffice to say I've discovered that somehow the wizards have found a way to bring the dybbukim here, and I'm positive they're near to finding a way to do it en masse. If that happens, the book of revelations will read like a Dick and Jane Primer in comparison."

"Why's that?" I asked; I kind of already figured out why, but I guess I was hoping I was wrong.

"Well," he said, "picture every last human being in the greater Miami area becoming a dybbuk and you might begin to appreciate the implications."

"Jeeesus," I said. "You're telling me the Wizards are going to start an all out apocalypse?"

"In a manner of speaking," Simon replied.

"The hell?" I said. "Isn't that a bit much?"

"The fuck it is," Reese said. I whipped my head around; I almost forgot he was there after all this time; that man is quiet and still as death when he wants to be. "What the hell else could they do, exactly?"

"Calm down, Reese," Simon said. "But he's right, you know, Kroger. What we have here is a whole people, indentured and incarcerated for something they have no control over: How they were born. This sort of unilateral fiat was what brought the Scions together in the first place. Vampires, Demons, Intermediates, Wizards, they all realized the only way to survive was some sort of unity, no matter how much they actually hated each other."

"The Knights created their own enemies," Reese said. "Because they couldn't keep their hands to themselves."

"You aren't wrong, Reese," Simon said. "But all the same, we can't allow all this to happen. *I* can't allow it."

"I get it," Reese said. "But what after?"

"First things first," Simon said. "Believe me, we have plenty to keep us busy."

"Well," Reese said. "I could give a shit about everything else. But if you bust Casey out for me, until this is over you've got everything I can give you, for free."

"Bust her out?" I asked. "Wait, you know where she is then?"

Reese lifted up one of his hands; he was holding a manila folder.

"Remember this?" He asked. "You dropped it by the door. When I went back for my gear I saw it on a box and had a look through it. Fun read. Dossiers and arrest records for what I recognized as two Intermediates, what I believe is a vampire, and a wizard. Guess which wizard."

Chapter Twenty Six

To think I was worried that I'd be bored this week. One quiet hour pretending to work in my cube would be just absolutely dandy right about now. I wouldn't make a peep about it, either. Hell, I'd even take bug duty. Almost.

We went on for another twenty minutes or so, or that was my best guess. I didn't have my phone on me, which I always glanced at to tell time—

Oh, that's right, *phone!*

"Hey Simon," I said. "You have a phone?"

"Still?" Reese groaned. I gave him a dirty look.

"No, Kroger, I don't," Simon said. "Don't you think holding on to that would be a bit dangerous at the moment?"

"You're kidding," I said.

"No, Kroger, I'm not," he said. "If you want to make yourself a huge, flashing neon target, that's your problem. Me, I think I'll pass. There was a GPS tracking device installed on this vehicle as well, but that wasn't especially hard to find. That's not even to mention what I had to dispel."

I hadn't really thought of that. It's probably for the best that I never got my stuff back. With the resources at the Knight's disposal I may as well have shouted LOOKIT ME on a ten million watt PA system.

"Although," Simon said, looking sideways at me for a second, "I *did* get a chance to see that video before I ditched my phone."

"Which video?" Reese asked.

"Look up 'Presentation fail' when you get a chance," Simon replied, and then went on before I could say anything more. "OK, We're here." He slowed down and merged into a turn lane.

Here turned out to be the St. David Catholic Church in Davie, which, judging from the banners and signs I could see, not to mention from the gigantic Ferris wheel and shiny lights, was deep into its winter carnival. The church sat alongside some huge empty field and they covered every square inch of it with some kind of ride or carny game. It wasn't anywhere close to as big as the county fairs I was used to, but it wasn't exactly just a couple bounce houses shoved on a parking lot, either. Like I said, it did have a big Ferris Wheel, and I could also see a zipper, a ring of fire, and a mini roller coaster, too.

Simon actually didn't end up parking anywhere near the grounds; instead he actually pulled into the next plaza up. When I asked him why, I almost kicked myself for not figuring it out.

Remember my little problem with churches? I wasn't making that up to get out of going with my Grandma. The last time I stepped foot on grounds occupied by a church, it was extremely uncool. Simon knew that, and that's why he didn't want to park on the Church lot. He said that he was pretty sure that the land the Church used for the fair shouldn't be a problem, though. I guess there was only one way to find out, right? Apparently that way was to just dive in headfirst and hope the water was deep enough.

We all got out, and Simon started off almost right away. He stood on my left, and made Reese stand on my right.

"Reese," he said. "Keep her between us. Cover one to six o'clock."

"Right," Reese said. "You know I can cover the whole damn clock, right?"

"I know," Simon said. "That doesn't mean it's efficient. Just do it. But by all means, if you spot something and it looks like I've missed it—"

"Gotcha," Reese said.

"All right," Simon said. "One last thing."

Simon reached into his shirt and pulled out something I couldn't see, except that whatever it was, it was attached to a thin silver chain around his neck. I saw his mouth move, and then there was a tiny flash of white light from between his fingers.

"What's that?" I asked.

"Our contingency plan," Simon said, and stuffed the thing on a chain back into his shirt. "Let's go."

So, like Simon said, they both kept real close to either side of me without actually looking like they were Marshalls escorting a fugitive, which didn't really stop me from feeling like one. Because, you know, technically I was. I still had no idea what the hell we were planning to do at a fair of all places, and Simon didn't much feel like telling me. He said something about intermediates compromising us since I didn't have the first damn clue how to counter them. Well, if Eveneshka wasn't just insulting me for the fun of it, Simon was right, because apparently my mind literally *shouts*.

Then Simon said that it was a safe bet that the Knights had increased intermediate patrols through the roof in the last couple of days and he wasn't up for taking any chances. Ok, fine, whatever, but in the end all that meant from where I sat was that once again I had no idea what was going on, which was getting seriously old.

But now check this out: It's kind of weird to admit, but as we got closer to the fair's front gate I actually almost relaxed for a second. I know, that's crazy talk, right? But it kind of happened without me realizing. If I had to try and explain it, I'd say it must have been a combination of a whole bunch of things. Like, the air was cool, there was a nice breeze, there were those pretty lights in nice patterns on the Ferris wheel and everything, and then there was the music and the smell of fair food. All of that together just felt nice. I know it sounds lame but it did.

So anyway, the fair wasn't all that busy, being the middle of the week, but it wasn't dead either. I guess that's because it was local and easy to get to? Sure, why not. We went through the front gate and no one even seemed to notice us, including the ticket collectors. I'm guessing Simon had his little suggestion prayer going, or it could have been the ticket collectors didn't give a shit. Maybe it was both.

"This way," Simon said, and we walked past the Ferris wheel, a tilt-a-whirl, and a funnel cake stand. We passed a game booth with the guy shouting at us, one of those things where you use a hammer to ring a bell, a rock climbing wall, and the zipper. When we came up to one of those "Fool the guesser" guys with a headset betting us he could guess all of our ages and weights, Simon stopped short.

"Guess your weight, sir?" Said the guy. He was short and a little on the chubby side and he was beginning to go bald, too. Honestly, he just looked overall like he'd seen way better days. A hell of a long time ago.

"I was hoping for a slightly more useful guess," Simon said.

What's not useful about that?" The man with the headset asked. "One dollar, if I'm not within five pounds you win." He motioned to a rack of hideous stuffed animals.

"Which gives you a ten pound margin of error," Simon said. "Which is ten more than you'd ever need. As I said, I'm in the mood for something more practical."

"What do you mean practical, sir?" Said the guy, and he almost looked like he was forcing his smile now. "If you're sensitive about your weight, I can guess your age within—"

"Practical," Simon said.

The guy looked pissed for a second, and then he puffed his cheeks up, blew out a huge breath, and reached up and whipped off his headset.

"Fine, Bradley, Fine," he said. "But make it fast. I haven't made a dime all night."

"Unless I miss my guess," Simon said. "It won't be fast."

The guy looked at Simon, and then at Reese, and then at me.

"What's with the backup?" the guy asked. "If you felt like railroading me, I think you could do that all by yourself with one hand behind your back on an empty stomach."

"They're not backup, Coleridge," Simon said. "And I'm not railroading you. I'm politely requesting your assistance."

Coleridge shrugged. "Semantics. But, I suppose you are as polite as any of you people get. Fine, what type of assistance are you *politely* requesting?"

Simon grinned. "How about extrapolating magically eradicated memories?"

Coleridge stopped and looked right at Simon for a few seconds without saying a thing. Then he puffed up a bit and his eyes got a bit wider.

"No shit?" he said.

"No shit," Simon said.

"H-awww-t," Coleridge said.

Umm, eww.

We didn't stick around in front of Coleridge's little stand for long after that; he motioned for us all to follow, and just a little too eagerly. I didn't much feel comfortable about it, but Simon or Reese didn't take the time to ask my opinion, which frankly was about what I expected. We all went ahead and followed Coleridge between two other concession stands and off the grounds.

"You never struck me as the forgetful type, Bradley," Coleridge said, once the four of us were more or less alone. "I always assumed you had always taken—er—adequate precautionary measures."

"It isn't me," Simon said.

"Yes, yes, I thought not," Coleridge said. "Just didn't fit. You can imagine my confusion. So, then, which of these two is the customer? Or are they both—"

"Just me," I said, and Simon shot me a look that was so quick I almost missed it. Coleridge looked over at me, and his eyebrows came together for a second.

"Of course," he said, and tilted his head. "The signs are rather obvious now that I look."

"Signs?" I said.

"In time," Coleridge said, and waved his hand. "What is your name—?"

"That's not especially important," Simon interrupted, and it was my turn to give *him* a look. I took a little more time with mine than he did.

Coleridge looked at Simon, and then at me, and shrugged.

"I suppose not," Coleridge said. "Very well, then, step into my lair."

Lair. Wow, this wasn't getting any better.

★ ★ ★ ★ ★

Ok, so it wasn't as bad as I thought for a second there. His *lair* was really nothing more than a beat up looking RV that looked like it was built in 1982 and driven back and forth across the country five times. I'm serious, if this thing didn't have at least four hundred thousand miles on it, then I don't know anything about anything. The tires were so bald in some places that I could see the steel poking through the rubber, and the bumper was so rusted that it looked like something big took bites out it. Come to think of it, it *was* as bad as I thought for a second there.

Coleridge stuck his hand in his pocket, rattled it around a little, and then pulled out something like sixty-seven keys all jammed onto one ring. I mean, I know I tend to go overboard a little with my key ring but this was just stupid.

He opened the side door, and it looked like it almost jumped right off the hinges but was held on entirely by filth and grit. We all got blasted with a gust of really stale air that was mixed with the stench of old Chinese food, reefer, and really bad BO.

"Can we do this out here?" I said. "I'm begging you."

"Afraid not, miss—?" Coleridge said.

"Kroger," I supplied. "And why the hell not?"

"Too risky," Coleridge said. "I've gone through great pains to make the interior of this vehicle safe from prying eyes. If what Bradley is implying is even partway true, I think that's a necessary precaution."

"To say the least," Simon said, and he put one hand on my shoulder and squeezed. Not too hard, but just hard enough for me to notice without flinching. "Quickly, please."

There was barely enough room for all of us in this thing; it was narrower than my loft and maybe one third as long, if that. There was a ratty old couch, a chair and table, a half assed kitchen which basically looked like a small counter with a hot plate on it, the sleeping area way in the back, and piles of random boxes and other crap I couldn't even identify. To be honest, what with all the clutter here there was probably more standing room in a cargo elevator.

"Anyone like some freshly brewed tea?" Coleridge said.

"No," Simon said. "We—"

"I'd murder one," I said, and I meant every letter of that, too.

"Excellent," Coleridge said. "Just be a moment."

I thought I heard Simon sigh as he sat down on the couch. Reese just stood where he was, looking out the window, while I took the chair. Coleridge turned his back on us and started fidgeting around with some small boxes on the kitchen counter.

"Chamomile or green?" Coleridge said, without turning around.

"Yes," I said.

Coleridge chuckled, and went on doing what he was doing. A minute or so later the glorious aroma jumped into my nose and just made every square inch of me feel as awesome as you could imagine. I inhaled real deep, and then folded my arms and leaned back.

"This is life," I said, and a second later I realized how stupid that was. Coleridge just chuckled again, and turned around to face me. He had a gross looking beat up tin cup in each hand.

"Sure you don't—?" he asked, looking at Simon, and gesturing with one of the cups.

"I'm sure I don't," Simon said. "I'm a coffee man."

"But it's ready—" Coleridge said, almost like he was disappointed.

"All the same, no."

"I just have to pour—"

"Coleridge," Simon said, and left it at that. Coleridge just shrugged and handed me one of the tin cups. The warmth felt so damn good I couldn't even explain it. Like bundling up against a rainstorm, maybe. I just sat there inhaling the vapors for a few seconds and I honestly felt like I could just have done that all the damn livelong day.

"All right, then," Coleridge said, and stood across the table from me. He took a quick sip from his tea and then looked right at me. "Let me see. Have you any pointers, Bradley?"

"Pointers?" I asked.

"The best one I can think of is *Raine*," Simon said. "Best association we have, I expect."

"Right," Coleridge said, rubbing his palms together. "Ok then, please remain silent and still, my dear."

★ ★ ★ ★ ★

"Wait," I said. "What exactly is he going to do?"

"Coleridge here has a rather extraordinary gift," Simon replied. "He can extrapolate lost memories based on the marks left on the brain, soul, and psyche."

"Correct," Coleridge said. "I can deduce any other number of things about an individual in similar fashions, but it is lost memories that I find most challenging and—exhilarating."

I was about to ask another stupid question, but then I got what they were talking about with pointers and everything else. Raine became a dybbuk, so it made sense to link her with any other memories you were trying to recover about those things. No one came right out and told me, but even I can put two and two together after a while, so I figured that's exactly what Coleridge was trying to do, however the hell he did it.

"Let's begin," Coleridge said. "As I said, please be silent and still."

★ ★ ★ ★ ★

I did that, and then I guess something started to happen, but I had a hard time telling at first. Coleridge just had me sit still and keep eye contact with him, and that by itself made me feel a little weird. Thing was, Coleridge was kind of strange looking to begin with, and seeing him look right into me just made it worse. Also, I saw his temples twitch a time or two and I saw some beads of sweat trickle down the side of his head. The more this went on, the greasier and grosser he ended up looking.

Just then I saw his lips move a little bit, like he was reading something to himself. He raised one eyebrow (again, I got jealous), and his forehead wrinkled up.

"...Son...?" he said, just loud enough for me to barely hear.

"Son?" Simon said. "As in somebody's male child?"

Coleridge held up a finger and made a small shooshing sound. He was looking at me harder than ever. About two or three seconds later he spoke again.

"They . . ." he said. "Want ...the ...Son?"

★ ★ ★ ★ ★

"Company," I heard Reese say. His voice was dry and flat.

"Hmm," Simon muttered. "How many?"

"I count seven," Reese said. "They haven't tried to surround us. Yet, anyway."

Coleridge and me looked over at the window; Reese and Simon were already glued to it.

"I see," Simon said. "Very well. No sense in wasting any more time. Let's all step outside, shall we? You too, Coleridge."

✶ ✶ ✶ ✶ ✶

So, we all stepped out of Coleridge's RV, and there, about twenty feet away in a neat sort of semi circle, was no fewer than three fully equipped and very angry looking paladins, three wizards, and, in the center, looking as fit and fine as you please, was . . .

Marsh.

It took a second, but she saw me, and when she did, man oh man, did I just about pee my pants. She didn't say anything, but she didn't really need to; that look said it all just fine. If I didn't know from that look that she meant business, one glance at her outfit said it all. She and the Paladins were dressed to the nines in full light combat regalia, the sort of thing you'd throw on for a job that was more than just routine field work. They were all wearing what they called anoraks, which basically were holy flak jackets that were twice as strong as normal flak jackets while being only slightly thicker and heavier than t-shirts. From experience I knew those things were tough enough to bounce bullets without being bulky at all. They were great for letting a Knight conserve energy for attack without giving up defense, and they saved my ass on more than one occasion, when I was allowed to wear them anyway. They were all wearing greaves, too—those were stylish cargo pants made of the same stuff as the anorak. Over all that they had their black uniform combat dusters made of the same material, and which were fireproof as well as perfectly insulated. I could also see that all of the Knights except Marsh had what looked like gleaming silver pistols slung low on both hips, which I recognized as those dual purpose weapons with nasty ass retractable blades I was never authorized to carry. Way to rub that in my face, assholes.

Yeah, they weren't messing around.

The wizards looked every bit as ready for a brawl. They were all in dusters too—and each one was wearing a different color. One was dark blue, one dark grey-green, and another reddish grey. Each of them also had a gnarled looking staff tied off at the top with hemp rope that matched their coats.

Simon just put his hands behind his back and stood quietly, looking at Marsh like he was waiting in line for a coffee and she was the cashier.

"I'm sorry, Bradley," Coleridge said, after a couple quiet seconds. "When I heard 'Kroger', I had no choice. Look, I like you. You're better than most, but they got to me first and to be honest, they're willing to go a lot farther than you. You might want to consider that moving forward. I have to admit that while I don't like it, it's damned effective."

"Noted," Simon said. "I suggest you disappear."

"On it," Coleridge said. "Good luck."

"Appreciated," Simon said. Coleridge bowed his head, and then turned around and ran. Simon didn't even so much as glance at him. No one said anything for a few seconds, and the only sounds were Coleridge's footsteps trailing off and faint noise from the carnival in the distance.

"Sir Bradley," Marsh said, finally.

"Millie," Simon said. Marsh frowned.

"I see that my deepest fears have been realized," Marsh said, and looked right at me. "And I am disgusted. Appalled. When that pig sent his message I could hardly believe what I heard, and yet here we are. Words simply cannot convey my revulsion at finding you of all people in league with this blasphemous apostate. It's almost tragic."

"Please," Simon said, "Let's not waste any more of our time. I know you're the chief Judge, and that you're acting under express orders from McCormick, the chief Exemplar, to apprehend those responsible for the murder of Brother Hanson, Sister Gregory and Sister McGowan. I also know that there are four of you, that your three Knights have been personally handpicked for their excellence, and judging from their markings, that you have three fifth rank elemental adepts in reserve. Nevertheless, if you don't just turn around and walk away, I'm going to knock the shit out of you."

Marsh didn't say anything, but I swear I saw her twitch. I'm also sure that I saw one of the Knights shuffle his feet a bit.

"We have no qualm with you, at present, good Sir Knight," Marsh said finally, a little bit quicker than I think she would have normally. "Your other transgressions are currently under official review, but ...as of now—" She pointed at me, but kept her eyes on Simon. "I only have issue with the apostate. I want her and her alone."

"Well, you can't *have* her, and her alone," he said. "So, I guess, technically, that means you *do* have a qualm with me at present, which I don't recommend you pursue. You can forget you saw us, or not. The choice is yours."

Marsh's eyes narrowed. "No, Sir Knight, it would seem that the choice is yours, and also that you've made it. I can't believe I've heard you correctly, though."

"You have," Simon said. "I say what I mean."

"So you always do," Marsh said. "Then am I to understand that you are would truly sacrifice all you have accomplished and throw in with ...abominations?"

"No, Millie," Simon said. "I'm trying to *stop* abominations. I'm afraid it is you and yours who are doing your best to make sure they win. You and the Templar and McCormick himself have ignored my warnings time and time again, and now we stand on the brink of annihilation. I hope you'll understand why I have elected to take matters into my own hands."

"That is not your place!" Marsh said. "You are only a sentinel!"

"Yes, I'm only a sentinel," Simon said, and spread his hands. "Policy isn't my thing. I like to actually get stuff done. So I have been."

"And in so doing," Marsh said, "You would betray the last beacon of righteousness and light in this wretched world?"

"If in so doing this wretched world is saved, and my oath and duty fulfilled? Yes."

Marsh snarled. "So...you intend to stand behind a mob of murderous, blasphemous, heretics?"

"I have been forced to do so by the shortsightedness and ignorance of Knights such as McCormick and yourself."

Marsh's face got darker, if that was even possible. "Well ...then I fear I have no choice. May the Light save you, Brother Bradley. You are under arrest."

"Last chance," Simon said. "I'm allowing you to walk away. I strongly encourage you to do so."

Marsh didn't say a thing, but she looked slightly to one side, and then to the other. The Paladins took a step forward, and the wizards closed up a bit, too.

Now, the next thing that happened kind of threw me for a second. I heard Simon's voice, like he was whispering in my ear. Problem was, he *wasn't* whispering in my ear. He was still several feet away.

"Kroger," he said. "Brace yourself. And be ready to run when you land."

"What?" I said out loud, like a goon.

✳ ✳ ✳ ✳ ✳

Lots of things happened really quick, and I'll do my best to get them in the right order.

First there was a huge flash of white light, and I couldn't see a thing, but I could hear a bunch of confused, angry shouts. Then someone, probably Simon, grabbed me by my shirt and yanked me in close like I was a giant Raggedy Ann doll. I thought I heard Simon mutter something, and then my whole body felt like unbelievably glorious energy shot through it, like nothing I could remember ever feeling.

Then I was flying.

It sure felt like it, or more like I was shot out of a cannon. Everything was upside down and spinning, my guts felt like they were being flattened against my backbone, and I felt completely weightless.

Then I thought I heard Simon, from a little ways away, yell, "PUSH!"

Then I felt like I was hit with a gigantic tennis racket, and I shot through the air in a whole new direction like a stone from a slingshot. The wind was blowing so hard against my face that, even though I couldn't really see yet, I could feel my eyes watering. Also, the noise was super incredibly loud, like when you lean out your car window when you're going eighty miles an hour.

A second or so later, my eyes came back to me, and I had just enough time to see that I was coming down. Really, really fast. On to some building's roof.

Right before I smashed into the roof and went straight though it, I caught a glimpse of something terrible. I mean, really, really, really terrible. Thing was, everything happened so fast, I didn't have time to react the way I should. But I had enough time for my brain to register what I was seeing, at least.

What I saw was a giant crucifix.

Chapter Twenty Seven

I didn't have time to be shocked or afraid. Hell, I barely even had enough time to think *holy shit*. I went through the roof, the paneled ceiling, everything, and landed flat on a pretty purple rug in between two sections of pews.

A church. *I just landed in a church!*

Remember when I said that my day could only have been made better by landing in a septic tank? Well, fuck that. I would have dove into one of those seventeen times if it meant I didn't have to land in a church.

Unfortunately, like always, who the hell cared what I thought?

Crashing through the roof and everything else didn't hurt at all. It didn't even tickle. Simon must have put one hell of a defensive prayer on me before I went flying through the air, and so that wasn't really surprising. But, as awesome as Simon may be, whatever prayer he used did roughly zero for me now.

I bounced a little and rolled a few feet down the aisle toward the altar before I finally came to a full stop. I'm surprised I even realized that much, because as soon as I crashed through the roof, the real fun began, and there almost wasn't room for anything else.

Ever put your hand on a flaming hot griddle? I mean, did you ever put your whole damn palm down on top of one for whatever reason? Ok, how about, did you ever do that and then immediately squeeze a knife blade with that same palm at the same time? No? Well, good for you, because that would be bad. But that's exactly what I felt like, over every square centimeter of my body. I think as the seconds rolled by real slow, I also started to feel like someone took an entire grease vat and upended it over my head. I couldn't move without making it worse, if that was even possible (which, apparently it was), and, despite how badly I wanted to, I just *would not pass out.*

This was the power of that exaction Marsh and McCormick hit me with when they burned the X onto my arm. They infused the brand with the full power of their faith, conviction, and flat out psychotic fanaticism, and then they threw some kind of demented inverse proportional vile shit on it. Basically, if I were to dare to step foot into a place like this, a place where people's faith and belief were strongest, I would get it in equal measure to how strong everyone's faith here was. Judging from how bad I was getting it, every Sunday this church was packed up with some seriously devout, pious and fervently faithful people.

Assholes. *Assholes!*

Every muscle in my body was stretched tight, like I was having a full on seizure. My eyelids were fluttering, my eyes rolled back into my head, and I started frothing at the mouth. I'm not sure how long the torture went on, but my best guess was way too long.

✷ ✷ ✷ ✷ ✷

"WAUGH!"

I whipped my arm around like I was trying to swing at something by reflex, and then I rolled onto my back.

Wait. What?

I was on my back at the moment, and, if I had to guess from how I swung and rolled, I had been lying on my side. Only something was wrong. I wasn't in any pain anymore, and, I wasn't in the church anymore. Hell, I wasn't *anywhere* I could recognize anymore.

I was lying on what looked like the middle of a street somewhere on the edge of some huge city, only the buildings were all gutted and smashed, and, um, some of the huge chunks of debris were ...floating. Hovering. And rotating really slow. There was a real gentle but also obvious breeze that I swear was actually whispering. Like voices were being carried on the breeze, but they were too faint to understand. Then the pavement started to bulge and roll a little bit under me, but only so much that it felt like I was on one of those massage chairs. It wasn't uncomfortable, but I have to admit it was kind of odd. Streets don't have massage rollers in them.

Then I heard a really weird sound, like BaBOO, baBOO ...baBOO baBOO. I sat up all the way, whipped around, and saw that it was this huge purple duck's head floating and rotating slowly that was making the sound. He looked more or less like a real duck, only his bill was making the 'O' shapes which didn't make any sense since duck bills can't do that. They're hard, not fleshy.

"Get them," I said, and pointed at the duck. That also didn't make any sense. Get *who*? What the hell was I talking about? Somehow it made sense to me while I was saying it, but . . .

"That's the fate plate," said a voice from behind me. I gasped and spun around. There, I came face to face with the first thing that made any sense since I woke up on the street.

"Crow!" I said.

★ ★ ★ ★ ★

"The glee plea," Crow said, and giggled. "I left them upstairs as toys."

"The stutter butter?" I asked; whatever the hell that meant. I tilted my head and my eyebrows went up; in my head I was asking a perfectly reasonable question, and Crow didn't seem fazed at all. She smiled and nodded, which for some reason confused me even more.

"Wait," I said. "Waywaywait ...What, is, is . . ." My head started to feel like it was straining. "Is, is, that doesn't even mean anything."

Crow looked at me like she was confused herself. "Yeah it doesn't," she said.

"Um, um, um, I'm not awake," I said. *Man*, was it hard to say that. I had to concentrate like I was trying to read words the size of pinpricks. "Ummaaa-I'm dreaming, this isn't real."

"I decide to know it is," Crow said. I just stared at her.

"SssTOP it," I said. "This is a dreeeeeam ...dream."

It was getting easier to say what I wanted to say the more I talked.

"I know it is," Crow said. Hell, *she* was beginning to make more sense, too. What, was I, like, forcing myself into a lucid dream? It was a very weird feeling.

"Yes it is, stupid," Crow said. "You're sound asleep, don't you know that?"

"Umm, I guess I do now," I said. "Where am I really?"

"Why'd I know, stupid?" she said, and swooped around behind me. "I did everything you wanted, so I'm back."

"Well," I replied. "It's great to see you. I've had a rotten time lately."

"Oops," she said.

"Yeah, big oops." I got up and looked around, but I still didn't see anything that made any sense, which I guess made sense in its own way. "I'm gonna go for a walk. That-a-way. Wanna come?"

"'Kay."

* * * * *

"I'm in trouble, Crow. Real big nasty trouble."

"So?"

"Well it's all because of something I did, and can't remember doing." I ducked under a stream of ink that a giant magic marker was squirting.

"So?"

"The worst part is, whatever I did was *really* important, apparently. If I could remember what I did then I think a lot of bad stuff won't happen. I think. That's what everyone told me."

"So?"

"Remember these?" I held out my hands in front of my face like a venus flytrap. "*Blaaugh.* Remember those? They're gonna attack and kill everyone. I'm connected somehow and I don't know why."

"So?"

"I forgot something really important about them, I think," I said. "If I could remember what it was, I could probably help stop those things."

"Oh. That's it?"

"Yes, Crow, that's it. All I know is one word: *Son. They want the Son.* It doesn't even make sense." I stepped on a mushroom and it squeaked like a clown horn.

"No," Crow said. "I mean, all you have to do is remember something?"

"Yes, Crow, that's what I just said."

"Well that's easy," she said. "I know where all that is."

"Wait, you *what?*" I said. I stopped and looked at her with my eyes wide open. "Say again?"

"I said I know where all that is, idiot. Or wait, no, I know where all that is, but I don't know how to find them."

"—what?"

"I mean I know where they are but I don't know how to find them," she reiterated.

"Ummm, ok, never mind," I said. "Forget explaining it. How about this. Why don't you just *show* me?"

Chapter Twenty Eight

I was falling. Sideways.

And then down, then up, then diagonally down, then sideways again in random patterns, through blinding blurs of color. This all started more or less right after I asked Crow to just *show* me what she was talking about, and she was obviously only too happy to do that.

It turns out what Crow was talking about was that she knew where all of my memories were, which, I guess, shouldn't have surprised me. I mean, if she could walk around in people's dreams, which is basically their subconscious, then why the hell couldn't she walk around in other parts of someone's mind? Apparently, she could do just that.

But then there was the second part of what she said. While she knew where all my memories were, she didn't know where to find *specific* memories. Here's the best way I can think of to explain it: Remember back when the world wide web was still kind of new, and a popular way to network your site was to join a web ring? Well, the main page of that web ring would have navigation buttons that would let you cycle to other sites in the ring, and there was also a 'random' button that would, surprise, bring up a random member of the web ring.

All Crow had was that 'random' button. She could basically plunge down into my memories and wait and see what popped up.

I have to admit, while this was going on I had an unpleasant flashback to Marsh's revelation exaction, but with Crow it was completely painless, and, dare I say, even a little cool. With Marsh, I was having things ripped out of me and I could only watch them go like I was watching them on TV. With Crow, I actually seemed to enter the memories myself and consciously relive them.

★ ★ ★ ★ ★

Here I am, in my grandmother's car, being dropped off for my first day at Blessed Nativity Catholic School for girls. I'm in my uniform, the classic shirt and tie and black skirt and knee socks, but I totally half-assed it. My tie is all loose and my collar is open and my shirt's wrinkled as hell and not tucked in. My Grandmother is singing some obnoxious song and I tell her to shut the fuck up and I totally let her have it every time she opens her mouth.

Okay, I was an asshole, I admit that. But I didn't need this memory, so I told Crow to move on.

Here I am, I'm five or six, and I just ripped off a candy bar from the corner convenience store. My mom caught me, and brought over a policeman to tell me what's what. He's a giant, ten times my size and all solid muscle. He's got a huge gun and handcuffs on his belt. He tells me what happens to big people who steal. I can't even look him in the face because I think he'll crush me like a bug.

Wow, that was really scary. But still not what I needed. I told Crow to keep going.

Now I'm beating up some girl named Nicki in sixth grade. She said something about "Dopey Kroger" like she did since kindergarten. I break her nose, knock her down and go on kicking her in the face and stomach.

Not my happiest moment. Keep it going.

Now I'm sitting on a couch with my Grandma right there next to me, gently patting and rubbing me on the back. I'm looking down and crying my eyes out because I just got into another fight, with some kids in fourth grade over some nasty things they drew and passed around class. She just did one of her kisses on my cheek, the kind where she goes smack-smack-smack and then tells me I taste like sugar. She goes on to recite this little poem she always did when I was feeling rotten, which meant I heard it so much I could recite it by the time I was seven.

"You are by God appointed, who hung the stars in space, for your one special purpose, and none can take your place. You're here to bring your light, as only you can do, and in the heart of Grammy, there's no one just like you."

I don't know what it is, but my Grandma's never ending religious sweetness in the face of all my ugliness has a way of making me feel worse every time. I swear I think I could full on slug her in the nose and she'd still go on smiling and talking sweetly. Ugh. Move on.

Now I'm in my bedroom at home, sitting at my desk. There's distorted death metal music blasting from my speakers, which I cranked way the hell up to drown out my mom and stepdad. I hate the stupid song and I don't even have any idea who the band is but it's loud and obnoxious so it guarantees I'll be left alone. The only light is coming from a half cracked black light tube next to my keyboard, which is plenty and then some. I hunch and lean over, almost putting my nose flat on the surface of the desk. I have one nostril pressed shut, and I take a deep, huge, hoover sized inhale. A second later I flop backward in my chair and roll my eyes back. After I finally exhale, a stupid slow grin creeps across my face as everything slips away.

Oh no. All right. Remember way earlier when I mentioned how channeling the Light was such an amazing high that I said it was like a shot of heroin on steroids? And also how I said I didn't know what shooting heroin felt like? Yeah. Well, like everything else addicts say about their addictions, that was a big fat lie.

Well not entirely. I never *shot* heroin, but I sure as hell *snorted* the hell out of it. All the goddamn time, like a fiend. So technically, when I said I didn't know about shooting up it wasn't all the way a lie. Let's just say that lying by omission is one of the many skills you have to develop if you're an addict.

I've been off heroin for years, but if you think I'm not still an addict I'm sorry to say you're wrong. Once an addict, always an addict; I just replaced one high for an even better high. In fact, I'm practically one thousand percent positive that if I never learned to channel the Light, I'd be face down dead in a gutter somewhere choked to death on my own sick.

I mean I was on the shit all the time once I found out how to get it, and I think I found out how to get it way earlier than I had any business finding out. I don't even want to go into what I did to get it, not now.

I think like almost any other addict would say, it was mainly out of desperation. I mean, I tried booze, cigarettes and weed (more or less in that order) and none of that crap ever gave me what I needed, which was to get the hell out of my own life. After my dad died and my mom went through one new bastard after another, I wanted to be anyone else but me. It started when I was around fifteen with a quick regular wake-and-bake after a semi-regular all night booze binge (the means for which weren't hard to come by at all if I led the right guys on) and from there it was more or less a snap to escalate and end up where I did. If there's anything I can say positive about that period in my life, it's that I didn't get knocked up, somehow.

Add this to the seven-story-tall pile of hate that made it impossible for my family to have me around. I mean I think I got into fistfights with at least three of my mom's boyfriends, and that's the least of it. Forget about when she actually remarried.

This one memory was exactly not what I needed. If weed was a gateway drug, then this was a gateway memory. All of the hell I went through in my brain day after day that led me to this point was nothing I thought I'd be able to revisit right now. I begged Crow to move on, and she did. Thankfully.

Now I'm deep in Paladin training after getting out of Blessed Nativity, which turned out to be a front for recruiting Paladins, Wizards, and Myrmidons. There's Rudy, he's a fresh pally like me. We're meditating, and trying to believe that we can lift this boulder in front of us. It took me forever to get this prayer right. It's really hard to unbelieve shit you spend your whole life being taught to believe.

Rudy was cool. I liked working with him. But I gotta go.

There's Reese, And Casey. Casey with her pageboy haircut and black hipster glasses, plaid skirt and thigh high striped stockings. That, or stuff like it was practically her official uniform. Instead of a staff she has a garden hoe. Pretty wacky, but wow, the stuff she can do. Anyway, they're talking to each other and then they stop when they see me. They did that a lot.

Never quite got why I kept getting the cold shoulder then, but, it makes more sense now. Keep 'em coming.

I'm knocking over our big screen plasma TV after a huge fight with my mom. The TV is completely destroyed. My sister tries to stop me but it's too late. She tries to restrain me but I elbow her hard in the face and run out the door. Before I run down the street I pick up a concrete block and heave it through my mom's van's windshield so she can't chase me down. Yes, I am blazingly high, and everyone knows it, especially my sister.

Fuck. That was only the *beginning* of the night that landed me in Blessed Nativity. Looking back, I got off so lucky it's goddamn ridiculous. If I were my mom, I'd have just let me rot in jail. But Grandma convinced her to let me have one last shot at reform by sending me to that Catholic school. Crap, this isn't easy to see again. Move on.

I'm with Casey and Reese, and we have a powerful succubus cornered.

Oh shit, no, I don't want to see this one. Let's go—

Wait. I'm still here? I said *lets go*—

Crow isn't letting me go.

Why isn't she letting me go? Is she doing this on purpose? Is she trying to make me suffer?

No, that's not it at all. She's not making me stay, she's just staying herself. I can somehow tell that she's staying because she *always* stays when she finds this one. She always stays for the whole thing.

I guess that means I have to stay for it, too. Terrific.

✶ ✶ ✶ ✶ ✶

Reese blurs behind one of the lesser succubi that was winding up some kind of spell to throw at me, turns her back into swiss cheese, and then whacks her head off like it wasn't anything at all. Casey is just about done draining the life force out of a group of shambling ghouls; they crumble to the floor.

"KROGER, GET READY!" She howls. "THIS BETTER WORK!"

I just finished slicing both of the vampires I was engaged with to ribbons, and I nod at her to show I heard. Casey was a little testy because this particular succubus wasn't just any old succubus. No, she was an archsuccubus.

Oops, speaking of, a lesser succubus just leapt at me. I block her attack with my standard issue riot shield, and let a rebuke fly right in her face. She's stunned just long enough for me to swing Sherman directly at her lovely neck. Good night nurse.

Anyway, we've been tracking this archsuccubus for a good while, ever since we found out she was behind the rash of killings and kidnappings our patrol was assigned to investigate. We thought we had her killed last time, but like most archdemons, killing her body doesn't really do anything except force her to go find a new body. That's because her spirit basically gains a separate existence on a higher plane. So we thought we had her, but we didn't. She came back stronger than ever, and went on a hell of a rampage. To put it lightly, we got our asses handed to us by the Knights for negligence.

Which, looking back, the negligence was all mine as both the leader of our patrol and the Paladin, but...

Whatever, so I busted my brain figuring out a way around our little issue, and I thought I found it. There was a very powerful Exaction that combined parts of an exorcism with annihilation, that was developed by a Sir Francis Justine in the fifteenth century. Basically, it used the Demon's mortal body as a bridge to its spirit, wherever that spirit may be, and it pulls that spirit into the same plane as its body, where the spirit would, in theory, be able to be killed for good.

I knew I had this Exaction down. Better yet, I believed I did. I got my team together and told them we were going for the kill this time. Looking back, I should have been able to tell that they didn't really buy that I could pull this off, and who could blame them? I mean, it's not like I was nearly as powerful as I thought I was.

Well, so there we were. We had the bitch's back against the wall, and we were mowing down her minions like they weren't there. We got really lucky and caught her off guard and mostly unprotected, so we knew this would probably be our only chance to pull this off.

That, along with my track record, was why Casey was a little pissy tonight.

Casey had been winding up a spell for the last minute, using energy "borrowed" from the ghouls and other unfortunate friends of the archsuccubus. She was about to let it fly, and it would give me the opening I needed.

Casey screamed out something I couldn't hope to pronounce, and then the air all around the archsuccubus looked like it just got hit by a train. I know that sounds crazy, but I'm telling you the air shook and rattled and buckled. Hell, Reese, Casey and me almost got knocked over.

The archsuccubus growled something I couldn't understand, but I had a feeling she wasn't thanking us for being awesome. I didn't give a shit; hell, she could have been reciting train schedules for all I cared. The point was, Casey blew her defenses sky high, and now it was up to me to finish the job.

And boy, did I ever.

I charged in, and let the archsuccubus have it full in the face.

"Liefern Zerstörung!" I yelled.

And then shit happened. Lots of shit.

Let's just say that if after Casey's spell the air looked like it was hit by a train, then now the air looked like it was twisted up, crumpled, *pinched, and then had a huge hole kicked through it. I mean, we're talking all hell AND heaven was breaking loose here. There was a big explosion, and then there was this huge spinning blue light behind the succubus, crackling and bursting with a kind of energy I'd never seen before.*

The succubus wasn't happy, mostly because I had a feeling she knew what was going on and what was about to happen. Well, too bad, so sad. I could see the look in her eyes; nothing but sheer terror.

I didn't bother to waste time taunting her. I just stuck Sherman straight into her heart up to the hilt, and then yanked the blade back out and sliced off the succubus's head before she could even double over. The big blue light behind her let out one last BOOM, and then it was gone.

That was it. It was over. My exaction worked, and we won.

✶ ✶ ✶ ✶ ✶

Ok, so you may be wondering why I didn't want to see this memory. I mean, it looks like a pretty damn nice one, doesn't it? It sure as hell does. Adobe Kroger triumphant. Hail to me, the conquering heroine.

Well okay. I'm just going to say it.

I didn't find out until later, but, that exaction I used, it had a very unfortunate side effect. Let me see if I can explain. I don't know, let's say you're doing an algebra problem, and you have two sides you have to work on to solve for x. Everything you do to one side, you have to do to the other side, or you can't solve the problem, right? Well ok, that's not the best example but you get where I'm going. You cannot do to one side and not do to the other.

That exaction I used forcibly draws an evil spirit onto our plane so it can be destroyed. Fine, it worked great as you saw. But what I didn't know was in order to do that *another* spirit from the directly *opposite* plane must also be forcibly drawn out. Why I don't know, but that's exactly what happened. That day, at the same time I tore the succubus's spirit from hell, I pulled another little extra spirit from heaven.

The little extra spirit was Crow. That's right, the big bad Paladin tore that innocent little girl out of heaven.

* * * * *

Did I know this at first? No, not really. Turns out she was bound to me after I did it, and she was lost, terrified, and confused. She found out that she could try to reach out to me in my dreams, and then, well, you remember how that ended up. Yeah.

Oh, and that thing she said that I had to play backwards to understand?

What she said was . . .

You stole me. I want to go home. I can't leave. You stole me and you won't let me leave. Why can't I go home? Home was warm and light. This is so dark and cold. I'm so scared.

* * * * *

I *did* try to get her home, and I did stuff I shouldn't have to try to get her there, too. But what choice did I have? I was caught and excommunicated over it, but I refused to give up my light. I couldn't. I needed it to finish what I started, to get Crow home. Which I swore to do if it killed me.

* * * * *

After that memory finished, Crow moved on and took me with her. She didn't make any mention of what she saw at all, which kind of freaked me out a little, but I was glad she didn't. It was already not all that fun to have to relive that colossal fuck up in my head every day for the last year, let alone to actually step back into it.

But here's the thing. I think Crow must have been using that memory as some kind of landmark or something, because from that point on we stopped jumping around into random points in my life and began following a much more straight line.

Which meant...Oh, fuck.

Yeah, Here I am, ripping crow out of my dreams and throwing Marsh's revelation exaction at her. There I am trying to bring Crow back from being totally catatonic. Now I'm whispering into her ear, promising to get her back to heaven...which is what finally snaps her out of it.

Now here I am with Reese and Casey. I'm telling them what I did and what I have to do to fix it. Neither of them seem to like it.

So now we're at Coral Castle, which is that strange little spot down in Homestead where this guy built a huge fortress out of coral rock all by himself. It's very late at night, and there's a thunderstorm going on. No rain, yet.

Coral Castle is sort of strange on its own, but tonight, it's worse. It feels like the air around me is pushing in on me and trying to push the breath out of me. I don't think anyone without the training I have would notice, though, and, of course, it helps that I know what's causing it. Basically, Coral Castle was built on a huge crossroads of powerful energy, and these kinds of places have a way of attracting all kinds of stuff. Over the years a lot of nasty shit gathered around this area, because it's the nasty things that usually want to find as much power as they can. This kind of upended the dominant energy of the place and turned it from a sweet gesture to a man's lost love into a dark pocket. I didn't know the term then, but that's what it was.

My plan is shaky but it's the best I can think of; frankly at this point I don't care what else happens as long as I can fix my screw up. I owe Crow that much. Casey and Reese seem to think my plan is more than just shaky, but I ask them to come anyway. I didn't know then, but obviously knowing what I know now, they only came because they literally could not disobey a Paladin.

So here we are, balls deep in pure evil energy, and there's lightning flying everywhere. Crow is with me, too, but I'm the only one who can see or hear her, like usual.

Oh, and we also have an incubus with us. But he's out cold; we wrangled him earlier that night.

I can hardly believe I'm even doing this, but like I said, I couldn't care less what happens to me, as long as Crow gets home. Casey begins her spell, and I wind up my exaction. One that I developed myself.

Ok, remember when I said I was amazed that Simon developed an exaction? Yeah, that must sound a bit off now that I just said I did the same thing. Well, the difference is that his worked. Mine, no, not really.

What I was trying to do was reverse the exaction I used on the archsuccubus, to rip this demon's soul out of its body and send it to hell. Not like an exorcism, no, more like a transplant. I was banking on the prayer letting me take Crow's spirit and throw it back into heaven, since, well, it ought to do the same balancing act it did before, right?

Newp.

All I ended up doing was linking this demon's soul to a higher, darker plane. In case you forgot what that means, I just made this Incubus about thirty seven times stronger. Yeah, I just turned this little minor demon into an archdemon. And Crow? She didn't go anywhere.

But you can sure as hell bet this brand new archdemon went somewhere. He went on a rampage. Guess what happened next?

Well, glad you asked. We're on the next memory now.

There I am in the center of a massive ring of Paladins in full uniform. McCormick is approaching with the goddamn branding iron.

"It's such a shame," he says. "That you will no longer be able to complete whatever vile task you have sought to undertake. You will never evoke the blessed light, for evil or otherwise, again."

I don't want to relive this! Crow, get me out of here!

Wow, Crow let me skip this one. Thank Christ. Guess she doesn't really care about the ones she isn't in. Yeah, that's totally it. Moving on to the next . . .

I'm at work arguing with Armando, again ...he does his whole bullshit rap about how all I do is "put stuff there" (his phrase for cutting and pasting code from the internet) . . .

Ugh Next.

I stutter like a motherfucker during a presentation at work. John is so embarrassed for me he has his face in his hand. Either that or he's trying not to laugh. Yeah, he's probably doing that.

Next.

I'm chugging a beer at some country bar with Jill and one of her on again, off again boyfriends...

No. Next.

Me and Jill and another guy . . .

No . . .

Me and Jill and another guy . . .

No . . .

Me and Jill and another guy . . .

NO!

Me and Jill and another guy and some of my other friends AND Raine.

Jackpot! We're getting closer ...next!

I'm fighting the Raine dybbuk . . .

Okay, okay, almost there ...next one—

I'm stumbling up the stairs in my black tank top, exhausted and drunk off my ass—

STOP!

★ ★ ★ ★ ★

This is it. This is almost the last thing I remember before blacking out and waking up half naked next to Smoot in the middle of nowhere. Whatever happened here destroyed my loft, got me thrown halfway across far-as-fuck-town, got Marsh wanting to make me eat my own ass, and may very possibly contain vital information that could stop an all out war!

But wait...would the memory be intact or what? Simon told me that Smoot's little problem made it impossible to even force information out of her. Would it be the same for information a wizard blocked out with a spell?

Only one way to find out, I guess. Let's see where this goes.

Chapter Twenty Nine

It was like I was reliving it, but, not really. Actually from where I stood it was like the first time all over again, and I kind of realized it was a memory but I also kind of didn't. Did that make any sense? If not, well, sorry, I don't know how else to explain it.

Whatever, ok, so there I was again. I was still drunk, but not as blitzed as I was earlier when I must have downed enough Guinness to drop a walrus. Still, I was at that point where I was feeling a hell of a strong downward pull on every inch of me that only got worse and worse the closer I got to my fantastic futon.

I fell over into bed, and I was still fully dressed, including boots. I lay there for a second until I realized that I should really at least take off my boots or I'd feel even worse. I decided to do that, but . . .

Right after this nap, I thought.

Ok now here's where it got weird.

I wasn't asleep yet. Even when I'm stone cold smashed it can take me years to finally nod off if I'm wired up, and I was super wired, and not in a good way, from how Jason and I parted ways. I don't know exactly how long I was lying there before my eyes shot back open, but it couldn't have been more than just a few seconds.

But then, like I said, here's where it got weird.

Everything started slowing down. I mean my breathing, my heartbeat, hell, all the dust in the air just started to slow down like a machine that was winding down after being shut off. Even the sound of traffic over the highway barrier through the window got slower and slower, and deeper and deeper. Finally, everything just ...stopped.

Seriously. I mean I was still wide awake and I could see everything, but nothing was moving, including me. I couldn't budge so much as an inch.

And then I felt like I was being crushed. Or, no, not crushed, squeezed. Very slowly, but very, very hard. Almost like I was being wrapped in a giant roll of cellophane that was being pulled over my whole body and tightened little by little. It was a seriously fucked up sensation, I'm not gonna lie.

And then, just when it felt like I was about to go *squish*, the pressure disappeared and everything snapped back into motion again. The traffic sounds, the dust, my breath and my heart. Everything was normal, like nothing happened.

What the hell was all that about?

Wait, wait, was that—

Hold on, I think I get it. Was that my own brain fighting to get through Smoot's spell? I guess that could have been it; it kind of made sense. The last thing I remembered was falling asleep with all my clothes on, so everything from here on has to be fresh.

So, here we go.

I couldn't fall asleep once I realized that if I didn't just cut the crap and get out of these clothes that I'd wake up in like a half an hour and feel roughly thirty seven times worse than I already did. I groaned and punched the futon a couple times, but in the end I got my ass up, swung my legs over the sides and undid my boots. I was so pissed and impatient that I threw the boots across the loft almost right after I got them off my feet. That wasn't much of a big deal though, because it's really hard to lose things in my loft. It's just too small. I got up, yanked off everything else, and then grabbed the first thing I could find from one of my plastic Walmart drawers. Turns out it was my R2D2 underoos, so they won the honors. On went the blue tank top with the cutest droid ever on it, on went the undies, and I belly flopped back on the futon so hard the poor frame shook and creaked.

I couldn't get comfortable for anything, not even if someone promised me five hundred dollars just to lie there and fall asleep. It just wasn't happening. I tossed and turned a couple of times, bunched myself up in a ball, stretched out and tried lying on either side or on my belly. Nothing doing. Finally I flopped flat on my back and spread out my arms like I was on a crucifix and closed my eyes as tight as they could go. That worked about as well as everything else, so I just sighed real hard and let my eyes open back up.

And there, like a foot over my face was the Raine-dybbuk, in its entire split star faced glory.

★ ★ ★ ★ ★

"HO!" I yelled, and the Raine-dybbuk lunged down at me. The dybbuk was as fast as anything, but my reflexes were on overdrive from the shock; I shot up one hand and got it round the throat. The flailing flaps of its mouth stopped just short of my nose and the dybbuk started struggling like a giant rabid dog. I turned my face to the side without realizing it; its breath was like a septic wrapped in a sewer. I almost gagged, but managed to avoid it.

I have to tell you, this is probably the most annoying way I've ever been woken up, and my mom was an absolute monster in high school. Don't even ask. The woman was insane.

I'm proud to say I sort of kept my head enough to remember what worked last time, and fortunately it was something that didn't need too much effort. I gathered up a tiny bit of the light and let the rebuke fly.

"Unterbrechen," I said, and struck out with my free hand. But the Raine-dybbuk must have been a damn good boxer, or just my aim sucked. Basically my hand only grazed the side of its face and the blast of white light shot right past it, mostly. I think it must have at least winged the dybbuk because it staggered a tiny bit. Well, I didn't waste any more time. While I didn't launch the dybbuk with the rebuke, it gave me enough of an opening to hammer it on the side of its ugly face, so I just did that little thing.

Now, on my own without prayers I'm not exactly a powerhouse, but I managed to knock the monster off balance enough to squirm and roll out from under it and onto the floor. That was all I needed, really; now that I was free I could even the playing field in a damn hurry.

But, I made a mistake. When I scrambled off a couple feet to put some distance between me and the Raine-dybbuk, I moved off toward the back end of the loft, toward my computer desk, mainly so I could yank on a low hanging string to light a bulb attached to the ceiling. That was all good, but basically I ended up putting the

257

Raine-dybbuk between my swords and me. I didn't think much of it at the time; well, ok, to be honest it didn't even enter my head. I was still in a sort of adrenaline shock and I guess I wasn't up to much mental multitasking.

I got back to my feet and assumed the most badass fighting pose I could manage standing there in blue R2D2 underoos. The Raine-dybbuk stared me down a moment, and then the petals of its face closed up a little bit, which let me get a better look at what the face looked like. When I did, I tilted my head and blinked.

"Umm," I said; my most favorite word, in case it wasn't already obvious. "You're not Raine. You're Jason."

The hell? Jason? From the pub? Wow, talk about a lack of observational skill. I should have realized it wasn't Raine much earlier, since Raine was like half Jason's size. But whatever, why was Jason here, and why was he basically giving me Raine part deux?

Jason didn't give me any time to think it over one way or the other. He jumped sort of diagonally through the air at me, kicked off the wall and was all over me before I could even wind up another prayer. I mean he was on me like mashed banana on plastic wrap. I didn't have a chance in hell of staying on my feet; Jason was a big guy and it was basically like he was shot out of a catapult. I went down, hard, and slid almost all the way to the back of the loft, too.

Jason barely gave me enough time to come to a complete stop before he tried to engulf my face in his maw, but I twisted mostly out of his way before he could clamp down. He still got my face halfway in his mouth, though.

"Shit—on—everything," I said. Jason was a big guy, like I said, but I get the feeling the whole dybbuk thing made him even stronger than usual. There wasn't any way I could fight him off in my stock configuration. I needed to get him the fuck away from me.

It was extremely difficult to focus, because, well, I had half my face covered in half of this monster's mouth and he reeked worse than anything. Also, I started getting some weird tingling feeling in my chest, like I was starting to freeze from the inside out. That didn't make me too happy, because if memory served from my little tussle with the Raine-dybbuk, in a second or two I wouldn't be able to move.

I gripped the side of his face as tightly as I could, and then—
"uhn-uhn-uhn—"

No! Not *now!* Why now? Why? Why always when I need to *exact?*

The cold inside me got even worse; I was probably about a half step away from feeling like I just jumped headfirst into a freezing lake. I had a feeling this was my last chance, so I scrunched up my face, bore down hard, and—

"Unt-t-t-terbrechen!"

I really needed to start using single syllable words to do my thing. You'd think I'd have done that long before now.

Anyway, glorious white light shot out from my clenched hand, and caught Jason full on. I launched him back like he was a doll, and he hit the rail next to the stairway. He flipped over the rails head over heels, and, I couldn't see for sure but judging from the racket I'm positive he fell all the way down the stairs.

That was all kinds of incredible awesome, but it also wasn't, and here's why. Have you ever had a leech on you? Well, good for you if you haven't, but whatever. What happens when a leech gets a hold of you is that they almost become a part of your skin, and if you just ripped them straight off they'll take your skin with them.

Now picture that on a much, much bigger scale.

When Jason went flying off me, it felt like someone ripped one giant piece of duct tape off my whole face. I got yanked up with him and fell forward flat on my face, and every inch of me that Jason got in his maw may as well have just caught on fire.

"Awww!" I yelled, and then I grabbed my face and rolled around while letting loose with a whole string of garbled curses that may or may not have been real words. Honestly, I think I invented at least six brand new swears right there.

I finally calmed down enough to lie still, but my heart was still going a jillion times a second and I was panting like I just sprinted for a whole mile. It took me a second or two after that, but I did eventually remember my trusty litany. I took a deep breath and let it loose.

The Light coursed through me, and bit by bit, the pain went away. When the blessing was all done I felt my face real gentle like, and everything seemed like it was the way it was supposed to be. Well, I thought so anyway. I'd check later.

I got up on my knees and whipped my head around, trying to spot Jason; I did a double take when I finally saw him on the far side of the loft by the front windows. He was on all fours with his mouth spread open, but he wasn't making any move at me. No, he was just sitting there like he was trying to stare me down or something.

I stared right back at him, but if you think that's all I did, you must be joking. I took another deep breath, focused my belief, and spoke slow and clear.

"Festigkeit," I said, under my breath. "Panzer. Geschwindigkeit."

The Jason-dybbuk's face opened and shut, and he let out a disgusting gargling hiss. A second later, out of the shadows, I heard another hiss that obviously didn't come from Jason. And then I heard another, and another.

I shot some real fast glances all over my loft, and what I saw didn't do much to relax me. There looked like there were maybe six or seven more dybbukim, some slinking along the walls and even the ceiling like gigantic cockroaches.

"Nuh-*uh*," I said.

All of the dybbukim spread their mouths as wide as they could go, and they all let loose with a hideous growl that sort of sounded like someone trying to yell and throw up at the same time.

Maybe it was just because I was still super pissed about the whole ripping off my whole face thing, but I wasn't the slightest bit afraid. No, I was just very, *very* mad.

I stood up straight, and started right off toward all of them. I slammed my fist into my palm, and there was a blast of white light when it hit.

"*Come on,*" I growled.

Well, they came on all right. In fact, they all jumped at me at the same time. I think it was about then that I realized I was nowhere near my swords, and I'm pretty sure it was because I was both angry as hell and high on my prayers that I didn't even give a shit about that.

The Jason-dybbuk got to me first, and I gave him one hell of a reward for his effort. I landed a full on haymaker directly to the side of his flesh-flower face, and he spun back like a top and slammed into one of his friends in midair. They both ended up falling over into the stairwell and they let out a high-pitched squeal that reminded me of a wild pig.

Before I even finished following through with that punch I was already positioning against the two dybbukim coming at me from the other side. I continued on through the motion of my punch and spun my body completely around, throwing a wheel kick at the nearest dybbuk. My heel slammed him like a ten-pound sledge and there was this gross squishing noise as his face folded like a wet rag. I came all the way back around just in time to throw a solid jab into the second dybbuk's face. Unfortunately, though, that wasn't very good judgment because all I ended up doing was shoving my fist right into his open maw.

That was about all I had time to do, even with my combat mobility prayer up. The rest of them all bowled me over like a wrecking ball and I slid back toward the rear of the loft.

They all latched on to me good and hard, and it was absolutely grotesque what they started doing next. They weren't trying to rip me to pieces like I thought they would, they were trying to...well, *absorb* me? That's the only way I can think of to describe it. One of them each got their maws totally around each of my limbs, and another began to work his maw around my head. They were sucking and sucking like they were trying to get an extra thick shake through a straw, and it sounded like that's just what they were doing, too.

Well, I think I let them have their fun long enough. I braced, flexed, wound up, and twisted sideways. I flung the dybbuk on my right arm against the wall, and the dybbuk on my right leg went spinning off over my futon and landed in the stairwell. I landed on top of the other two dybbukim but didn't so much as pause. I rolled back in the other direction and sent the other two dybbukim flying the same way. One of them landed square on my computer desk and just pulverized it. My huge flat screen monitor sailed off the surface and face planted after doing a full somersault, and then the whole desk just flipped up and came down on top of the dybbuk. My tower case got crushed and bent all the way inward, and I'm pretty sure the motherboard got snapped in half. Crap. I paid for all that with last year's bonus.

That left only the dybbuk sucking on my skull. I said *skull* instead of *head* because you'd obviously get the wrong idea.

I went into a squat, reached up and grabbed hold of the last dybbuk, and yanked him off of me. My shield prayer kept him from being able to actually leech on like Jason did, but it was still like pulling a suction cup off of a glass door. Well, I heaved that jerk face right into the three other dybbukim that were still standing and knocked them all down.

Nice try assholes. Advantage: Me.

They didn't know they were severely outclassed, apparently, because they got right back up and came right for me all over again. They lashed out with their hands and maws, but I was all geared up now, so to speak. I swatted their attacks aside and then punted one of them across the loft, and he knocked down another dybbuk on his way there. I heel kicked another one right in the gut, and elbowed another in the side of his head before I grabbed a third and threw him. Let me tell you, I was knocking them around like nothing at all. This went on for maybe a half a minute before they all backed off and regrouped by my futon.

"HA!" I said; I was sort of leaning forward at them like I was king shit. "Haaa! AAHHHAHAA—*HA!* Say *what?* What else?" I was on one hell of a natural high, let me tell you. I was back in that goofy fighting pose, hopping around like Muhammad Ali. If I didn't look absolutely ridiculous I'd eat my shoes, but I didn't really care.

Well, they didn't charge at me again, which would have been cool. No, they just stared at me a second, and then they did something else. They started climbing all over each other and making disgusting squishing noises; I mean it was so gross you wouldn't believe it. On top of that, their bodies started to stretch, bulge, squeeze and kind of melt into each other like some kind of demented silly putty. It was maybe one of the sickest things I'd seen in a long time, and I've been around the dark web a time or two. They kept this up for a bit, and I couldn't do a damn thing but stand there and stare, like how everyone always has to slow down on the highway to gawk at a car wreck.

They finally, well, sort of molded together into a larger, nastier, throbbing and pulsating version of themselves. One dybbuk each was an arm and leg, three of them wrapped up to make the body, and the last one split apart its whole body to make a giant star shaped maw. I swear, I couldn't help but tilt my head like I was looking at some seriously twisted fetish video.

"Nuh-*uh*," I said.

The giant dybbuk slammed forward on its huge fists like a great big skinless gorilla, and the whole loft shook. He cracked my futon in two and dust and pieces of ceiling came falling down all over. I almost fell over myself but I steadied my feet just in time.

"What," I said. "That it?"

You can just bet the giant dybbuk spread its maw wide and roared like a canon blast, showering me with gross goo and phlegm and blasting me with an indescribably putrid stench. I think the only thing I can think of to match that smell was when I opened up my bathroom sink's u-bend to clear out a clog. Holy hell, this was at least three times worse, and no I am not even joking.

So this giant dybbuk hauled off and lunged at me, and right about then I was seriously realizing that the big guy was between me and my swords.

You make one tiny mistake…

★ ★ ★ ★ ★

Well this thing wasn't messing around. He took one giant sledgehammer swing at me much faster than he ought to have been able to. I blocked it with both arms, for all the good it did me; I wasn't braced too well and he just weighed a whole hell of a lot more. He knocked me right into the low slanting ceiling and I smashed a crater in it and bounced hard and fast straight to the floor.

"Bastard," I growled, and rolled and tumbled out of the way of a follow up swing, which almost collapsed the floor.

This asshole was fast, but I was faster. I was up and at him before he could draw back again, and let him have a full on leaping kick straight to his midsection. I thought it was an ok shot but he just kind of shook a bit and didn't even really slow down. He was already swinging at me before I could reposition and I had to almost fall flat to avoid getting smashed again. Well, he missed me but knocked in my bathroom wall completely; it crumbled with a glorious racket.

He was overextended from that last swing, so I gritted my teeth and leapt at him, thrust my fingers into his side like knives, and added a rebuke for good measure. There was a big flash of blue-white light at the point of impact; I was pouring a whole lot of concentrated holy power into this. He let out a kind of higher pitched growl that time which I took to mean that maybe I managed to hurt him. Thing was I was having trouble getting my hands back because the bastard's skin was trying to close up around my fingers. This gave him just enough time to swing back one of his meaty elbows and launch me like a ball in a batting cage. I ended up in the corner, and I heard a kind of terrible discordant BWAANG as I hit the floor.

This wasn't working out too well. I mean, I got him good that last time, and I could tell because he wasn't coming at me right away, but my arms and legs were just too damn short. I couldn't get at him without being a sitting duck. That, and he was obviously fast enough to stop me from getting at my swords; I had no doubt about that. Still, I had to do something. Maybe I could use these few seconds while he recovered to think of—

Just then I remembered the BWAANG.

My mind kicked into overdrive. "Nuh-*uh*," I said.

★ ★ ★ ★ ★

Right under my ass was my poor, abused, road worn, beat-up five-string banjo. The impact had cracked his bridge into pieces and his strings lay flat across his clear head. I winced for a second, and then realized that I could probably play him just as well now as I could with a bridge. I'm serious, after two years I still couldn't do shit with this thing that didn't sound like animals being skinned alive.

Plus, what the hell, I got him off eBay for eighty-five bucks.

The point was, his neck was made of one single solid heavy piece of wood with a metal truss rod, and his pot was solid metal as well. He was an old piece of shit, but he was a *substantial* and *hefty* old piece of shit.

I made a pass over the banjo and spat out my prayer as fast as I could. Mercifully, I didn't stutter; it was probably the luckiest reprieve of my life.

"*Ich im Namen des Lichts segne*," I hissed. "*Ich gebe meinen Geist und Seele.*"

The big dybbuk-thing was facing me now. I grabbed my banjo's neck with one hand and made a blazingly fast sign of the cross with the other.

"*Stärke, Nützlichkeit, Schönheit—*"

I was clubbed with a double handed hammer blow that sent me flying clear out through the back wall of the loft and into the stormy night.

✶ ✶ ✶ ✶ ✶

I barely had time to stop bouncing and rolling on the muddy grass before I saw the huge dybbuk jumping down the whole three stories into the back yard after me; he landed with a massive *thump* that I easily felt from forty feet away. See, he whacked me so hard I almost landed right up against the two story highway barrier, and I had a sneaking suspicion he was probably only getting warmed up.

That made one of us. The rain seemed to wait until I was out in it to really pick up, and it must have been fifty degrees out but felt like thirty since I barely had anything on. I was already soaked and mostly covered in mud, and I almost lost control of my prayers, but I shook myself and reaffirmed them all.

So I got to one knee and stared down the huge dybbuk, who was mostly only a vague shadowy shape, until a brilliant lightning flash lit up the whole place like a rave. In that split second, I saw the big ugly in all his magnificence, and if he hadn't seen me yet he sure did now, and he let me know it, too. He hunched over and roared. But I didn't really care about that; all I cared about was that lightning flash showed me where my banjo landed. It was about maybe fifteen feet away from me, directly in the big dybbuk's path.

The dybbuk took off charging at me, roaring like you wouldn't believe, but I charged and roared like a maniac right back at him. When I got to my banjo, I'd like to tell you that I did a totally sweet arm-free cartwheel and scooped it up in one smooth motion, but that would be a huge lie. I just bent and grabbed it mid stride and almost tripped. Hey, the ground was slippery, ok? And no one saw it so who cares.

I gripped the banjo right near the headstock and it glinted with a faint blueish light for half a second. I fed myself into it like I always did with Sherman or anything else, letting the light course through its neck and pot, believing that it was nothing less than an indestructible divine instrument of furious retribution.

The big dybbuk wound up another 'to-the moon' shot, twisting his whole torso around and getting his whole self into it. I did the same thing, hauling back my banjo like it was some giant silver war hammer with ivory insets and shiny gold trim.

We both swung in opposite directions at once, and when his fist hit my banjo, there was a small explosion of blue and white light, and the big dybbuk went spinning and almost fell over. I followed up immediately, letting my momentum carry me in a full circle, and slammed him right in his midsection. There was another blast of white light, and he went down like a cheap whore. Hello, crotch, meet my friend, steel toed boot. He skidded back across the mud and wrecked the tiny utility shed before he came to a stop.

Oh, yeah. Now that's what I'm talking about. Hey, you try doing this with some sissy plywood folk guitar and see what happens. I don't think so. No, it's a banjo what's meant for killin', and boy, did I take the time to prove it, too. I didn't pause. I charged right away.

He got up pretty quick, but I wasn't about to give him a chance to do much more than stand up. That's not to say he didn't try. He took another wild swing at me, but I whacked it away with my own swing, and then spun and thrust the banjo into his stomach like a spear. He doubled over, and then I went upside his ugly face like I was swinging a golf club. There was another explosion of white light, and he spun once and went down hard, face down about fifteen feet away, sending mud splashing everywhere.

The banjo was almost throbbing in my hand at this point, almost like it was every bit as eager to split this gigantic bastard in half as I was. I wasn't about to disappoint it, either.

"*Springen*," I said, and jumped through the air at him with my banjo up over my head like I was about to split a log. I brought it down, and I was positive I would have smashed him like pudding, but I never got the chance. There was a blast of red light, and something hit me so hard I went flying almost all the way back to the highway wall, and I have no idea where my banjo went; it probably ended up somewhere in Dade County. I bounced and slid through the mud and finally ended up on my back looking up into the rain.

I was surprised as hell, but not too terribly hurt or even dazed. Whatever the hell that red flash was didn't really hit me super hard, it mostly just *shoved* me super hard. I chalked that up to my shield prayer. I got up on my elbows and looked around. There was another lightning flash, and I had a quick, clear glimpse of the whole back yard. I saw the wrecked shed, the huge divots in the grass, and the giant dybbuk lying where I left him, but that was all—

Then there was another lightning flash, and that was when I saw her standing right next to the dybbuk. I blinked a whole hell of a lot, and I must have done one of those goofy ass quadruple takes. I took a second before my mouth worked, but I did finally get it moving.

"—Casey?" I said.

Without the lightning flash, all I could see was a sort of dim outline, but that one quick glimpse I caught of her filled in all the blanks. It was Casey Crumb, my old teammate, with her jaw length hair, hipster glasses and garden hoe. She was dressed a little more bummy than usual though, from the quick shot I got of her it looked like she was wearing the first thing she could find on her way out the door. Basically she had an oversized t-shirt with a picture of somebody's face on it and some baggy looking capris or something. She had no shoes on.

"Hey, Kroger," she said, like we just met for a hot dog and soda. "You are a massive pain in my ass, I tell you what."

"Hh-hh-hh-Huh?" I said. Wow. I sounded like I was panting like a dog.

Casey chuckled. "Okay, now I know it's you." She turned and looked down at the dybbuk, which was getting up, but really slow. "Tell me one thing, though."

"What?"

"How the *hell* did you knock this thing around so easily?"

"...What are you talking about?"

"Every Paladin I've tested these things against couldn't so much as scratch them. How do *you* of all people manage to keep getting the better of them?"

I blinked. "Wait—you...you? *You* sent this thing?"

"She shoots, she scores," Casey said, and she paused a second to look the dybbuk over, kind of deliberately. "But I have to admit I'm confused. By my observations, tonight there should have only been *one*, and now there seems to be a whole bunch of them. And apparently they've fused their bodies together also. That's new. Any ideas?"

I got up and got into a kind of crouch.

"whh ...hhh ...whhhu ...*what? You* made these monsters?"

"No," she replied, and then the blade of her hoe started to glow red and make real faint crackling sounds. I could see her a lot clearer now, but she looked terrible, like you do when you shine a flashlight up at your face from below. I could also see that the dybbuk was just about on its gigantic feet, too. "They were already there, I just helped them get *here*."

My eyes went wide, and then I started trying to talk really fast, which was a bonehead move. "You—these things alm-ma-ma-most k-k-killed me!"

"That was sort of the point," Casey said, and then she lowered her hoe more or less in the dybbuk's direction without turning away from me. Red light arced out from the blade like it was completing some kind of weird circuit and started dancing all over the dybbuk. The monster stiffened a little and groaned like it was in pain but it was too tired to care. "I couldn't very well kill you myself, could I? Do you have any idea what they'd do to a wizard who *disobeyed* a Paladin, let alone murdered one? No thanks."

Casey thrust out her hoe at the dybbuk, and then red light looked like it burst out from every fold, crevice and orifice on his body. He threw his head back and howled, and his giant starfish face spread as wide as it could go.

"Now," Casey said. "If a Paladin died fighting a nasty demon monster, well . . ." She looked right at me and tilted her head. "...That's just part of your job, isn't it?"

The dybbuk slammed both of his fists into the ground, and I swear I felt the ground shake from all the way over where I was. A second later he was charging at me like a juggernaut wrapped in an avalanche.

I was all shaken up and for some reason I couldn't totally stand up straight yet, but I guess the dybbuk missed when I called time out. He just kept on coming and I had to either do something about it or I'd be in a seriously bad way.

So, I got up in time, but this time he didn't try to wallop me. No, he decided to show off and just rip the ground up from under me instead. I'm serious, he just crashed his big meaty hooks into the ground and heaved, scooping up a whole huge chunk of it. I went flying. If I were a cool person I would have done a cute little twist and flip dismount like from a balance beam and landed with my arms up in the air and said TA DA but if you've heard a thing I've said up till now you should know that's not what happened. No, what happened was I landed flat on my chest and almost bent in half backwards.

I rolled and he barely missed his "how strong are you" circus mallet double-fisted blow that sent more mud and mess flying everywhere. By now I was so filthy and freezing I didn't know or care what the hell I had to do, just as long as I ended it quick so I could bundle up before I caught pneumonia and died. Yeah, yeah, I know you can't catch pneumonia from the cold.

I managed to square off against him finally, swatting his punches back with blasts of light or dodging as best as I could. It must have looked awful funny, like when a little swallow darts all over pecking at a huge hawk. But the dybbuk was faster and stronger than he was only a minute ago, no doubt thanks whatever Casey the wonder kid did. He swung and missed just barely, but he ended up hitting the ground so hard I almost lost balance from the impact anyway. That was all he needed. One back handed fist later I shot straight through the two story highway wall like an armor piercing bullet, and landed smack the middle of I-95, bouncing and scraping across the wet concrete like a skipping stone.

"Awww! Ow! AWWW!" That was me hitting the hard, wet tarmac and rolling like a grounder to center field. Almost all at once I heard horns blaring and tires screeching and smelled burning rubber.

WHAM! I got just *clobbered* by something that I swear was a diesel train but turned out to be a skidding pickup truck. I rolled up the hood, spider-webbed his windshield and kept on rolling up and over and off to the side. I got clipped in midair by something else and went off spinning like a helicopter blade and bounced off some other car's hood like a goddamn pinball.

"Awww! Ow! Awwgh! MOTHER F---AWWWW!"

Horns were going off in every direction, brakes were howling, cars were crashing and piling up, and I was the guest of honor at a blanket party. I don't have any idea how long it lasted, but I'm sure it was just shy of fifteen goddamn hours. Finally I hit something, or something hit me, and I stopped moving. I ended up flat on my stomach, and I tasted blood in my mouth and I ached from every last little part of me, but I was still conscious, however I managed that. That shield prayer of mine was obviously tougher than I ever could have thought possible; all that I just went through in the last five minutes should have pasted me. Holy sweet crap. I mean, like I said, I had seen Simon shrug off bullets with this same prayer, but I think stopping gunfire is like small change to it. I just know Simon could do it a whole hell of a lot better than I could, like usual, so I don't even want to know what he could stand up to if he really wanted to.

Anyway, as it turned out, after all that I was eventually knocked off the road and I rolled onto the median. I guess I rolled hard and fast and sort of bounced off the concrete divider and ended up like I was.

I blinked, and for I second I forgot what just happened. I couldn't make heads or tails out of anything. I mean, the world was sideways and I heard things but they were all mushy and distorted and way, way too loud. The veins in the side of my head were pulsing in time with the noise, and I felt like I was about to lose everything in my stomach. Honestly I was shocked I didn't already.

I strained my eyes against a painful glare, and then I saw that damn giant dybbuk hurtling through the air right at me.

My eyebrows just went together and I mouthed *Oh, come ON.* That was all I really had time for. The dybbuk landed on a crashed car about twelve feet from me, mashed it down to a pancake, and then leapt the rest of the way at me. He scooped me up and slammed me almost like he was spiking a football against the pavement, and I don't think I have words for how much that hurt. So of course he did it again, heaving me clear over his head in a big giant arc like he was tracing a rainbow or something and smashed me back into the pavement again. I guess at that point he got bored with that activity so what he did was he threw me southbound down the highway like a hail mary touchdown pass, and believe you me, he must have put everything he had into it because I think I was airborne for a whole week.

I figured that was pretty much it. I had no idea if my prayers were still up or not, and I sure as hell wasn't in any frame of mind to reaffirm them again. I guessed I would find out soon enough one way or the other.

So of course eventually I had to hit the top of the arc and come back down. The monster-thing threw me southbound, against traffic, so I was sailing off toward a bunch of poor bastards who hadn't hit the massive pile up caused by my ping-pong ball impression. The wind was freezing and the rain felt like thousands of tiny nasty little needles.

Have you ever had a flying dream where suddenly you realize you shouldn't really be able to fly and you start to drop back down? I kind of have those a lot, so for a second I was pretty sure I was having another one of them right now. If only. I mean, don't get me wrong, those dreams are always a massive let down, but at least there's no actual sudden stop at the end. Usually I wake up right before impact.

This time unfortunately I think I forgot to wake up. Yeah.

"Awwwww!" I remember being awake enough to yell out when I hit the pavement again, bounced twice, and rolled. The pain was severe, but it couldn't really have been too fatal if I was awake enough to yell, right? Well, clearly at least I was still conscious. I remember also I heard those blaring horns and those squealing breaks and screeching tires piling one on top of another until my ears felt like they were going to explode. I never heard so many in-my-face examples of the Doppler effect in my whole life, not by a damn sight. I didn't get hammered right away, so I guess the drivers down this far on the highway were better at swerving to miss a body that appeared out of goddamn nowhere. I had enough time to get on all fours and get out of the way of a minivan that barely missed me, and I just started scrambling like a kicked puppy. I didn't even know if I was going toward the side of the highway or just up the highway, but at this point I was moving mostly on pure momentum and figured anywhere was better than sitting still.

So yeah, I wasn't getting hit by any oncoming traffic at that moment, but apparently that itself had serious consequences. In order to miss me, whole columns of cars were creating a kind of sick chain-reacting avalanche of metal and crashed glass. I mean, when one car swerves or brakes, the one behind it has to do the same, and the one behind that, and so on...

...aaaand there, as if on cue, came two things I really didn't need at once. The whole ground heaved and shook, and I gasped and whipped around. I gawked like an idiot, like I was surprised to see the dybbuk there. What, did I think he'd just magically vanish or something? But wait, there's more. All this time like I said, cars, vans, and trucks were falling all over each other, braking and running off the road and blasting their horns. It was a serious ruckus, but then all of a sudden something big, something deep, something seriously *booming* drowned it all out. Yeah, it was a tractor-trailer's horn, and the unmistakable sound of severe jake-braking. I looked back toward that sound, and saw a gigantic semi jack-knifing and skidding straight at me. I couldn't think of anything to do at that point but stay where I was on all fours and stare.

So I was caught between this giant dybbuk and this careening giant truck, and I had no idea which one was likelier to turn me into unidentifiable gunk faster. I was in so much pain right then I swear I may as well have been on fire. You know how you feel the day after you get monstrous sunburn? Like you could brush the round edge of a plastic laundry basket with your back and it would feel like you just got knifed? I felt like that, all over. My prayers were obviously still in effect, since I could still move and think, sort of. Although at the moment I was wondering just how much of a good thing that was, because I figured not knowing what was about to happen might have made the medicine go down a bit easier.

Not like it would have made any difference one way or the other. I wasn't doing anything to change the outcome, so whatever was going to happen was going to happen. So, here's what happened.

The dybbuk didn't see me right away, but when he did it was almost funny. He spotted me and roared with every last ounce of air in his lungs (well, that is, if he had lungs, I don't really know), but was what funny was, it was right then that the semi fired off its horn. It was like both of them were letting me know just how thoroughly they both planned to wreck me, and that they both just wanted to remind me that I wasn't going to like it one little bit.

I knew I wasn't going to make it out of the semi's way unless I could suddenly discover how to teleport, and if there was such an prayer Simon never apparently figured it out so that must mean it didn't exist. Also, I'd already demonstrated my complete inability to cope with the dybbuk over the last few minutes, so that was out. What did that leave?

Roughly nothing, if you're keeping score.

The Semi was braking so hard it looked like it was almost bending in half, and finally the trailer broke off but kept on swinging, and then that trailer went tumbling top over bottom, cart wheeling and rolling straight at me. Honestly, at this point I'm not too sure what I did next, but I think I must have hunched up my shoulders and maybe dipped my head like if I ducked low enough I'd be fine and the trailer would miss me.

Well here's the best part, the trailer did miss me, but it wasn't because of any lame hunching up or ducking I did. Turns out the trailer missed because it did a full somersault before it got to me, and it was back on its wheels just as it passed over me so there was plenty of room under it for me.

The dybbuk wasn't quite so lucky. The trailer just kept going on its way and pulverized him like a rolling pin, and the whole mangled mess of metal and dybbuk mashed up into the rest of the debris.

This was when I started finding the whole business completely hysterical. I'm telling you, I half expected to hear some guy yell "AAaaaand CUT" and then everyone would step out, laugh and slap each other on the back and go on and on about how great the scene turned out. The guy who yelled CUT would high five everyone and then he'd tell the whole set to take a break for drinks and smokes.

I don't think it should take a genius to figure out that all that didn't happen, but it was nice to think about for a few seconds. I guess maybe it helped keep my mind from snapping.

I really had no idea how else to react so I just snorted and started laughing. Yep, there I was, drenched, dirty, beaten half to death, half naked in the middle of piles of wrecked cars and burning trucks, and I was laughing like a loon. Well, for a few seconds anyway, and then I threw up. For like twenty years. I mean everything came up and out and went everywhere, including, very possibly, my whole stomach along with it.

If I ever binge drink on a weeknight again, I give you full permission to knock me down and stomp on my face until I bleed the stupid out of me. I'm being totally serious.

But whatever. The important thing was I was hardly done with my business when the dybbuk burst out through the wreckage of the trailer like a bomb going off. He tore his way out like a wrestler tearing off his shirt and hurled and chucked bits of the trailer all over the place. When he got out, he took a huge piece of the trailer and threw it at a wrecked car and sent it rolling like a toy. Then he swung his huge fists down on the hood of another car and launched it into a massive somersault. Then he gave similar treatment to a pickup truck and a van.

I could have sworn I saw people still trapped in all those cars, and that was what snapped me out of it. For a second I forgot about myself and I started feeling really, really pissed.

By pissed I must have meant stupid because get a load of what I did next. I let my head drop, smacked the pavement with both palms, and pushed myself up to my feet. I was about as steady on my legs as a twig in a hurricane, but I didn't fall over right away, which would probably have been better, since it would have stopped my brilliant strategy dead in its tracks. Of course, I didn't fall over, like I said, so my plan went ahead full force. So get this. What I did was yell at the dybbuk.

Yeah. I yelled at it. That was it.

"HEY," I screamed, and swatted myself on the chest with my palm a few times. "Why don't you try that on *me?*"

Apparently I forgot that he already *did* try all that on me and did a quite a good job too. I blame the head trauma.

I want to say that maybe he was going nuts on all those wrecked cars because he was pissed off for letting me get away or something because as soon as I got his attention he stopped what he was doing and looked right at me.

I didn't have much of a plan after that, so I just smiled and waved like I was the Queen of England, and a second later I snorted again like a wild hog and started laughing. I kept on laughing, too, even as the dybbuk darted at me and snatched me up in his big smelly meaty mitts.

I got whipped around a little bit like a rag doll before he steadied his grip and got me right in front of his giant flower shaped maw. Once he did that he spread his gross fleshy petals wide and roared point blank right into my face. I got hit with such a strong blast of his rancid breath that I'm practically positive my face got all mooshed and squishy like I was skydiving. On top of that, I was pelted with foul crap that felt like shit scented Jell-o. I swear to god, I never ever wanted to smell anything ever again after that. I wanted to just rip off my nose and have done with it.

But you know what? At that point something weird came over me. Maybe it was because I figured I was a goner one way or the other, I don't know, but for whatever reason I just didn't care anymore. Not even a little bit. Mainly I was kind of annoyed.

I waited for him to finish his little bellowing rant, and then I just looked him straight in what was supposed to be his face.

"What's this all about anyway, man?" I said.

He let out a gradually increasing growl, which turned into a sort of splutter. Globs of that Jell-o stuff was dropping from the lining of his maw.

"What?" I said. "Speak up and speak English, huh?"

He hissed, he spat, and then he kind of sounded like he was winding up a giant hock, but then something happened that gave me the chills.

He talked. I think.

"sssssSSSSSSSSONNNN...." he said, or that's what I heard, in a voice that sounded like a cross between a giant snake and a clogged pipe getting cleared out.

Well, if that didn't just confuse the hell out of me. What, did he just call me his son or something?

"Son?" I said. "Umm, wrong plumbing? Oh, and If you're still there, Jason, I'm telling Jill you're a dick."

Just then I felt a massive chill tear through my whole body. My muscles went stiff and my teeth clenched as hard as I think I ever could make them clench. And then, out of the corner of my eye, in and among the wrecked cars, I saw movement.

Lots of movement.

I turned my head to see, and it didn't take long for me to wish I hadn't bothered.

There, crawling out of the pile of cars and trucks and vans, were more dybbukim. It looked like there were over twenty or thirty of them, maybe even more I couldn't see.

"sssssSSSSSSSSONNNN...." the big Jason-Dybbuk said again, and then he leaned in and began to close those fleshy petals around my head. All at once the sounds around me got muffled and the lights blurred and went out.

But then something else happened.

I sort of saw something.

No, that wasn't it. I didn't *see* it because I'm positive that my eyes were shut tight. Also I wasn't really even experiencing any kind of visual sensation. No, it was more like I just *understood* it. I don't know how else to explain it. I don't know how it happened, but somehow the dybbuk and I were sharing minds.

It wasn't *Son* he was saying. No, that's just what I *heard* him say. He meant something else altogether, and what he meant was something terribly huge. Oh my Christ, could he be serious?

Casey thought she was sending these monsters after me, and I guess she sort of did, but the truth was, the dybbukim were already looking for me. I mean specifically me. Not someone like me. *Me.* Adobe Francine Kroger. Because...Adobe Francine Kroger was the *Midnight Sun.*

All at once, everything fell into place. Somehow, instinctively, I understood it all.

But before another second passed, there was a booming explosion and everything started spinning like I was on the world's most terribly designed roller coaster.

And then, I couldn't see or hear anything, any more.

Chapter Thirty

That was the end of that. Before I knew it I was whipping around in that weird place between memories like I was falling a thousand miles an hour and gravity couldn't make up its mind where it wanted to pull me.

"Stop, Crow, stop," I said. "I need ...I need to get out of here." I have no idea if you can throw up in your dreams, but I didn't really want to find out just at the minute. Crow was nice and prompt; before I could even finish talking, I was back in the weird city where everything was spinning and floating. Or I think that's where I was. It didn't look the same at all, but in my head I knew that's where I was, somehow.

"Okay," Crow said, and then she swooped in right next to me. "Bored. What now?"

"Well," I replied, and looked around. "Am I still alive? You know, out there?" I pointed in some random upward direction.

"Yeah, stupid," Crow said. "If you were dead we couldn't both be here."

"Ok," I said. "Well then I need to wake up. Now."

"Why?"

"Because I have to."

"So?"

"Crow, all that stuff I just saw, I have to get back up out there and tell someone."

"That all?" Crow said. "Fine. That's easy. Here we go."

"Easy? Wait, how are you—"

I gapsed like I was trying to suck in the whole atmosphere, and my chest felt like it was trying to twist itself inside out. It took a couple seconds before I got everything (sort of) under control.

"With me, Kroger?" said a voice, which I recognized a couple of seconds later as Reese.

"Hmhuh?" My vision was all blurry and I couldn't see a thing.

"Wake up," he said. "I'm gonna move you. Here goes."

✱ ✱ ✱ ✱ ✱

I don't remember much else after that in detail except a whole bunch of thumps and rattles, honestly. It went on for I don't know how long or how little. It could have been anywhere from thirty seconds to thirty minutes for all I knew. My head was throbbing and pounding at the same time, if that makes any sense, and I felt raw pain over every part of me that wasn't completely numb.

Finally I could see, but I could only look straight up. I tried to turn my head but I was locked in place. I groaned.

"You're strapped down all over," said Reese. "We'll get you out of there in a second."

"Good job, Reese," someone else said. I recognized that voice, too. "...Simon?" I asked.

"Yes," Simon replied, and then he leaned over me so I could see him; he looked like he was giving my face a sort of once over. "Reese said you landed in St. David's, smack in the middle of the sanctuary. Honestly I had no intention of that happening, but Smoot pushed you in the wrong direction. Rest assured I gave her a good tongue lashing."

"Awesome," I said. "Hurts. Lots."

"No doubt," Simon said. "I imagine you now know how it feels for a vampire caught in direct sunlight."

"Go me," I said. "Are we—where's—you know—whatser- name—?"

"Marsh?" Simon said. "Don't worry about Marsh. She's... *regrouping* at the moment. Reese, What about the ambulance?"

"Went perfect," Reese said. "Hijacked it enroute. Hendrie met me and took it from there."

"Hijacked?" Simon asked.

"I didn't kill anyone," Reese snapped. "Let's get Kroger out of this."

They both got to work, and gradually the pressure on my limbs and chest eased off and I felt like I could move again, sort of. Not that I considered that a very good idea.

"So now what?" Reese said; he was getting to work removing the brace on my neck. "Did we get anything useful from Coleridge or was that just a big wash?"

"*They want the Son*," Simon said. "You heard what I heard, no doubt."

"Yeah," Reese said, nodding. "Which means less than nothing to me."

I heard them going back and forth a little bit, but their voices kind of slipped off. Something Simon said brought some background process that was idling in my brain to the foreground, and everything else was going blurry.

"Guys," I said.

They went on talking like I wasn't even there.

"Guys," I said, a little louder.

They still apparently hadn't heard. They went on yapping. I rolled my eyes and took a deep breath.

"GUUUYYYS!" I howled, about as loud as my sore throat would let me. You can bet they turned and looked at me then.

"What?" Reese said, real irritated like.

I started to get up, and managed to get up on my elbows, more or less. I glanced around to get my bearings for a second; it looked like I was on a gurney in the middle of some kind of storage room, lined with shelf after shelf of junk and piss-poor quality lighting coming from bare light bulbs dangling down from the ceiling.

"I know everything," I said, and flicked my wrist. I wanted to make a big sweeping motion but I didn't think I could have held myself up on only one elbow just then. "About all of this."

"What are you saying, Kroger?" Simon asked.

"I remember what happened," I said. "Last night. And why."

"What do you mean you remember?" Simon said. "You told me the reason you forgot was Smoot's spell."

I nodded. "It was."

"So, you're telling me it wore off? That's impossible."

I shook my head. "No, I mean I, well, I kinda ...*punched through* her spell."

Simon's eyebrows came together. "How?" He asked. "There's a reason Smoot's kept on such a tight leash, Kroger."

"Because she's a wizard," Reese said.

"Aside from that," Simon said, "She's just only *slightly* powerful. Kroger, what do you mean you *punched through* her spell?"

I waved my hand. "I'll tell you later. Right now, the only thing that matters is, I remember everything from last night, and you weren't wrong, Simon. It's damn important."

Simon looked at me a second without saying anything. Finally he just let out a breath.

"Ok, Kroger," Simon said. "I still don't quite understand how, but I'll bite, since we're otherwise stuck. Let's hear it."

"Well," I said. "For starters, what I remember explains all this. The dybbukim, Casey . . ."

"Wait, *what?*" Reese said, and he leaned forward a bit. "What was that?"

"Hang on, Reese," I said.

"No, *you* hang on," he growled, and got all up in my face. "What about Casey?"

"Do you mind?" I said, leaning back.

"Yes," Reese snapped, and leaned in further. "What about Casey?"

"I'll tell you!" I shouted back. We were practically touching noses.

"Well, what the hell are you waiting for, Kroger?"

"A beer!" I said. "Stout!"

✳ ✳ ✳ ✳ ✳

So there I was, nice cold longneck from some c-store nearby in hand, sitting slumped like a beaten woman on the gurney, legs dangling over the side. I took a nice long pull, let the luscious flavor sit for a second, and swallowed as slowly as possible.

"Thanks, Reese," I said. "Holy shit did I need this."

"Whatever," he said. "Hit me back later."

"Now," Simon said. "Not to sound like a Nervous Nelly, but we don't have much time, if any. Why don't you get started?"

"Yeah, right," I said, and took another quick swig. Honestly what I wanted to do was drain the whole bottle in one shot like usual, but I had a feeling they wouldn't take the time to run back out and replace it, so I decided it was better to take it slow. I exhaled one more time and then set the bottle down next to me.

"It's like this," I said. I wiped my mouth on my arm and looked up at the ceiling. "Coleridge had it right."

"He usually does," Simon said. "I'm not too worried about that. The problem is we never got an explanation."

"I know," I said. "I have an explanation, obviously."

"You do? You're saying you know what he meant by 'they want the son'?"

I nodded. "Yeah, I do. We got the wrong idea, though; same sound, different word. It isn't someone's S-O-N the dybbukim want. Coleridge meant S-*U*-N."

The guys didn't say anything, but Simon's eyes narrowed just a little bit. After a second, though, Reese spoke up.

"So...? Ok. S-U-N. How exactly does that make it any clearer?"

"It makes it clear as hell," I answered.

"In what universe?" Reese said.

"Cut it out," Simon said. "Kroger, get on with it."

"Right. Anyway, what that means, Reese," I went on, and looked at him, "is the dybbukim want the *Midnight Sun*."

Simon put his hands behind his back, straightened up, and his face suddenly went hard as stone. Reese just looked confused.

"The fuck's that?" Reese said.

"Literally," Simon said, his voice calm and level, "it's a natural phenomenon that occurs in certain parts of the world, usually the Arctic or Antarctic regions, during which the sun shines all day and night."

"What?" Reese said. "What's that got to do with anything?"

"I said that's what it literally means," Simon said. "I get the impression Kroger didn't in fact mean it literally."

I shook my head. "No, but the idea isn't that far off, though."

"Go on," Simon said, and held up a hand to stop Reese from talking, thankfully.

"You told me about the dybbukim," I said, "Like you said, Simon, they were the first living things God made. They lived closer to God than anything else ever has, only—" I trailed off.

"God was dissatisfied," Simon prompted.

"—Yeah," I said, and took a breath. I had no idea why, but I had a hard time saying that. "He didn't like how they turned out, so, well, he got rid of them. Threw them away. They went from being neck deep in pure joy to full on misery. Well, they don't know why that happened, but all they want is to get back to where they were. Back—home. They want the light of God, but it was taken from them, and there wasn't anything they could do about it."

"...and...?" Simon said. I got the feeling he was prompting me to confirm something he had just figured out for himself.

"Well," I said, and then held out my right arm. The nasty X shaped brand stood out clear as ever like it always did. I saw Reese's eyes flick down at it real quick. "I had God's light, too. And then Marsh and McCormick and everyone else tried to rip it away from me." I started running a finger down one of the X's lines. Out of the corner of my eye, I thought I saw Reese twitch. "Only they failed. I kept the light, because I wanted to. Because I chose to."

I dropped my arm, and Simon and Reese just stood there a second, looking right at me. Finally, Simon took a breath.

"...And in so doing," he said, "You became—"

"The Midnight Sun," I finished. "The light that p-p-prevails in the deepest darkness. That's what the dybbukim say, anyway. They all wish they could be me."

"Why would anything want to be you?" Reese said.

"Because I'm someone who was told *no you can't have it* and said *fuck you, it's mine, I'm keeping it anyway.* And I won."

I thrust out my palm right into Reese's face.

"*Unterbrechen!*" I said, and a flash of white light shot out point blank into his face. Reese dodged it easily, but I smiled at him.

"Two for flinching," I said, and let my arm drop. "What, you forgot that one's useless against people?"

Reese frowned at me, but that was all.

"That," I said, "because I can still do that, even though McCormick and Marsh and Holloway and Wolfe told me I wasn't allowed, is why the dybbukim want me, and specifically me. Unlike every other Knight, I don't *rent* my power—" I looked real quick at Simon, but if he cared about what I was trying to say there he didn't say anything—"I *own* it. I took back and kept what they tried to take away. If the dybbukim can become one with my power, then they will also be able to take what they weren't allowed to have, even if God said so. Short version: they can all come home."

"You mean," Simon said, "That the dybbukim want you, and specifically you, because through you, they can completely transpose every human being on this planet."

I nodded.

"This is fascinating," Reese put in. "And you know this...how?"

"They sent me a business plan," I said. "What the fuck, I don't know. One of them was devouring me and suddenly I just knew everything about everything. Ask *them* how it worked."

"What about Casey?" Reese said.

It actually took me a second to realize what I heard. I blinked, and then looked at him like I couldn't believe my ears.

'What?" I asked.

"What about Casey?"

"Really?" I said. "Were you ignoring me this whole time? The part about all humans becoming monsters? Cataclysm?"

"What about Casey?" He said, and slammed his hands down on the gurney. The gurney shook and my beer fell over onto the floor; I made a mad grab for the bottle but I totally missed. All the rest of my beer ended up all over the concrete and the longneck spun off under one of the shelves.

"Oh, you dick!" I said.

"Cool it Reese," Simon said, and put a hand on Reese's shoulder.

"No!" Reese shouted, and swatted Simon's arm away. Or, I should say, he *tried* to swat Simon's arm away. It looked like Reese probably would have had better luck punching through a brick wall with a feather, honestly. Reese's arm just slammed into Simon but Simon's arm didn't so much as budge.

Reese glanced at Simon's arm, then at Simon's face, and back at his arm again.

"I said cool it," Simon said, and gave Reese a little tug. Well, it *looked* like he just gave Reese a little tug, but Reese actually stumbled back like five feet. "How exactly is that helping anything, Reese?"

Reese was kind of snarling and rubbing his shoulder, and he looked like he was trying to do his best to stare Simon down. That didn't last long. Reese exhaled and looked away. "Ok," he said, and all of a sudden his voice got a little softer. "I'm sorry. I just...want to hear that she's all right, ok?"

"I...yeah," I said. "I know, look, I didn't mean—"

"It's ok, just forget it," Reese interrupted, his voice trailing off.

"Right, Kroger," Simon said; he was still looking at Reese. "Please continue. And when you get around to it, why don't you tell us what you know about Casey?"

"Sure," I said, and looked at Reese. "I'll tell you. But this is probably gonna make you mad, Reese. Fair warning."

Reese looked at me, and his eyes narrowed.

"What's...that mean, Kroger?"

"If you must know, *Connelly*," I answered, "Casey's behind the whole thing."

"WHAT?" Reese bellowed. "WHAT ARE YOU---"

"*Shut up!*" I screamed, and, for some reason Reese did just that. He looked about as surprised as I felt, honestly. We just stared at each other for a second or two as if neither of us really understood what just happened. Finally, though, I spoke up.

"Do you want to hear the truth or not, Reese?"

"What kind of 'truth' is that bullshit, Francine? What do you mean, she's behind the whole thing?"

"Just that. We already more or less knew a wizard was doing it. Like Simon said, no one else would have the motivation or the ability. Well, that wizard is Casey. The truth is I saw her last night and talked to her and guess what? She admitted she sent the dybbukim after me. She wants me completely and all the way dead, Reese."

Reese Blinked.

"Go on," I said. "*Please* deny that last part."

Reese didn't say anything. I clicked my tongue, rolled my eyes, and took in a loud breath.

"Didn't think so," I said. "Good to know we're on the same page somewhere."

"Kroger," Simon said. "Continue, please. What did you learn from Casey?"

"Stop," Reese interrupted, and his voice sounded calmer than usual. "No. Kroger, Casey did *not* do this."

"Reese," I said through my teeth. "You told me yourself that she said she was going to the *store*. You were ready to kill me over it!"

"Because I thought she was under your orders!" Reese said.

"Well she wasn't!" I shot back.

"Stop," Simon cut in. "Reese, be quiet. Kroger, tell us everything you remember." Reese exhaled and stomped away a few steps, but he didn't say anything else.

"Fine. Let me start from the beginning," I said. "It's like this." I gave them all the details of my fight with the Jason-dybbuk and the giant all-in-one-dybbuk and what Casey told me about how surprised she was that my power seemed not only effective, but also *ridiculously* effective against the dybbukim. I told them all about how dybbukim were springing up all over the place after the fight adjourned to the highway, and how I have no idea what happened in the end because the big dybbuk engulfed me and then I was knocked out.

"Smoot," Simon said, when I finished. "Smoot happened. I wasn't able to make it to the scene personally until well after the fact, but that's blatantly obvious. She did go out that night, and if the aftermath broadcast over the news didn't have her mark all over it, there was of course the fact that you were hit with her greater mass amnesia and were pulled along when she recalled."

"Aftermath?" I said.

"*Horror on the Highway*, they're calling it," Simon said. "Almost a mile stretch of northbound 95 covered in piles of wreckage—but not one single body."

"No—bodies?" I said. "But..." At that moment, all I could think of was Jason. If there were no bodies, then...

Simon shook his head. "None."

I bit my bottom lip, but I couldn't think of a thing to say. Fortunately, Simon pushed on from there. "No one that was anywhere near to the scene remembers hearing or seeing anything, either," he said. "Smoot cleans up well."

"But the bodies, how could there not be—*ohhhh...*" I said. "All those dybbukim ..."

Simon nodded. "From what you just said, there were no bodies because they were all transposed. Thanks no doubt to their proximity to this giant dybbuk who had obviously gotten somewhat intimate with you."

"But..." I said. "That doesn't answer the question. Dybbukim still have bodies. What happened to all of them?"

"Like I said, Smoot cleans up well."

I blinked, and then my jaw dropped wide open.

"She—did she—she *destroyed* all of them?"

Simon shrugged. "I wasn't there, but Smoot always remembers which spells she cast and in what order, somehow; I got as much out of her later. And one spell she mentioned was what she called a *full spatial reversal*. Did she by any chance mention that she was out of stash?"

My eyes went up and to the left for a second. "Now that you mention it," I said. "Yeah. What about it?"

"Then yes, she destroyed them all," he said, as casually as if he was telling me it was five-thirty. "She carries a pouch full of Jimson weed joints to fuel her more ambitious spells. If she said she was out of stash, then she had to have burned through one hell of a lot of power. That was probably when she used the full spatial reversal, which would account for the lack of bodies."

"...*Jimson weed?*" I said, my eyebrows rising. Then I remembered that tiny little white cigarette Smoot flicked into her mouth when she was squaring off against Bob. I also remembered a massive burst of power just after that.

Simon nodded. "Datura stramonium; an extremely potent magical catalyst for those who know how. But we're getting sidetracked, Kroger. You've just confirmed everything I suspected. The dybbukim can manifest en masse, even if I was wrong about how it occurs. I had thought it was the wizard's doing, but from your account, Casey was as perplexed as you were."

"Seemed like it," I said.

"Wait," Reese interrupted. "I'm just supposed to buy that you conveniently remembered Casey doing all this?"

"Reese," Simon said, "The truth is I had the opportunity to trace back the carnage on the highway. Everything fits with Kroger's account, from the path of destruction, to the hole in the highway wall, to the state of her apartment and back yard. The evidence was in plain sight and ample. I even found her banjo."

"You found my banjo?" I said, perking up. For some reason even that ridiculous little point of light in all this crap was enough to brighten me up a bit.

"Later," Simon said. "There was also a black pickup truck halfway up the street, idling, with one door swung wide open. I didn't think anything of it at the time, but it's safe to assume it belonged to this Jason."

I felt ice in my chest when Simon said that. I remembered running to the window to see if I could catch Jason before he left, but by the time I got there he was already gone. He must have already been transposed by then, and . . .

"How do you know it was Casey?" Reese blurted, which broke my train of thought, thankfully. "What if it was this Smoot character?"

"Impossible," Simon said. "Smoot would not have ventured out on her own unless she sensed the presence of a dybbuk. I saw to that by putting in a post hypnotic suggestion, which was the only way I found to give her what amounts to a standing order. Essentially, I told her to remain where she was until she sensed the peculiar energy of the dybbukim; her sensitivity to that sort of thing is monstrous. Once she sensed them, she was to then transport both her and myself to the dybbukim. Aside from that, she would have no desire to leave her house and would vehemently resist the notion of doing so."

Simon was right about that. I couldn't have budged Smoot out or her bedroom for pie.

"Well, then it was someone else!" Reese said.

"It was Casey," I said.

"You can't prove that!" Reese said.

"Yes I can," I said.

"How?"

"Because—the dybbukim came at me through Raine and Jason!"

✷ ✷ ✷ ✷ ✷

"—What...?" Reese said.

"You and Casey were together, weren't you?"

"What—"

"Shut up, I'm not that stupid," I said. "Okay, I admit that I didn't know everything about what was going on and I got both of you in deep shit and fucked you both over. I got that. I can't even imagine all the shit you and Casey went through over me."

It took a second, but Reese answered.

"You don't want to imagine it," he said. "I wouldn't even wish that much on you."

I looked at Simon, and he nodded back at me. "He's right, Kroger."

"There's more," Reese said. "Do you realize that once they found out we were together—" his voice started to shake—"to keep me in line, they made me *watch*."

I glanced at Simon again, and he just gave a single slow nod. I looked back at Reese for a couple seconds before I said anything.

"I saw Marsh beat the shit out of Smoot," I said. "It couldn't have been better for Casey."

Reese just shook his head and looked away; I had to take in a breath before I could go on.

"So," I said. "On top of all that, they came down harder on you for my screw ups. I ruined the only escape you guys got from everything. Your only chance to be even remotely happy."

"You're preaching to the choir, Kroger," Reese said. "What's your point? What's this got to do with this Raine and Jason?"

"Because—I really—liked them," I said, and I have to tell you, I was amazed how hard that was to say. "I mean, a lot."

Reese and Simon didn't say anything right away, so I went on.

"That's it," I said. "That's why I know it was Casey. She wanted me to suffer like I made her suffer. She wanted to destroy any chance I had to be the kind of happy she couldn't be."

"...Isn't Jason a guy's name?" Reese asked, finally.

"Yes," I answered. "I know what you're thinking but---it wasn't ...physical, just—I don't know, our brains clicked. I realized he made me feel comfortable just being me. And then he said something about my dad...I guess it took me by surprise."

Reese blinked, and then he did about the last thing I expected him to do. He sputtered and started laughing.

"What the hell, Reese?" I said; I was flushing really bad. It wasn't easy for me to open up like I just did under perfect conditions let alone in front of these two. I think it must have been obvious as hell that I was blushing too because I'm so goddamn pale.

"I knew you were full of shit," Reese said. "You're forgetting something kind of important here."

"What's that?" I said.

"I became a dybbuk too," he said. "And so did everyone else. Remember?"

I froze. Holy shit, he was right. That sort of blew a hole in my idea, didn't it?

"So what are you saying, Kroger," Reese said. "Do you *like* me?" He made finger quotes around the word.

"Oh my *Christ* no," I said.

"Also, are you saying that Casey would sacrifice me just to get back at you? That contradicts everything you just said. Bullshit. You have no idea what the hell you're—"

"She's right, Reese."

That was Simon. His voice was calm and composed, but it cut Reese off like a chainsaw. Reese looked at Simon like the man just told him he was pregnant.

"What's that mean?" Reese said.

"Kroger is correct," Simon said, "But she has it backwards."

"How's that?" I said.

"I was mulling it over while you two were inanely jabbing at each other," Simon said. "Think. Casey's entire motive, as Kroger told us, was to attack Kroger without being caught. This is perfectly plausible given the consequences. It wouldn't make much sense, then, for Casey's plan to need micromanagement, as this would make it far more likely that she *would* be caught. No, she'd want to cast one single spell, one that was practically impossible to detect, that would trigger on its own based on some external stimulus. Fire and forget.

"Now, in order to make this one spell as difficult for Kroger to notice as possible, she couldn't make the spell trigger on something that Kroger herself did or felt. Casey knows Kroger is a Paladin of sorts—"

I scowled at him, but either he ignored me or didn't notice. Probably the first one.

"—and Casey is experienced enough to know that Paladins are trained to be sensitive to these things. If Kroger's emotional response were to trigger the spell, Casey had to have known there'd be a chance Kroger would notice it."

"So what's your point?" Reese said.

"That Casey would have done the next best thing," Simon said. "Rather than make the spell trigger from Kroger's emotional response, Casey made the spell trigger off of someone *else's* emotional response, *to* Kroger."

"Huh?" I said.

"Her spell turned you into a conduit for the dybbukim," Simon said. "And it activates when someone, as you put it—" He grinned— "realizes *they* 'like' *you*."

I blinked.

"It's an elegant solution," Simon said, "And I would expect no less from a wizard of her caliber. The goal was to transpose the victim once they experienced a powerful emotional reaction to Kroger, and that powerful emotional reaction made the target all the more vulnerable to transposition. It's like kicking open a double wide door."

I blinked again.

"So what's all that mean?" Reese said.

"Umm . . ." I said, falling back into my comfort zone, obviously. A second later I turned to Reese and smiled. "I'm pretty sure he's saying that Raine, Jason, that warlock, and . . ."

"Don't you say it!" Reese said, and pointed at me.

I had to do it. Lord knows Reese does his best to push my buttons all the time.

"...and *you* got the hots for me?"

"Fuck you, Kroger!" Reese said. He jumped at me, but Simon caught him on the shoulder and yanked him back; Reese flew clear across the room and hit the wall. He knocked over a trashcan and ended up wearing whatever was in it.

"Take five, Reese," Simon said. "Save that energy for later."

"Lick a sack," Reese said, from under the trash. "This isn't over, Francine."

Wonderful. It was nice to finally ding Reese a good one, but I really shouldn't have done that; the last thing I needed to do right now was to piss off Reese more. Between Simon, him, and the wall my allies in this mess were thin on the ground. Reese was already on a short fuse, and I had to defuse him quick.

"No, no, wait," I said, kind of quickly. "You're forgetting something."

"Which is?" Simon asked.

"Bob already had a dybbuk there, remember? From his kennels. That's how they all got transposed."

Simon thought a second, and then nodded. "Yes, that's right; in that case there already was a dybbuk present. Still, everything you've told me about Raine and Jason seems to fit with my supposition as well as anything. I think it's probable enough to use as our working hypothesis."

I had a feeling Simon was right, basically because I remember feeling like I needed an oxygen mask the first time I saw Raine, but nothing happened then. It could have been that Casey hadn't done her thing to me yet, but I think it's more because it worked the way Simon figured. It did seem to fit.

"One way or the other," Simon went on, "The main thing is, the dybbukim can manifest en masse, and very quickly once they've got their catalyst."

"Meaning m-m-me," I said.

"Yes, Kroger, meaning you. Did you learn anything else from Casey we might be able to use?"

"Well," I replied, "Fact is she didn't spend a whole lot of time explaining herself. But she did say she tried the dybbukim out on other paladins before sending them after me. Guess she wanted to be sure they were up to the job."

Simon nodded. "Brother Hanson, Sister Gregory and Sister McGowan," he said. "All murdered. And Marsh believes the Scions were the cause of it all. Hence the edict. She's also convinced you are colluding with the Scions somehow, which is why she was rather vigorously pursuing you."

"Wait," Reese said, from across the room. He hadn't bothered to even get up, so he was basically talking to the ceiling. "I don't get something. Why did Casey even show herself? She wouldn't have had any idea you were excommunicated. She had to know that if there was any chance you'd get away, she'd be implicated in the attempted murder of a paladin and obviously the others too. If she was lucky, it would take her *all year* to die. She's not that stupid, Kroger."

"I think it was because I was winning," I answered.

"Wha?"

"Simon said that the dybbukim are basically immune to a Paladin's power," I said.

"They are," Simon said. "They negate most conventional effects all together."

"Well," I went on, "That apparently doesn't apply to me. Like I told you, I was fucking them up with exactions a first term acolyte could do in her sleep. My Rebuke hit them like a bus, for crying out loud. Casey said she didn't know what to make of it."

"...I'm going to go out on a limb," Simon said, after thinking for a second, "and posit that it just might have something to do with your unique condition." He pointed at my right arm, and I glanced down at the X shaped brand. "That's the only thing I can think of that makes you a distinct case. It may be that the dybbukim cannot bear to confront your exactions directly because, as you said, your Light represents everything they wish they could be, but could not be. Perhaps a full-blown direct assault with that is more trauma then they can bear; like suddenly achieving full self-knowledge and not liking what you see." He shrugged. "All that is just a guess. As for the dybbukim's ability to somehow circumspectly harness the essence of your Light to enter our world, well...Casey obviously had no idea about that, if her reaction was any indication, but—"

"How could she?" Reese said; by this time he got into a sitting position. "She wouldn't have known anything about Kroger's condition anyway."

"—But she's every bit as responsible as if she did know," Simon said.

"What?" Reese said. He stood up and pointed at me. "Kroger just said Casey's spell only brought the one dybbuk. The others showed up on their own!"

"And if you struck a match in the middle of the woods, dropped it and walked away," Simon said, "Whose fault is it that the forest burned down?"

"That's—no, that's not the same thing," Reese said.

"Reese," Simon said. "Whatever Casey planned to do, whatever her intentions, she was playing with forces far beyond her ken. If she is the one who set the dybbukim loose, than every result of that is on her head. It is because of her and her alone that we face the destruction of our entire world."

"No!" Reese yelled. "Fuck that! It's because of you and her—" he pointed at me—"and all of you sanctimonious assholes! You did this to her! *You* made this happen!"

"Reese," Simon said, and he made that one word sound calming, and like a threat and a warning all at once.

"...Maybe if you all would just leave people alone..." Reese went on, but I could see Simon's voice knocked the wind out of his sails.

"I've already told you I don't disagree, Reese," Simon said. "And as you can see by the fact that I'm standing here, I'm in the same boat with you. But we can't allow Casey to bring about the end of the world."

"I can stop her," Reese said. "Let me just talk to her and I'll make her stop. Then we'll both disappear and I swear you'll never hear from us again."

"I think she's past that, Reese," Simon replied. "You were transposed too. Don't you think she may find that odd?"

"That—"

"Think about all that implies, Reese," Simon said. "How would that look to her, if we're correct about the impetus of her spell?"

"Well...first of all we don't know that for sure," Reese said, a little hesitatingly. "But either way, I can talk her down. Please, I know I can."

"It's too late for that," Simon said. "There's nothing left to do but stop her."

"If we do that they'll execute her," Reese said; he backed away a step and pointed at Simon. "On the spot."

"She's responsible for the murder of three paladins," Simon said. "Not to mention—"

"Good for her!" Reese said; he kept backing away. "She should get a medal!"

"I know her situation was untenable," Simon said. "But if we don't stop her she will have essentially murdered *everyone*. She has to reverse this spell she put on Kroger. One more transposition in a crowded area is all that's needed, and that could be the end. There's no other way."

"No," Reese said, and then he stood silent for a second, his eyes flicking back and forth between Simon and me. After a breath or two, he spoke up. "No, I think—no, you've—no, wait, I've got it, yeah! We've got it all wrong. Yeah, see, we've got it wrong. The problem isn't Casey. No, in fact, there's one sure fire way to fix all this right now."

"And that—wait! *Reese!*" Simon said.

It happened so fast I could barely react until it was over. Reese whipped out a pistol, pointed it at my chest and shot off three rounds as fast as he could squeeze the trigger. All of a sudden I was flat on my back on the concrete and I had no idea what just happened.

Until the pain kicked in.

And then I had a pretty clear idea.

Chapter Thirty One

My sister used to always say the coolest things. Of course, I only realize now that they were actually cool, back then I thought she was just being an annoying prissy dipshit.

Right then, as I lay on my back, I remembered one certain specific thing, and I heard her voice saying it clear as day in my head.

You get what you give.

Sure she didn't invent that phrase and probably heard it in a song or read it on a greeting card or something, but it's remarkable how the simplest overused phrases ring the most true. What people tend to forget is that there's a reason some things become clichés. It's because they hold enough truth to bear repeating.

That last bit I just said wasn't me; that was another thing my sister said. She was about a thousand times smarter than me, and that's being generous on my account. She was generally better at life in just about every way you can dream up. She was better at school, better to our parents and family, she always took initiative and she never got intimidated when things got tough.

Me, not so much. If I wasn't family I don't think she'd so much as acknowledge I was even alive these days. Or, maybe she might. She was and still is, after all, a way better person than me.

Point was, I remembered her telling me *you get what you give* all the time, and, like usual, she was dead on. I gave out lots of shit in my time, mostly to people who deserved it least. In fact, I think, in some twisted fucked up way, the fact that they didn't deserve it almost made it easier for me to do. It's sick, I know. But then I wasn't a particularly awesome person.

I gave out so much shit that finally I got shipped off to a catholic reform boarding school, which, as it turned out, was about the best thing that could have happened to me. It's corny, but it's true. That place turned out to be quite a bit more than just a reform boarding school. No, it was actually a recruiting and training ground for the

Knights. That place gave me the first real chance I had to make something out of my waste of a life, even though I got dragged into it fighting tooth and nail.

But Adobe Francine Kroger is who she is, fancy uniform and title or no. Even while I thought I was some kind of cool superhero I was just the same old selfish screw up. The only difference was that now I was dangerous, and not because I was a badass. No, I was dangerous because all of a sudden what I did actually mattered and had consequences to someone besides me. But did I even think about that? Hell fuck no. Everything was all about how being a paladin was such a great thing for me. How it could finally turn my life around and make such a huge fantastic difference. For *me*.

Then, there was Crow. Even when I was trying to finally make good on one of my biggest screw-ups I was being selfish. Looking back, I wonder if the reason I was trying so hard to get Crow back into heaven wasn't to do the right thing, but just to make myself feel better. If I was being totally honest with myself, I think it was entirely for the second reason. Forget that I ripped an innocent spirit away from peace and paradise; the important thing was how did that make *me* feel?

I've never put someone else before me, not ever. Hell, as recently as a day or two ago I kept on badgering Simon to tell me how he turned the Raine-dybbuk back into plain old Raine. I never even asked if Raine was actually going to live. And then I sent Crow to find out for me, but that was only to stop me from feeling guilty about not bothering to find out earlier.

Well, I definitely got what I gave. I gave nothing but misery, and so that's all I deserve. I'm actually not surprised I ended up on the floor bleeding out with a bunch of bullets in me. In fact, now that I had a moment to think about it, I would have been disappointed with anything less.

I couldn't breathe. I was choking and gagging and I couldn't stop doing either one. I don't know how long it went on, but—

"—Kroger?"

Smack smack smack smack.

"Come on, Kroger let's go—"

I blinked myself awake, and all of a sudden I was looking up at Simon. He was smacking me in the cheek.

"Cut it out!" I growled, and snapped my head to the side. "Get off me!"

"Stay here a second," He said, and he got to his feet. Then he started doing something but I couldn't see what it was.

"He—he *shot* me!" I said.

"I know, Kroger," Simon said. "But he only hit you once. I stopped the rest. And don't worry, I made sure you'll be just fine."

I patted gently around my chest and stomach area, bracing for the worst, but there wasn't any sign of damage that I could see or feel. Sure enough, Simon did good work. Shocking, I know.

"Where the fuck is he?" I said, and I tried to get up. I was still kind of sore, so the most I could do without much effort was sit up and scoot along the floor a foot or two so I could lean against a wall. "Did you get him?"

"No," Simon answered. He was cupping something in his hands just in front of his face, but I couldn't see what it was. "Right after he fired off his shots he made a very fast exit. I could have still caught him, but I decided to be sure you would survive instead."

"Well that's very neighborly," I said. "Holy shit, what in the fuck set him off?"

"It's rather obvious," Simon said. He didn't bother to look at me or anything, he just went on looking into his cupped hands. "He thought that everything would be solved if you were dead. No Kroger, no Midnight Sun, and the dybbuk apocalypse is a non-issue. Logical and efficient, and, yes, it would likely solve everything."

I blinked. Hearing it spelled out for me that plainly and bluntly, for one brief second I almost agreed with Reese for doing it. Cut off the head and burn the stump, kind of. Then I realized that what I was thinking about here was my death, and I got shocked back into reality. I guess it just goes to show that it's easier to make that kind of decision when it isn't your own ass on the line. Of course, once I began to consider it, I couldn't much help but have another thought I didn't much care for.

"If you agree that killing me would solve everything, why did you save me?" I asked.

"Your condition is your fault," Simon said, "but not its rather disastrous side effect. In that at least, you're innocent. Regardless of the consequences, I can't allow you to come to harm over it. Not while there's an alternative."

"...What's the alternative?" I said.

"Like I told Reese, we need to find Casey and make her reverse this spell of hers, which—" I saw him drop his hands all of a sudden— "as of now may prove slightly more complicated."

"I don't get it," I said.

"Smoot isn't responding," he said. "Which I'm forced to assume means that she can't."

"Smoot—What do you mean, they caught her?"

Simon shook his head. "They never lost her. This could mean one of two things, though. Either they found out about how she keeps breaking free of their lockdowns and have taken appropriate countermeasures, or, she's dead. Likely both."

"Oh," I said, which was extremely lame, but I couldn't think of anything else. I couldn't even imagine what Smoot would be going through if Simon was right. Death would probably be better. I didn't have much time to think about it, though, because after like one second Simon yanked me up to my feet like I was a toy.

"Wauuh?" I said. I wobbled around a bit and almost fell back down, but I managed to plant my hands on the gurney before I did.

"I have to find Smoot," Simon said. "You're coming with me."

Before I knew what happened, Simon ushered me down along a narrow gap between the wall and one of those huge, long shelves. It looked like we were really hauling ass because the shelf was so close by and everything was just whizzing past my face.

"Where are we going?" I said.

"I'm going to have to take a rather big risk," Simon said. "But there's isn't much choice. If Smoot was found out, it may be too late to do anything anyway."

"What do you mean?"

"If they discover how Smoot and I have been communicating and collaborating," he said, "Then they will not only be able to find me but also all of the sensible, rational Knights who have thrown in with me. If that happens, it's over."

He pushed open a big metal door with his side and motioned me through. We came out on a cracked-up, abused looking sidewalk on some deserted side road that didn't look like it was in anything close to a savory neighborhood.

"What about Reese?" I said.

"I'm afraid we'll have to proceed without his assistance for the time being," he said. "And he seems to have stolen my car. This way."

That wasn't what I meant, but I didn't have time to press the issue. Simon all of a sudden broke into a full on sprint, and I had to really haul to keep him from full on dusting me.

"How are you feeling, Kroger?" he called over his shoulder.

"Like shit, thanks! Why?"

Simon didn't answer. Instead there was a blast of white light, and all of a sudden he was running so goddamn fast it was like I was running away from him full tilt in the opposite direction. I almost lost sight of him before I got my head together and gathered up my prayer.

"*Geschwindigkeit*," I said, and felt the burst of speed shove me forward. I have to admit I got a good bit of steam going, but I wasn't gaining an inch on Simon. No, all I managed to really do was gradually slow down how fast he was pulling away. Still, I did keep him in sight, which I guessed was all he needed me to do. What a goddamn show off. It was like he yanked my banjo out of my clumsy hands and shredded the hell out of it right in front of me.

He took one sharp sudden turn after another, dashing down back alleys and between buildings, and I kept up, but only barely. I think all together we floored it for about maybe just over half a minute, and when he finally stopped short I damn near crashed right into him before I finally managed to stop myself.

"Easy, Kroger," he said. "How do you feel?"

Honestly, I felt like a wreck. I was sweating, I was doubled over panting, and I felt the beginnings of a massive headache. Simon, of course, wasn't even breathing hard. I swear to god I hate this man.

"I'm, I'm not too hot," I said.

"I can see that," he said. "Hold still."

He took both of my shoulders in his hands and looked straight into my eyes. His mouth moved a tiny bit, but I couldn't hear what he said, if anything.

"You need to eat, and soon," he said, after a second. "You're about a hair's breadth from blunting yourself again."

"Y—you think?" I said.

"Don't worry, I'll take care of it. This way."

"But," I said. "Wait, which way? This is a dead end."

"Not really," Simon said. "But I'm sure it will be in about five seconds."

"Huh?"

Simon didn't say anything; he just grabbed one of my shoulders and sort of rushed me forward toward the end of the alley. In a second I saw that I was wrong; this wasn't *technically* a dead end, since there was a dilapidated looking metal door right there that was absolutely covered in random blotches of spray paint.

In fact, after a quick look I realized that every color of the rainbow was there somewhere in that mess. Red, orange, yellow, green, blue—

For some reason, after seeing all those colors, something clicked in my head. I couldn't put my finger on what it was, though, and I didn't have much time to think it over, either. Simon just shoved the door open, pushed me through, and—

All of a sudden I was standing on a brightly lit, bustling sidewalk. I had to sidestep to avoid getting mowed down by a cyclist, and almost bumped into these two guys holding hands.

"Sorry!" I said without thinking, and one of the guys just held up his hand and nodded at me. They kept on walking like nothing happened, and then more and more people walked past me in both directions. I was surrounded by noise of all kinds, from slightly muffled music, car horns and motors, people babbling, and the plasticy thump of some guy sitting and playing a upside down bucket like a drum.

"Huh?" I said.

"Let's go, this way," Simon said, and off we went.

"Um, where are we?" I asked.

"Las Olas. About thirty miles from where we just were. I'll explain on the way."

Chapter Thirty Two

I blinked, but after a second everything kind of fell squarely into place. All of a sudden I knew why that spray paint on the door kick-started something in my brain. All those colors made me think of only one thing, and that was—

"Smoot," I said. "That door—"

"Exactly," Simon said. "Very good." We dodged around a group of people. "Ever since I've undertaken my independent *enterprise*, if you will, I've found it necessary to circumvent certain rules without sacrificing their benefits."

"That is to say—?"

"That is to say, I've had Smoot construct a number of unsanctioned Nexuses. Only I am able to use or authorize access to them, and even if that weren't so, only I know where each one leads."

"What, are they like portals?"

Simon nodded. "You were never authorized to know this," he said, "but as you may have guessed, many of the more senior Knights have rather had a knack for rapid mobility. That would be because every church in the purview of the Knights is connected to every other by way of a Nexus. They are perhaps the strongest deterrent the Knights have against attack since, if you attack one church, you effectively must fight them all. The Knights have the most powerful interior positions ever devised."

"Woah," I said.

"Now," Simon said. "My problem is several fold. First, I must Locate Smoot and gather all of those Knights loyal to me as expediently as possible. Also, I cannot leave you unattended, given the most recent developments. However—"

He glanced at me a second.

"In order to do the former, I cannot do the latter."

"What do you mean?" I asked.

"If I am to locate Smoot and gather everyone else as quickly as I need to, I must use the officially sanctioned Nexuses. Unfortunately... those exist only inside the churches."

My heart sank. I didn't need Simon to go on, but go on he did anyway.

"And as such, if I were to bring you along—"

"No thanks," I said.

"Exactly. Stop right here Kroger."

Here turned out to be a tiny little open-front pizza joint called Moe's. Just from one glance it was obvious that it was standing room only in the place, not that it had a lot of sitting room to begin with. I mean it was packed tight and jumping. All the same, Simon walked up to one of the tables, where some chick and a couple of surfer-looking guys were sitting and shooting the breeze. There was half a huge cheese pizza on one of those big silver round trays on top of a pillar in the center of the table.

"Time to go, folks," Simon said, looking at each of the people in turn. "Don't worry about your bill."

The chick and the guys took one second to look Simon in the eye, and then got up and left without a word or so much as a glance at their pizza or drinks.

Wow. Leave it to Simon. Yet one more thing I wished I could do. Someday . . .

But whatever. Simon motioned me into one of the now empty chairs. He sat down across from me.

"Eat up," he said, nodding at the pizza. "There should be enough calories in all that to stave off blunting for a while at least."

He didn't have to tell me twice. I dove on the nearest slice and stuffed almost half of it into my mouth in one go, and, by the way, this was one of those gigantic New York style pies where the slice was practically the length of my forearm. Christ, I was in heaven. Salty, cheesy, saucy, greasy heaven.

"Easy," Simon said; his eyes focused somewhere over my shoulder and then he nodded his head. A couple of seconds later a waitress plunked down a large red cup full to the top with fizzing, popping, glorious soda. Christ, what more could I want?

"Sweet," I said, and snatched up the glass and downed half of it before putting it back down. It was perfect. Just the right amount of syrup.

Simon didn't say anything for a minute or two, and I took advantage of the reprieve. I got through a second slice and almost an entire refill before he spoke up.

"So, here's the situation, Kroger. I have to leave you right here."

I looked up at him but went on chewing.

"Only long enough for me to do what I need to do," he went on. "Listen carefully now, I only have time to go over this once. Understand?"

I nodded.

"Right," he said. "I chose this place because it is one of the several sanctuaries I personally sealed against magical incursion. Any scrying will be useless, as will any magic cast by wizard, demon or Paladin other than myself within the restaurant's confines. Now—"

He turned in his chair and pointed across the street. "Do you see that flag, Kroger?"

I squinted a bit. "What, the Cuban flag?"

"No, the next one to its right."

"The Pride flag—? Ohhhhh...." I nodded, and all at once I understood.

Simon grinned. "Do you see?"

"Yeah," I said. "You're saying that's another—?"

Simon nodded. "Yes. The door directly under it is another of Smoot's Nexuses. My friends and I would use it to gather to this sanctuary. You, if necessity dictates, will use it to escape."

"Why that one?" I asked. "What about the one we just used?"

"Using the Nexus we just came through is out of the question," Simon said. "If the Knights do in fact have Smoot, and I have every reason to believe that they do, then they will have taken measures to trace back all signs of her energy. Essentially that means they will have detected the use of that Nexus and will have taken the next logical step, which is to turn that Nexus into a tar pit."

"Tar pit?"

"That means, the next person to use it will walk straight into their hands. It's what I would do, and I can't allow myself the luxury of underestimating the likes of Marsh, Wolfe or Holloway. So, here—"

He reached behind his head, fidgeted a bit and then pulled out a small talisman on a chain from under his shirt. He held it out to me.

"Take this. Wear this and you will be able to use the Nexus." I cupped my hands and he dropped the necklace into them; the metal felt warm, soothing and alive. "If anything, and I mean *anything* happens before I get back, use it. Do not pause. Once you're through, run as fast as you can out of the alley you'll find yourself in and turn left. Take that road three blocks and turn right at the stop sign. Two blocks up from there you'll find a bus stop, which is another minor sanctuary. Wait there for Sister Hendrie. Do you have it?"

I nodded. "Out the alley, turn left, three blocks, right at stop sign, two blocks, wait at bus stop." I bunched up the necklace in one fist, and ripped off another huge bite of pizza. "Got it."

"Very good," Simon said; he slid back his chair and stood up. "Good luck, Adobe."

My mouth was full to bursting, but as I watched Simon leave the restaurant and disappear into the night, I was way too shocked to chew.

It took a bit for my jaw to start working again, but I managed it. I don't know why I found it so startling that I just heard my first name, I mean, I've been hearing it my entire life whether I wanted to or not. But not from that man. Not like that. Not ever.

I mean, he'd been plenty generous with other forms of address, like the ever popular dumbshit, dipshit, idiot, moron, fucking dumbshit, fucking idiot, fucking dipshit, fucking moron and of course, the standard fallback *Kroger*. Sometimes he said my first and last names together, as in *Surprise, it's Adobe Kroger*. But there was always a kind of bored, sarcastic sneer lying just below the surface; only not this time. It was so weird to hear I had no clue how to react.

"Huh," I said. I blinked, shrugged, and decided to just finish up my mouthful and wash it down. After that all that was left of my slice was the crust, so I turned that sideways and bit off one end.

"Huh," I said again, and shook my head.

The waitress stopped by with yet another refill. By this time I was pleasantly full, though, so I just took my time with this one. The place was still busy, but no one bothered me to ask how everything was or if I needed anything else. It was like I was more of an actual guest than a customer, if that makes any sense.

I took a moment then to have a closer look at Simon's talisman. Like I said before, I loved how it felt in my hands; it was like every last part of it was as smooth as snow that no one stepped around in yet. The chain was what looked like flawless, gleaming silver that almost made me think of extremely fine chain mail armor, and I automatically thought that you could probably take a chainsaw to those links and the chainsaw would lose. I'd bet a sawbuck I was right, too.

And then there was the charm. I'll have to be honest, I was expecting something else, like maybe a gloriously appointed crucifix or some other kind of mystic religious kabalistic symbol or something like that. But it wasn't anything close. No, it looked like a small silver foot and talons of some kind of bird of prey.

My eyebrows went up (Yes, both of them. One of these days I'll get the whole one eyebrow thing right). Then I just shrugged and clasped the talisman to my neck and let it drop under my shirt.

✷ ✷ ✷ ✷ ✷

The street noise sort of fell into the background and became more white noise than annoyance, like one of those apps you can get for free on your phone.

Crap. My phone. Damn, I still never managed to make one goddamn phone call since all this shit started. What day was it anyway? I just realized I didn't even know that. Yes, I know it seemed a bit silly to keep harping on the whole phone call thing, but to be perfectly honest I could really use a small injection of mundane normalcy just at the minute, thanks, no matter how small an injection it ended up being.

That was when it hit me. I was sitting in a restaurant, which would most likely have a phone I could use. Go me for figuring out that brain buster, huh?

Well, I didn't waste another second. I got up and made my way over to the counter, and, wouldn't you know it, one of the girls there was indeed taking an order on a miraculously functional telephone. She looked like she was kind of in the weeds, though, so I decided to just sit back down and wait a bit before I bothered her to ask to use it.

And that was when I saw Casey Crumb standing out on the sidewalk looking right at me.

Chapter Thirty Three

Yep, there she was, with her jaw length raven black hair cut, hipster glasses, hoe and all. And this time she didn't look like she just rolled out of bed, either. No, this time she was literally dressed to kill. Thigh high purple and black striped leggings, black shit kickers with a purple stripe across them, black mini skirt with a purple polka dot pattern, purple undershirt and black overcoat that ran down to mid calf. She even had on purple lipstick that perfectly coordinated with her outfit.

And there I sat in a stained extra large blue and white tee shirt, faded baggy jeans, imitation converses, and my nasty ass natty hair tied up in a knot. I was already outclassed, and neither of us had said or done shit yet.

Casey took a step forward into the restaurant, but then she stopped short all of a sudden. She blinked, and then she looked slightly to one side, and then another. A second later she took another step forward.

Or, I should say, she tried to. She kind of just ended up jerking back a bit like she just ran into a really, really clean window she couldn't see. She looked at me for a moment, and then she held out one hand in front of herself, almost like she was groping in the dark. She waved it back and forth a couple of times, and then she reached out with her other hand, which was the one holding her hoe. This time, it looked like she was trying to hold the hoe out in front of her but couldn't do it for some reason. A second later she smirked, dropped the hoe on the sidewalk, and walked right up to my table.

"May I?" She said, and took a seat right across from me.

✶ ✶ ✶ ✶ ✶

"Umm," I said. But Casey just started talking as if I hadn't made a sound.

"Simon Frederick Bradley," she said. She put her chin in her hand and looked at me kind of sideways. "I wouldn't try to stand up to that man if he were tied hand and foot. Of all the Knights, he is the one who truly scares the dog piss out of me." She shrugged. "Not gonna lie."

"What is this, Casey?" I said, not that I had a whole hell of a lot of doubt what this was. I couldn't think of much else to say though.

"But," she said; again she was apparently ignoring me. "Even *he* is only one man, trying to do so much, and given everything he is trying to account for, there will inevitably be at least one minor thing that slips past him. This little restaurant is as potent a Sanctuary as any I've ever had the privilege to imprisoned in, and I'd bet my life he substantiated it all by himself. I saw immediately it'd be worthless to try to do anything fun in here."

"Cut the shit. What do you want?" I said.

"You see," she went on, "it's true I could never have found you my own way if I lived to be a million. Like I said, this place is the real deal. Magic just won't work. But—"

She nodded at something over my shoulder. Slowly, I turned and looked. A plump old Italian looking guy was rubbing down a cup with a dishrag, and looking right at me.

"Moe and I have an understanding," she said, and made a telephone shape with her thumb and pinky. "He let me know you were here."

I turned back and did my best to make it look like I was looking her right in the eye. Honestly though, I was actually trying to draw a bead on the Pride flag across the street, and if I could somehow make it there before Casey could do anything. Yeah I know, that's real brave of me, but I needed to get as far from this chick as possible before her friend Moe decided to go on helping her by asking me to leave this nice little Sanctuary. More than just my own ass was at stake if Casey decided to sick a dybbuk or two on me again anywhere near this crowded place, if that was still her plan. I didn't really have much choice but to assume it was.

Before I had more than a second to think all that over, though, Casey spoke up.

"So this is how it is, Kroger," she said. "I can't do anything cool to you while you're sitting here. But all the same, you're going to come with me, or I will walk right out of here and kill your entire family. Any questions?"

My heart just about blew up. I felt the blood rush to my face and my jaw clenched.

"What—did—you—say?" I said, and I almost didn't recognize the sound of my own voice. It sounded flat, lifeless, and, well, frankly a bit scary.

"You're out of time, Kroger," she said, and then she leaned forward, stood up, turned around, and started walking out of the restaurant. "Choose."

★ ★ ★ ★ ★

You're probably wondering right about now what I chose to do. If you want the truth, at that moment I was wondering the exact same thing.

Problem was, I was kind of in a little bit of a tight spot. Everything I just talked about from seeing Casey on the sidewalk to watching her leave took about one whole whopping minute. In that one whole whopping minute, I had several bombs dropped on me, each one bigger and worse than the last. In order, they were:

a) Oh holy fuck, it's Casey Crumb.

b) Crap, she's coming this way.

c) Whoever this Moe guy is, he gave me up.

d) Casey has my family?!

e) She's leaving and if I don't follow her . . .

I mean, I barely had time to process everything, and now I was being forced to make an impossible decision in something like half a second. So, given all that, what do you think jumped into my brain?

I'm glad you asked. Here's what it was.

Tactics.

★ ★ ★ ★ ★

Tactics—let's see, there's a break in the crowd, Casey isn't all the way out and she doesn't have that hoe of hers yet. I could jump at her from the table top, push her down, roll her to the right away from her hoe, and pray like hell. Make a ruckus, maybe everyone will freak out and panic long enough for me to knock Casey out and haul her away through the Nexus across the street. From there I take her to Hendrie who'll get me to Simon and then everything will be fine.

I loved this plan.

Casey was built a bit thicker than me, and if memory serves she was also three inches or so taller. But that doesn't mean anything when you factor in momentum and good old-fashioned gravitational marriage. Casey crumpled under my weight as if I was a boulder and we both fell forward and down, hard. Remember my plan? Well, this was about as far as it went. I had counted on us both landing right outside on the sidewalk, but we went sort of to the side and ended up cartwheeling over some couple's table instead. We took the whole table with us---I mean soda, pasta, pizza and all. All the food was freshly served, too, so I got a face and chest full of scalding hot cheese. Casey got a metal pitcher full of ice water square on her head and got her face buried in meat sauce. Everyone started screaming in surprise and panic before we even made it all the way down to the concrete outside.

Another thing I'd counted on was landing on top of Casey to both cushion my fall and give her an extra little wallop as all my weight came crashing down. Well that was another tits-up because I landed full force on the pavement before I could even so much as throw out my arms to brace myself. My cheek smacked down, and I saw stars and tasted blood. For a second I was so dizzy, I felt like I was standing up leaning against a wall instead of prone on the ground, and I momentarily forgot what just happened and where I was.

But fortunately I was only dazed for a second. I got it together enough to realize that I was outside the Sanctuary, and that meant Casey could sling all the magic she wanted. It also meant, though, that I could pray.

New tactics—Casey was probably in the same shape I was, which meant she was probably coming around too. I had no idea if she had her hoe yet, or if that even mattered, but I had to assume that she had it either way. This meant my first order of business was living through whatever she planned to do while I got ready to play her some chin music.

So, defense over offense it was. I wound up my shield prayer.

"Panz—"

Just as I was about to finish, something yanked me up into the air. I couldn't see exactly what it was because I was being shaken all over the place, but I saw what looked like a huge muscled man, and heard a weird combination of a growl and a hiss. I guessed about then that Casey obviously hadn't come after me alone. I thought that maybe I should have felt flattered by how dangerous she thought I must have been to need backup.

"—errr," I said, and I hoped the little break in my substantiation wouldn't mean I blew the prayer.

It didn't. And the prayer kicked in just in time, too, because this growling hissing guy threw me straight up in the air like a cap at the end of graduation.

"Waauuu—aaAAaa—UUFF!" I spun through the air like a propeller and landed hard on the hood of a parked car. The car buckled under my weight and the car alarm went off like an inch from where my ear ended up. It was so loud I felt like someone ran a spear through my skull.

"Awwww!" I howled, and I slammed my hands onto my ears and started kicking, writhing and rolling. That didn't really last long though, because I tumbled right off the hood something like a second later and landed flat on my back. I maneuvered onto my side just in time to see a boot swinging right into my face.

The force of that kick was so seriously strong that I almost got snapped in half backwards, and my whole body spun around like a lever. Other than that, though, I didn't feel anything. Go me for picking the right prayer to use, because I had the feeling I was going to need it a hell of a lot more before too long.

I wasn't wrong about that, either. I got up on all fours at the exact same time the big muscled guy threw another kick right at my midsection. He sent me flying down the road like a badly punted football, and I bounced and skidded and rolled to a stop something like twenty feet away.

Actually, despite his best efforts, muscle guy just did me a favor. He gave me distance, which meant he gave me time. I got into a super cool kneeling position almost right after I stopped moving, and I saw Mr. Muscles charging at me to continue his fine work that was so rudely interrupted.

Well, unfortunately, I was going to go on interrupting it. I fired up all my combat prayers and met the motherfucker head on, shrieking with glee.

★ ★ ★ ★ ★

Now, I know it seems I've spent a hell of a lot of time making it sound as if I was a total half-assed incompetent screw up, so let me take a second to explain why that is. Honestly, there is a part of it that stems from the fact that I really do still have a lot to learn and a long way to go in life, just like everyone else, really. But I think also the other main reason is something I've come to call the Watson syndrome.

You all know Dr. Watson, the constant companion and biographer of the world's greatest consulting detective. Over the years he kind of got a bad rap, I think, for being a kind of simpleton always twenty steps behind his ingenious friend. But anyone who read the original stories should know that Watson was actually a badass ex-army surgeon and a raging ladies' man to boot. You can't be a doctor and be slow upstairs, folks. No, but nonetheless he had his fair share of *Duh, I don't know* moments or he was just plain stupefied a lot of the time because the man he was trying to keep up with was *Sherlock fucking Holmes.*

I have a super bad habit of fixating on similar kinds of exceptional people who are, let's be honest, masters of their crafts. Like, Simon Bradley or Reese Connelly. Yes, next to them I don't have anything to say, but like I said, those men are just, well, *geniuses*, end of statement. Yes, I can't touch either of them in their bailiwick, but, all the same, like Watson, I do have some nice little chops of my own.

★ ★ ★ ★ ★

When I got up close, I saw that Mr. muscles wasn't any kind of normal human being (as if that wasn't already obvious). His face was livid and grotesque, and his mouth was way wider than it had any business being. Not to mention his teeth were closer to knives than anything else. It took me all of half a second to go out on a limb and guess that Mr. muscles here was in fact a vampire.

Well, hoo-ray. Finally, something easy.

He made the first move when we got in close, which was perfectly fine with me once I saw how god-awful clumsy he was. The fact is, just from watching his first wild left hook I could tell that he fought like a street brawler; which meant he was all power and no finesse or strategy. I'd bet a donut that he was one of those guys who went all in with every swing, and that every one of his swings would be exactly the same, too. If so, this asshole was about to get all of my pent up frustration dumped all over him.

I sidestepped and deflected his swing with my left hand, smacking his arm away and downwards. At the same time I lifted my right arm, fist clenched, and took aim at the side of his ugly face which was presently as wide open as the Grand Canyon. I gave him everything I had straight on, and I scored a perfect bulls-eye, too. His whole body whipped back around like I just went upside his skull with a sledgehammer, and he let out a sound that was like a roar mixed with gagging. I followed up immediately with a low left hook to his solar plexus, which doubled him over, and followed that up with a right uppercut to his nose. He staggered, and I heel kicked him sideways across one of his kneecaps, and then spun around and slammed a fist into his left lower back. Now he was on one knee, arched backwards and screaming like you wouldn't believe.

"Night," I said, and grabbed the vampire's head in both hands from behind. I twisted his neck all the way around as hard as I could, and then twisted it again in the opposite direction. I spread my arms and let the vampire go; he crumpled in a heap onto the street, and didn't move again.

It was only just then that I got fully aware of what was going on around me. To say the least, my little ruckus had caused quite a stir with the locals; it was probably aggravated by our little tussle in the middle of the street, which brought traffic to a standstill. To put it as lightly as possible, I was surrounded by random indistinguishable sounds of flat out confusion and commotion.

And it was about to get a hell of a lot worse.

There was a blast of red light and a noise like one of those two hundred dollar fireworks going off five feet from your ear. I jerked sideways almost by reflex and then dipped my head and covered my ears with both hands. A second later there was another ear splitting crash, and then I heard what sounded like a car's horn blaring. I spun around just in time to see a black SUV somersaulting through the air, hood over tailgate, right toward where I was standing.

I didn't give myself time to stare at it or swear; I just dove toward the curb to my left and curled up between two parked cars. The suv landed on its roof and pancaked, sending shards of glass and metal all over the street. Its horn was obviously stuck because it just kept going and going.

I think that must have done it for everyone on the street, because now there wasn't anything to be heard but full-blown panic. I lifted my head a bit and saw people running all over the place in every direction, bumping and shoving and pushing each other, just trying to get the hell out of there.

Just then the car in front of me, which I think was a Prius, all of a sudden flew cartwheeling into the air toward the opposite sidewalk. The Prius landed squarely on a blue pickup and just smashed it all to hell, and then both of their alarms went off at the same time. All that distracted me for only a second, though, because I saw something about half a block away that demanded my attention a whole hell of a lot more. It was little miss Casey Crumb.

She was a hell of a sight, I tell you what. She was standing dead center in the road, her feet solidly planted, her hoe held in front of her in both hands like a poleaxe. But that was just for starters. She looked like she was standing in the middle of a sort of shimmering cylinder of air, you know, like a mirage, and there was an occasional arc of green lightning sparking and popping all over her. Her hair and coat were blowing all over the place like she was in a wind tunnel.

"That's enough, Kroger!" She called. "Step out here or I'll blow this whole block to hell."

Well, so much for tactics.

What the shit was I thinking, anyway? Why the hell did I waste time with that stupid vampire? Why didn't I ignore him and at least make sure Casey was at least knocked out before mixing it up? All I accomplished with everything was to piss Casey off even more than she already was, if that was possible.

I don't mind telling you that I looked to my right and saw the pride flag flapping in the breeze, and for the space of half a second I seriously contemplated running for it. But, I didn't. For one thing, Casey had just made a rather compelling argument just now about blowing up the whole block, and I don't think she was bluffing, either. For another, there was that little comment she dropped earlier about my family. Yeah, I was fucked either way, really, but in the end I decided that it was better me than all of them, so I went ahead and did what Casey told me.

I got up and slowly walked to the middle of the street, and turned to face her. There we stood, like a pair of gunslingers at high noon, only Casey was dual-wielding miniguns and I had a straw with a spitball. All around us people were screaming and running, but if you can believe it I barely even noticed anymore.

"Do you know the things I've seen, Kroger?" Casey said. "What I've been forced to endure? No, I don't think you do; see, you just don't have the right things on the menu."

I didn't have anything to say against that, because more than likely she was right. Instead, I said the only thing I could say in my defense.

"I didn't know, Casey. I never knew. If I did I would never have allowed it."

She snorted. "Ok. Here's how it is, Kroger. There are 13 exemplar, 169 templar, 2169 judges, and 28650 sentinels. I say they've all been alive long enough. Your day is over, as of tonight."

"What do you mean?" I said, although by the time I asked I already had a pretty damn good idea what she meant.

"Tonight, we will attack you, and win," she said. "And you won't be able to stop us. Once we show everyone that the Knights can bleed, your holy house of cards is finished."

"Who's we?" I asked.

"Please," she said, kind of sarcastically. "Your stalling skills need work. But you should feel honored. Of all the Knights on this planet, you were the only one I insisted I be able to kill personally. But you've been a hell of a bitch about that, you know? I went through a lot of trouble to make it nice and meaningful and elegant but . . ." She shrugged. "I guess I'll just have to settle for this."

She thrust out her hoe like a spear, and then a beam of green light about as big around as a parking meter's pole shot out from its blade and right at me. I didn't have time to do anything but flinch.

★ ★ ★ ★ ★

Now, I'm no genius about wizard magic so I have no idea what kind of spell Casey just cast, but I don't think it would have been a long shot to assume it was a miniature version of the Death Star's super laser. Basically that means I think the whole point of that spell was to slam me with enough raw magical energy to vaporize me before I could even have enough time to think about it.

The trouble was, I apparently *did* have enough time to think about it, because, there I was thinking about it.

I had my arms up in front of my face, as if that would have done any good at all against what was obviously a full-blown power blast that Casey spent a good amount of time charging up. I didn't think that my shield prayer was *this* strong.

I slowly lowered my arms see what was happening. When I did, I was probably more confused than I was a second ago. There was Casey, her hoe still pointed directly at me, and there was the Death Star beam flowing out of it like some kind of fucked up fire hose, and the sheer force of it was tearing a groove in the pavement directly underneath. But here's where it got weird. Once the green beam got to within two feet of me, it split off to either side and flowed around me like I was a rock in a riverbed. I looked around and saw that the beam came back together once it got past me, and it was digging a hell of a ditch in the pavement a few feet behind me before the beam dissipated into nothing a foot or two further back.

"Huh," I said.

★ ★ ★ ★ ★

Casey finally let her death beam drop, and then she just stood there just like she was a second ago with her hoe held out, like she was frozen solid. Then she slowly tilted her head, and even from where I was standing I could see her mouthing *what ...the ...fuck ...?*

I was on the verge of saying the exact same thing, if you want the truth. I mean, I still had my shield prayer up and everything, but there wasn't any way in hell it could have stopped something like that spell cold. I've been hit with blasts that sort of resembled what Casey just did before, and even with my prayer up it hurt like a bitch and I got knocked around like a doll. This was totally different. It was as if the damn spell just ignored me altogether.

That was when I noticed it—there an ever so slight pulsing sensation and warmth right near my heart. Both of those things definitely were not there before.

It hit me all at once, and I grinned like a deranged lunatic. The talisman! The talisman protected me!

"Simon, you fantastic son of a bitch," I whispered to myself.

"Oh...oh *yeah?*" Casey said. "Fine!" She lifted her hoe with both hands like it was a flagpole. Almost immediately, a massive bolt of searing white lightning shot down from the night sky with a sound like a whole volley of guns going off. The lightning hit the blade of her hoe and, unlike a normal bolt of lightning that comes and goes in the blink of an eye, this one kept right on dancing and arcing all over and around Casey's body.

Well, as you could probably guess, being the practical sort, I wasn't about to just sit around waiting to see what would happen. That was mainly because I knew damn well what would happen. I mean I didn't exactly think Casey was planning to give me a massage, and though apparently this miraculous little eagle's foot Simon lent me was a talisman in the literal sense of the word, I couldn't afford to assume it would render me permanently invincible.

So, I did the only thing I could do. I charged at her, as fast as my combat mobility prayer would let me.

"No! Kroger!" Casey screamed; her eyes shot open wide and then she leveled her hoe at me. Actually, it was more like she was *struggling* to level her hoe at me. It looked like she was trying to swing it underwater if that makes any sense, like she really needed to put her back into it, and she was growling and snarling like she was lifting weights. For a second it looked like she almost lost control of the lightning, but only for a second.

She finally got her hoe pointing right at me, but by then I was ten feet away.

"NnnGRAGH!" She said, through clenched teeth, and the lightning shot straight for my chest at point blank range.

✶ ✶ ✶ ✶ ✶

Casey didn't disappoint. That lightning spell of hers was something else.

Only I didn't get so much as scratched.

No, the bolt came to within about a foot of me and then forked off in all different directions, and I mean *all* different directions. One bolt hit a van to my right, and the van folded in half and exploded. Another bolt just blew a fire hydrant to pieces and ripped a gouge in the sidewalk behind it; water burst out from the concrete like old faithful. Another bolt tore into the second story of a storefront, leaving a burning gash mark like it was slashed with a knife made of fire; bits of broken glass and wood flew into the air like confetti. Another bolt left a scorched trail on the street a dozen feet long and kicked up fist-sized chunks of concrete. Another took out a street light in a blinding shower of sparks, and another blasted a sidewalk bench to splinters.

I took in all of that sort of out of the corner of my eye. I didn't have any time to give it any more attention, because I had something else much more important to think about.

My aim.

✶ ✶ ✶ ✶ ✶

I can't do what Casey just did. Not at all. I couldn't chuck a guided missile strong enough to split a building no matter how much I tried, and forget about being able to do it from half a mile off. As I said earlier, a Paladin's power is mostly limited to the reach of her arms and legs or whatever weapon she's holding. Since, obviously, I wasn't lucky enough to be holding a weapon just at that moment that left me with one option.

My fists.

Yep, all I had against Casey's power to turn reality inside out was the first two knuckles of my left hand. And I couldn't afford to miss, because I had enough time a split second after the lightning hit me to notice something that couldn't have been good. Simon's talisman suddenly started burning like it was a griddle left on the heat way too long. Now don't quote me on this but I had a feeling that signified that it was close to reaching its limit. Or, it could mean the exact opposite for all I knew, but I doubted it. So basically I had to assume that any more wizard crap out of this chick would mean my death. That meant I needed to drop her, now.

By the time I got in close Casey must have already figured out what was going on, because her eyes went about as wide as they could go. I'm sad to say that I didn't give her a chance to do anything else. I know; I'm a miserable person.

My fist felt like it practically mashed Casey's face inside out. I mean her face felt so soft and delicate it was like punching a pillow filled with the most luxurious down you could think of. There was no resistance in her at all. Her glasses flew off to who the fuck knows where and she spun three times before she landed flat on her face on the pavement. I couldn't help but wince a little when I saw her head bounce off the ground once before she finally stopped moving completely. Her hoe clattered along the concrete for about ten feet before it hit the tire of a parked car.

And that was that. Casey was out cold. All of the power that was pulsating through the air vanished like someone just tripped over the power cord and turned off the TV. If you want to know the truth, for some reason I felt kind of let down and disappointed about that.

I looked at Casey, and then I looked down real slow at my fist. A second later something gradually started to click in my brain. It was something so obvious and simple that only I would have missed it for so long.

Basically, it was this. Casey, and for that matter, all the other wizards I've had the pleasure of knowing could do things I couldn't even begin to understand or duplicate. You could threaten me with death by water boarding and I don't think I would ever figure out how to call down lightning from the sky and turn a garden hoe into a tesla cannon. As Casey said earlier, I just don't have the right things on the menu. All of my time spent training whatever talents and potential I may have had took me off in a completely different direction based on a completely different set of rules.

But here's the thing. Casey or any other wizard couldn't do what even a half assed ex-acolyte like me could do because, like Casey just said, *they* don't have the right things on the menu. Not necessarily that either of us were flat out incapable of doing what the other could because of some inborn defect, it was just that we developed our abilities differently. My whole point is that the Casey menu was strong where the Adobe menu was weak, and vice versa. It was almost as if these two different 'menus' were trying to...I don't know, *complement* each other?

To put it in Adobe terms, I was useless outside of my box, but Casey was useless inside it. She was the queen bitch until she got within my area of expertise, and then suddenly she wasn't shit. All it took was one sloppy left hook and all of her showy sparkly power meant nothing. Hell, I don't even think I would have needed a combat prayer to finish her off, either. Seeing as that I did put a combat prayer behind that punch, I was seriously beginning to wonder if I just flat out killed her.

Crap. Once that thought found its way into my brain, I came real close to panicking for a whole hell of a lot of reasons. But I didn't have any time to do a damn thing about it, because before I could so much as get my thoughts in order—

"FREEZE! SHOW ME YOUR HANDS!"

Chapter Thirty Four

I was so shocked I spun around without realizing I'd done it. All of a sudden I was staring down a pair of cops pointing their weapons at me from behind the hood and trunk of a cruiser parked diagonally across the street about twenty feet behind me. The cruiser's lights were flashing and the spotlight was pointed at me so I couldn't really see the cop's faces too well. Talk about oblivious; until they shouted at me I had no clue they were even there.

"I said stop! Show me your hands!"

My hands shot up. Way up. It was practically a reflex. My brain hadn't kicked back into gear yet.

"IT'S KROGER!" One of the cops yelled.

"Down on your knees!" Said the other.

"Wha—? I—" Obviously I was still kind of unable to think straight.

"On your knees Kroger! Hands behind your head!"

These cops knew me? No, it was more than that. It was—

Shit! Of course the cops would be after me, if the Knights were after me. Perfect. What kind of story did Marsh and her goons bake up? Oh, what the hell did it matter anyway? I could have gotten framed for anything from domestic terrorism to killing a cop or whatever it would have taken to get the police after me in full force. I guess even though I knew it was coming it was still surprising to see it actually happening.

But here was the thing: If I let these guys take me in it was over, and if I ran or fought back it was over because they'd just keep coming after me harder than ever until they got me. Either way, Adobe Kroger was fucked.

"ON YOUR KNEES NOW!"

No more time to mess around. These guys sounded seriously serious. I got down on my knees.

"HANDS BEHIND YOUR HEAD, INTERLOCK YOUR FINGERS!"

I did that. I saw the cops come out from behind their cruiser, weapons still trained on me. One of them reached down to a pouch on his belt and pulled out a pair of handcuffs; that one walked around behind me while the other one stood a few feet in front of me, his weapon pointed straight into my face. I looked back at him while his partner took one of my wrists and slipped a cuff around it, and he stared right back at me like he wanted nothing more than to just squeeze that trigger and blast my brains out.

And I think that look of his was what did it. That look of his could have been easily mistaken for just plain old fashioned hate, but that wasn't what it was at all. No, this was something else altogether. I'm not sure how or why this thought jumped into my head, or why I was so sure I was right, but it did, and I was. What I was seeing was the look of a genuinely good man forced to stare down the face of genuine evil.

Somehow I could see, or at least I imagined I could see everything that motivated this cop to do what he does, and the huge main reason was to free the world of things like what he thought I was. In other words, things that stopped the world from being good.

Over the course of the last couple days, in between everything else, I've found out quite a few things about the Knights, that glorious organization that was the one thing that managed to give my life its first and thus far only semblance of meaning. I didn't like any of those things I found out, either. But this, this was the last straw. I decided then and there that one of the most evil things anyone could do was to exploit the intentions of a good man. Smoot was right. I was dealing with some dark, dark shit.

"I'm s-s-sorry," I said to the cop, as his partner was cuffing up my other wrist. Through the glare of blue and red flashing lights I could see the silhouettes of a crowd of people gathering round to see what was going on. I could also hear a low, dull babble that I guess was the sound of all those people gabbing away.

"You shut up," the cop said. "You have the right to remain silent. Anything you say c—c-c-c—"

He stopped short, and blinked. That was when I saw it.

On the tip of his nose, there was a small black dot. It wasn't there before.

It felt like everything just dropped into slow motion. I watched everything unfold and there wasn't anything I could do to stop it because it was like it already happened, if that makes sense.

The dot on the cop's nose spread out until it was a line that ran all up and down the center of his face, and then more lines spread out from the same center point until it looked like there was an asterisk all over his face. And then . . .

His face split apart into six fleshy petals, and I saw rows and rows of teeth running all around in circles down his hollow gullet.

I think I screamed, but I don't remember hearing my own voice. The dybbuk lunged down at me, mouth wide.

I did the only thing I could think of: I ducked backwards, but I must have momentarily forgotten that my hands were cuffed because I kept right on going and hit the ground, hard. That bought me enough time to raise my legs, though, and I managed to snag the dybbuk's head between them.

"What the fuck?" Said some guy's voice. It sounded real close by so I took a wild guess and figured it was the other cop. Not that it really mattered. I felt a terrible, terrible cold rip through my body, and I almost went numb.

"NO!" I cried, and I whipped my body to the side, taking the dybbuk with me. I rolled and for a second I was straddling him, but I didn't hang around.

"*Springen*," I said, and I pushed off of my knees and sort of flailed backwards through the air in a messy, ungraceful arc. I made up for it by landing on one knee in a super cool pose, totally by accident.

I looked up, and what I saw almost stopped my heart dead.

I saw that both of the cops were dybbukim. And there must have been twelve more behind them.

"No No no no ...." I said in a quiet pathetic voice. I whipped my head around in all directions, and all I could see, creeping out from behind the glare of the cruiser's lights, were more dybbukim.

This was it. It was over. I was standing in the middle of downtown Fort Lauderdale, and every second that went by was bringing everything closer to the end. I did this. This was my fault. All because I was too selfish to live with the guilt of a mistake, all because I refused to surrender my bond to the Light for some unknown and unreachable chance to make myself feel better for screwing up, all because I wanted to be able to look myself in the mirror, I was about to bring about the end of everything.

I could have run, but to where? I was in the middle of a populated urban area, and I would probably just spread the dybbukim even faster if I—

Of course! The Nexxus! But wait, first—

I whipped around like mad, and I managed to spot Casey. She sure as hell wasn't knocked out anymore; no, she was half crawling, half dragging herself down the street, her hoe in one hand. That persistent bitch must have transposed the first cop while my back was turned! I had to get out of here and she needed to come with me whether she wanted to or not. By the time that thought crossed my mind, though, the dybbukim were closing in tightly around me, and fast.

Well, here goes.

I snapped the cuffs apart with one sharp tug, and spread my hands out in either direction.

"*Unterbrechen!*" I yelled, and a blast of white light shot out in both directions, and, as I was expecting, bowled the dybbukim over like ninepins. I charged through the throng, and ended up using one dybbuk's shoulders as a springboard to get over the outermost edge of the crowd.

I overshot Casey by a good six feet, and slid to a stop like a runner trying to beat a throw to home plate. I twisted around a bit to my side, and then our eyes met. Oh, and if you think I waited for us to actually stare each other down and maybe narrow our eyes dramatically you're crazy. No, what I did was push off with my arms and legs, and I launched myself forward along the ground like a torpedo. I twisted and threw a wild jab and, by the grace of whatever luck I had left,

I got her right between her eyes. Her head snapped back and then forward on to the concrete, and she quit moving after that.

A second later I was on my feet and had Casey up over one shoulder in a fireman's carry. I looked back and forth over the storefronts on the opposite side of the road and, after a couple seconds, I finally spotted the pride flag.

I pushed off as hard as my legs would let me, and I came straight down on a dybbuk that was crouching on the roof of a town car. The pride flag, and that precious door underneath were just ahead. I jumped again, but I miscalculated and hit the wall directly over the door, hard. I dropped Casey, and my arms flailed all over and I ended up tearing off the pride flag on my way down.

I landed in a heap, but my shield prayer held so I was perfectly okay. I automatically apologized to Casey before I realized what I was saying, though.

The dybbukim were all over us like gigantic ants before I could even get on my feet. I sent Rebukes flying wild in every direction, and the tide fell back just enough for me to get Casey on my shoulder again.

And then I saw it—the street was packed tight, standing room only, with dybbukim. There were easily hundreds of them.

That was enough for me. I pushed open the door and began to step through, but something sharp, cold and wet closed around my leg. A dybbuk had managed to latch on.

"No!" I screamed, and shot one more Rebuke. The dybbuk let go but quick with a high-pitched squeal. Without looking back or waiting one more second, I stumbled through the door and slammed it shut.

Or I should say I *tried* to slam it shut, because I wasn't fast enough. A dybbuk got its hand jammed in the door and stopped me from closing it all the way. Good sweet hell, did it make the loudest, most painful sound I ever heard. I mean scratching a chalkboard would have been like soothing raindrops next to it. And then it felt and sounded like the door was taking artillery fire, quite literally. There was a fury of thumps and thuds and the door was buckling and shaking against me. I was leaning against the door with everything I had, and my feet were shuffling as I tried and failed to push the damn thing shut.

"Mother-fucking-shit-sucking-two-balled-BITCH!" I growled through my teeth. This wasn't working, even with my prayer it felt like I was gradually losing. The sheer weight of the crowd on the other side of the door was just too much.

And then somehow my brain suggested something, almost like it was doing its job. I know, I don't get it either. Thing was, the door was big and heavy and metal. It was just right for what I had in mind. I thought. Maybe.

Well, it couldn't possibly be any worse than what I was doing right now. I guess that was something. Sort of.

I let Casey's body slip down from my shoulder and into both hands, which I have to admit took a little bit of squirming especially because I had to keep pressure on the door at the same time. When I finally did it, it must have looked like I was some guy from a movie carrying his dead girlfriend just before he does the big *Noooo*.

Once that was all done, I bent one knee and braced a foot against the door. I guessed I was as ready as I was gonna get. I closed my eyes and took a deep breath.

✶ ✶ ✶ ✶ ✶

I pushed up and away from the door, and at the same time I heaved Casey forward and away. Behind me the door began to swing open.

I corkscrewed in mid air and swung the heel of my left leg around just in time to make contact with the door. The second my foot hit, I substantiated my prayer.

"*Festigkeit*," I said, and a surge of power shot through my muscles. Here was the part I wasn't sure about. See, I already had this same exact prayer going already, and I had no idea what would happen if I substantiated it all over again. I've reaffirmed prayers in the past, which basically meant I focused long enough to make sure they were maintained. But I never resubstantiated with the intention of redoubling the prayer's effects. I was about to figure out whether or not it would do what I expected.

I'll save you the suspense. It did what I expected and how.

The door swung shut so fast that it was closed before I even got halfway to the ground, and it slammed so hard that it almost sounded like a full on explosion. I hit the ground sort of sideways and I had to roll a bit before I got oriented again. When I did, though . . .

"Woah."

There was a huge splatter of blood all over the wall on one side of the door, and it was riddled with guts of all shapes and sizes. Over to the left there were still shuddering pieces of limbs, a head, and most of a torso. It took me another second to realize that I was covered in blood, too. Like, seriously, and mostly in the face.

But the door was closed, and the horrible sound of all of those gargling, choking throats was gone. All I could hear was blessed, dead silence.

Chapter Thirty Five

I think I took over ten breaths before I realized I was just sitting there like a goon. I didn't have time for this; I needed to get going, fast. I sort of half crawled, half shuffled over to where Casey was lying; she was still as limp and lifeless as ever.

"Please, please, don't be dead," I said, and touched her neck with two fingers. It took me a second but I found a pulse. Sweet Christ that was a relief. I closed my eyes and let out a huge puff of air. I didn't waste another second. I got her over one shoulder again and took off running down the alley, trying my best to remember Simon's directions. After a moment I could hear his voice like he was standing right next to me:

Run as fast as you can out of the alley you'll find yourself in and turn left. Take that road three blocks and turn right at the stop sign. Two blocks up from there you'll find a bus stop, which is another minor sanctuary. Wait there for Sister Hendrie.

Off I went, like I was on rails. I kept up a nice steady jog most of the way, which I feel the need to brag about since I never got past week three on my couch to 5k attempts. The streets were for all intents and purposes deserted, thankfully, and so the only sounds I heard were the soles of my sneakers slapping the pavement and my own steady breathing. Also, I was able to hug the shadows most of the way, which went a long way towards making me feel a little safer lugging a body around with blood all over me.

My mind started wandering after a block or so; I really couldn't help it. My feet, my heart and my breath created a weird kind of relaxing rhythm that cleared my head somehow or other. After a second, though, I honestly wished it hadn't.

Mainly all I could think about was the army of dybbukim I left behind. It wasn't like I had any choice in the matter, though. It was either

A) Cut and run or
B) Add fuel to the fire or
C) There was no C.

There. Was. No. C.
No, wait.
There *was* a C.
There was a C, wasn't there? Yes, yes there was. There most certainly *was* a C, and a hell of an effective C, too. Reese saw that C full and clear and plain as day. I could just kill myself and end it, couldn't I? How's that for a C? Why, That C would . . .

No, no, fuck that C. Fuck it sideways. That C was out of the question, at least until Crow was back where she belonged.

Wow. I just realized something. What kind of self-centered monster was I?

The whole reason we were standing on the brink of possible annihilation of the human race was because I needed—no, not even needed, just *wanted* to assuage my own goddamn guilt. Because I screwed up in a monumental way through my own over confidence in abilities I never had and never will have and didn't feel like living with it, I was bringing about more destruction than I ever could have imagined. I hadn't changed at all. Everything was still all about me.

Because I didn't know what I was doing when I tried to get Crow home and only made everything worse, I had to face the consequences. Marsh and McCormick had fun with that one. Trouble was, I was too stubborn—no, I mean too *selfish* to accept the consequences because I thought I was entitled to fix everything under my own terms regardless of what everyone else thought, simply because I chose to do so.

And now, thanks to my own choice, I've become a conduit for the death of my entire species.

But here's the thing, and this is what really scared me most of all, I think. Even knowing all that, I wouldn't have changed a thing. Not for pie. Even knowing everything I know now.

And that's the one thing that stopped me from wanting to even consider option C, which Reese had arrived at so brilliantly. Yes, I think if I were dead the threat of a worldwide mass dybbuk massacre would die with me, but that wouldn't really work for me. It wouldn't work for the same reason I refused to give up my light when those bastards burned a scar into my skin that could never heal.

But even though that was probably the only thing I've ever felt absolutely sure of in my whole waste of a life so far, why shouldn't I feel an equal amount of disgust with myself over it? I mean, who the hell am I to put my own desire to get Crow home over everything else, given what that turned out to cost? I must really be the most evil person I know. Worse than all the demons I've ever fought. Worse even than Marsh.

No.

Yeah, even her.

But you know what? Even after all that, somehow I realized I couldn't give two shits out of a dead dog's ass, and anyone who had a problem with it can go fuck themselves.

✳ ✳ ✳ ✳ ✳

I didn't have any way of keeping track of time, but it felt like I made it to the bus stop in less than five minutes all together. I have to tell you that it was as nondescript as a bus stop could get; all it had was a beat up old bench and a small sign attached to a concrete streetlight. Still, it was hard to miss the place since the streetlight shone directly on it, making it look almost like it was a spotlight on some stage somewhere.

I was still completely alone from what I could tell. Honestly, it looked like there hadn't been anyone else but me in the area for the last three months, and I couldn't blame everyone for keeping away. This whole area looked like it just gave up and rotted away completely like a disease-infested corpse.

Now that I was here, though, I realized something, which was that there was a kind of big gap Simon left in my course of action. What I mean by that is, he told me to get here and wait for Sister Hendrie, but I had no idea how to let this Sister Hendrie know I was waiting for her. Hell, I didn't know if I even needed to let Sister Hendrie know that I was here, or if she was looking out for me, or however the hell this was supposed to work. Basically, that meant I just ran out of things to do, and that wasn't a happy thing.

Well, seeing as that was the case, I did the only thing that seemed to make sense in context. I plunked Casey down on the ground in front of the bench and had a seat. A second later I leaned back and let all my prayers drop. It felt kind of weird when I did that, too, almost like a combination of relief and disappointment. I don't know how else to explain it.

I let out a huge sigh and shut my eyes. There really wasn't much else I could do, and that was the problem. Not doing anything meant I was free to think, I mean, really seriously think, and that wasn't what I needed right then. I didn't need time to dwell on shit and not have anything to do about it. I hate that most of all.

Fortunately for me, I got interrupted.

"Done."

"HO!" I jumped and almost fell off the bench. It's not like I was scared, just really surprised to go from dead silence to hearing that sudden sound from out of nowhere. I recognized the voice almost as soon as I heard it, though.

"Crow?"

"Yeah, idiot," she said. She swooped down in front of me from out of nowhere and hung in midair like she always did, looking like she was floating underwater. "What now?"

"W-w-what do you mean what now?" I said; I was still getting situated on the bench.

"I went and found out where that guy lives so you can give him Six bucks," she said. "It took forever because he didn't go home for a while and he slept a lot, too. He just drove and rode and flew all over."

"Wh—oooh, yeah, the guy in the red car," I said. "Where does he live?"

Crow answered like she was reading off of a teleprompter. "17 Shepards Cottage, High Street, Barbraham, Cambridge, CB22 3AG. I think."

"Where the hell's that?" I said.

"Why'd I know, idiot?" she said. "I just saw it on one of his envelopes he opened."

"Oh," I said. "Thanks, I guess."

"What now?" she asked. "I wanted to go home, but it's all gone."

"Oh, yeah, that," I said. "Yeah, that's—oh, I don't know. Honestly, Crow, I don't have the first damn clue."

"When *do* you?" she said, and swooped around so she was more or less sitting next to me.

"Not often," I said.

"Not ever," she corrected.

"True enough," I said, and sighed. "Everything's going real bad, Crow. It's all my fault, too."

"I know," Crow said.

"You know?" I looked at her. "You know what's going on?"

"No," she said. "I know it's your fault. It's always your fault."

"True enough," I said again, and I couldn't help but smile sarcastically at myself. "I guess admitting that is the first step toward growing as a person."

"You're never gonna grow," Crow said, as if she was telling me the earth was round and I thought it was flat. "You're way too stupid."

"Hey now," I said. "You don't have to be mean about it."

"I'm not being mean, idiot," she said. "It's the truth."

"Oh is it?" I said. "You know, you don't have to add *idiot* to every sentence you say to me. I get the idea, already."

"Whaddaya mean, idiot?" she said.

"I know I made a lot of mistakes, especially by you," I said. "I think I'm setting my own self on fire over it plenty without you constantly dumping gas all over me . . ."

I stopped, and I had no idea why. I didn't know it just then, but I just at that moment I realized something, or, I should say, I *started* to realize something. I wouldn't put my finger on it exactly for a little while yet.

"What are you talking about, idiot?" Crow said.

"Um," I said. "I—I'm not—" my mind was still making a kind of vague connection, but I couldn't make it fully so I dropped it. "Nothing, forget it."

Crow shrugged. "Ok. What now?"

"Like I said, I don't really know. I'm kind of backed into a corner at the minute. I'm waiting for someone to help me out of it."

"You mean for a change?" Crow said.

I scowled, but only a little. I'm not sure why, because Crow threw that lame line at me more times than I could hope to count, but this time it kind of really stung.

"Crow, I know it's really not my place to ask, but would you mind cooling it for a bit on that?"

"What are you talking about, idiot?" Crow said.

"I—Ugghhhhh, never mind," I said.

"I'm not," she said. "Oh, she's moving."

"She's—" I said, and then I realized what Crow meant. I looked down just in time to see that Casey had gotten to her feet and was making a break for it.

✶ ✶ ✶ ✶ ✶

"Shit," I said, but it didn't come out shocked or surprised, just really annoyed. I can't believe I was so out of it I didn't notice and probably wouldn't have noticed if Crow hadn't said something. But it's not like it mattered, not really. Casey was obviously not in really good shape because she was more hobbling along than running. All told, it was really kind of a pathetic sight.

"Casey," I said, and got up and took off after her. Actually, I barely needed to even jog to start gaining on her. It was practically one step up from walking after someone who was trying to crawl away.

She half turned around and pointed a shaky finger at me. "Y— you stay the fuck away from me!"

"Casey," I said. By then I got a hold of her by her shoulder and she stopped short. She whipped an arm around and tried to knock off my grip, but even without any combat prayers Casey was soft as silk next to me. I spun her around and grabbed her by her overcoat. We were face to face, and the look Casey gave me wasn't what I was expecting. The look wasn't wasn't anger or fear or frustration, it was more like contempt.

"You better kill me this time, Kroger."

"I don't want to, *Crumb*," I retorted. I was getting really sick of having my last name thrown at me like I was gutter trash. I copied her tone perfectly, even if I do say so myself.

"Why, so you can watch them execute me?"

"I don't *want* them to execute you," I said.

"Oh, of course not," she said. "You'd have them throw me into shadow again, first, wouldn't you?"

I Just kept my eyes locked onto hers for a few seconds. I really, really wanted to hit her again, but that wouldn't end up solving a thing. Well, I guess it would make me feel better for a few seconds, but that was it.

"Crow," I said.

"What, idiot?" Crow said from somewhere behind me.

"...Crow?" Casey asked; she looked genuinely confused, and one of her eyebrows went up. For fuck's sake, can everyone on the planet do that except me? "What the hell are you talking about?"

"Could you get her, please, Crow?" I asked.

"Ok," Crow replied.

✱ ✱ ✱ ✱ ✱

Casey was sitting next to me on the bench, as straight as if her spine was a solid metal pole. Her hands were on her lap and she was looking in my direction, sort of.

"Got her, Crow?" I asked.

Casey, or, Crow, nodded. "She's much easier than that other lady."

"Gotcha. Ok, could you ease off enough so she can talk on her own?"

"I guess," Casey, or Crow said. A second went by, and then I heard Casey's voice again.

"You better kill me," Casey growled, which sure as hell sounded more like Casey than Crow using Casey's voice. I guess that meant Crow did what I asked. I leaned in a bit.

"Casey, you'd like that, wouldn't you?" Casey didn't answer, but she sort of grinned back at me, which I could tell took a little bit of effort. "You'd like it if the big bad Pally snuffed you, wouldn't you? It would justify everything you've done, wouldn't it?"

"What I've done is only what should have been done a long time ago," she said.

"What? Killing innocent people to turn them into weapons?"

Casey blinked. I had a feeling she hadn't been expecting that from me.

"...I'm not killing them, I'm transposing them. Not that you'd understand."

"Oh, I do understand," I said. "These dybbukim are people on some other plane. You force them to swap places with people on this one."

Casey looked like she wanted to say something, like she had something planned to say I mean, but my answer threw her off.

"Y—how?" She said.

"Forget it," I said. "Tell me how throwing someone on to some other plane is any different from killing them."

"Because—because I can always switch them back afterward," she said, kind of lamely.

"Funny," I said. "I don't recall ever seeing that happen. Do you even know how?"

"...Fuck you," she said.

"Sure. So tell me. You whipped up some spell to turn me into a gateway for these things, didn't you?"

"...Wow," Casey replied, and her face got a little dark. "Did you like, skip to the back of the book or something?"

"If there's any book I wish would end soon," I shot back, "It's this one. But anyway, you set this thing to fire off when someone starts to like me. Am I right?"

Casey whipped her eyes toward me, and then she snorted. "Well holy shit, there's no fooling you, is there? But actually no, you're only half right, I'm afraid."

"What's that mean, Crumb?"

"...It has to be *mutual*," she replied, with a super tight, nasty looking grin.

I blinked, and then scowled. "You're an evil cunt, you know that?"

Casey just laughed as best she could without being able to move much. Holy shit did I ever want to dislocate her jaw. Instead, I counted to ten in my head (in German so I had to think about it a bit more, to give myself more time) and then:

"Ok, whatever. Why couldn't you just send a demon or a construct out to do your dirty jobs? Why this whole roundabout process that needs a person's *life* to work?"

Casey took a breath, and did her best to stop chuckling. "Since I apparently don't have much else to do, why not tell you the rest of it. It's because the dybbukim exhibited a tremendous resilience to your goddamn pious magic. That, and the Knights had no idea what they were or where they were coming from. So, it was easy to pin their origin on the Scions. From what I saw, that worked like a charm."

"And that was important because you wanted to start a war between the Knights and Scions," I said.

Casey grit her teeth, but didn't say anything.

"Yeah, I know the whole deal," I said. "You figured they'd both be so busy fighting each other that you could move in and knock the Knights down. Did I miss anything?"

It took her a second to answer.

"Yes," she said. "Only that the war has already begun, and you've already lost. Just so you know, I've taught several other wizards to transpose dybbukim, so it will only be a matter of time before all of the churches within fifty miles are completely over run. And you can forget about your precious Nexuses, we've solved that little problem too." She smiled. "Once the churches in this area are destroyed, the rest will follow soon after. So, as I said, your day is over. Do whatever the fuck you want with me."

"Ok," I said. "I'll take you up on that. But first, you need to remove this spell of yours, now."

"...Yeah, about that. No."

"You aren't exactly in the best position to refuse, you know."

Casey gave me a crooked grin. "Who cares? Like I said, it doesn't matter anyway. You're too late. Besides, I'd be happy to kick it if I knew whatever happened afterward, you'd never be happy again. I'm telling you, just thinking about that makes me want to prance through a meadow of daisies singing 'Ode to Joy'."

"...As fucked up as that is," I frowned, "that's not why you need to remove it."

"That so?"

"Yeah, it is. I don't know how much you managed to see before I knocked your lights out, but there's one small detail about this spell of yours you need to know."

"Oh really? What's that?"

"You didn't seem to understand why you sent only one dybbuk after me and we ended up with a crowd of them. Still curious? It happened again tonight in case you missed it. Oh, and I saved you from them. You're welcome."

Casey just looked at me. I leaned back and threw my arms over the back of the bench.

"Would you like me to explain why this little strategy of yours could very well end all human life as we know it?"

"I would *love* for you too," said a voice that was definitely *not* Casey. The sound of it almost froze the blood in my veins. My eyes went wide and I half jumped, half stumbled off the bench. I turned and looked, and had my worst fears confirmed. I wasn't imagining it. It was definitely . . .

Marsh.

Chapter Thirty Six

She wasn't alone, either. She had with her two Knights in full light combat regalia, what must have been a wizard judging from the sparks dancing all over his baseball bat, and . . .

Reese.

Reese?

"It's Kroger," Reese said. "Just like I said."

"Yes," Marsh said. "Sister Hendrie was indeed quite useful. You've done well, myrmidon."

"So, I did what you needed," Reese said. "Now it's your turn."

"You will get what you want, myrmidon," Marsh said. "Make no mistake about that, and sooner than you may think. It would seem the apostate has saved us the time of locating your wizard."

Casey was still sitting still and straight, but her face told a whole other story. I don't think I had ever seen someone turn pure white before.

"But hello, what's this?" Marsh said, and took a step or two closer. "I believe I've seen this before. Yes, indeed."

I had no idea what the hell she was talking about, but I found I couldn't move or talk. Marsh took another couple steps and looked at Casey, tilting her head.

"It would seem that the apostate is up to her old tricks," Marsh said. "Well, I'm afraid that ends, now."

It wasn't until Marsh stretched out her arm that I realized what she was doing, and by then all I could do was watch; it was over so quickly.

✴ ✴ ✴ ✴ ✴

Marsh yanked her hand back, like she was pulling on some kind of invisible rope. At the same time, I saw Crow leap out of Casey's body, and her tiny little blue-white self froze in midair about two feet away. I had enough time to hear Crow let out one tiny squeak before Marsh slashed her arm through the air.

A half second later, Crow arched her back and then just ...broke apart. Into a thousand pieces, like she was made of glass. The pieces drifted in the air for as long as it takes to blink, and then they all faded into nothing.

What happened next ...well ...Wait, gimmee a second.
I—
I'm sorry, I just, I just have a real hard time dealing with remembering that.

Ok.

It felt like everything stopped, like when the film would catch on a two-reel projector and the heat would start burning a hole through the picture. Finally, though, it seemed like the projectionist got his shit together and fixed the film because everything started moving again. Fast. But it was still kind of unfocused.

I remember howling so loud my throat almost started to burn. I remember charging at Marsh. I remember letting loose every prayer I knew at once. I remember swinging at that bitch with everything I had left in me. But, she was better than me. Faster, stronger, and much more experienced. She blocked one shot, and another, and another, and then she got me square in the face. I growled but I didn't even slow down. I tried to grapple her but she got me in the ribs so hard I thought her fist went straight through me. I kept trying to grab at her anyway for whatever good that would have done, but a second later I was hit with pain so excruciating I couldn't even stand up. I think I remember hearing my own voice screaming as if from a distance, and then everything went upside down, and out. Hard.

It took me a second to be aware of anything, at all. Or maybe it was ten seconds or a hundred, or maybe even ten thousand, I had no idea. Also, when I said *aware of anything at all* I meant that quite literally because it seemed for a good long while I was off drifting in a sweet, silent void far away from everything. I should have known better.

The first thing I noticed was a weak, far off pulsing sensation, slow, but steady. After I noticed it and focused on it I could tell that it was coming from inside my own ear, and the more I focused on it the louder and more painful it seemed to get.

I managed to get my eyes open, and although I couldn't really tell where I was exactly, I could tell that I was on my side, cheek on the floor.

Slowly, the pulsing sensation became a throbbing, and it seemed to slowly spread out and over my whole head. The more it spread, the more it hurt, until it was so severe that I was clenching my jaw against it before I knew what I was doing.

And then, something that was the next best thing to a bowling ball hit me full on in the face, and I cried out with a voice that felt and sounded completely ruined.

"Get her up," I heard Marsh's unmistakable voice say. A second later someone got a hold of both of my arms and yanked me vertical. There was no chance of me standing up, but they seemed to be ok with letting me slump to my knees, which is exactly what I did. I must have looked like every beaten prisoner you've ever seen, what with my sagging shoulders, hunched back, and lowered head. For the moment, I was staring at the floor, which seemed the safest thing to do just then.

"Look at me, apostate," Marsh said. I hated where this was going already.

All the same, though, it wouldn't have accomplished anything to piss her off, so I went ahead and did what she asked. I raised my head.

And, sure as hell, there was Marsh glaring down at me. Only—
—I saw behind her—
—an altar, and—a crucifix!

I couldn't help it, I screamed out loud and almost fell over backwards. I would have done it, too, but a pair of really strong hands stopped me and held me in place.

I couldn't believe it. I whipped my head left and right and every other direction, taking in everything I was able to see. I was kneeling on a soft, elegantly designed, oval shaped section of carpet. This carpet was sitting at what could be called the apex of a triangle formed by three sections of wooden pews with wide aisles in between each one. The pews were sort of arranged I guess like stadium seating; they rose up a bit after each row and there was a huge balcony in the back. All along either side of this humungous room were floor to ceiling stained glass windows with images of the Stations of the Cross.

I guess there wasn't any way around it. I was in a church!

Only—

I looked back at Marsh, and my face must have been a sight to see because she actually cracked a smile, which I swear is maybe the second time I've ever seen her do anything like it.

"Oh yes, apostate," Marsh said. "You are not mistaken. You are in fact within a sanctified dwelling of the Lord."

I didn't say anything. I couldn't. I took some more quick looks around and noticed some things I didn't think were as important as the tiny fact that I was in a church. There were at least ten other people in here, sort of in a loose circle around the oval of carpet. There were a couple Knights and three myrmidons from the look of their uniforms, and three wizards, two with baseball bats and one with what looked like the wood handle of a mop. And then, mixed in with all that, I saw Casey. She looked different without her glasses; almost, I don't know, smaller. Also, from what I could see, Casey was the only wizard without a focus. Seeing her alone, with a sort of blank, almost desolate expression made me realize just then that I couldn't see Reese anywhere.

Finally there was the bruiser holding me in place. I twisted around and got a good look at him; he was a massive brick wall of a Knight who, judging from what I could see of his insignia was an Acolyte Sentinel third class.

Just like I was.

"Under normal circumstances," Marsh said, "being here would not be pleasant for you. The Exaction responsible for that, with which I supplemented your richly deserved excommunication, has been for the moment, rescinded."

I was about to give her my best confused look, but suddenly I heard something that sounded something like a very large caliber gun going off somewhere outside, maybe a block or two away. It made me jump, I don't mind admitting. A second or two later there were several more of them, but they weren't nearly as loud, so I guessed that was because they were further off. I could also hear, faintly, what sounded like a crowd of voices yelling over each other.

"Yes," Marsh said when our eyes met again. "As if you didn't know, open warfare has been precipitated by the foul filth you have thrown in with."

Holy Christ, I thought. *Open Warfare? You mean it's actually happened and already started?*

"As of this moment," Marsh continued, "One quarter of downtown Miami has already has been overrun with violence, rioting and looting. Additionally, many of our main districts, including this one, have come under what appears to be organized assault. You, apostate, shall assist us in ending it before it spreads any further."

I tried to think of something to say, but I came up short except for:

"How am I supposed do that?"

"Oh, but that's really quite simple," she said. "You will tell me how to find all of your co-conspirators, the true architects of tonight's blasphemous treachery."

"Help you find my what?" I said.

"You and I both know you are unfit to be anything more than the meanest foot soldier. You take orders; you do not give them. You will help me find the one who *does* give orders, the only one with a mind capable enough to be responsible, which I regret not realizing sooner. Where is Simon Bradley?"

"What are you talking about?"

"As I have told you, apostate," Marsh said," I have blocked the exaction that assaults every cell in your body when you enter consecrated ground. But it needn't remain that way. Observe."

Well.

I don't think I need to elaborate much on what happened next. But, just in case, let me just say that Marsh wasn't bluffing, and, like she told me, I observed. I observed the holy shit out of it. I'm not sure if it was intentional or what, but when Marsh went ahead and put that vile exaction of hers back on, the pain didn't hit me all at once. No, it started in my midsection like I was skewered with a trident, and then tore through my back and belly like that same trident ripped right through me and back again. I couldn't do anything but crumple and scream, although I'm going to have to go ahead and brag that it was a nice, full, back of the throat scream, not a high pitched sissy squeal. Go me. Marsh let me thrash around for a few seconds, and then finally, the pain stopped.

"Though you are an apostate," Marsh said, like nothing happened, "you were a paragon of right and virtue, once. That is the only reason I brought you here, to grant you one final chance to make good. To recant the evil that, by your own volition, has all but annihilated the best of you."

"The best of me?" I sputtered. "The fuck would you know about the best of me?"

She poured on the pain again, and this time it spread all around my whole torso. I think I bit my tongue, but that was the least of my problems.

"A Knight of your limited experience," she said, a second or two after she let the pain drop again, "managed to defeat an archsuccubus. It was an achievement to be held as an example for all. But then you willingly facilitated the creation of another archdemon. Soon after, you consorted with traitorous wizards and demonic forces to bring about these monstrous creatures responsible for the death of three of the finest young Knights I have had the privilege of teaching. And on top of that, you consorted with wicked spirits for the purposes of domination and manipulation. Do you not see how far you have fallen?"

"The wha—" I said. My brain was still doing somersaults after that last trip into the deep fat fryer, so I missed about everything she said, except for one tiny little part that jumped out at me. Somewhere in all that crap she said *wicked spirits*. Once I realized that, I asked the next question without taking one more breath.

"What did you do to Crow?" I croaked, and I have no idea why I bothered. I knew damn well what happened to Crow, but for some stupid childish reason I guessed I could still pretend it didn't happen, as long as I didn't hear . . .

"Crow?" Marsh said.

"The g-g-ghost. What did you do to her?"

"Ahh," she said. "So you've gone so far as to name it. Well, It has been exorcised, of course. I have sent that malicious spirit back to the depths of hell, where it so rightly belongs."

"She—" I said. "-she—hell ...."

Of course. Who was I kidding? I knew that from the moment I saw Crow burst apart. That is the one and only destination for any spirit hit with a full-blown exorcism, whether the spirit possesses a body or flies free, that's the only place it goes.

So. That meant the innocent little girl spirit I tore out of heaven, the one I tore away from peace, tranquility, happiness and contentment, was now trapped forever, in hell.

I gasped and panted and let my cheek hit the floor after Marsh removed that exaction one more time. I was drenched in sweat and I was having a hell of a hard time staying awake.

"Now," Marsh said. "Let me make one thing clear. You are your own destroyer. It was you who brought yourself to this end, through the atrocities you committed and helped to commit. If you do not recant of your own free will, and assist us in undoing the evil you have wrought, your soul will be damned for eternity."

Damned. She said—damned.

I don't know if it was delirium over the heaping helping of name brand torture or what, but for some reason hearing that word, the word *damned*, kick started my almost broken brain into motion like a rusty decrepit steam engine making one last try at the big freight run.

"Damned," I said.

"Yes, apostate."

"Does that mean ...I'll ...I'll go to hell?" I said.

"None other."

My next thought came out as clear as any I could ever remember having.

"Good."

My screams were becoming much less like growls and much more like screeching. Marsh was letting the pain go on longer and longer each time, and this time it covered every inch of me as far as I could tell. When she let it drop, I dropped too, like I had no bones left in me. The Knight that was holding me up quit holding me up and I hit the floor like I weighed five hundred pounds.

"You—" I said, after about ten seconds of panting and drooling. My voice came out almost all breath, like I had the world's worst case of laryngitis. "You—why are you doing this? If you want to know something why can't you just use revelation? You'll see I don't know shit!"

"Unfortunately," Marsh said. "Revelation has proven to be less of a panacea than we had thought. Particularly if the individual still holds the belief that continuing to conceal is just and noble. I think you are in a distinctly suitable position to hold that belief."

"What are you talking about?"

"You are an disgruntled excommunicated Paladin, who believes that those who enacted your punishment are agents of evil. You saw your own evil as righteousness and sought to lash out at those who were truly righteous. You sought to destroy all that is good *because* it is good. I think you would believe in your purpose strongly enough to resist Revelation."

"That," I said, "Or maybe you just get off on this."

My body exploded with pain I couldn't even begin to describe. When it was over, I felt the aftershocks for at least seventeen seconds. I was full on trembling and whimpering.

"It would seem that you still haven't quite grasped your position," she said. "So allow me to make it very plain. You will die, apostate. You have no choice about that. The only choice remaining to you is the ultimate fate of your soul. So, again, I ask. Where is Simon Bradley?"

"L—l—listen," I said. "You want the truth?"

"I'm listening," she said.

"Fine," I said. "You want it you got it. You said that—that what I did to destroy that s-s-succubus was the best of me. Well...guess what? It wasn't. It was the WORST. What I did after, what ended up making the archdemon, *That* was the best of me. So, get it over with! I *want* to go to hell!"

"Do you really?"

That last voice wasn't Marsh's. No, not even close. It was a calm, smooth, almost soothing male voice. I heard a couple of gasps and shifting steps, and Marsh herself turned off to the side like a rope jerked her.

"Father McCormick?" She said.

"Sister Marsh," said McCormick, and he slowly stepped into view alongside Marsh. He looked down at me, and smiled.

★ ★ ★ ★ ★

"Adobe Francine Kroger," said McCormick. "Acolyte Sentinel third class, Six points Cathedral, House Whytehearte, fifth abbey. It has certainly been an interesting few days, hasn't it."

I looked up at him as best I could, mostly sideways because I had a hard time lifting my head. I don't mind admitting I was both weirded out and comforted at the same time by the way he looked back at me. It looked like he was half concerned and half ...leering? I don't even know if that makes any sense. I was also pretty sure he heard every last word of my little rant just now, but if he did, he sure as hell wasn't letting on.

"Is that a question or a statement?" I said. "I would have to say *yes* and *no shit*, respectively. Hurry up and kill me already."

Marsh stepped forward a bit, but McCormick held up a hand and stopped her short.

Oh, now, let's not be so precipitous," he said. "I don't believe you sincerely want to die. On the contrary, I believe that you desperately want to live."

"That so?" I said.

"Yes. In that respect I don't believe we are all too terribly different, you and I. I too, passionately want to live. Above all else, that is my desire."

"Congratulations," I said. "Have a nice life."

He smiled. "Oh, I assure you I have every intention of doing just that. And I know that you do as well, despite your protestations."

"Oh, but you'd be wrong," I said, imitating his tone as best I could.

"No," he said, "I don't think I am. Brother Edelson, remove her shackles, please."

"What?" Marsh said. "How can you—"

"She is not to be harmed," McCormick said, looking at Marsh quietly. "As it happens, in this instance we were greatly mistaken about her—she is entirely innocent of tonight's events."

"What—?" Marsh said.

"I know what you have told me; I haven't forgotten," McCormick said. "But she is every bit as much the victim as you or I. She had no choice but to act as she did in the police station and thereafter. You see, she was under severe coercion from one of the most gifted and powerful Knights to grace our world in near on a century. She had to obey or die."

Marsh kept her mouth shut, so McCormick turned back to me. "Brother Edelson, if you would please, her shackles."

"Yes, Father," said the bruiser behind me, who, I figured was Edelson. He fiddled for a bit and my wrists came free. Then he hoisted me up onto my knees. That was when I noticed that McCormick hadn't come in alone. In fact, he had a small crowd of his own with him. There were at least eight Knights in full combat regalia, about six or seven myrmidons and four wizards with bamboo poles.

"Everyone, please be seated. I have sent word to London and Berlin for Wolfe and Holloway to join us here; I intend that all branches of the order be made aware of the evening's developments. They should arrive at any moment. Once they are here with their contingents, I shall begin." He looked at me, and then he motioned to a pew. "Would you like a seat, Ms. Kroger?"

"What is this?" I said; I stayed right where I was, but everyone else was filing into the nearest pews. Well, everyone that is except for a pair of Knights who, by their uniforms, were a bit high up on the ladder. The wizards with the bamboo poles stayed, too.

And Casey.

Those Knights, the wizards, and Casey took up positions on the altar behind McCormick, like a row of ceremonial bodyguards. Marsh glanced at them for a second, and then moved to the front row of the pews to my left.

"What indeed?" McCormick said. "It would seem that there was a minor plot of sorts hatched tonight, one that, if successful, could have had rather far reaching consequences. I am here to assure all of you, sister Marsh especially, that any imminent threat of that plot achieving its goals has been soundly eliminated."

"Has it?" Said Marsh. "But father, I have heard differently. In fact, You can hear that less than a mile from here—"

Marsh wasn't just blowing air, either. You could still hear faint crashes and commotion from somewhere outside.

Still, McCormick cut her off with another wave of his hand. "We have nothing more to fear from the radical elements that have attempted this middling uprising," he said, "and I can speak with full confidence on the matter. As I have said, the other heads of the order should arrive at any moment, now that the attempted sabotage of the primary Nexuses has been handily foiled."

"It has?" Marsh said. A couple of big booms went off, just then, and I swear they sounded a little louder, but maybe I was imagining it. Marsh and McCormick obviously noticed also.

"Indeed," McCormick said, and he sounded as calm as ever, like those noises hadn't even happened. "It would seem our radicals rather drastically underestimated the efficacy of our security. No church was cut off from any other for more than few moments. Ah, and here we are, It appears Wolfe and Holloway have arrived."

Sure enough, a column of Knights, some in light combat regalia, others just in dress uniform (which looked more or less the same, but was mainly for show), came out from a huge double door on the rear wall. They fanned out and streamed down the aisles to the left and right of the center group of pews. There had to have been at least thirty Knights all together, including maybe ten wizards and myrmidons bringing up the rear.

"Father Wolfe, Holloway, brothers and sisters," McCormick said, and made his way up to the pulpit. "Thank you for coming so quickly. Please, if you all would, have a seat."

"Certainly, Father," Holloway said, and made a hand motion. The column behind him turned and filled the second empty row to the front, and the rest filled in the next rows up. Holloway himself took a seat up front next to Marsh. Wolfe did the same thing Holloway just did, without saying a word. Once everyone was settled, including Edelson, I was left on my knees in front of everybody, and I have to admit it felt slightly awkward. I didn't have time to do anything about it, though, before McCormick spoke up. By then I decided to stay put.

"Brothers, sisters, loyal servants of the light," McCormick said, looking for all the world like a preacher delivering his Sunday sermon. "Tonight we have faced a series of rather troubling events. I am here to assuage any worries or concerns you may have about the effects of those events, which, thankfully, have been relatively minimal. However—"

He paused and let his eyes sweep the room.

"The effects are of little concern next to the cause."

"How do you mean?" Holloway asked.

"As Sister Marsh can readily corroborate," McCormick replied, nodding at Marsh, "The provocateur of this attempted coup was, it ...pains me to say, one of our own, and not just any one of our own. The one responsible was—" he took a breath—"Brother Simon Frederick Bradley."

The whole room gasped almost all at once, and then I heard the babble of a bunch of people talking in whispers. McCormick held up his hands and lowered his head.

"Attention, please, Brothers and Sisters," he said. "Attention!" A second or two later, the room quieted down.

"That is only the least important point," he said. "Yes, it is shocking and tragic to see such a exceptionally gifted genius as Bradley come to this end. But as I said, that is the least of it."

"How could that be the *least* of it?" said a Knight three rows back, which set of another chorus of babbling. McCormick quieted them all down again.

"It is the least of it next to Bradley's motive," McCormick said. "At first glance, is does indeed seem damning enough that Bradley apparently sought usurpation of our established order. Unfortunately, that is not the case. No, I'm afraid what he sought was far more... fundamental."

"What are you saying?" Marsh said.

"What Bradley sought—" McCormick said, "was nothing less than the total annihilation of God's world."

Chapter Thirty Seven

Almost as if McCormick had done it on purpose to punctuate his sentence, an explosion louder and closer than any of the others went off and rattled the entire room. A second later I saw flashes of red light through the stained glass windows, and then another explosion. This time, McCormick didn't really have much chance of calming everyone down.

Knights shot to their feet all over the place; Marsh and Holloway were shouting orders and pointing. As for me, well, I had to get up and move to avoid getting trampled. I ended up backing toward the altar, which gave me a clear view of everything. Every Knight, wizard and myrmidon was swarming up the aisles like a well-oiled military machine.

Except, I noticed, for the Knights and wizards on the altar, which included Casey. They just stayed right where they were.

The three columns of Knights and the others were maybe three quarters of the way to the huge double doors when it happened. The doors burst open and inward with a blast of red light and a massive, ear pounding crash; the doors cart wheeled down the empty rows of pews and smashed a neat line of splinters and debris through them, coming to a stop against the back wall to either side of the altar.

I'm not sure if it was that, or the sight of what was now standing in the open doorway that stopped everyone short, but I guess that's six of one, half dozen of the other when you think about it. The point is they stopped.

There, in the doorway, his hands behind his back in a sort of restful military pose, was Simon. Next to him—red hair, scarf, rainbow flannel, and cricket bat held slung diagonally across her back with one hand, was Smoot. On either side of both of them stood two Knights, all with nasty looking, glowing scimitars drawn. On the left was a young girl with short dark brown hair and a thin red headed guy, and on the right there was a beefy looking guy with a crew cut and a girl with half of her hair shaved. All four of them, I noticed, were wearing not light but *heavy* combat regalia, which was roughly the same as walking around in a main battle tank. I've only ever seen that gear in demonstrations, never in action, and it looked even more ferocious now. Basically it had the look of full Kevlar body armor, if that body armor had blue glowing seams.

But that wasn't all. There was Eveneshka, Horace the Baku, and a giant, red scaly thing with arms like barrels, a chest like a god damn mountain, hooves for feet, and a massive, thick muscular tail.

"Father Caelin McCormick," Simon said, his voice sounding louder than anyone's voice had any business being. "You're under arrest."

★ ★ ★ ★ ★

No one moved or said anything for maybe five or six seconds. I sure as hell didn't blame them, either. It was Simon who broke the silence.

"It's over, Father," He said.

It felt like every head turned to look at McCormick. Mine sure did.

"Is it, Bradley?" McCormick said. "You are aware that you are addressing an Exemplar?"

"Not at present," Simon said. "Brothers and Sisters, I accuse Father McCormick of the murders of Brother Hanson, Sister Gregory and Sister McGowan; of collusion with the Scions, and attempted genocide."

★ ★ ★ ★ ★

Well, that sure got everyone buzzing amongst themselves, I can tell you. But that was all. Not one person in the room took one step toward Simon or away.

"I daresay you've slightly overstepped yourself, Bradley," McCormick said. "Especially since it would appear to any casual observer that at present it is *you* who are in collusion with the Scions."

The big red scaly creature grunted.

"Oh, him?" Simon said, and glanced at the red guy. "Oh, naw, man, he's cool."

"A rogue wizard, a hostile intermediate, demons...you aren't making much of a case for yourself, Bradley, and to be perfectly frank, brothers and sisters, Bradley has done quite a competent job of proving all that I have just finished telling you."

"Just finished, did you?" Simon said. "You had just enough time to squeeze that all in, after demolishing the New Horizons Nexxus after yourself? Your forces held us up longer than I thought."

"No sense trying to talk around it, Caelin," said Eveneshka. "It was—on the whole—elegant, but your haste has made you sloppy. I can hear all of it."

"She has a point, you know," Simon said, gesturing to her with his chin. "She's good."

McCormick smiled. "I think I've heard enough lies from this traitorous heretic and his underlings. It has ceased to be amusing. Brothers and sisters, take him!"

★ ★ ★ ★ ★

If McCormick had been expecting everyone to howl a battle cry and charge at that small group in the doorway, he would have been disappointed. All everyone did, from what I could tell, was glance around at everyone around themselves, I guess maybe to see if anyone else would do it first.

"WHAT ARE YOU WAITING FOR?" Marsh screamed.

At the same second Marsh said that, a whole lot of things started happening. But it was only because I was looking at McCormick already that I saw the most important bit. That bit was that I saw McCormick glance quickly at Casey. Almost too quickly for me to notice, but I definitely saw him do it.

A split second later, Casey jumped at the wizard nearest her and clocked him across his face. In almost the same motion she grabbed his bamboo stick and pointed it at McCormick.

There was a flash of purple light and a very *very* loud bang, loud enough to turn every head in the room. McCormick yelled out in pain and slumped slowly to his knees, almost like he was melting, and there were dozens of purple arcs of lightning dancing all over his body. Everyone in the room could see it plain as day; Casey was holding out her bamboo pole, attacking McCormick.

The Knights on the Altar grabbed Casey and slammed her to the ground almost immediately, or, I should say, they *tried* to slam her to the ground. In reality, they never got the chance to do anything more than grab. In a blur of motion I could just barely see, Reese appeared from out of nowhere. One of the Knights screamed, bent backwards, and fell with a nasty looking blade in his side; the other Knight caught an elbow in the face and lost his balance. Reese threw a kick to that Knight's midsection that send him tumbling down the altar's steps.

By now, even the undecided in the crowd made up their minds, and it looked like an avalanche of black coats was converging down the aisles to the altar. Apparently they all decided that stopping whatever the fuck Casey just did was more important than not knowing if they should charge Simon or not. Or who knows, maybe they thought whatever just happened was Simon's plan. Maybe they thought he had just been distracting them so he could signal Casey to assassinate McCormick, I have no idea. The fact was, they were all charging back down.

I whipped my head back to McCormick, and that was when I saw it happen, almost in super slow motion.

His face split apart into six fleshy petals.

As I saw it happening, I felt as if I was laying down my feet on the last few inches of solid ground before a five thousand foot drop, and I was stumbling. On top of that, I all of a sudden felt that even though the noise in the room was deafening, I could barely hear it. I backed one step, two steps away from the altar, and then I was caught up in the oncoming mob.

✸ ✸ ✸ ✸ ✸

I felt a strong chill sweep through me, and then it began. The faces of the Knights all around me split open, one after the other, like a bunched up mess of dominoes.

"KROOOGERRR!"

There was only one person that booming voice could belong to. I have to tell you, it sounded like that voice drowned out everything, and I am not exaggerating. If it makes any sense, it also felt like that voice smacked me upside the head and told me to wake the fuck up and get moving.

So I just did that little thing.

"*Springen*," I said, and pushed off the floor with everything I had.

I shot up over the crowd, and, I saw something I was already half expecting; Simon was midair, coming straight at me, with a wicked looking war hammer on a long pole in one hand. He must have jumped right after I did. We crashed into each other like boulders swinging on ropes, and then Simon wrapped his free arm around me and gripped me so hard it almost felt like he was going to snap my back in half.

Simon twisted his whole body like a drill and chucked his hammer off to his left, and then twisted one more time and chucked me in the same direction.

I barely had enough time to see what was going on, but I did see Simon's hammer rolling through the air like a gigantic glowing blue wheel. The hammer hit the wall, and when it did, I swear the hammer may as well have been a round from a field artillery piece.

The wall just, I don't want to say *crumbled*, because it did more than that. The wall liquefied and burst outward like it was just a wet piece of paper that someone dropped a marble on. Now, instead of the fifth and sixth Stations of the Cross, there was a hole big enough to drive a train through. Fortunately, I was a lot smaller than a train.

I came down on some pavement, bounced twice, and rolled; I didn't feel any pain though, just a bunch of jolts. I couldn't believe it, but Simon must have substantiated a shield prayer on me. Somehow he managed to get off a prayer on his weapon and me and throw us both in the exact same direction while he was spinning in midair without making a mistake, and he had maybe half a second to plan it all out and do it on top of that. What the living shit fuck *was* he?

I didn't give myself any time to worry about that. Simon yanked me out of there to get me as far away from the dybbukim as possible, and you can bet I planned to help in any way I could. But I was getting ahead of myself. First, I needed to get my bearings.

It looked like I was in the middle of an empty parking lot next to the church, maybe a football field away from the building. Simon had one holy hell of a damn arm, I tell you what. At the moment the church itself looked less like a church and almost like a dance club, what with all the blasts of red and blue-white light going off like fireworks inside.

And then, there was a sound like a whip cracking, only like seventeen thousand times louder, and the ground under me shook. I almost fell over, but I managed to avoid it, at least until the pavement started to crack like thin ice. I mean, this huge gash at least one hundred feet long and maybe half a foot wide tore out from the church through the parking lot and ended up practically between my feet. At that point it was kind of like trying to stay standing on one of those jerking metal funhouse floors, only worse. I went down. A second later there were more and more of these loud cracks and gouges in the concrete, all spreading out from the church, as if—

Holy shit.

Right in front of my eyes, the ground under the church just caved in as if someone was doing a controlled demolition, and the church collapsed, imploded, and sunk out of sight.

But that was just the beginning. Before I could even react a bright red lightning bolt tore down from the clouds and struck somewhere in the hole where the church used to be. And then another one struck, and another, and another, and then three or four at once. The noise was so severe I felt like someone was driving spikes in my ears. But what happened next was even better.

An area of pavement about fifty feet away began to swell and bulge like a balloon, or maybe a soap bubble; and then it exploded like it was a giant fire hose, only instead of water, it was shooting chunks of stone and dirt. Almost right away, another bubble twenty feet away from the first swelled up and exploded, and then another, and another, until finally I felt the ground under my feet bulging.

"Wah!" I said. Yes. I said *wah*. That was it. I continue to amaze myself. But I guess I was a bit more interested in what was going on under my feet than I was thinking up something cool to say that no one would hear anyway. I jumped with everything my mobility prayer would give me, and I got clear just in time to avoid getting pasted by pieces of concrete bigger than both of my fists put together.

Only now, there seemed to be a hell of a lot more than just big nasty flying debris to worry about. No, now there looked like there was goddamn lava spurting out of the holes too, only the lava was dark blue instead of red or orange.

And this dark blue lava wasn't just staying put and flowing like nice, normal, sane rational lava, either. No, this abnormal, insane, irrational lava was beginning to form up into what looked like a bunch of oversized, vaguely human shapes. And when I say oversized, I mean more like twice sized. Width *and* height.

Now, I had never seen anything like these, but I had managed to do a little bit of reading while I had the Knight's resources at my disposal, and I took a wild stab at these being elementals. Of the fire variety.

Only, why the shit were they showing up now?

Whether or not I personally understood that wouldn't have changed a goddamn thing, though, not with everything else that was going on, like Casey transposing a fucking Exemplar and using me to transpose the heads of all branches of the order—

Just then a thought flickered into my head, but only for about a quarter of a second. I didn't really have enough time to register more than one quick thing about it before it was gone. Basically, something didn't sit quite right about Casey transposing McCormick.

Again, one way or the other, it didn't matter just at the minute. I was patient zero of the apocalypse, and living demonic fire beasts were slowly surrounding me.

★ ★ ★ ★ ★

I needed to get the fuck out of there. I looked around for escape route, and I did a double take as I spotted just what I needed just then. It was a thing of pure beauty. There, about thirty feet away, half buried by rubble, was Simon's hammer.

★ ★ ★ ★ ★

Oh, Christ, yes. A weapon. A goddamn weapon. Holy sweet flaming fuck, *a real consecrated weapon*. It could be that maybe you don't really appreciate just why this was so fantastic, so let me explain. Since all of this crazy shit started happening, I've been forced into some rather uncomfortable situations over and over again with nothing to go on but my fists. If you don't mind my bitching a little, it was beginning to get a tiny bit old. It was like asking a NASCAR driver to run the race in a beetle.

So, if it was the last thing I did that night, I was going to get that hammer and fuck something up with it.

I know what you're thinking right now—you're thinking *but Francine, you had a weapon against the giant Jason dybbuk, didn't you?* Yeah, I guess technically. But my poor banjo was what you'd call ad hoc. Although it did do the job, it wasn't built for it. This hammer on the other hand…

This was *Simon's hammer.*

From the moment I got my hand around the handle, I could feel it. It was warm, almost alive. I lifted it into both hands almost like I was afraid I was gonna break it, which was bullshit but I couldn't help it. This was like nothing I'd ever experienced before.

The hammer was more like a maul, about as long as you'd expect a spear to be end to end, and the head looked like it was forged out of one single piece of gleaming silver. It didn't have a blunt end and a sharp end, like most war hammers; no, it was shaped kind of like a rubber mallet. Also, it looked like it should have weighed something like thirty pounds but the thing was lighter than air.

But that was only the start of it. From the moment I touched this weapon, I could tell that any prayers I put on it or myself would only be gravy. This thing only actually needed me to find an unlucky target, or five, and it would take care of the rest.

I looked up, and I saw that there were at least four fire elementals in my way, which frankly felt like I was almost like staring down a crowded trench with a machine gun in my hand.

I charged at the nearest one and swung. The hammer was, like I said, practically weightless, and swinging it was as easy as swinging my empty arm, only kind of better. I hit the elemental in what would have been his knee if he had any bones, and there was a blast of blue-white light at the point of impact. His lower leg just crumbled and broke off like it was a huge, burned out charcoal briquette. It went flying and spinning off through the air, and when it hit the ground, it smashed apart into ash. The elemental lost his balance and tipped forward, which let me get him in his chest. I tore off a massive chunk of that, and then served his left arm the same way. After that, he fell over completely and his whole body collapsed into black smoke.

By then two more elementals were in range, and they were pissed. One of them lifted one of his flaming fists and something that looked like a chunk of magma shot out from it. I dove toward him and rolled; he ended up missing me by maybe six inches but I sure as hell felt the heat from it. Honestly, it felt like when you put your hand too close to the heat of a flame and your hand starts to roast—only over my whole body.

I took his feet out from under him with wide swing, and he toppled like a redwood. I got showered with ash that singed me and burned holes in my shirt and jeans.

The other elemental brought one of his fists down on me like he was trying to smash a roach, only I swung back at him and broke his whole arm in half. He rocked backward, and I took out his other arm. A second later I split him in half at the waist, and he disintegrated.

I was so caught up in the sheer awesomeness of me that I didn't notice until just now that while I was goofing around, more and more fire elementals had been sprouting up all over the place the whole time. Like, dozens of them, some twice as big as the others, and they had me completely boxed in.

I did a slow three-sixty, blinked, and took a deep breath. "Come one, come all," I said.

Then, there was a hell of a ruckus over by the huge hole where the church used to be. I mean that literally. A column of fire maybe fifty feet around shot up from the hole and spat out a shower of burning rocks the size of motorcycles. The fire elementals jerked to a stop.

After a couple seconds the column of fire disappeared as quickly as it came, and the burning rocks came down one after the other, smashing into buildings, pavement, and elementals like tiny meteorites.

And then, a bright red bolt of lightning blasted up out of the hole, followed by a shockwave of red energy at the bolt's highest tip. For a second, nothing else happened, that is until I saw a black shape hurtling through the air, roughly in my direction. The shape got bigger, and bigger, and bigger, until whatever it was hit the ground right on top of the outer ring of elementals and ran over and through them like a gigantic bowling ball. It rolled right past me, missing me by at most ten feet, and smashed through a bunch more of the elementals until it finally stopped short.

By now, it wasn't just some unrecognizable big black shape. No, I could see exactly what it was. It was a giant, giant, *giant* dybbuk.

Chapter Thirty Eight

For a second I almost felt like I would have been better off with the elementals. I gripped the hammer tightly, and I felt its warmth flow all through me.

The dybbuk was obviously shaken up, but it wasn't out. It was already pushing itself up, and that was when I appreciated just how giant this giant dybbuk was. He was only halfway to a kneeling position and he was already two stories high and maybe one whole story wide. Up close, I could see all the normal sized dybbukim fused together on its arms and legs and body just like the Jason dybbuk. Only, instead of five or six, there had to have been . . .

...Well, how about maybe everyone that was in the church?

The giant dybbuk made a deep, groaning sound that made my bones rattle, and ashes of dead elementals flaked off of him as she straightened up.

All I could do was let my eyes go up, up, up, up, and slowly back away. I don't think the dybbuk noticed me yet, and I wanted to get a head start before it did. Even with my mobility prayer, I didn't think I had a chance of keeping ahead of this thing for long.

And then I got a break. All at once, the elementals attacked it.

It was like watching a bunch of preschoolers trying to tackle their teacher, only in this case the teacher didn't really care if she punted the kids like footballs or threw them like sacks of grain. I didn't wait around to watch, though. I turned and ran.

Only I didn't get far.

★ ★ ★ ★ ★

A blast of red light and a sound like a rifle shot went off right in front of me and knocked me flying. I dropped Simon's hammer and slid to a stop ten feet or so away.

"DAMN IT, SMOOT," I head Simon howl. I lifted my head just in time to see Simon and Smoot running past me. Smoot had her cricket bat slung across her back like always. "YOU PUSHED MCCORMICK RIGHT NEXT TO KROGER! WAS I NOT CLEAR?"

"SORRY MAN," Smoot yelled, managing to make even a yell sound like she was stoned.

"NEVER MIND," Simon continued. "TAKE THEM! LEAVE MCCORMICK TO ME! KROGER, GET OUT OF HERE!"

"YEAH, MAN," Smoot said. She stopped short and looked left and right real fast, getting her whole body into the motion like she was hamming it up on stage. Then she looked down at a brown satchel on her hip, lifted the flap and peeked inside. She nodded, and then she raised her free hand, palm up, like she was motioning for someone to raise their voice. A red arc of electricity popped on her cricket bat, and then another, until it looked like a jacob's ladder on speed.

And then, the ground began to shake. Gently at first, but—
May I never piss off this woman.

When I was little once my sister bet me that I was such a weakling that I couldn't even crush a hard-boiled egg in my bare hand. I'd sure show her, I said. She went and fetched an egg, and I squeezed as hard as I could. Of course, she handed me a raw egg, and needless to say I ended up wearing the goo all over my shirt, arm, and face. She called me a moron and walked away laughing like usual. I swear she was better at everything, even stupid shit like that.

I only brought that up because was Smoot was doing could only be called a bigger, louder, more cataclysmic version of what I did to that poor innocent egg.

I saw the ground under one of the elementals fold up and around the elemental like someone's hand clenching tight. The elemental disintegrated in a huge cloud of ash and dust after like a second or two. And then, this same thing started happening again and again and again and again all around me until it was going as fast as popcorn popping. The noise was overpowering to both my ears and body, almost like being beat up in the pit at a bona fide punk show.

The giant dybbuk was mostly free now, and it looked like it was trying to figure out where it was. That only lasted a second, though, because all of a sudden he threw back his head, spread his giant fleshy petals as far as they could and let out a sound that knocked me to my knees, with my hands on my ears. It was so loud, I was screaming but I couldn't hear my own voice. I could see, though, that there was a spark of blue-white light up by the dybbuk's shoulder.

Holy *shit*, Simon.

The dybbuk started thrashing around, grabbing at its head and shoulders like a man trapped in a swarm of bees; I think I missed getting smashed by one of his huge feet by something like seventeen inches. I ended up scrambling in some random direction to get clear; I looked everywhere for Simon's hammer but I couldn't see it. What I did see, though, was Smoot standing as still and calm as you please, her cricket bat over her back, looking up at the giant dybbuk.

"HANG ON, MAN," she said, again in that ridiculous calm shout of hers. I swear to Christ I wanted whatever this chick was on. She put her index finger in front of her face, like she was shushing the dybbuk or something, and then . . .

Four rectangular columns of earth, each one maybe the size of a school bus standing on its end tore up and pressed against the giant dybbuk like a four way vice grip. The dybbuk was stuck in place, but only for a second. It was still fighting like hell, and coming really close to breaking out.

Smoot didn't even flinch, though. She just moved her free hand and one of those flaming rocks from earlier that was sitting nearby rose up in the air and shot at the dybbuk's face like a cannon ball. The rock hit dead on and bounced; then the rock froze in midair and smacked the dybbuk again, and again, and again until the dybbuk quit struggling. When it did, the rock fell back down.

"DO IT, MAN," Smoot yelled.

✳ ✳ ✳ ✳ ✳

I could hardly believe the shit I just saw Smoot do, and she didn't even look like she was breathing hard. But that was just the prologue.

After a second or two of quiet, I saw one single flash of blue white light, and then . . .

It looked like the giant dybbuk was ...melting.

I don't know what else to call it; that's exactly what it looked like. Bits and pieces of the dybbuk just fell off one after the other and its body started to look like it was shriveling and shrinking. The more it shrunk, the more the four columns of earth trapping the dybbuk in place sank back down into the ground.

By the time the dybbuk's body shrank by about half, I could see what was actually happening. The dybbuk wasn't melting. No, what was happening was that all the little bodies that made up the one big one were breaking away and falling off, and I could see that they were human, or at least they looked like it.

Then I understood. Simon just re-transposed the *entire giant dybbuk at once.*

★ ★ ★ ★ ★

In less than a minute, all that was left of the giant dybbuk was a huge mess of bodies. I glanced real quickly over them all and saw that most of the bodies were Knights, but I also saw the big red demon thing that came in with Simon, and the Baku, and Reese.

"Keep back, Kroger," I heard Simon say. I looked up and saw him on the other side of the bodies. "It's not quite over yet."

"No," came another voice I had no chance of mistaking. I looked in the direction of that voice, and, sure as hell, I saw McCormick in the middle of the pile of bodies, slowly getting to his feet.

"No," he said again. "It is not."

★ ★ ★ ★ ★

"You certainly are intolerable, Bradley," McCormick said. He was walking slowly through the mess of bodies, kind of with a limp. "But I suppose I should have expected trouble from you."

"How could you do it, Caelin?" Simon said.

"Yeah, man," Smoot said reproachfully, and blinked. "—Do what?"

"You're asking the wrong question," McCormick said still looking straight at Simon, apparently ignoring Smoot. "You should rather ask how could I not?"

"You couldn't have thought you would get away with it," Simon said. "And that blind with Crumb, you must admit that was laughably clumsy."

"I never said I could ad-lib," McCormick said, and shrugged.

After hearing that, something came together in my brain. It was the little thing I almost realized before but didn't exactly have time to think about. Only now I got it. What did it for me was when Simon called it a *blind*; I've read enough Sherlock Holmes to know that means a distraction.

The thing that I got was this: That little purple lightshow Casey put on to transpose McCormick didn't make any sense.

I had witnessed Casey transposing that poor cop right in front of my eyes, and there sure as shit wasn't anything remotely like what I saw with McCormick. No, in fact there wasn't anything but the transformation. No muss, no fuss, no bother, just face to starface just like that, and the cop didn't make a sound while it went on. Come to think of it, neither did Raine when it happened to her.

This made me think of something Simon said about Casey being smart enough to keep it discreet, seeing as how badly she stood to catch it if she was caught. So, that whole thing with the purple sparklies and McCormick screaming didn't fit. It was as if Casey wanted everyone to see it was her . . .

Or McCormick did.

Yeah. I mean, everyone was focused on Simon and his little group, and then it was like *No, look at me!* Everything from how Casey got a hold of the other wizard's focus to how the spell was cast was just, as Simon put it, a blind.

So . . .

✳ ✳ ✳ ✳ ✳

"And as for *how I could think I could get away with it,* as you put it," McCormick said, "Surely you realize who you are speaking to. There was, in fact, only one small problem, the only thing capable of obviating my designs. You."

"Me?" Simon said. "You mean to tell me that an Exemplar, one of thirteen human beings so close to God that they are practically part angel, can be stopped by a mere Sentinel?"

"I never said *stopped*," McCormick said.

★ ★ ★ ★ ★

McCormick looked like he was barely able to stand up, but in the next second he sure as hell didn't move like he was barely able to stand up. Quite the goddamn opposite.

He swung one arm like he was backhanding someone, and growled. A blast of white light went off right on top of Smoot, and knocked her back like a toy. She didn't make a sound.

Almost in the same motion, McCormick leapt and flipped through the air like he was a circus acrobat, and landed toe to toe with Simon. And then I stopped being able to follow anything.

I saw one crash, flash, blast, crack, and explosion of blue-white light after another, and I could sort of see Simon and McCormick swinging, kicking, blocking, and countering, but they were moving so goddamn fast I could hardly tell who was doing what to whom. Finally, McCormick growled again, and he swung one arm in an overhand sledgehammer blow, which Simon stopped with both hands. When McCormick hit Simon's hands, there was an incredible explosion of white light that let out a shockwave that damn near knocked me flat out. Simon didn't even flinch, though; no, he just moved like he was pushing something heavy off to the left. A second later another explosion of white light blew a crater in the ground twenty or thirty feet away, and McCormick stumbled back a step.

"You dare?" McCormick said, and whipped his right arm from one shoulder down to his waist. Blue-white light shot down from his shoulder to his hand, and all of a sudden what looked like some kind of weird cross between a claymore and a scimitar just materialized in his grip. A second later he was swinging at Simon from, as far as I could tell, almost every direction at once. I'm serious; it almost looked like there were three or four McCormicks jumping and leaping all around Simon.

Simon didn't look like he had any weapon of his own, either. And to be honest, it didn't look like he cared. Simon didn't look like he had any trouble deflecting McCormick's sword, and he also had no trouble getting past McCormick's guard. Simon landed one punch, then another, and then finally Simon got a hold of McCormick's sword hand.

McCormick tried to break free, but Simon twisted his grip and McCormick growled again. A second later Simon gave McCormick a full on sidekick into his midsection. There was a blast of blue-while light, and McCormick flew back through the air, landing about seventeen feet away in a pile of ash. McCormick had lost his hold on his sword in the bargain, and now, Simon had it. He slung it up to rest on one shoulder.

"I wouldn't keep escalating, if I were you," Simon said. "You do, and you'll just end up blunted."

"You insolent, arrogant egotist," McCormick said. He was slowly getting back on his feet. "Do you think you can stand against GOD?"

"I'm not standing against God," Simon said. "Or at least not at the moment. I'm only standing against you, and all that implies."

"To stand against me," McCormick said, "Is to stand against the true, pure will of God."

"No," Simon said. "It is to stand against God's mistakes."

McCormick didn't say a thing at first. When he did, he didn't sound quite as angry as I thought he should have. No, in fact, he just sounded kind of...sad.

"Oh, Bradley," he said. "This is even worse than I feared. You truly do believe that, don't you?"

"No," Simon said. "I know it."

"God makes no mistakes," McCormick said. "To imply as much is the height of heresy."

"No," Simon said. "It's the truth. You are wrong, and so was God. That is why this, the most beautiful of all worlds, exists. It is with this world that God finally succeeded."

"No," McCormick said. "This world, a world that dares to question the very existence of God, one that places the insignificant mind of man above the will of their creator, cannot and must not exist any longer. No, these so called wandering spirits, these dybbukim, the true first children of God, exist for one purpose and one purpose only: To be close to HIM. It is only they who deserve to be so, not those who would place their own feeble reason, judgment and will above HIS."

"Doesn't the fact that *we* are the ones closest to God tell you anything, father?" Simon said. "That if God wanted our unquestioning devotion above all else, that he would not have replaced his first creations? Would he not have simply stopped there? Basking in their endless adoration?"

"Every word you speak," McCormick said, "Only damns you further. You have taken the power granted you by God, and are daring to presume to wield that very power against him?"

"It is not I who is doing that," Simon said. "But even if it were, it would change nothing."

"Then . . ." McCormick said. "I wash my hands of you."

McCormick bent his knees for as long as it took to inhale, and then there was a huge burst of blue light all over and around him. McCormick's body launched forward like a rocket on rails; he was leaning forward, one arm reaching for Simon, and McCormick was bathed all over in crackling blue white energy. I swear I saw some of that crackling energy vaguely taking the shape of giant wings on McCormick's back.

They came together in another blast of energy, and the ground all around them was torn to pieces as if someone just set off about twenty sticks of dynamite. Lord knows it was loud enough for that, and I sure as hell felt the force of it. I got knocked down flat.

I couldn't believe the power I was witnessing. I had never seen anything like it. Never have I ever dreamed I would see an Exemplar in action like this. Hell, I had only heard hints about what Exemplar actually were, and now...

Holy sweet shit.

One time when I was younger my parents took me to see a space shuttle launch. I'm not positive but I want to say it was the Atlantis? I don't know, whatever, that's not important.

The point was, I was maybe three miles or more away from the launch pad, and all I could really see when it lifted off was a tiny bright white circle way off in the distance that I could cover up with the tip of my pinky. But the noise . . .

Holy shit, it was so powerful it shook the ground I was standing on and I could feel it rattling my bones. I could only imagine what it must have felt like if I was so much as a mile closer, or maybe, for the love of Christ, right on top of it.

I had a feeling it may not be too terribly far off from being this close to an Exemplar letting loose.

✳ ✳ ✳ ✳ ✳

I felt like I was being pummeled by stones, over and over, only, the stones weren't being thrown at me, it was more like the stones were being teleported directly into my body. The light was so blinding I could barely even see what the hell was going on, but my ears and body kept reminding me that whatever it was, it was severe.

My list of people I pray I never piss off just got bigger. Again. I needed to get away from this, to find cover. I couldn't take much more of this. It was like trying to sit in front of a woofer eight feet high on full blast playing a dubstep bass drop. I started to crawl away, but that ended up being like trying to crawl between two lines of people who were all kicking the shit out of you. I gave up and just lay flat, begging for it to end.

Which it did, after like thirty-seven years.

✳ ✳ ✳ ✳ ✳

When it finally stopped, my ears were ringing, I was bruised all over, and I was coughing up blood. I'm positive I was hemorrhaging and then some.

And I heard a sound that was awfully familiar: I heard McCormick growling, only it sounded different this time. He didn't sound pissed, he sounded like he was in pain. Serious pain. And the growls were coming and going and getting louder each time.

I looked around just in time to see it.

Simon was literally pounding McCormick into the ground. I mean literally *literally*. Simon was throwing one full on haymaker after another, and after each one, McCormick got closer to the ground. First he was kind of bent at the shoulders, then bent at the waist, then on one knee, then on his side holding himself up with one arm, and then finally prone.

Then Simon punched him on the side of the head four or five times, until it looked like McCormick's head was half underground. Then, Simon stomped on his head like seven times, or maybe more, I lost count. Then Simon stepped away, reached under his overcoat, and pulled out something that looked like a silver and pearl flintlock pistol. He cocked the hammer, pointed it at McCormick, and then a ball of white light the size of softball shot out and slammed into the old man. He groaned.

Simon fired three more times, and McCormick kept groaning. Simon kept firing until McCormick finally shut up. I frankly lost count how many shots it took.

"I warned you about escalating," Simon said when it was finally over, and slipped the pistol back into his coat.

"Simon," I said, in between gross hacking coughs.

"Adobe," he said. "What are you still doing here?"

"G-g-etting m-my ass kicked," I said. I coughed up another glob of blood.

"Hold on," Simon said, and he came over to me. "Take it easy. Here."

He passed his hand over my face, my chest, and my stomach. Within a second, all of the pain flew right out the window like it was never there. Hell, even any *memory* of the pain was gone, too. In fact, I actually felt better than I usually do after a full night's sleep.

"Oh, *thank* you," I said. "What happened? How did you—?"

"Later," he interrupted. "Short version, McCormick is insane. Stay here, I'm going to see to Smoot. I'm fairly sure he only sealed her power off, but all the same."

Before anything else could happen, though, a shaky, gravelly voice broke in.

"Insane...am I?'

Both of our heads whipped around at the same time. There was McCormick, staggering slowly to his feet.

"Really, Caelin?" Simon said, and he sounded more impatient than anything else. "What exactly made you think you could accomplish anything by getting up? I'd love to hear it."

"Your power is *extraordinary*, Bradley," McCormick said. "Why, I don't believe I could have ever imagined a Knight like you could be possible."

"Well, like I always say," Simon said, "I have no talent, just sheer dogged determination."

"Whatever the case," McCormick said. "You have thwarted my greatest efforts. I shudder to consider what you may become."

"What's your point, Caelin? Aside from stating the obvious."

"That I do not want a Knight like you to be possible."

"Too late."

"No," McCormick said. "I don't think so, you see, I did acknowledge that your power and skill are quite formidable. However, I did not say that you were infallible."

"Never claimed it," Simon said. "But I suggest you shut up and sit down before I make you do it again."

"No, I don't think I will," McCormick said. "You see, that little ingenious exaction you developed—that sends the true children of God back whence they came—while it requires some effort, it is not so impossible to reverse as you may think."

Simon's eyes opened wider, very slowly. At the same second, McCormick' s face spilt open into six fleshy petals.

✳ ✳ ✳ ✳ ✳

McCormick leapt at Simon like a giant cat. Simon had enough time to get ready, but all the same he got bowled over. They were grabbing at each other and tumbling and rolling all around, and I heard something I don't think I'd ever thought I'd ever hear: Simon grunted in pain.

McCormick had his fleshy maw closed tight around one of Simon's arms, and Simon was trying to shake him off. He was having a hard time, though, because McCormick had Simon's free arm locked up. I couldn't really process what I was seeing for a second, because I'd never seen Simon in any kind of trouble. In fact, he actually looked worried.

That was when I remembered. I mean, I'd only been told it a thousand times.

Casey said that the dybbukim *exhibited a tremendous resilience to your goddamn pious magic*. Simon himself said the same thing.

I was seeing the proof right in front of me. It was as if Simon was totally powerless.

And then, everything else fell into place, too. Simon may be powerless now, but *I* sure as hell wasn't. Not against a dybbuk.

I knew what I had to do, and I didn't waste another second. I charged at McCormick, and wound up the best possible belief I had that McCormick was the one evil standing between all life and total destruction. It was actually easy as hell.

"*Unterbrechen!*"

McCormick flew so far I may as well have slammed him with a wrecking ball. He let out a pathetic super high-pitched squeal and he bounced along the ground like a basketball. In fact, he looked like he would have kept going for a hell of a long time if some huge chunk of concrete hadn't gotten in the way.

Simon looked at me for a second, nodded, and jumped up to his feet. He ran over to McCormick, heaved him up in one hand, and then he hit McCormick's face, chest, and stomach, really quick, like wham-wham-wham.

The fleshy petals closed up and fused shut, and in a few seconds McCormick looked like his perfectly normal self, if you could call him that. McCormick was looking at Simon like Simon was an oncoming diesel train and he himself was tied to the tracks.

"I'm afraid, Caelin," Simon said, panting, "That you've left me no choice. This insanity ends *now*."

Simon thrust out the first two fingers of his free hand against McCormick's forehead. After half a second Simon yanked his fingers away, and there was a burst of white light.

McCormick collapsed down to the ground like he had no bones in his body, and didn't move again. Simon just stood there, looking down at McCormick, breathing hard. Neither of us moved or said anything for about ten seconds, in the sudden quiet, until I decided to interject something brilliant.

"Umm," I said.

Simon glanced at me, and then looked back down at McCormick.

"Now," Simon said. "*Now*, it's over."

Chapter Thirty Nine

Well, no, not really. I mean, I guess technically, the whole immediate threat of a dybbuk apocalypse was over, but that was really it. In fact, things were about as far from over as I could possibly imagine.

Simon found Smoot and got her back in to working order; it turned out that all McCormick did was lock out her magic, which Simon was able to reverse. At about the same time all the Knights, wizards, and not to mention Reese (you know, all the people that were part of the giant dybbuk) started to come around. Before anything else could happen, Simon told Smoot to burn all the rest of her stash (which is what she kept in that big brown satchel of hers) to cast the most powerful greater mass amnesia she could, but to please don't forget to remember to shield him and me from it.

Smoot did that, and afterwards she was so exhausted she could barely stand up. Simon carried her piggy back, and then we three got the hell out of there.

The whole neighborhood for as far as I could see was in total chaos. Cars were on fire, buildings and businesses were smashed up, and fire hydrants were busted and shooting water way up into the air. It looked like something straight out of a disaster movie. We ducked down back alleys and side streets to avoid being seen by what looked like a mix of roaming gangs, police, and for all I knew, national guard.

Simon said he was looking for one of Smoot's Nexuses that could get me and Smoot to safety, before he went back to find out if anyone he brought with him survived the battle. He said he doubted it, because he saw several of them die right in front of him. If Smoot hadn't been there, he said, he wasn't sure that he would have survived the tidal wave of dybbukim.

Then he explained everything, as if he heard me ask the question before I actually did.

Turns out McCormick, the most revered Exemplar in the order, had gone a little funny. Something about the process of becoming an Exemplar-which turned them into a sort of part angel/human mashup had gone to his head. Or that's what Simon thought anyway. Basically McCormick thought that we didn't deserve to be close to God and he found a way to do something about it. It was him who discovered how to transpose a human and a dybbuk, using his own self as his guinea pig. After a while he developed complete control over the process and could undertake it and reverse it whenever he wanted. Of course, even though he was sort of a special case (since he had access to a level and type of power that most other Knights and wizards couldn't dream of) he needed to keep his direct involvement to a minimum. So, he...*recruited* a discontented wizard named Casey Crumb to do some experimentation. That was, if by recruited you meant *subverted her subconscious will.*

Once Casey successfully transposed a test subject and sent it against a Knight, McCormick had everything he needed. Here was a creature that the Knights could not stop, and those same creatures also happened to be what McCormick thought deserved to be closest to God. He had his goal in sight, and once he could discover how to transpose en masse there wasn't anything the Knights could do to stop him.

The only trouble was, how could he transpose en masse? Casey was a brilliant wizard but the transposition spell was extremely difficult and exhausting; it was very hard for her to manage to cast the spell on maybe at most two or three people a day. McCormick needed to catch the Knights by surprise with thousands of dybbukim before they could figure out how to beat them.

That was solved by the happy accident that the wizard he picked hated my guts.

On her own, Casey figured out how to use me as a trigger to set off the spell on someone who started to have feelings for me, basically to give back what she thought I deserved for ruining her life.

That night when the Raine-dybbuk came after me, that formally lovely monster-thing discovered something very strange about Ms. AFK. She didn't have much time to do anything about it before Simon sent her packing, but afterward, she took that knowledge back with her. It was probably the most important discovery a dybbuk could have made. All of a sudden the dybbukim had a way to come home.

In order to make it work, they just needed to want to return while one of them was close to me, and that was it. My connection to God's Light, that I kept because I wanted to, that kept me closer to God because I wanted to, was all the bridge they needed. Any human being close to me and another dybbuk was open to being transposed.

Once McCormick figured this out, he sent all of the resources the Knights had after me. It was only because Simon got wise about the dybbukim at about the same time, and a whole lot of dumb luck, that kept McCormick from flat out succeeding.

The screwed up thing was, Simon didn't put all the pieces together until practically the last possible instant, after he rescued Smoot from McCormick's co-conspirators. By sheer luck, Eveneshka, that intermediate that insulted me a lot was there, too; apparently her safe house got raided and she and everyone in it were dragged in for interrogation. Well, thanks to Eveneshka being who she was, Simon soon got privy to the essential parts of McCormick's plan.

McCormick showed up with his people almost right after, and Simon and everyone else fought it out with him. Lots of demons got killed, but in the end McCormick ran for it through the Nexus and destroyed it after himself. Simon was able to tell where he went, though.

From there, Simon and Smoot gathered up everyone else they could in such a short time now that Smoot could help speed that up. She used that recall spell of hers and got all of them as close as they could to the church where I was being held with Marsh. The church's defensive prayers were still in full force, though, so Smoot could only transport them all as close as about five blocks away. From there they had to fight their way through demons, Knights, and wizards that were already fighting each other, thanks to the bogus revolution McCormick himself had helped stage to distract the Knights, using the wizard's own desire for freedom as the means. He let it get just enough out of hand to keep all the sentinels in the area busy, but not enough to call over any Knights from everywhere else. No, he only wanted the heads of the other branches of the order to show up when he was ready to take them all out by transposing them using yours truly.

Well, from there, I already told you what happened. Except for the small matter of *why did all those fire elementals show up?* Simon told me, if you wanted to know. Turns out there was a reason certain churches where built where they were, and it's not because people clamor for them. The truth is there are little spots on our plane that are very "close" to spots on other planes, and the Knights thought it would be good policy to keep those spots locked down hard. In the case of our church, the spot was a portal to the elemental plane of fire, and McCormick himself blew it open when he thought he was losing. Smoot managed to get it shut before it could get out of hand, though.

Simon said that McCormick shouldn't be a problem from here on, since he basically used a hell of a nasty exaction to cut the connection between McCormick's mind and his body, which meant McCormick was essentially a vegetable for the rest of his life. This prayer also let Simon see into McCormick's mind and instinctively know certain things McCormick knew, which let Simon fill in all the blanks.

So, it looked like everything was fine, right? So, why did I say *It wasn't really over?*

Well, lots of reasons. If you want the truth, things were just getting started. For starters, There was the problem that Casey's transposition spell was still on me, and—well, Casey didn't survive the fight. No, she wasn't turned into a dybbuk along with everyone else because of a safeguard McCormick put on, and she was killed by one of them. Who knows, it may have even been Reese who did it. Simon said Reese got transposed after McCormick broke through Simon's exaction, like he demonstrated he could do.

So, this shit could still start all over again. I'm not going to sit here and tell you that I'd expect Casey's spell would fire off ten times a day, but it only really needs to happen once.

Oh, and that's not even to mention the whole huge whopping throng of dybbukim I left behind in Las Olas. Simon said that lots of those had been accounted for, but there was no way of knowing how many weren't. For all I knew, there were still a good amount of them still roaming around God knew where. All that would have to happen is for one of them to bump into me, and then, well, shit.

Simon said Smoot could try to remove Casey's spell, but it would be like trying to crack a 256-bit encryption algorithm through brute force. In other words, it could take a while.

Terrific.

Simon said it would also technically be possible to teach me his exaction that re-transposes a dybbuk, but that could be a huge issue too. He said the best bet would be to just reverse my excommunication, so that I would no longer be the Midnight Sun, but . . .

He said that would only be possible to do that if all the people involved in the excommunication ritual would suddenly believe I didn't deserve it anymore, so it would more likely to do both of the other two things in one day than to have that happen.

"At this point," Simon said, "It's probably inevitable that you'll have to stand trial for all this, as will I." He smiled, kind of off center, and shook his head. "It won't be pretty. I had precious few friends in the Judges on up as it was."

I looked at him, and rolled my eyes. Now that the worst of the danger was over, I wasn't distracted anymore by being worried about dying every second, so I had time to think. That was not a good thing. I had time to remember a whole lot of other things, including Marsh ripping out that innocent little girl's spirit and—

Damn it.

It was my fault Crow was where she was now. My fault that she was suffering only God knows what unimaginable terror.

"Good," I said, after a second. My voice was quivering. "A trial. You know what? *I can't fuckin' wait.* Hopefully they'll execute me. That'll save me a step."

"What's that mean?"

"One way or another," I said, and turned to look out the window; I would have looked at Simon but my eyes were starting to water up, and I didn't feel like showing him that. "I'm going to hell. And however I get there, I'm getting Crow out."

★ ★ ★ ★ ★

After I hung out for a bit at one of Simon's little safe houses, he drove me home. He knew I technically *had* no home at the moment, but at least I had blueberry and from there I could go wherever, probably to my mom's. You know, if, for example, North Korea had no vacancy.

Along the way I had more time to think, and while I spent most of that time letting my mind go in circles I finally worked out what I was trying to work out earlier, when I was sitting on the bus stop with Crow. Honestly, although it wasn't really earth shatteringly profound, it did help me put everything in a bit more perspective. Here's basically what it was.

At the time, while I was sitting there waiting for sister Hendrie, Crow was laying into me like she usually does, only about ten times worse. What I mean was she kept ending each sentence with *idiot* or *stupid*, or she kept putting me down, hard. It was getting to be a bit much, even for her, but now that I think I figured it out, it all made sense.

The thing was, Crow lived inside my subconscious a lot of the time; I mean she danced around in my dreams, or just hitchhiked along while I was awake, somehow. It had something to do with the Exaction that I used to rip her out of heaven. I'm not sure how or why that is, but that's how it was.

This is important because, while I was growing up, I spent a lot of time making a lot of people miserable. Not to oversimplify, but I should just come right out and say that I was a thoughtless bitch. Part of me likes to think that maybe I've started to grow up a little, but that really doesn't change the past worth a damn. And then the royal mess I made of things once I finally got dangerous enough to do serious damage didn't help things much, either.

Putting myself down over all that, in case you didn't notice, was practically my number one hobby. If that's all Crow hears while she's in there, what else would she think would be appropriate to say? For all I knew, she used the word *idiot* the same way I'd say *hi there.*

Well, regardless. I didn't have time for that anymore. Damn it, I was a Paladin. I had the power and the ability to fix this, and I would if it was the last thing I did. Crow would go home, if I had to throw myself into the fires of hell to do it. Who knows, maybe I'd even flip Satan off as he burned me to dogmeat.

The sun was coming up when we pulled up to my apartment building; it was still taped off with crime scene tape. Of course it still would have been—it took me a second to remember how quickly all this happened.

I had to give Simon back the talisman, which honestly almost felt like I was stripping naked. Don't ask. As a consolation, though, Simon helped me slice those cuffs off my wrists, and then he even managed to get all my stuff back from the police station, in a nice big Ziploc baggie. I finally had my wallet, my phone, and my keys. My phone, surprise, surprise, was dead.

"When you get that charged up," Simon said, "You may want to give a certain someone a call. She was discharged this morning, no complications."

I glanced at him a second, and then smiled. "...Oh. Thanks. Really."

"I'm sorry about Jason, too," he said. "Unfortunately I don't know how to bring anyone back, once their counterpart is destroyed. Smoot was too thorough."

My smile dropped off, and then I looked down a second, let out a huge breath, and nodded. "Yeah. Well, One more thing on my list, I guess."

"Speaking of one more thing," he said, and reached over to the back seat. He came back with a good-sized black backpack, which he plopped on my lap.

"What's all this?" I asked.

"A full set of light combat regalia," he replied, and I snapped my head around to look at him, eyes wide.

"...Really?"

He nodded. "I had a feeling you just might be needing it soon. Take this, too." He reached under his coat and pulled out an ornate pearl and silver pistol, which looked like it was straight out of the revolutionary war. Unless I was seeing things, this was the same gun he used to blast McCormick a new one.

"You never can tell," he said. He held it out to me, stock first.

"Ummm . . ." was all I could manage. I stared almost cross eyed at the gun, like I was hypnotized or something, but after a second I held out my hand and took it anyway. It felt like it didn't weigh anything; I turned it over in my hands a couple times, and I could hardly believe how fucking beautiful the thing was.

"Ummm," I said again, "...how...how do I *work* this?"

"Just send your best Exaction through it," he answered. "It'll do the rest."

"...Oh. Thanks, man. Really. I'm serious, no bullshit."

He nodded. "No harm in being prepared. I managed to...*deflect* the authorities from their search for you, but all the same."

"Deflect—?"

"Let's just say they have a few things they need to ask *me*." He smiled. "I'll be in touch, Adobe. Good luck."

"...You too, man," I said, and my voice was sorta shaking a little.

I got about halfway out of the car, and then something crossed my mind. Something I think I would go on wondering until I understood it, so I decided just to get it over with.

"Hey," I said.

Simon looked at me and raised one eyebrow. Again, I got jealous.

"How the hell did you beat McCormick? Before he cheated, I mean."

Simon grinned. "Ah. Well, nothing to it, really," he answered. "He only believed he could defeat me. I *knew* I could defeat him. Before too long, I suggest you learn the difference."

I found out it was Thursday morning, which means I was out of the loop for two days. I was practically positive I was in some seriously deep shit at work, since I no-called-no-showed twice in a row. I wanted to call to make sure, but as I said, my phone was dead.

Well, maybe the electricity was still on in my loft? Worth a look, I guessed.

Up I went, up the squeaky stairs, past the bathroom on the landing, and up the narrow stairs. The foul stench that smacked me across the face the last time I was here only appeared to have gotten worse, so after one breath I had to seriously try to breathe through my mouth only. It didn't work all that great, and I didn't feel like using one hand to hold my nose shut. I just dealt with it. I looked around and had a hard time believing this disaster area was my own perfect, private sanctuary only two days ago. I could barely recognize it.

I checked one outlet after another, but no dice. There wasn't a lick of juice in the whole place. Figures. The only way I had to charge my phone, then, was from my car charger. I sighed, dropped the backpack on the floor and slumped down on my knees. That was when I saw it.

"Nuh-*uh*," I mumbled, and crawled across the floor to the far wall. The wall had a huge hole in it, probably from when the Jason-dybbuk started thrashing all over the place. There was a crawlspace behind the wall, where I stashed boxes full of stuff I never bothered to unpack. I didn't care about any of that, though. No, what caught my eye was the ever-familiar pommel and grip.

I reached out and took a hold. When I did, a stupid grin split my face almost in half. I couldn't help it.

"Sherman," I said, cradling my model 1860 cavalry saber like a baby, "Thank God you're okay."

He was still in his sheath, and, from what I could tell, as fit and as fine as ever. I guess either the cops missed him or didn't care about him enough to take him. I guessed it was the first one because I couldn't find Slinky anywhere. Oh well.

I closed my eyes, took a breath, and held Sherman's grip against my forehead.

"Get ready," I whispered. "You and I have a lot of work to do."

While I sat there for a few seconds just taking deep breaths and letting my mind wander, I remembered something else. I went over to where my computer desk stood once upon a time, and scrounged around a bit until I finally managed to find my Dad's photo. I was glad I found it, but also sort of not at the same time because the frame was fucked and the picture itself didn't get out of it scot free. It had a big rip and a crease in it, but other than that it was salvageable.

Once that thought crossed my mind and I actually processed it, I couldn't help but laugh. If that wasn't a perfect description of my whole god damn life I couldn't tell you what the hell would be.

I removed the picture as gently as I could and brushed the dust off of my dad's young, vigorous face. I just sat there for a bit, wishing I could unload all of the shit on my brain on him and ask him what the hell he thought I should do. Then more than anything I wished I could tell him everything there was to know about me, about everything I did and what I wanted to do. He never got to see me make anything of myself, and more than anything I wish he had the chance. Well, maybe if I can get everything together before I see him again, I'll have something to brag to him about. Jason said my dad was lucky to have a daughter like me. I wanted to earn that sentiment.

★ ★ ★ ★ ★

So, I hopped into Blueberry, started her up, and plugged in my phone. Unfortunately, my phone developed this quirk that if it goes completely dead, you can't power it on until the battery gets to at least 10% charge. I think it started doing that because I drop it an average of four times an hour. Anyway, seeing as I didn't really feel like idling, I went ahead and got on the road to work.

It was a hell of a relaxing ride. I didn't bother to turn on any music; I just rolled down the window, let my elbow rest on the door, and listened to the wind. I occasionally glanced in the rearview mirror and saw Sherman and Simon's backpack lying there in the backseat. Somehow or other, that seriously comforted me. Anyway, traffic was light, and the trip took less time than usual. My phone didn't even make it to 10% before I pulled in to the parking lot. Whatever. I'd go ahead and plug my phone in to my workstation while I wait to get chewed out, I guess.

I took the long way around to my desk, so I could walk in front of my boss's office. He was usually in by now, and if possible I wanted to get this shit over with.

His office light was out, and the door was closed. Hmm. Oh well. Temporary stay I guess.

I went to my desk and noticed I was the only one on my team that was in so far. Slackers. I shrugged, powered up my workstation, and plugged in my phone. I leaned back while my machine booted up, and let out a huge sigh of relief to be back in this tiny cube. I figured I'd snap out of it in a minute, but for now, it felt damn good. My machine chugged and beeped, and I started slowly swinging back and forth in my chair. That was when I saw that someone wrote '8,000,000 views!!!' on my whiteboard in red dry erase marker. I groaned, rolled my eyes, and told myself that it was okay because more than likely, the Internet was bored with me already.

Once my workstation finished booting, I fired up a terminal and logged in to my source control to get all the committed updates from the other developers, which was always the first thing I did. When I typed in the update command, I got . . .

No files.

What?

No files? No commits in two days? Did anyone even do anything? I shrugged again. Slackers.

My phone was still charging but it wasn't to 10% yet. It was like the poor thing was dead twice over and really wanted to stay that way. I got my workspace in order while I waited. I loaded up my dev environment, opened up the last file was working on, and tried to remember where I left off. I had a feeling that wouldn't be a snap.

Finally, my phone hit that fabled 10%, and I powered it on. It started going through its boot sequence.

Then, I heard someone's footsteps coming into the pod. I figured it was John or Armando. I braced for the *where the hell were you* stuff, but I just acted natural and went on doing what I was doing.

Then I heard someone rapping their knuckles on the glass of my cube wall. I turned around and saw . . .

Tony, my boss's boss.

✶ ✶ ✶ ✶ ✶

"Adobe, may I speak to you?" He said, kind of hasty like.

"Umm," I said. "Sure. ok."

"Ok, come with me," he said.

Cool, here it comes.

✶ ✶ ✶ ✶ ✶

He sat me down in front of his desk and took a seat himself.

"Are you feeling better?" He asked. "You were out yesterday."

I was confused, but only for a second. He only thought I was out for one day? And he thought I was legitimately out sick? Ok, not too bad.

"Yeah," I said. "I'm still a little under the weather, but I should be fine."

"Good, good," he said. "...Well, I'm just going to say it. I'm afraid that since you were out yesterday you missed layoff day. We had to let a dozen go, and unfortunately you...were on the list."

"...Oh," I said.

"Yeah," he said, nodding.

✶ ✶ ✶ ✶ ✶

And, that was that. I cleaned out my stuff with him watching. When I was done with that one of the IT guys that got spared the cut escorted me out and took my pass card. It was over in something like seven minutes, and I was outside in the parking lot standing in place like a big dumb goon. I'd get my last check and that was it. No more job.

Whee.

Well, at least my phone was powered up, so I had something to fiddle with while I thought things over. I unlocked it and saw that I had texts, missed calls and some voicemail. One text came from my phone provider letting me know that my bill was ready to view. Another came from the Red Cross, since I texted a donation once a few months ago and they were soliciting more. That started a train of thought in my head; maybe I should just go volunteer there or something, lord knows I'd make a killer medic. Yeah, that sounded great. Moving on. After that there's a text from Armando, saying he just got laid off but he might have a nice lead, and would I be interested in forwarding my information to whoever. Sure, that sounded great too. Then there's…

My heart jumped, and my cheeks started to get all red. The next text was from… *Raine.* She replied to me! Oh my god, she replied to me. That drunk text I shot off the night after O'shea's, she replied! I tapped my thumb on it so fast I almost opened Armando's text again by accident. I was already breathing a bit faster as my phone brought up the message, because I was so excited to hear or read anything at all from her, especially right then.

Me too, the text said. *I was worried. I thought I ruined everything. Tried calling but it went to voicemail. Call me <3*

I just went on standing there, reading it over and over and over. My heart was literally racing, and there was a light kind of little *woosh* in my belly, like when you're in freefall. I couldn't help it; I read every word of that text in her voice, and that led my mind to go all over the place. I kept picturing those eyes, that slightly crooked girl-next door smile, her adorable large teeth, her untidy bootlaces, how one sock was up higher than the other, how she looked raising one eyebrow, her soft twangy voice…

Oh my Christ. It was almost too much to take. I couldn't believe that, after this ungodly hell I just got shoved through, right on up to losing my job, that I could possibly feel anything like this, ever. I'm telling you, it felt practically surreal, like someone was playing some kind of …

And then I panicked. I looked at the timestamp on the reply.

"Fuck!" I cried. "No!"

Raine replied literally like twenty minutes after I texted her. That was Monday night, and now it was Thursday!

"No no no no *no*," I whimpered, and I almost mashed the little phone icon to call her, but I stopped short. I couldn't call her when I was in this mood; I had to calm down first and think out what I was gonna say. I mean, well, I don't know what I meant. I guess I mean I left her hanging for two days going on three, and it wasn't like I had a good reason I could give her.

I pressed the edge of my phone against my forehead and closed my eyes, trying to calm my breathing. It didn't help much that I just kept on picturing Casey Crumb, wherever the hell she ended up, skipping through a field singing 'Ode to Joy', and when I did, I lost my cool all over again.

"That bitch is so lucky she's dead," I growled to myself.

But it wasn't any good; I couldn't calm down, and I couldn't call Raine when I was like this. I needed...

I didn't even know what I needed.

No. Wait. Yes I did. I knew what I needed, and now more than ever, I needed it.

I calmed myself, cleared my head, and did my best to steady my breathing. I stopped fighting the anger, the confusion, the frustration, the helplessness, the uncertainty, the self-loathing, the doubt, and let it all lay over me. The trick was to detach and disassociate. Forget and ignore. The last three days didn't happen. I didn't cause Jason's death. I didn't almost cause the end of the human race. I didn't let Marsh throw Crow into hell. I didn't just lose my job. I didn't just leave this most amazing human being, who makes me dizzy just thinking about her, with the impression that I blew her off. I am not here. Nothing is here, not even nothing.

There we go. I was taught well. I can do this in my sleep, and I often do.

Now it felt like I was alone, floating in the dark. The dark was so thick I could feel it compressing every inch of me; to get out I'd need...

The Light.

The Light they tried to steal from me, The Light I kept anyway.

The Light I kept, because I refused to let it go.

The Light that I will never lose, because it is mine. I don't need anyone's permission to use it, and I never will again.

There it is. It's the size of a softball in my palm.

This time, though, it's going to be a little bit different. I'm going to load up this little bit of light with everything that's tearing my brain to bits and then blow it all sky high. I don't have time to let all that shit bury me, and so out it goes.

There, the light is the size of a basketball. Now a beach ball. Now it's as big as that boulder that almost crushed Indiana Jones. Just a little bit more, now I hold out my hand and then…

Release it.

There was a massive *krak*, a flash of white light, and a blast of force shot directly out a few feet from me that left a gash in the concrete. That was loud. I glanced around real quick and noticed that, yes, I was still all alone out here. Good.

Unlike the last time when I hurled out raw holy power, though, I didn't feel like I just got beaten up. No, this time I felt…

Tired, but in a really good way. Like, energized. Like I just ran a mile after weight training. Actually kind of refreshed.

Wow. I blinked a few times to make sure I wasn't going crazy, and then I looked at Raine's text again. After a second, I pressed her name, and it started ringing.

By the fourth ring I was almost breathing fast again, but then she finally picked up. When she did, I honestly almost felt like I was just pushed out onto a stage in front of ten thousand people.

"Hey!" she said, and I thought her voice sounded like a combination of surprised, rushed, and maybe a little bit happy tacked on there at the end. "Sorry, I couldn't find my phone, it was under something. Anyway, hey you!"

My mouth opened, but all it did was tremble for a second. For the life of me I couldn't make the stupid thing budge.

"Adobe?" she asked. Oh my god, hearing her say my name…It honestly almost short circuited my brain. I managed to get control back, sort of, long enough to think of something to say. The only problem was…

I got stuck.

I got motherfucking stuck. Now. Of all times. I'd rather have gotten stuck trying to substantiate a shield prayer while I was staring down a gun than to get stuck now, but if you think my defective mouth cared what I thought you're crazy.

All I was trying to say was "Yes", but all I could do was stand there exhaling the first syllable. When I say exhaling, I mean exactly that: It sounded like I was panting, or had the wind knocked out of me. Both of my eyes were blinking against my will each time I tried to get the word out, and my head tilted back the more I tried.

"...Hello?" Raine asked. I was so frustrated at that point my face scrunched up. I went on panting.

"Can you hear me? What's that? Hello?" She asked.

With a massive effort, or maybe just sheer dumb luck, I finally got the goddamn word out.

"Ye-*hess*," I said, and by then I had almost no breath left. "It's me."

"Oh, are you OK?" She asked. "What's wrong? You sound---"

"Oh, n-n-no, I'm-ma-ma-ma I'm fine. It's just, I'm just, it's just I stutter."

"Oh, oh, I'm sorry, I didn't---"

"No no, it's OK, it's OK, really! It's fine. Really. Are you feeling OK? You were in the hospital, are you OK?"

"Oh, yeah, yeah," she replied. "I'm all right, I just got out this morning. It wasn't anything really serious, but they were worried I had a concussion. I'm so sorry, I felt so stupid for that."

"St-stupid for what?" I was seriously surprised. I had no idea what she meant by that.

"Well," she said, and there was some hesitation in her voice. "I mean..."

She didn't say anything more, even after I waited a second or two. So finally I spoke up.

"What is it?" I asked, gently.

"I'm sorry, I'm---I'm a little nervous," she said. "I gotta sound ridiculous---"

"No, no!" I interrupted. "What's wrong?"

"I don't know---I, I guess I thought I ruined everything or something, and...well right in the middle of about the best moment of my life I faint and hit my head and then I don't hear from you for two days and I...I mean I really *really* like you, I mean, a lot, you know? And I didn't hear anything and I didn't have any idea---"

I couldn't believe my ears. Here I was, the one who didn't call or text back for two days (even though I had a pretty good reason), and this girl who could floor me just by walking in the room was thinking it was *her* fault?

No, I wasn't letting this go on for one more second.

"Raine," I said, kind of assertively, and she cut off.

"...Yeah?" she said, softly.

"I'm real sorry I didn't call, that was m-m-my fault, not yours. Long st-story short, I had a ma-ma-massively bad c-kkch-couple of days, but that's an explan-na-na-nation, n-n-not an excuse. Knowing that you thought it was anything you did is k-k-kkkch-kinda mmmm-more than I can take, you know?"

I waited for her to say something to all that, but she didn't. So I went on.

"Are you free?" I asked. She sounded seriously taken off guard when she answered.

"Am I...*Oh*, um, *yeah*, I mean I just got home and the doctor wants me to take the next few days off, but---"

"Do you want some c-c-kkkch-ompany?"

"Do I want---"

"I've come into a lot of free time suddenly. I can pick up donuts. Do you like blueberry cake? The Internet says they're known for their recuperative properties. My confirmation bias is happy."

She giggled in a kind of surprised way, and then:

"...um...*yes?*"

"Great. I'll at least need your address."

"...Yeah, yeah, I'll text it to you," she said, and I swear I heard the smile in her voice. Just hearing that settled everything; I could take a day or two off, even from everything I had to do. Besides, she and I had some things to discuss, like maybe something about some dreams she's been having. As in, it was time to do more than dream. I was already thinking of some subtle or not so subtle ways to broach the subject.

"See you soon...?" She asked.

"Whether you w-w-want it or not," I answered.

After I hung up, I felt like I could have picked up a tank and thrown it through a building. In fact, I was on such a high that I looked through my missed calls, just daring any of them to be from my student loan lenders, like they usually were. Right then I would have called them back just to tell them all to fuck off.

Sure enough, there were a few calls from them, and, wouldn't you know it, from my grandmother, too. As it turned out, Grandma left another of her voicemails on top of that. Normally I would have rolled my eyes and ignored it, but then something made me listen to it.

Here's how it went.

Hello Adobe, this is your Grammy, I just wanted to give you a call and let you know that you are a bright light in a dark world. You are a very special person, and no one can take your place. You're contributing so much to your family and the world. I pray every day that you have God's blessings all day long, to strengthen and maintain the bright light in your soul. I love you and think about you every day. There is no one just like you. Bye bye dear.

I just stood there listening to the recorded voice asking me if I wanted to play the message again, save it, or delete it. It looped maybe three times before my phone went off, letting me know I had a text. I smiled, and hung up the phone.

"Hmm," I said, and made my way to my car. "Maybe."

Printed in the United States
By Bookmasters